New York Times bestselling author **Christine Feehan** has over 30 novels published and has thrilled legions of fans with her seductive and sensual 'Dark' Carpathian tales. She has received numerous honours throughout her career including being a nominee for the Romance Writers of America RITA, and receiving a Career Achievement Award from *Romantic Times*, and has been published in multiple languages and in many formats, including audio book, e-book and large print.

For more information about Christine Feehan visit her website:

www.christinefeehan.com
https://www.facebook.com/christinefeehanauthor

Praise for Christine Feehan:

'After Bram Stoker, Anne Rice and Joss Whedon (who created the venerated *Buffy the Vampire* series), Feehan is the person most credited with popularizing the neck gripper'
Time magazine

'The queen of paranormal romance'
USA Today

'Feehan has a knack for bringing vampiric Carpathians to vivid, virile life in her Dark Carpathian novels'
Publishers Weekly

Also by Christine Feehan

DARKEST AT DAWN

OMNIBUS

CHRISTINE FEEHAN

piatkus

PIATKUS

First published in the US in 2011 by The Berkley Publishing Group,
A division of Penguin Group (USA) Inc., New York
First published in Great Britain as a paperback original in 2012 by Piatkus
Reprinted 2012

Dark Hunger previously appeared in the anthology *Hot Blooded*, published by Jove Books.

Collection Copyright © 2011 by Christine Feehan
Dark Hunger Copyright © 2004 by Christine Feehan
Dark Secret Copyright © 2005 by Christine Feehan

A CIP catalogue record for this book
is available from the British Library.

ISBN 978-0-7499-5757-5

Printed and bound in Great Britain by
Clays Ltd, St Ives plc

Papers used by Piatkus are from well-managed forests
and other responsible sources.

MIX
Paper from
responsible sources
FSC
www.fsc.org   FSC® C104740

Piatkus
An imprint of
Little, Brown Book Group
100 Victoria Embankment
London EC4Y 0DY

An Hachette UK Company
www.hachette.co.uk

www.piatkus.co.uk

Contents

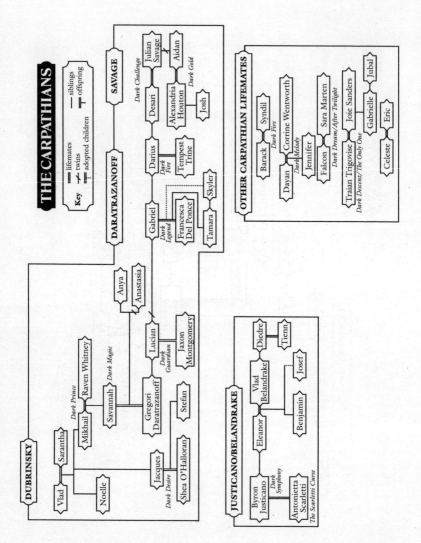

THE CARPATHIANS

Key
═══ lifemates
── siblings
▲ twins
═══ offspring
═══ adopted children

DUBRINSKY

Vlad ── Sarantha
Mikhail ═══ Raven Whitney — *Dark Prince*
Savannah ═══ *Dark Magic*
Noelle
Jacques
Shea O'Halloran — *Dark Desire*
Stefan
Gregori Daratrazanoff

DARATRAZANOFF

Anya
Anastasia
Lucian ═══ Jaxon Montgomery — *Dark Guardian*
Gabriel ═══ Francesca Del Ponce — *Dark Legend*
Tamara
Skyler
Darius ═══ Tempest Trine — *Dark Fire*

SAVAGE

Desari ═══ Julian Savage — *Dark Challenge*
Alexandria Houton ═══ Aidan — *Dark Gold*
Josh

OTHER CARPATHIAN LIFEMATES

Barack ═══ Syndil
Dayan ═══ Corinne Wentworth — *Dark Fire*
Jennifer
Falcon ═══ Sara Marten — *Dark Melody*
Traian Trigovise ═══ Joie Sanders — *Dark Dream/After Twilight*
Gabrielle ═══ Jubal
Celeste Eric — *Dark Descent/The Only One*

JUSTICANO/BELANDRAKE

Byron Justicano ═══ Eleanor ── Vlad Belandrake
Antonietta Scarletti — *The Scarletti Curse* — *Dark Symphony*
Benjamin
Josef
Diedre
Tienn

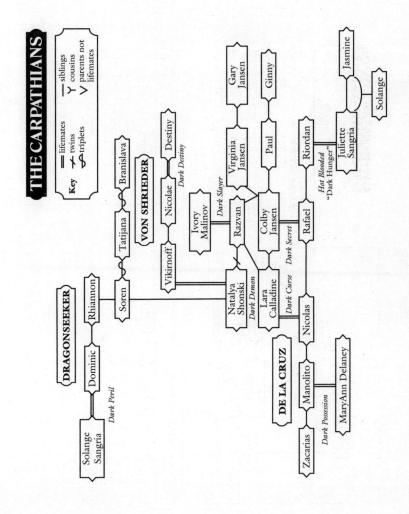

DARK HUNGER

*This story is dedicated to Diane Trudeau
and all the ladies at the RBL board.*

May you always know how to live life to the fullest!

1

"You would have to pick the most humid night of the year," Juliette Sangria whispered to her sister. She wiped sweat from her forehead and crouched lower in the shrubbery to keep from being seen.

A spotlight swept the area of thick vegetation where the two girls were hidden, but it couldn't penetrate the lush shrubbery and multitude of vines and creepers hanging from the trees. Jasmine waited for the light to pass before shrugging. "I saw them bring in three animals tonight. We have to get them out before they hurt them or perform experiments on them. You know that's what this place is all about."

Juliette swore under her breath and melted back into the shadows as the spotlight slid by them in a long sweep. She was certain the light was more for the superstitious guards, always afraid of the encroaching jungle. She knew from experience the jungle never slept and always tried to regain what man took away.

The building was concrete and mortar, fairly new, but already covered with moss and fungi, a dark, moldy green as the jungle crept back. Creeper vines climbed the walls and wound around the top of the building as if seeking a way in. There were no windows, and Juliette could imagine how hot it was inside for the animals, even with the thick walls. Humidity was always high here, and the research center had been built in the most unlikely of places. She knew it was built in this remote location simply to hide the fact that animals on the endangered species list were being used for illegal research.

"Jazz, we'll only have six minutes to get as many animals out as possible. Some of them will be highly agitated. If any are beyond our help, you have to leave them. Is that understood?" She knew her sister's affinity for wildlife. "These people play for keeps. I think they'd kill us, Jazz. Promise me, no matter what, you'll get out in six minutes and head for home and stay there. I'll hang back and make sure they don't recapture any of the animals."

"You'll lay a false trail into the jungle to keep them off of me," Jasmine said.

"That too. We both know I can lose them. Yes or no, Jazz, do you give me your word? We aren't going in otherwise." Juliette would take her younger sister home and come back another night if she didn't promise. She detested that these men could come into her jungle and capture and torture animals and get away with it, but she wasn't losing her sister over it.

"Six minutes," Jasmine confirmed and set the alarm on her watch.

"Then let's do it. I'll take out the guard at the main entrance and you cut into the security system."

Jasmine frowned as she nodded her acceptance of the plan. Juliette always made it sound so easy. Distracting and taking out the guard was always dangerous. She moved into a better position, covering her sister and getting closer to the main box where the wires were stored. Few people paid attention to that little box, but Juliette and Jasmine knew it contained the highway for the main alarms. At night, only the guards were in attendance and they were always nervous and highly superstitious. They seemed as afraid of what was out in the dark interior of the jungle as they were afraid of what was inside the building they guarded.

Juliette unbuttoned her blouse to just below her breasts so that the thin material gaped open, revealing the generous swell of soft, inviting skin. She pulled a thick banana from her pack and slipped around the building, slowly unpeeling the fruit as she went. As she emerged from the thick shrubbery, she paused deliberately in the sliver of moonlight, bringing the banana to her mouth and running her tongue over the tip of it. The light shone through the thin fabric of her blouse, caressing her rounded breasts so that her dark nipples thrust invitingly against the fabric.

The guard's attention was immediately riveted to her breasts. He licked his lips and stared. Juliette smiled at him around the banana. "I had no idea this building was here. I'm camping with a small party of friends just beyond the stream." She used tentative Spanish as if she didn't know the local dialect. Juliette turned slightly, giving him a more intriguing view of her body, and pointed back into the darkened vegetation. She turned back to him, allowing her gaze to sweep him up and down, to linger for just a moment on the sudden bulge growing in his trousers. "Oh, my, I certainly didn't expect such a big, strong man as you."

He couldn't talk, staring at her mouth as she sucked on the fruit, her lips sliding up and down suggestively. Juliette pulled the banana from her mouth, gaining ground, her hips swaying, her smile flirtatious. "Are you hungry? I'll share." She held out the banana and seemed to notice her blouse gaping open for the first time. "Oh, I'm sorry, it was so steamy in the jungle, I can hardly stand having clothes on. Doesn't the heat bother you? It makes me feel . . . soooo hot." One hand went to her blouse as if to close it, but her fingers trailed over the ripe swell of her breast.

The guard swallowed hard, staring at her. She held the banana to his mouth. "Are all the men in the jungle as handsome as you?"

He took a bite of the offered fruit, he couldn't help himself. He was smiling down at her, still staring at her breasts when she used the pressure syringe on him, tranquilizing him. He was heavy, but Juliette was strong, and she dragged him into the cover of the bushes, sending up a small prayer that no predatory animal would find him defenseless, propped up against a broad tree trunk. She hastily prepared the scene while Jasmine penetrated the alarm system. From her pack, Juliette spilled a small amount of liquor on the guard's clothes, settled the flask in his hand and removed the bullets from his gun, flinging them into the dense undergrowth.

Juliette and Jasmine stayed in the shadows, avoiding the open where a camera might pick them up as they hurried through the large building. The first few rooms appeared to be empty offices, but just beyond them, they could hear the uneasy sounds of animals in distress. The laboratories were fairly large, each holding several cages. They separated, glancing quickly at their watches and blowing a kiss for luck as they took separate sides of the huge building in the hopes of freeing as many animals as possible.

Both had the ability to calm and control even the largest of cats. It was more difficult when the animals had been teased and abused or tortured, but both women were certain of their talents and they moved fast and efficiently, their teamwork well practiced.

Juliette kept an eye on the time as she opened cages and directed animals. The last laboratory held the biggest animals. A sun bear, a jaguar, and a sloth. She cursed under her breath as she saw that the sloth was beyond all help. The sun bear had several injuries from someone poking it with a sharp instrument, but the jaguar was still in good shape, one of the newest animals the laboratory had acquired. She spoke softly, soothing the pacing animal, growling once low in her throat when it leapt at the cage walls in agitation.

It took a bit longer to manage the lock and herd him out of the room down toward the entrance, using her telepathic link to guide him. She took three steps after the cat when she felt a tremendous draw toward her left. To her dismay there was another door.

The door was heavy, a thick, soundproof vault with several bars and locks. Juliette glanced at her watch a second time. She should be running to get out, but something outside herself demanded she investigate. Praying Jasmine kept her promise to depart and head home immediately, Juliette set to work on the door.

Riordan lay on the cement floor in a pool of blood, dispassionately watching as it seeped toward the built-in drain. His blood looked like a thin, pale gray trail of liquid pooling in an ever-widening puddle. It was unthinkable that he had been trapped like this, that one of his kind could be shamed and dying at the hands of his enemies. He was an immortal, a Carpathian male, no fledgling, but a man of honor and skill. He lay in a pitiful heap, unable to gather the strength needed to move. Unable to summon help from his own kind.

His brothers would be seeking him now, wondering why his mind was closed to them. He dared not draw another into the trap as he had been drawn. He would not be bait to ensnare more of his kind. The enemy had found a way to poison the blood of their people, to immobilize them long enough to drain their blood and keep them weak. He had thought he was skilled enough to push the poison from his body. In the past he had done so on numerous occasions, but the new poison held him helpless and weak and paralyzed against the continual torture.

There was no way to transmit the news to his prince, no way to warn of this new, even more lethal drug their enemies had devised. Riordan struggled into a sitting position until he lay, propped against the wall he was chained to, examining the compounds racing through his system. They had used some sort of electrical charge to stimulate the cell deterioration in his blood. He allowed his breath to escape in a long, slow hiss of deadly promise. Of deadly despair.

He would not die easily—his body would continually regenerate—but without the necessary blood, without the healing earth, it would happen, slowly and painfully. It was the last death he had ever envisioned for himself.

The drug was crawling through his body, a chemical monster nearly as lethal as the dark demon lurking deep within him. Before he died, he intended to transmit as much information on the poisonous compound as he could to his brothers. He would issue a warning, but he would not do so until his death was imminent. He would not betray his kin. He would not be used as bait to draw in the others. His prince needed to know that a master vampire was using the humans, playing puppet master. Riordan had to find a way to escape, there was no other option. He could not allow his life to end until he carried the vital information of this treachery to his people. He could not let pain and despair, his ever-present companions, weaken his resolve.

Riordan closed his eyes and crawled deep into his mind. Almost at once he heard the soft click of the lock at the heavy metal door. Fearing his immense power, his captors never came to him at night. He did a cursory scanning to touch the mind of the human entering the laboratory, his prison, but to his shock, he could not read the thoughts. Hehad the impression of a human female.

He sat very still, his mind working at a furious rate. Had his captors managed to find a way to shield their thoughts? They were protected most of the time by his own weakness. During the daylight hours he was helpless and vulnerable, but at night they had been cunning enough to stay away. Although they had drained his blood and his strength, hewas mentally strong enough to command one of them should they venture near at night. This was his chance to escape or seek a way to end his life before they could use him against his own species.

He studied the mind of the single person entering his prison. She was a young female. He kept his eyes closed, conserving his strength, waiting for that one moment he knew would come. He would reach past the strange barriers in her mind, rip past each strange compartment until he had total control. He would force the human female to do his bidding. Escape or death, whichever it took to win this battle. He could smell her now, a clean, fresh fragrance suggesting the outdoors, the rainforest after a cleansing downpour. A hint of exotic flowers, and something else—something wild. Something not quite human. Riordan felt his muscles tense at the unfamiliar odor, a strange quickening, a heat spreading throughout his body, but he held himself under control.

Nothing could prevent his attack. It was the first mistake any of them had made, and he would use it, capitalize on it. The demon in him was struggling to break free, listening to the steady heartbeat, the ebb and flow of blood in her veins. Hunger gnawed at him endlessly, mindlessly, brutally. He waited, unmoving, listening to the soft padding of her steps. There was only a whisper of sound, yet he smelled her excitement, the edge of fear and adrenaline. She was moving closer.

All at once the soft footfall ceased, her breath exploding out of her in a soft hiss of shock. "Oh no!" There was a rush of movement toward him, the rustle of clothes. Riordan clearly heard the shocked horror in her voice. She had not been expecting him.

Juliette couldn't believe the terrible sight, the man pale beyond imagining, his blood draining away on the floor. The heavy chains wrapped around his chest seemed burned into his very flesh. His hands were manacled, and blood seeped from a multitude of wounds. She couldn't believe he could suffer so much and still live. She knelt beside him and felt for his pulse.

Riordan opened his eyes to stare into her face as she squatted beside him, heedless of the blood smearing her clothing as she leaned in close. Her fingers settled gently against his neck. Her large, strangely turquoise eyes filled with compassion. "Who did this to you?" Even as she whispered the question, she was pulling out a small instrument from a toolbelt hooked around her waist to work at the lock on the heavy cuffs. She carefully avoided looking at the cameras she knew were locked on him.

"We don't have too long. Can you walk? They'll send security after us and we'll have to run." He was a big man and Juliette didn't think she had a prayer of packing him out in a fireman's carry. She would try it though. She had come to this place thinking it was a research lab for exotic jungle cats. She had never expected to find a half-dead, obviously tortured man imprisoned within the walls. She had never seen so much blood, such a ravaged face, such intense eyes. The cuff dropped off of his left hand, and she stretched around him to work at the second one.

Her hair fell across her face in a silky fall of blue-black strands. Faintly shocked that he could see the individual colors, Riordan could only stare at her hair. For one moment he couldn't think, couldn't even breathe, drag air into his lungs. It was impossible, yet the hand he raised to the fall of black hair was smeared red with blood. Red, not a muddy gray. His fingers brushed her hair back over her shoulder with exquisite gentleness, an instinct bred into his bones, exposing the line of her neck to him. She didn't seem to notice, working meticulously on the lock of the thick steel cuff. Her skin was soft and inviting. Like satin. He bent his head forward, slowly, steadily, the fangs lengthening, the demon roaring, his body clenching. His breath was warm against her skin. His teeth almost touched her pulse, that vulnerable pinpoint beckoning seductively.

Her blouse gaped open, revealing exquisite breasts, lush and full and soft enough to pillow his head. He wanted to slip his hand inside her shirt and hold warm flesh as he bent to her neck.

She made a sound, frowning, still absorbed in her work. Riordan inhaled, taking the scent of her deep into his body. He didn't have control of her mind, and he was too weak to waste what was left of his strength on working out the intricate puzzle. The moment the heavy steel dropped from his wrist, he whipped up his arms, locking her body to his as his teeth sank deep into her neck.

White-hot pain lashed through Juliette's body, danced like a whip of lightning through her bloodstream, heating her body so that every nerve ending was alive and pulsing with fire. The pain gave way to a dark, erotic, slumberous ecstasy she was helpless to resist. Juliette was certain she struggled, but he was like iron, her softer body battering itself against his hard one, and he didn't seem to notice. She felt the strength growing in him, spreading through him, even as her own strength seemed to slide away from her. There was a part of her that seemed to be separate, standing apart, watching and feeling in a kind of horror. There was fire in her blood, moving through her body, muscles clenching, tightening, going boneless, pliant in his ironlike grip.

Riordan glanced up at the camera trained on him, his mouth twisting in a humorless smile, flashing his white teeth. With his eyes staring straight at the lens, he lowered his head and stroked a caress across the pinpricks on her neck with his tongue. That look would tell them everything. He knew each of them, knew their scent; he knew his enemies. Their stench was in his very lungs, and he was a hunter. He had gone from prey to predator with one small infusion of blood. It wasn't enough to completely heal him, but it was enough to allow his escape.

He lifted the woman's limp body easily to his shoulder, moving with a graceful show of strength. He had every intention of drawing his enemies to him and away from his family. But first he would destroy everything they had built out in the jungle. They hid their laboratoryaway from prying eyes. They hid their hideous torture chamber deep within the jungle, thinking they were far from the law, far from justice, but he would show them who owned this part of the world, who had owned it for a long, long time.

The woman erupted into a wild struggle, attempting to squirm away from him.

Riordan tightened his hold on her. "Stop it," he ordered. "You have no way to escape. It is impossible. Lie still." His voice was a soft, menacing command.

Juliette lay quietly, feeling the enormous strength in his arms. She fought down her panic, trying desperately to think. Her body had become lead. It was an effort to lift her arm, make a fist, pound on his back. She was dizzy and sick. His emotions were swamping her, a wild swirling of dark danger beating at her. She had never come close to feeling such overwhelming emotions. They welled up like a volcano, explosive, violent, very intense. She sensed something wild and untamed, a predator without equal. Her neck throbbed and burned and she wondered what manner of demon she had unleashed.

She actually felt the strength gathering in him. *Felt* it. A seething cauldron of enormous power. It built in him and seemed to spill out of him, out of his pores, bursting from his masculine body so that the building frame shook and creaked ominously, until the very air was so filled, the walls actually bulged outward in an attempt to contain such power. Juliette clutched at the tattered remains of his shirt, her fist bunching the material in her palm, needing something, anything to hang on to.

"My sister might be in here." She managed to whisper the words, terrified Jasmine would be caught in the massive destruction of cement and mortar.

"No one is in the building but us," he assured. He moved then, his speed so incredible everything around her blurred. Juliette squeezed her eyes shut tightly to prevent the dizziness from overcoming her. Her stomach lurched and she clung grimly. She could feel the powerful muscles bunching beneath her, the rush of air over her body. She could have sworn at one point they left the ground, moving through space so quickly they were flying.

2

Fear amounting to terror tore at Juliette. She had no idea what she was dealing with, but he was a powerful predator and from the condition she found him in, his anger was justified. She could feel a controlled rage simmering deep within him. Shockingly, they seemed linked together, she feeling his emotions, he feeling hers. She summoned her courage, her eyes still held tightly shut to keep dizziness at bay, keep from being overwhelmed with fear and the rush of wind in her face as they raced through the chamber of horrors. She needed all of her senses working if she was going to escape. She had to be alert for that one moment, that one chance when he would momentarily be distracted. She tried to gather her strength. It seemed a monumental task in the face of being upside down, her stomach rammed hard against his shoulder. He held her with one arm tightly across her buttocks, easily, casually, as if he barely remembered she was there. Her stomach rebelled and she was weak and light-headed. *But his touch seemed familiar, intimate even.* His fingers were splayed across her bottom, absently caressing the roundness of her muscles even as he was striding quickly through the building. Almost as if his touch remembered her body, knew her intimately in some way. Juliette couldn't focus properly no matter how hard she tried, aware of his fingers more than she would have liked.

The very foundation of the building shook; wrenching apart, the earth beneath them buckled and rippled violently. Sparks began to snap and crackle around them as the wiring popped from the beams, cracking and splintering overhead. Light fixtures swayed precariously. Fissures appeared in the floor, along the wall, great, ominous cracks. There was a roaring in her ears, loud and insistent. The man locking her to him moved smoothly, fluidly, a certain poetry to his motion, not jarring her badly knotted stomach. *Breathe*. She heard the word as a soft whisper in her mind. Almost a caress, intimate. *Breathe*. As if warm air from his mouth was breathed into her ear. As if his lungs moved for her lungs. Her body still felt leaden, her arms hanging heavily down his back. She tried to concentrate, tried to gather her strength to wait for her moment, but that single word had disturbed her. Changed her. *Breathe*. It whispered through her body, swam in her bloodstream, spread insidiously throughout her body so that her very heart beat the rhythm of his heart. And the word was in her mind, not spoken aloud.

As the building vibrated, he took stairs three and four at a time. He leapt from the crumbling cement wall, a good twenty feet in the air, landing easily on the balls of his feet, still careful not to jar her. Flames were licking at the blocks of concrete, trying to find fuel, greedily looking for something to devour as he took her into the shelter of the jungle.

At once the dark green leaves enfolded them, swallowed them, a haven of rich, lush vegetation. The darkness was nearly impenetrable beneath the heavy canopy of foliage overhead. The fallen trees and thick shrubbery didn't slow him down. He moved as one born and bred in the jungle, silent and deadly, protecting her with his body as he raced through the darkened interior, putting distance between them and the crumbling laboratory. He seemed to know exactly where he was going, when most were disoriented deep within the forest. Before he had run with speed and power, now he began to falter, his legs shaking as if he were suddenly weak. Blood still ran from his wounds and trickled down his body from the many lacerations.

Juliette flexed her fingers, grasping his tattered shirt. She didn't have the energy to cry out a protest, limp and lifeless, hanging like a sack over his shoulder, but she was certain he was half-mad with pain. All at once they were back on the edge of the trees where civilization had hacked the jungle back to build small townships and villages. The jungle, as always, was creeping forward to reclaim what had been taken, providing cover all the way to the very edge of the village.

He stopped near a thick tree trunk, a shadow in the darkness. She felt his stillness, his gathering of information, scenting the wind. Her heart began to pound in anticipation, a loud, terrifying beat. He was hunting prey. Deep within her very soul, she knew he was hunting human prey with her leaden body draped casually over his shoulder. She wanted to struggle, to scream, to warn his victim. No sound emerged; her body refused to obey her. Her heart nearly exploded in her chest, wild and frightened.

Breathe. It came again. A soft command in her mind—gentle, intimate. A caress she felt on her skin, a stroke she felt in her hair. On her bare breast. Air moved through her lungs, through his, and her heart found the steady, natural beat of his.

She heard the padding of footsteps, the murmur of voices carrying in the night. Coming closer. Closer still. Who would be so foolish as to wander near the jungle this late at night? There were many predators in the forest. He moved then, shifting her into his arms, cradling her close to his chest, his black eyes burning deeply into hers for a long moment. She could only stare helplessly, half mesmerized, half paralyzed. Slowly he lowered her feet to the ground, keeping his arm around her to hold her to him. To hold her up. She was dizzy and weak.

His dark examination was the most intimate thing she had ever experienced. The connection between them was growing. His gaze drifted over her body, touched her exposed breasts with the heat of a flame. Juliette couldn't summon the strength to button her blouse so she stood swaying and vulnerable in front of him. As if reading her mind, her captor drew the edges of the material together and slipped the buttons in place. His knuckles brushed against her skin, sending a shiver of awareness down her spine. He bent his dark head toward her, a slow, almost seductive movement. Her heart thundered in her ears as his sculpted mouth came close to hers. A whisper away, no more. Mesmerized, she could only stare at him, waiting, forgetting to breathe. Abruptly, he turned his head toward the small group of houses.

Juliette saw two men moving toward them, walking straight as if on a path, yet they were walking through dense shrubbery. Neither spoke, nor looked right or left. Neither seemed to be aware they were close to the jungle where predators lurked. Juliette tipped her head back. It fell against his chest, too heavy for her to hold up on her own. His arm tightened, locking her even closer to him so that the heat of his body seeped into the cold of hers.

She could only stand there helplessly as the two victims walked closer and closer. There was a stillness in her captor, the coiling of a snake. She felt him gathering his strength, holding it in place while his prey came closer. The two men walked right up to him as if drawn, as if programmed. A shudder ran through her as one tipped his head back, exposing his throat. Her captor bent his dark head in that same, unhurried, almost casual manner, and sank his fangs deep and drank.

Juliette's heart pounded frantically, adrenaline racing through her bloodstream. *They cannot feel. They are not afraid, why should you be afraid for them? I am not hurting them. You always forget to breathe.* There was the merest hint of amusement in his melodic voice, an intimacy that took her breath away.

Her entire body clenched, searing heat touching her in places like the stroke of fingertips. Her breath caught in her throat. He was dangerous, far more than she first thought. His voice was a weapon, seduction a tool. And she was susceptible to his sensual mouth, his burning eyes and his velvet voice.

Juliette forced energy into her body, using her fear, her adrenaline and his momentary distraction while feeding. She attempted to jerk out of his arms, using the sudden surge of built-up terror. His arm remained clamped around her like a steel trap, unmoving, almost as if he didn't feel her resistance.

Riordan allowed the first human male to sit down on the ground, swaying weakly, and he reached for the second one. He needed fresh blood to replace the enormous loss he had suffered through his confinement and torture within the walls of the laboratory. With the infusion of blood, he hoped to heal enough to begin restoring his body to full power. With renewed power and without the constant electrical charges to stimulate the artificial poison he might be able to remove the substance from his system. Carefully, he helped the second human to the ground, retaining possession of the woman by holding her body close to his. He felt her. Every inch, every curve. Her skin was unbelievably soft. He bent his head to her thick mane of flowing hair, inhaling the scent of her. It took a tremendous amount of self-control not to bury his face in the silken strands.

She was very frightened, the fear swamping her despite the fact that he had tried to soothe her. Her brain patterns were different, the mostdifficult he had ever encountered. He caught her chin firmly in his hand and tipped her head back so her strange eyes were forced to meet his gaze. Her eyes were shaped liked a cat's, a deep turquoise in color, and he could tell by her pupils she had excellent night vision. Her lashes werelong and the same inky black color as her hair. He stared down into her eyes, a simple hypnotic technique that should have calmed her instantly, but instead he could hear the frantic rhythm of her heart pick up.

"You rescued me. Thank you," he said softly, gently, compulsionburied in the silvery tones of his voice.

Juliette tried desperately to regain her energy. Her legs were veryheavy, her arms still leaden. He was the only thing holding her up. She was dizzy, and every time she stared into his black eyes she felt as if she were falling forward. She blinked rapidly, trying to find a way to regainher ability to think clearly. "What's wrong with me?" Her mouth was dry and her voice sounded far away to her own ears.

"I took too much of your blood," he answered softly, honestly. "It was the only way I could escape from that hellhole. There is no need tofear me, I will replace what was lost." His arms tightened possessively.

Juliette pushed ineffectually at him. "Just go away. I don't want you to replace anything at all."

"I am Riordan, your lifemate. I have searched these long years tofind you."

"You are some kind of bloodsucking something or other and I just want you to go away." Juliette nearly sank into the bushes, but he liftedher, preventing her from falling. It disturbed her that he had suchstrength when he had been so brutally tortured. Blood or no blood, heshould have been as weak as a kitten. His chest held long, raw burnmarks, almost as if the chains holding him had been made of acid. "You have to take care of these wounds. They'll get infected in the jungle. You can't have any open wounds at all." Why she cared made no sense. She just wanted him to go away. He cradled her as if she were a child hanging limply in his arms, her head lolling back on her neck. She was very aware of her throat, so vulnerable to his sharp teeth.

Riordan stared down into her peculiar eyes, searching her mind for away to calm her fears. He heard a soft grunting cough coming from the darkened interior not very far from them. She reacted. She tried not to, but there was elation, hastily suppressed in her mind, and her body tensed for the briefest of moments. He felt her response beginning in her mind, he was already that tuned to her and they hadn't shared his blood yet. She took a breath. Before she could make a sound his hand clamped around her throat. Her frightened gaze jumped to his. Riordan shook his head.

You will remain silent. I will kill anything that comes to your aid. Is that understood?

Juliette nodded. She didn't understand the tremendous connection between them. She felt what he felt. She could almost see the black, volcanic thoughts swirling in his mind to match the dark violence churning in his belly. He frightened her in a way that had nothing to do with his teeth and evident abilities. Long ago she had heard the whisper of another race of beings, and she suspected he was of that race. Carpathians. Nearly immortal. Hunters of the vampire, guardians of the many species, yet always alone, always apart. She knew little about them, only that they were extremely dangerous to her kind.

He had not killed either man he had fed on, even with the black anger stirring in his gut and the terrible need for vengeance riding him hard. She should have feared for her life, but it was something altogether different that frightened her. The way he looked at her was entirely predatory. Entirely sexual. Entirely possessive. And her whole being responded with heat and fire and secret longing and shocked terror.

Riordan allowed his hand to slip from her throat. He bent to place his mouth beside her ear, although when he spoke he used telepathic communication rather than speaking aloud. *I am taking you far from this place. The hunters will know I am weak. I must rid my body of their toxins before I can attend you. Close your eyes if traveling through the air frightens you.*

You frighten me. Leave me here.

He made a sound. Not out loud, but deep in his mind—a snort of derision. His face was an implacable mask, lines of weariness and pain were etched deep. If she could have, Juliette would have touched those small lines with gentle fingers. She wanted to take that look of bleak loneliness from his face forever.

You only fear that you have lost your freedom. You do not fear that I will harm you. You feel my need of you, do not pretend you cannot.

Juliette turned his words over in her mind. He couldn't read her as clearly as he pretended, which was a good thing. He was torn up, a stranger, a demon for all she knew, but something deep and feminine and animalistic responded to him with every fiber of her being.

She watched the earth drop away, the clouds whiten and mist form around them. Below her the canopy looked unbroken and impenetrable. He knew the jungle nearly as well as she knew it. He had a specific goal in mind. She rarely left her part of the forest to explore the deeper, more mountainous areas, but she knew that was where he was taking her. She would be a hundred miles from home, maybe more. Juliette hugged her secrets to her. She just needed to find her strength, go along with whatever he wanted until she was able to make her escape.

His laughter was low and without humor. *I am not in the mood to go chasing you through the forest.*

What good news. She looked up at his masculine face. He looked a man, not a boy, one who could be frightening, even a little cruel should he choose. Why would she be remotely attracted to such a man? It was unthinkable, yet she couldn't look at him without feeling the effects.

Maybe you should be afraid of me. He sounded more weary than sarcastic. *Are you going to tell me your name?*

She tried to think clearly, tried to remember the old legends told around the campfires, told by her mother's people about such a race. Did giving her name give him more power over her? She couldn't sort through the haze in her mind quickly enough.

I think it essential to know your name. Are you going to give me something to call you or shall I make it up?

Juliette. My name is Juliette. She didn't want him calling her some endearment in his mesmerizing voice that she might come to believe. In any case, she couldn't imagine him having any more power over her than he already did.

Thunder rolled over their heads, booming through the clouds so that the tree branches below them shook and the space they traveled through vibrated in alarm. Juliette felt Riordan's body jerk. She clutched at his arms.

I will not drop you. We are being pursued by the undead. I don't like the sound of that. If only she wasn't so weak. She didn't have a weapon, nothing at all that could help. *Is the undead what I think it is?*

I will not be trapped twice. There was such finality in his voice she shivered. *And yes, it is a vampire tracking us.*

How is he trailing us? You aren't leaving tracks behind.

He smells my blood. His voice was grim.

Juliette was silent, sensing Riordan was growing tired with the effort he was making. Her stomach flipped when he dropped unexpectedly to the ground below. The canopy was thick and leaves slapped at them as they plummeted through, skimming branches and hurtling toward the ground at such a fast speed she thought they would crash. She kept her eyes closed tight and only the thought of a vampire hearing her kept her from screaming.

Suddenly they were floating, coming to a halt. Riordan placed

Juliette on the ground, her back against a tree. Her eyes widened with horror as he stared at his hand, his fingernail growing to a lethal-looking length. Juliette drew in her legs, stifling a gasp as he tore a long cut in his own wrist. Blood dripping, he flung droplets in all directions and took off running with blurring speed, away from her, winding through the trees, spreading the scent along the leaves and shrubbery over a long distance.

Juliette held her breath for a long moment, waiting to be certain she was alone. For some reason, Riordan shocked her by abandoning her to the vampire. He was clearly using her as bait. She dragged herself to her feet. So much for sexy, brooding heroes. Obviously the more tortured, the less heroic. "Maybe you weren't really all that sexy after all," she muttered out loud, furious that he would leave her. Her legs were wobbly and she was dizzy, the ground tilting and rolling. It didn't matter. She was not going to wait for the vampire to descend from the clouds and find a helpless victim. If she had to crawl, she would find a way to escape. She let go of the tree and took two tentative steps. The ground rushed up to meet her. Before she hit the ground, a strong arm circled her waist and she was dragged up against Riordan's hard body.

3

"What are you doing?" Riordan hissed the words at her, clearly annoyed.

Juliette glared at him. "I thought you left me."

"I am your life mate. Your protection and health must be placed above all things. I would never leave you."

If she weren't so tired, she would have rolled her eyes in exasperation. She did the mental equivalent just to let him know he was an idiot for not explaining things she had no hope of understanding on her own. She glanced down at his wrist. The jagged tear was closed but looked raw and angry. "You laid a false trail of blood for the vampire, one stronger and fresher, didn't you?"

"Of course. It will hopefully delay him long enough for me to regain more strength and remove the poison from my body." He gathered her into his arms. "He will attack the skies blindly in hopes of finding us. You must remain silent."

Juliette was becoming annoyed at being hauled around like a sack of potatoes. "I'm not exactly a cringing baby. I got you out of that place, didn't I?"

For the first time a faint smile flitted across his face. It nearly stopped her heart. "That was before I showed you my teeth."

"Is that a little vampire humor?" she asked, but her stomach was doing a curious little flip. He looked so weary. She might have given in and put her arms around him to comfort him if she weren't so certain touching him was dangerous.

He bent his head to hers, his breath warm against her skin. When he smiled, she could see no signs of his incisors, but it didn't stop a small shiver from running down her spine. Unexpectedly her womb clenched. She didn't think that was a good sign. There was definite chemistry between them and it seemed to be growing. It wasn't logical and she just wanted to get away from him.

"The vampire will try to attack us in the air. He will not really know where we are, but he will hope to score a hit. It is essential you remain quiet. It will be very frightening."

She snorted derisively. "And you aren't? Let's get out of here."

He took to the skies again with dizzying speed. She felt him stirring in her mind, an attempt to reassure her, but she wanted to keep him out. Mind-to-mind contact was far too intimate. He could read her thoughts and even, possibly, her strange attraction to him. It bothered her that she was susceptible to him. There was no way to tell whether it was physical attraction or whether he was manipulating her in some way. She definitely had no intention of sticking around long enough to find out which it was.

Without warning the clouds rained sparks, red-hot embers, slivers of molten fire that fell like raindrops in a steady barrage. Riordan bent his body protectively over Juliette, cursing that he wasn't at full strength and couldn't provide the shelter they needed as they streaked through the sky. Despite his best efforts, several slivers penetrated her arm and burned through her skin nearly to the bone. He heard her gasp, but she turned her face against his chest, against the terrible burn marks there, and remained silent.

The embers burned his back and shoulders, raised welts and stung like angry bees along his arms. He was infinitely weary and wanted desperately to go to the healing ground in the way of his people, but Juliette could not do that, and he would not leave her unprotected while human and vampire enemies searched for them.

She was an unexpected gift, drawn to him by their connection, two halves of the same soul. She didn't want the connection, but it was there and it was explosive. In spite of the relentless pain, he was all too aware of her soft, generous curves and the heat and scent of her body. It only added to his physical discomfort and raised the level of her wariness. With her face nuzzling his bare chest, his insides were turning to mush. She had no idea how much faith and trust she showed him with that simple gesture.

I'm hiding from the embers. She denied his thoughts.

You are hiding from yourself, from the truth.

You could be the most infuriating, exasperating creature on the face of this earth.

Perhaps, but nevertheless, you find yourself inexplicably attracted to me. There was purring satisfaction in his voice.

Riordan took them lower into the comparative shelter of the jungle canopy and made his way toward the small forest stream where the plants he needed grew in abundance. Lightning slashed the night skies, lighting up the forests in flashes, sending animals scurrying for shelter. He moved through the trees until he found the darker, overgrown spot he needed for safety.

"If we are lucky, the vampire is weaving his way through the forest miles from here. Let me look at those burns." Riordan set her down and crouched beside her, drawing her arm straight out to examine it.

"You're hurt worse than I am," Juliette objected, her heart pounding. It was the way he was looking at her wound, his black eyes moving over her skin as if he took it as a personal affront that she'd been scored by the slivers of fire. "I can live with it."

"I cannot," he said simply and bent his head so that his dark hair, wild and tangled from the journey through the sky, cascaded around him, hiding his face.

She felt the warmth of his breath first. His lips, featherlight, a mere brush so that her heart quickened and her body tensed. His tongue swirled over the blackened welt. Electricity sizzled through her entire body. The breath went out of her lungs and her mouth went dry. She jerked her arm in reaction, but he held on firmly.

"I am sorry if this hurts, but I have a healing agent in my saliva. It should remove all pain. Just relax." He didn't just say the words, he breathed them against her skin. She felt his voice crawling through her pores, winding around her heart and lungs and every other vital organ.

Juliette closed her eyes against the waves of heat coursing through her bloodstream. Bloody and torn, swaying with weariness, Riordan was still the sexiest man she'd ever encountered. There was his voice, his eyes, the way he looked at her, the way he turned his head, his hard, masculine body, but most of all, the danger emanating from him. He was a powerful predator and it showed, yet his touch with her was amazingly gentle, almost tender.

She swallowed hard. "It isn't right that you're trying to heal me when your body is so torn up. I can wait."

"I feel your pain beating at me."

She made an attempt at finding humor when her body was stirring to life and her thoughts were turning to things better left alone. "See why we shouldn't share minds? It would be so much easier if you didn't have to feel my pain on top of yours." She frowned. "I'm in your mind, why can't I feel your pain?" She could feel how tired he was, but he had to feel pain with all the lacerations and burns.

His tongue swirled a second time. Then a third. "I am shielding you."

He could rob a woman of sanity. Juliette couldn't look at his gorgeous face without wanting to wipe away those terrible lines. His touch was beyond gentle, was causing her stomach to do flips and somersaults. Beads of sweat trickled down the valley between her breasts, and she was certain it had nothing to do with the humidity. The small burns miraculously stopped stinging under his ministrations. When he finally lifted his head and looked at her with his dark eyes, she saw the stark hunger smoldering there.

Riordan allowed her arm to slip from his fingers before moving a short distance away from her to the stream.

Juliette half sat with her back against the tree trunk watching Riordan carefully. "Thank you. It really does feel much better." She studied the lines in his face. "Is there really poison in your system?"

He glanced at her, his black, black eyes blazing a trail right to her heart . . . or her body. He began to carefully ease out of the bloodstained and tattered shirt. All the while his gaze remained on her, making it difficult to breathe. "Unfortunately, yes."

"Why? Why would they do that to you?"

"Because I am different. I am a creature to be loathed and hated. And because, I fear, they wish to kill our prince."

The burns on his skin were horrible to see. "Did they heat the chains? Is that how those burns got there?" Juliette wanted to rush to him, press her lips to those terrible marks. He had to be in such pain, yet he had attended to her first.

"They had vampire blood and they painted the chains regularly with it. They knew the blood was toxic and would burn as acid does. And they hoped the scent of blood, when I was drained and starving, would drive me out of my mind." He gave her a faint smile. "Perhaps they succeeded."

Juliette shook her head. "You're saner than they will ever be. We're both a bit shaky, but we made it out of there."

"Thanks to you. I am sorry you have to see me this way. As soon as I remove the poison, I'll restore your strength to you."

"I'm not as dizzy. I think my body's already recovering. You just worry about you." She wanted to look away as his face grew paler, as he made a tremendous effort, using every ounce of reserve strength in an attempt to analyze the poisonous compound used to paralyze him. A part of her mind was merged with his, or perhaps it was the other way around, but she could see the data flowing through his mind and was amazed that he understood each separate composite. "Who are you? How do you know all this?"

He leaned back against a moss-covered boulder. "I have lived a long life and learned much over the years. There is little else to do when you have nothing to live for. Knowledge is power and it keeps one alive, even when one no longer wishes to remain in a barren world." His dark eyes slid over her. He reached out his hand.

Juliette had no idea why she put her hand in his. The moment his fingers closed around hers her body came alive, and it felt right. Juliette wanted to pull her hand away from the heat of his, but he looked bone weary and tormented and she didn't have the heart.

"You changed that for me. You gave me back colors and emotions. I have four brothers. I have lived with them for years with only the memory of my affection for them, yet in that one moment when you spoke to me, I *felt* that deep love for them again. How could I ever repay such a gift?" His voice was soft, almost as if he were talking to himself.

"I love my sister and cousin so much. I can't imagine not being able to feel my love for them. I'm glad I could, in some way, restore those feelings to you." She tightened her fingers around his. "Have you always lived in South America? You're obviously familiar with the jungle." She knew he was resting, gathering his strength to break down the poison and push it from his system. She could feel him continually scanning the skies, worried the vampire might have tracked them in spite of his sacrifice of precious blood to lay a false trail. He had fought vampires on many occasions and she briefly touched on those hideous battles through their link. The creatures were grotesque and evil and worse than the human monsters she'd encountered.

"Many years ago, when our current prince was still young, his father sent many of us out in the hopes we could stop the spread of evil. I was fortunate that my family was sent together. It made it easier to endure being so far from our kind, so far from our homeland. We made this our home." He squeezed her fingers as if for courage and started to let go.

Juliette tightened her grip, tugging until he looked at her. "I'm strong enough to help you. I'm keeping you out of my mind, but I can let you use my strength."

"You do not have to, Juliette." He liked saying her name, was pleased she wanted to aid him, but he was not the gentle man she believed he was in her mind. He was far more ruthless than she knew, and he had no intention of allowing her to escape him. "I would not want you to expend energy you cannot afford."

He was warning her. Juliette felt a chill go through her body, but she chose to ignore it. He was drooping with pain. His wounds seeped and wept and every now and then, in spite of his efforts to shield her, she glimpsed the torment he was in. "I don't mind. I'm just sitting here anyway." She gave him a tentative smile. "How did they manage to capture you?"

His expression darkened. "I heard a cry for help on the common telepathic link all Carpathians use. When I followed the cry back to its source, I found a vampire, not a Carpathian. Unfortunately it was impossible to tell that he was vampire until it was too late. I was injected with the paralyzing formula and drained of blood to keep me weak." His gaze settled on hers, stayed there, a hypnotic, mesmerizing stare. "You are not shocked to hear of my species. You were frightened of me because I took your blood in such a manner, and for that I apologize, but the fact that I needed it did not fully surprise you. How is that?"

She was silent for a moment, weighing her words carefully. She felt him in her mind, seeking answers, but he was not nearly at full strength and the poison was hideously painful. With her brain patterns so different and the strength of her protective walls, he simply waited for her spoken answer. "When I was a child we often spent long periods of time in the jungle. At night my mother would build a campfire and we'd tell stories. She told us of a great people, Carpathians from the mountains in Europe with extraordinary skills and gifts. They were blood-drinkers."

"How did she know of them?"

"Our family goes back hundreds of years. Apparently my ancestor met a small group of Carpathians here in the jungle." She looked at him steadily. "Five brothers. They were said to have a vast cattle estate and human family to work their lands while they slept beneath the ground during the sunlight hours."

Juliette waited for a response to her revelation, but Riordan only stared at her for a few more moments in silence, then simply withdrew, pulling back into himself. He moved outside his own body, gathering himself into a ball of pure energy. It was fascinating to observe his healing abilities. She stayed merged with his mind, watching him not only break down the chemical compound so he could view each separate element and identify it, but also send the information to someone else with a warning to pass it on to the prince of their people and as many of their hunters as possible.

Sending the information over a distance was draining and Riordan faltered.

Where are you? The demand was strong in her mind. Male and frightening, it carried a command, a hypnotic draw that was very powerful and sent shivers of fear down Juliette's spine. *Riordan. I feel your pain.*

Riordan hesitated. *Do not come to me. I will be able to push the poison from my body and replenish myself.*

Juliette found herself holding her breath. She didn't want to meet the man behind that voice. There was a merciless, ruthless, frightening quality to the voice.

She felt Riordan touch her with his mind, a reassuring, caressing stroke.

I will not allow you to be recaptured. You were sent to check out the research lab to see what they were doing. The Morrison research laboratory was a front for a vampire controlling the human society that hunts our people. I have destroyed the building. The animals they captured on pretense were allowed to go free. I will come home when I have healed.

Where is the vampire?

He is hunting us. Riordan broke off the communication and glanced over at Juliette. "My eldest brother is very exacting about our staying alive."

"Families are like that. My sister will probably be worried about me. I need to get back home." She watched his face, hoping to read his response, but his sculptured features went carefully blank.

Riordan stared down at his arms. She felt the gathering of his strength. Very slowly the poison began to respond, moving with reluctance as he shepherded the damaging compound toward his pores. Some of the droplets oozed through his skin, golden, thick liquid carrying the ability to paralyze his race.

Juliette pulled a small plastic container from the bag hanging around her waist. She leaned forward and pressed the lip of the container to his arm, capturing as much of the liquid as possible before she screwed the lid on tight. "This might come in handy if your people need to study this."

He leaned against the boulder, his head back, fighting for air, his strength gone. Juliette immediately opened her mind to his, sending him as much of her remaining strength as she could give. She knew the jungle, better than most, every rustle in the undergrowth, every sound the birds made. Something evil was stalking them, and the jungle was alive with the news. In her present state she couldn't escape, but she had no doubt Riordan could fight if given the strength.

He wasted no time removing every drop of the toxic compound as quickly as possible. The moment he was certain he had gotten rid of all of it, he dunked his head into the stream, rubbed the cold water over his arms to scrub off the thick, sticky residue. Riordan spun around and reached for Juliette, dragging her onto his lap, cradling her against his chest.

She felt a jolt through her body, an electric shock as their bodies came into contact. Her mouth went dry. "What are you going to do?"

"Exchange our blood. Your blood will help me get us somewhere safe where I can heal, and my blood is ancient and will restore the strength you have so generously given to me."

"Will it tie us together?" Her voice might have been an invitation, but her palm went up in a defensive gesture, fingers splayed wide against his chest.

"Yes." His strong fingers slid over her chin, pushed stray tendrils of hair from her shoulder. "But we are already tied together." He bent his head, his face buried in the warmth of her soft, vulnerable neck. The water from the small stream was cold as it dripped from him, down her skin, cooling the heat from the oppressive humidity.

A soft moan of pleasure escaped as his teeth sank deep. She settled deeper into his hard frame, moving with restless urgency as her blood went thick with heat. Her lashes drifted down, her hands sliding limply into her lap.

"I claim you as my lifemate. I belong to you. I offer my life for you. I give to you my protection, my allegiance, my heart, my soul and my body. I take into my keeping the same that is yours. Your life, happiness and welfare will be cherished and placed above my own for all time. You are my lifemate, bound to me for all eternity and always in my care." Riordan spoke the words in a black velvet voice.

Juliette felt his voice vibrate through her body, touch her deep inside. Somehow his words brought them together, skin to skin, organ to organ so that they breathed with the same lungs, shared the same heartbeat, possessed the same soul. He flowed through her, a dark temptation, learning her secrets, sharing his. Kissing her until her body caught fire and ached for his. There were hot blood and flames licking at her. She shook her head, suddenly caught by the ritual of the entire thing. A ceremony as old as time.

4

Juliette opened her eyes cautiously in the hopes that none of her recent experiences had been real, that she'd just been having nightmares. She had participated all too eagerly in the exchange of blood, in the exchange of kisses. "Damn, damn, damn," she muttered and pushed herself up from the bed of foliage she was lying on.

She could hear the steady drip of water. She was in a cave, and the leaves and twigs that formed her bed were man-made, not at all natural. Riordan had provided her with the safety of a shelter and a soft bed while he had "gone to ground." She carefully avoided walking over the spot where she was certain he lay in a bed of rich soil. She felt him there beneath the dirt and leaves, buried deep. Still, not breathing.

Juliette dragged air into her burning lungs and backed away from the spot. She had a mad desire to fling herself to the ground and claw the dirt away to get to him. A sob welled up in her throat. She took another step back. "It was a ceremony of some kind, wasn't it?" she whispered. "My people do not marry." She backed up another step, although this time her feet dragged. "You're an extraordinary man, but I'm not what you think and I never could be."

She had no choice; she had to get home to her sister. Juliette tugged off her boots and tied the laces together. She shrugged out of her blouse and then her jeans, tying the two garments tightly together with the boots. She stood there completely naked, holding one hand over her throbbing neck. Her body called to him. Her mind called. Her very heart tried to find the beat of his. Hastily, before she gave in to the grief and madness welling up in her, Juliette tied the clothes securely around her neck.

She closed her eyes to block out all visual distractions and calm her mind. She would need every ounce of strength to leave him. When he had recited those ritual words, Riordan had carefully explained that they were tied together and should she wake without him she would feel the separation as intense grief. "And you weren't kidding," she said aloud. "I feel like my heart's been torn out. Whatever it is you are, whatever it is you did, it definitely works on me."

What are you doing? There was alarm in his voice. She could almost feel his fingers brush over her face, trail down her throat, slip over her breast. Her entire body reacted, recognizing his touch, reacting with heat and need.

Her eyes opened wide and she looked wildly around. *Where are you? Why can't I see you? How can you touch me when you aren't here?*

I am locked beneath the earth until the sun sets. You cannot leave me, Juliette. You know you must not.

Another gift? You can touch me, but I can't reach you? It was shocking that his touch seemed so real, could arouse her body and affect her heart when he wasn't even a substantial presence.

Tell me what you are doing. Why would you leave when you feel that we belong?

You don't know me. He had his secrets, but so did she.

You refuse to allow me into your mind and heart.

I can't. Her hand went to her suddenly raw throat. The thought of leaving him was painful. Hearing his voice only added to her torment, but she had obligations and she couldn't put them aside because her heart and soul and body cried out for his.

You can't escape me. Your blood flows in me and mine in you. He sighed. *I can see your mind is made up. When it becomes too difficult, reach for me, I will answer. In the meantime, try not to get into too much trouble.* Abruptly he broke the connection between them.

Juliette felt the loss like a physical blow. She took a deep breath and released the air slowly, calling up her other self, calling up the part of her that could give her the strength to go home where she belonged, when she really wanted to crawl into the earth with Riordan.

The change took her slowly, almost reluctantly, as if a part of her brain was fighting rather than embracing her other form. Spotted fur slid over her skin, muscles and tendons contracted and stretched. Stiletto-sharp claws sprang from her curving hands. She landed heavily on all fours while her body went through the change. It was always a slow process and somewhat painful, but never like this time. Juliette wept as the jaguar took her over.

The cat was small and stocky. Roped muscles and a flexible spine allowed her to flow across the cavern floor, seeking a way out to the jungle where she belonged. Rain fell softly as she emerged from the damp cave. She paused to get her bearings before taking to the trees and running along the twisting highway of branches high above the forest floor. She couldn't maintain this form for long periods of time, so she had to use it efficiently to travel across the greatest distance before shedding it. She ran as quickly as possible, threading her way through the leaves and foliage.

The rain barely penetrated the canopy, dripping steadily on the leaves but rarely touching her fur. Steam rose from the forest floor, but the jaguar didn't feel the heat the way Juliette would have. The boots banged against her neck and chest as she made her way through the trees and shrubbery. The birds screamed a warning to one another at her approach and monkeys chattered and threw sticks and leaves at her. She snarled at them, but hurried onward, not stopping to teach them manners.

After a time, she began to shake, her legs suddenly growing weak. She stumbled twice, tripped on a branch and leapt hastily to the ground. She was miles from the cave; the sun was setting and Riordan would be rising. Hopefully he would only find the scent of a large cat and she would be gone. Even if her blood called to him, she was a great distance away with a good head start.

She shifted into her human form, her sides heaving and her lungs burning for air. Leaves and twigs scraped her bare flesh. She looked hastily around to make certain she wasn't crouching in anything poisonous. The last thing she wanted was blisters on her skin. More than once she'd managed to shift at the most inappropriate time. She had little control when the form became too difficult to hold.

With a sigh she dragged on her clothes. Humidity was so high the material clung to her skin. Juliette was skilled in the jungle, but without the jaguar's fur and claws, it was much more difficult to make her way through the trees. The canopy kept out much of the light, and with the sun setting, the interior went dark quickly. She had excellent night vision, but it wasn't going to help much with night predators.

She passed the miles alternating between a run and walk. She tried to listen to the steady rhythm of the rain, but it sounded like a heartbeat. She tried to block out the scent of Riordan, but it clung to her body. Tears made a relentless path down her face, blurring her vision. Grief was a heavy weight that slowed her steps and robbed her of air.

Every step was a fight to go forward, to keep from turning around and running back to find Riordan. Worse, her mind continually tried to tune itself to his. Fighting herself was more exhausting than fighting the jungle. She needed a place to rest. Juliette found a small circle of boulders, nearly hidden by overgrown ferns. Within the ring of boulders a deep pool fed by a small stream shimmered in the moonlight. She sat down, lifted her face to catch the mist like drops that managed to work through the thick foliage overhead. Thunder rolled. Lightning lined the clouds. A roar shook the ground, the trees, caused small waves to race across the surface of the water. Juliette's hand fluttered over her heart. He had risen.

Juliette was gone. His first reaction was to roar out his pain and frustration. Now Riordan let out his breath in a long, slow hiss of exasperation. He wanted to shake her. The physical attraction between them was a wildfire. That alone should have been enough to bind her to him. She was in for a long, difficult time, out there alone without him. The ritual bonding words would force her mind to attempt to connect with his. He had explained it to her, had tried to spare her the misery he knew she would be going through.

He was already feeling the effects of their separation. Worse, he was feeling her grief, a torrent of emotion every bit as deep as the well of passion he touched in her. She felt things intensely. Riordan raked his fingers through his long hair. He needed to find prey fast. He needed more time in the ground to heal, but more than anything, he needed Juliette. He lifted his head toward the heavens and roared a second time. She had opened the dam of his emotions. He remembered nothing of anger and jealousy and fear, but now the feelings were crowding into his mind mixed with grief. It was a potent combination and a dangerous one.

He found the tracks of a large cat, but not the footprints of a woman. His heart beat hard in his chest, pounded with fear for her, with need for her. She had managed to disguise herself, leave no trace behind, but the call of blood and the ties that bound them together were far too strong to ever break. He moved quickly through the cave, shifting on the run, bursting into the air as a thick stream of white mist. The sky was orange and red, dazzling and vivid and near blinding to a man who had seen only shades of gray for so long. Even with the heavy mist for protection, his head burst with the sheer brilliance of color. He streaked through the trees, staying below the canopy, using the protection of the foliage while he acclimated himself to his new sight.

A bird shrieked, his only warning. He hit something and bounced backward. Droplets shimmered briefly through a dropping silver net, falling through on the outside. Instincts took over. He shot upward, through and above the silver. In his present form he was able to slip through, but he felt the thin blades, razor-sharp, cutting deep.

Riordan! Juliette sounded panic-stricken.

The trap had been set specifically for him. Juliette knew he would come after her. He had not fully penetrated the barriers in her mind. Could she betray him? Was it even possible for one life-mate to betray another? Riordan doubted it, but he didn't have time to think so he simply didn't answer, pulling his mind from hers. The echo of her anguished cry tore at his heart, but he refused to be swayed, streaking through the canopy and shifting into the form of a bird. He went still, hiding among the birds in the tree, examining the trap that had been set for him.

It had been sprung without an operator. He had merely flown into it, which meant there might be other traps out there waiting for him. Blood trickled down his beak and seeped through his feathers. Far below, on the forest floor, the silver net lay tangled in a heap. He could see traces of his blood on the thin wires.

Humans, puppets of a vampire, had constructed the trap, and only a master vampire could have kept his presence from Riordan. He was dealing with something extremely powerful and evil.

Something willing to mingle with humans and use them for its own ruthless purposes.

Fear for his lifemate clawed at him. She was somewhere alone and unprotected. It couldn't have been Juliette. What would be the point of rescuing him only to lead him into a trap? He touched her mind, heard her weeping. His heart shattered. For a moment he couldn't breathe, couldn't drag air into his lungs. How could her soft weeping affect him so deeply?

Juliette, it is nothing, a trap that failed.

There was a small silence. He pictured her wiping at her tears, felt the anger stirring in her mind. *I hate that you did this to us. Tied us together until we can't breathe without each other.*

Destiny tied us together, Juliette.

You had a choice.

I did not have a choice. I was shocked to find you. I had never expected to find you. Tell me why you are so resistant. I can help you with whatever it is you feel the need to do. You are not so opposed to our joining as you want me to believe.

He felt her shock that he had penetrated her barriers to such an extent. He felt her hurt that he might think she was part of a larger conspiracy to harm him when she had risked her life to get him out of the laboratory. He felt her withdrawal, but he could not let it matter. He would find her. He had no other choice.

Carpathians often traveled in the form of an owl. The vampire had prepared to capture him in the form of mist, knowing hunters often used the fog to travel in. The vampire could very well have planned a trap for a bird winging through the sky. Riordan chose the shape of a smaller cat, a civet, able to move fast on the highway of branches above the forest floor. Any trap designed for an animal would be for a wolf or the much heavier leopard, forms routinely used for fast travel.

He was much more cautious as he leapt from branch to branch.

His mind continually tuned itself toward Juliette. Riordan was used to being in complete control, without the danger of intense emotions, and his newly acquired feelings threw his normal balance. He sighed. *I am as ensnared as you.*

The silence was so long, he feared she would refuse to answer. *I would not say ensnared. I am merely obsessed, and obsession is very disturbing.*

I do not mind if I am the object of your obsession.

I mind. I refuse to be obsessed over anything, or anyone, let alone a man.

He felt the heat in her voice, the raw desire. Somewhere, Juliette was thinking of him, fantasizing over him. There was a silence, and he caught the shimmer of images in her mind. Their mouths welded together, her hands stroking his body, her lips traveling over the terrible burns on his chest. Riordan's temperature rose sharply. Thunder pounded in his head. His body went tight and uncomfortable. The small cat stumbled as the sexual drive hit it hard.

You cannot do this to me. He knew his voice was husky and slightly harsh but he couldn't help it. His body burned, was on fire. Each step was painful and mixed with the cat's animalistic emotions, his own beast roared for his mate.

Why not? You did it to me. I don't think my fantasy about touching your body or kissing you is nearly as bad as you touching me without physically laying a finger on me.

The little cat leapt over a twig holding a spray of leaves and nearly didn't make it, almost somersaulting into a thick snake coiled around a branch. The cat hissed and spit as it gave the snake a wide berth.

Riordan nearly groaned. Juliette wasn't stopping her fantasy at touching his body or kissing him. She was doing delicious things with her lips, working her way deliberately down his body to engulf him in the heated silk of her mouth. He groaned aloud, the small cat shuddering. It was becoming an effort to hold the form while hunger beat at him and desire swamped him. He had not taken the time to fully heal himself and if he were to regain his strength he would need sustenance.

More than anything he wanted to find Juliette, to bury his body deep in the haven of hers, relieve the terrible pressure building with unrelenting madness in his body. He could almost feel her mouth gliding over him. He could taste her heat and spice, feel her soft skin beneath his fingers.

A sound shook him out of his reverie and the small cat went instantly still, crouching low high in the forest canopy. He heard a soft sound in the distance, muted by the natural sounds of the night. Insects hummed. The sap ran in trees. Bats dipped and wheeled in the air. Bushes rustled as small rodents dashed around looking for safety. Larger predators hunted. But the sound was human—and feminine.

Riordan remained still, allowing his senses to flair out into the night, scanning the area for intruders, for traps, for the identity of the human hidden a few miles from him.

Juliette. His heart accelerated. He shifted to his natural form as his incisors lengthened in anticipation. She was close, just ahead near the stream. He could hear the water bubbling over rocks and emptying into a pool of sorts. She had to be there, cooling her body from the heat of the jungle, from the fire raging out of control between them. When he was absolutely certain they were alone, with no one near them for miles, he began to make his way toward her, using the foliage for cover.

I want you. He breathed the words into her mind. Meaning them. Needing her.

There was the smallest of hesitations. *Well, maybe I want you too, but I have things that I have to do, obligations to fulfill. I can't just change my life to suit you.*

Her voice was breathless, sensual. She was feeling the same heat, the same needs. Riordan was beginning to understand what life-mates were all about. He had been away from his people too long and he had forgotten the close bonds. He had forgotten whatever one lifemate was feeling, so did the other. Relationships were highly sexual and always intense.

He found his way to the small grotto where she rested. He sat above her, high in the trees, pleasure blossoming deep and wild just looking at her. She was so beautiful she robbed him of speech, of breath. He could look at her for eternity and never tire of it.

5

Juliette lifted her hair from the nape of her neck and wiped the sweat gleaming on her body. It was very hot and her clothes were sticking to her skin. The moon's reflection in the deep pool shimmered with cool invitation. She slowly unbuttoned her blouse and allowed it to fall to her elbows.

Riordan's breath caught in his lungs. She shrugged the top off and tossed it to land on a large fern growing out of the boulders. Juliette dipped her hand in the cool pool and poured the water down the valley between her breasts. Her head was thrown back and her breasts jutted forward, high and firm and enticing in the moonlight. Her body was no girl's, but that of a woman, with generous curves a man could lose himself in. She looked a night temptress, a woods fairy, nearly insubstantial as the water ran down her soft, alluring skin to her belly and lower still, disappearing beneath the darker material of her jeans.

His body tightened into a hard, painful ache just looking at her. Her hands were graceful as she pulled the pins from her hair and the thick braid tumbled down well below her waist. There was something terribly sensual about a woman unbraiding her hair,

Riordan decided. His chest hurt it was so tight, his lungs burning for air. Her hair floated free, a mass of blue-black silk he longed to crush in his fingers, to bury his face in.

She crouched by the pool, threw water on her face. Droplets ran down her throat, down to the creamy swell of her breasts, and lay on her skin waiting to be licked off. Riordan shifted his weight in an attempt to ease the fullness of his clothes. He didn't dare warn her she wasn't alone: she would try to run from him, and it was necessary to find out the secrets she kept locked away from him.

A faint breeze fingered the leaves of the trees so that they glittered silver and black in the night. Her scent was ripe and feminine, an allure all its own. He felt a growl rising in his throat, the beast roaring for freedom. Temptation was a woman cooling the heat of her body there by the pool in the moonlight. Riordan sank his nails deep into the branch to keep from going to her. His head pounded, his blood thick and hot. Every movement she made was a seduction. And what the hell was she doing walking around half-naked all alone where any predator could come upon her?

Juliette rose with her lithe, sensuous grace, her breasts swaying in time with the seductive movement of her hips. He couldn't take his hungry gaze off of her. Honor and gentlemanly behavior were completely overridden by primitive possessiveness. She was his lifemate. She belonged to him. Her lush body was everything he could ever want. He wanted to start at the top of her head and kiss his way down to her toes, lingering in every intriguing shadow and hollow along the way. His gaze narrowed as he saw her look around, scrutinizing the trees and bushes before stepping up on the highest boulder. She lifted her face into the air and sniffed, as if scenting the wind. Apparently satisfied she was alone, she stepped back to the edge of the pool, her hands going to the zipper of her jeans.

Riordan bit down hard on his bottom lip, hoping the pain would distract him. He couldn't have looked away if his life depended on it. She tugged at her jeans. The humidity was high and the material clung to her skin, so she had to squirm and shimmy to get them over her hips and down her thighs. Her breasts jiggled invitingly as she did a little dance to rid herself of her clothes. Tight dark curls formed a vee at the junction of her legs, a tempting arrow to draw his attention. At once he caught her feminine fragrance, the call of woman to man. Her body was burning, catching fire from his thoughts. He was broadcasting his hunger far too loudly.

Juliette was very susceptible to his needs. Dark cravings ate at him, hardened his body and sent erotic images teasing his brain. She was there waiting for him, her body open for his, craving his with the same terrible need that could never be assuaged. He closed his eyes and thought about how it would feel to plunge inside of her welcoming sheath, hot and tight and wet, slick with need for him.

Juliette made a single sound of distress as her body reacted to the waves of sexual hunger, the lust rising in him, lust she'd helped to create with her blatant fantasies. Riordan drank her in through half-closed eyes, his lids heavy and his body on fire. He wanted to see her hands travel over her soft skin, taking the path his hands would take. Up her thighs, over her rounded belly, up her narrow rib cage to cup the weight of her breasts in his palms. He wanted her thumbs to tease and flick her dark nipples, bring them to a heated peak in anticipation of his hot mouth suckling strongly.

He could already taste her, feel the soft mound of flesh in his mouth. He needed to pillow his head there, spend the night lavishing attention on each breast, on the dark inviting nipples, yet it wasn't enough. He wanted to feel how hot she was. How wet. How much she needed his body deep inside of her. His palms itched to feel her thighs, soft and rounded with firm muscles. He would slide his palms upward, feel the heat of her entrance before widening her stance, wanting her legs open to him. Gently he would slide one finger deep inside of her. He actually felt fiery heat, slick and moist, and it nearly stopped his heart. He wanted more. Wanted to feel her body grip and hold, clamp tightly around his.

He couldn't bear the feel of his clothes another moment and he dispensed with them easily with a single thought in the way of his people. The small breeze instantly caressed his body, touching him all over, adding to his sensitivity. He wished it were her fingers wrapping around the hard length of him. His erection was full and heavy and merciless, a pulsing, throbbing pain he could hardly endure.

Damn you, what are you doing to me? Her voice was breathless in his mind. Husky. Sexy. Fraught with an elemental need.

Damn you back. My body is on fire. I want your mouth on me. I want to be inside of you. I do not want illusion. Your stubbornness is going to kill us both.

Juliette had never felt such unbearable lust. It rose up from the very depths of her being and consumed her. She had always known there was passion deep inside of her. The heat of the jungle made her feel sensual when others found it oppressive. She often felt sexy, even seductive around men, but never had she felt such building heat. It was uncomfortable and unsettling, an edgy pressure demanding urgent relief. Her breasts ached for the feel of his mouth. She didn't want a gentle lover, she wanted him to feel the same smoldering, dangerous passion welling up in her. She wanted an explosive joining, his hard body driving deep and mercilessly into her. She itched and burned and hungered and there was no relief, no matter what she did.

Are you near me? She couldn't keep the invitation out of her voice. She looked around her, unconsciously enticing him with her body. She stretched her arms over her head, turned slowly in a circle. She knew she had a beautiful body and she wanted him to see it. He had done this to her, put her in this terrible state of passion, and it was up to him to assuage her unrelenting lust.

I am watching you. Can't you feel my eyes on you? You are so beautiful. Touch yourself for me.

There was seduction in his voice. A purring command, a promise of exactly what she needed. Sex—hot, elemental. A fierce lover who would slake her burning need. Juliette turned her head so that her silken hair flew around her like a cape, settling over her shoulders and body, sliding over her sensitive skin. She felt his heated gaze burning over her and she smiled.

I'm so much hotter than you can imagine. I'm slick and wet, dripping for you. She licked her fingers, a slow deliberate curl of her tongue before sucking her own tangy juice from her fingers. *I'm burning up. Are you going to just watch me all night or are you going to do something about it?* Juliette had never been so bold in her life, but then she'd never felt such intense pressure. She was angry with him for making her so out of control, and if she was out of control, she was determined he would feel the same. And she wanted him right there, right now, and didn't care that he knew it.

Riordan didn't wait for a second invitation. He floated across the sky toward the pool, settling to earth behind her. She had a beautiful back and a perfect, rounded bottom. His hands slid over the curve of her hips, starkly possessive, and he dragged her roughly against him, wanting her to feel the thick, hard length of his erection pressed tightly against her bottom.

The breath slammed out of her lungs and hot fluid rushed to pool between her legs. His teeth skimmed the nape of her neck, her shoulder, and his hands slid up to cup her aching breasts. The soft weight filled his palms, his thumbs slid over her taut nipples, stroking caresses.

"I never thought I would find you. I spent centuries without hope, and you came to me in my darkest hour." His lips drifted up her neck to her ear, whispering the words while his hips pushed into her, rubbed to try, unsuccessfully, to ease some of the pressure.

His touch set every nerve ending screaming for relief. "I found you." Juliette didn't recognize her own voice. She shook with hunger. His body was everything to her, his mind thrust deep inside of hers, heightening her pleasure at his touch, sharing her passion, the intensity of her desire until she couldn't tell where hers began or where his left off . "I can't wait anymore. I want you inside of me."

His hand slid between her legs, felt her wet welcome. She nearly sobbed with pleasure, pushing against his hand. Her arm went back, circled his neck, dragged his head around so she could find his mouth, drown in his kisses, devour him, her teeth nibbling at his lips, her tongue dueling and dancing wildly with his. "I *need* you inside of me, Riordan. I'm going to burn up if you don't hurry."

He bit wildly at her mouth, her neck, bent her back so he could get to her breasts. He'd been fantasizing about her breasts for so long he couldn't stand not tasting them, drawing her into his mouth, suckling strongly, while his hips frantically surged against her enticing buttocks.

She screamed at the pull of his mouth, her hand tunneling in his hair, clutching his head to her while he devoured her breast. Every pull of his mouth sent wet heat pulsating through her body and trickling down her leg. Her cries nearly sent him over the edge. He bent her body forward, planting her hands on the boulders while he thrust his fingers deep into her to test her readiness. She pushed back into his hand, riding, bucking, sobbing for him to enter her.

He caught her hips and held her, looking down at her beautiful body. His lifemate. Sultry, sexy—everything he could ever want. Crying out for him. Pleading for him to take her, to unite them. *Demanding* he take her. He was so hard he thought he might shatter. He surged into her thick wetness, one long stroke that felt as if it blew the top of his head off. Fire raced up his penis, spread through his body, a volcanic eruption that reached all the way to his toes.

Juliette's body was tight and hot and gripping his as he withdrew so that he shuddered with pleasure. She sobbed again, pushing eagerly back onto him as he thrust forward. He was large and thick, and driving through the soft folds was sweet torture. "Are you all right?" He was so large and she felt so small. He pressed her forward, adjusting their positions so she could take more of him. "I want all of me inside of you."

"I want every last bit of you in me too," Juliette answered. "Can't you feel what I'm feeling? Harder. Faster. I need you to be crazy, because I feel crazy." And she did. She felt wild and heated and sensual and she wanted him out of control and driving into her with everything he was. Pouring his heart and soul and his very essence into her. "More, I want more."

Juliette gave herself up to the wild pounding. Every hard stroke sent vibrations of sheer pleasure rushing through her body. Every cell, everynerve ending, every tiny part of her burned and blazed. Her breasts ached and swung with every thrust, her hair brushed the ground and silky strands fell in her face. Her body was hot and sweaty and exploding in ecstasy. She took him with her over the edge, her muscles clamping around his thick erection and dragging every last drop of his seed out of him.

For Juliette it didn't end, her body rippling with aftershocks, colors bursting behind her eyes and fireworks going off in her mind. She didn't want him to move, wanted to savor their joined bodies. He was magnificent, long and thick and more than she could possibly have imagined.

Riordan slid out of her body reluctantly. When she made a soft sound of protest he drew her back into his arms. "We have time. All the time in the world, and I want to touch you. I love kissing you." His hands skimmed her breasts, moved up to frame her face. "And I hunger for the taste of you. I want to bring you more fully into my world."

She turned her face up to nuzzle his throat. "Do you know what I am?" She kissed the hollow of his throat, her hands sliding possessively over his body. Stroking his flat stomach and kissing her way along his chest. Her hands caressed his penis, shaping and teasing and memorizing the long line of him. "I'm a jaguar. A shape-shifter. Are you certain I am what you want?"

Riordan answered her in the only way he could. His body was sensitized and reacting with more demands. His incisors lengthened as his penis did. He bent his head and buried his teeth in the pulse beating so strongly in her neck.

She cried out, threw her head back and circled his neck with her arms, pressing her body closer to his. He had not used his tongue to prepare her for the shock of the connection, but Juliette felt it only as white-hot heat coursing through her bloodstream, as whips of lightning lashed every nerve ending into a sexual frenzy.

He held her possessively, his hands tender, but commanding, shifting her so that the tips of her breasts rubbed against his chest and her hair was out of the way. So that his straining groin pressed against her soft belly. *You taste like an exotic fruit, tangy and spicy and hot. I wonder what you'll taste like when I crawl between your legs and drink my fill there.*

Her entire body clenched. She closed her eyes and pressed closer to him. She wanted everything from him, with him. She wanted it all.

His tongue swept across the pinpricks on her neck. His hand circled her throat, his thumb tipping up her face so that she was compelled to look into his eyes. *See what I taste like.* He commanded it in a purring, velvet voice, so mesmerizing she half fell into a dream. Riordan opened a line with a sharp fingernail, caught the back of her head in his palm and pressed her face forward until her mouth was pressed to the heavy muscles of his chest, just above his heart. She could feel it beating, accelerating as her lips moved over his skin, as she drew his dark gift into her body.

He brought her out of her enthrallment when she had taken enough for their second exchange, his mouth ravishing hers. He could kiss her forever, over and over and never get enough. Their mouths clung, tongues tangling wildly. Abruptly he pulled away, scowling at her. There was an ominous danger to his smoldering gaze.

"What?"

"Do not *what* me. You were thinking of another man."

Juliette ran her tongue over her bottom lip. "I was not thinking of another man. I merely thought I'd never been with a man as sexy as you. There's a difference."

His hand circled her bare arm, brought her close to him. "You have been with another man."

"Jaguars are sexual creatures, Riordan. We need sex at times." She leaned forward and lapped at his chest, right above his heart. "Why should that bother you?"

"Juliette, we are bound together. I would know if you had sex with another man. You could not hide it from me."

"I wouldn't try to hide it from you." She pushed at the wall of his chest but he was a rock, and even with her unusual strength, she couldn't move him.

"I would kill him."

"Why would you kill him? He isn't the one bound to you."

"Exactly." Riordan turned away from her, a black anger he didn't understand enveloping him. To cool off, he waded into the pool and looked back at her. She stood there with the moonlight spilling over her luscious body, her expression a mixture of amusement and exasperation. She was so beautiful he hurt just looking at her. "I am not human, Juliette, and you can never think for one moment that I am. I am a predator and I will protect what is mine."

"Did I say I wanted another man? No! I was thinking no one else could compare with you. I was *not* thinking I wanted someone else. How could I, after what we just shared? Are you going to be an idiot and act jealous all the time? That would make me crazy."

He ducked under the water to rinse the heat from his skin. He stood up, the water lapping at his hips. "Come here."

"You didn't answer me."

He sighed. "Yes, I am going to be an idiot and act jealous all the time. The idea of another man touching you, making love to you, makes me want to tear out his heart."

"Well." Juliette smiled and waded out to him. "I'd want to tear out the heart of any woman who tried to seduce you." She reached him, tipping up her face for his searing kiss. "We'll both have to work not to be jealous idiots. I can't see myself wanting anyone else when I have you."

"I will not mind if you wish to seduce me." He kissed her again, long, addictive kisses that had a bite to them.

"How lucky for me." She bent down and hit the water with her hand, sending up a spray that doused him thoroughly. Laughing, she dove away from him, swimming beneath the water to the center of the pond.

6

Riordan watched her swim, her pale body slipping sensuously through the water. The clear liquid shimmered over her feminine form, enhancing every curve and secret hollow. Catching the glimpse of another man in her mind had been a shock, and he wasn't certain why it would be. She was a very sexual woman. She was bold and knew what she wanted. He wanted that kind of woman, as sexual as he knew himself to be, yet the thought of another man leaning down to suckle her breast or plunge deep into her body made the beast in him rise. It was dark and ugly and utterly dangerous.

Juliette would attract the attention of men with her shapely body. She was the epitome of a sexual creature. Riordan dove underwater and began to swim laps, back and forth, driving himself to keep his fury at bay. If she ever wanted another man . . .

I thought lifemates wanted only each other. There was curiosity in her voice.

You are the only lifemate I have ever had. I am new at this.

He sounded so disgruntled she laughed and swam to the other side of the pool. There was a smooth shelf formed from boulders beneath the surface near the edge of the water. Juliette sat on it and watched him swim back and forth like a shark. *Does it really bother you so much?*

Riordan heard the soft tremor in her voice. *Of course it bothers me. I am a possessive man. But it matters little, Juliette. We are lifemates. We are bound from this time forward and there will be no other.*

Is that a decree? She didn't know why she was suddenly close to tears. She wasn't ashamed of her past. She didn't want any other men now, but she couldn't help that she had been born into a species that made it nearly impossible not to have sex at certain times. She wasn't about to apologize for who she was.

Riordan caught the echo of her thoughts, the painful tightness in her chest, and knew he'd hurt her. Had that been his intention? He hoped not. He would despise himself if his newly acquired emotions were so out of control that he could punish his lifemate for something she did before he met her.

He swam slowly across the pool until he was directly in front of her. "I do believe I am the idiot you called me. I apologize for my jealous streak. I also find I have a rotten temper which I shall do my best to control." He grinned at her, a sudden melting smile that brought life to his dark eyes. "It is the passion in me. My blood runs hot and I am caught. Fortunately . . . " He moved closer to her, his hands circling her ankles. "I can make up for my shortcomings in other ways."

"Don't you dare." She could see the mischief on his face.

He yanked on her legs, catching her by surprise, so that she slid toward him, her legs over his shoulders. *I thought I would find out how you taste. If you're as tangy and spicy all over as I imagine you are.* Without giving her the slightest opportunity to squirm away, he lowered his head between her thighs.

Juliette jumped, but his hands cupped her bare buttocks, fingers digging deep to hold her still. His teeth scraped the inside of her thigh. She heard herself moan softly. Felt the first surge of moist welcoming heat.

"Lie back for me," he said softly, "relax, float. Just feel. Just feel this time, Juliette."

She loved the way he said her name with his peculiar, very sexy accent. She loved the way his eyes went dark and smoldered and hungered and burned over her body. His hair touched her sensitive skin, her body trembled. She felt his hand pushing against her heat. She stared up at the night sky, watched the droplets of rain come down in slow motion. Some landed on her face, some on her bare breasts. Water from the pool slid over her stomach, a silken blanket arousing her further. Juliette gave herself to him completely.

His finger pushed into her, stroking deep caresses, teasing and dancing until she moaned with pleasure. His mouth replaced his hand, a hot pulsing of fire that left her breathless, unable to scream, unable to breathe. Pressure built fast and hard and raged through her body for release. When her orgasm hit, it was explosive and violent and shook her to the very core of her being.

Riordan slowly lifted his head from between her thighs, holding her secure when she might have drowned, might have just sunk to the bottom in a heap of heated feminine flesh. He pulled her through the water to him, rocked her gently while her body continued to sizzle and spark and ripple with pleasure.

Juliette wrapped her arms around his neck and laid her head on his shoulder. "I accept your apology."

His arms tightened possessively. He floated over to the small shelf near the water's edge. "I hoped you would feel my sincerity."

"Do you think a woman can fall in love with a man she barely knows?"

"I do not know, but she can fall in love with a man after she has walked in his mind and knows who he is and what he stands for."

She kissed his neck. "I never once dreamed I would have a man in my life. Never once."

"That is only because you could not conjure up the image of such a charming man." He sank down onto the shelf looking pleased with himself and pulled her onto his lap, cradling her close. "I have four brothers." He pushed the wet hair from the side of her neck and threw it back in a long, wet trail over her shoulder. "Our prince sent us out so many years ago this country has become our home. I am the youngest in the family, and my brothers worry for me, all of them. Nicolas and Rafael are out of the country at the moment so you are safe from meeting them en masse. We have very close ties to a family of humans . . ."

"The ones who work your cattle empire," she interrupted.

"Ranch. It is large, but it is no empire. Yes, they run the ranch. They have young orphaned relatives in the United States and two of my brothers went to help them smooth the way to bring them home."

She looked up at him suspiciously. "What does that mean? Smooth the way. By using their voices with hypnotic suggestions? Their eyes mesmerizing people?"

He grinned again, softening the lines in his face. "Is that what you think I do?"

"You're shameless about it," she confirmed.

"It worked on you, and that is all that matters."

"You wish it worked on me. I just happen to like the way you're put together." She laced her fingers through his. "So you have a big ranch and live there with four overprotective brothers and a human family as well."

"My other brothers, Manolito and Zacarias, the eldest, are probably heading this way as we speak to check on me as if I were an infant."

She brought his hand to her mouth. "I'll testify you're long past the infant stage if you'd like."

"I doubt if it will be helpful. I can handle my brothers. I am just warning you that their protection will extend to you. We have to avoid them until I know you're so completely captivated by my charm, you will not run away from them."

"I live with my younger sister, and my cousin. Jasmine, my little sister, is beautiful inside and out." Juliette frowned. "She is able to shift once in a while if she is under tremendous stress, but she can't count on the ability as I do. My cousin and I are the protectors in my family. Not just in my family but for all women in our bloodline."

He was silent, waiting for her to continue. He sensed a terrible sadness and tightened his arms around her to give her comfort and support.

Juliette leaned her head against his shoulder, her hair floating on the water around them like seaweed. "I have to go back home and make certain my sister and my cousin are safe. I have a duty to my family, Riordan, just as you have one to your people. We don't have men to protect us. Our men do not mate for life, nor do they stay with us. Some of the men try to kidnap and hold our women prisoners just to be able to keep the bloodline pure. Very few of us are capable of shifting in to our other form. And it will continue to become fewer and fewer. They treat these women like breeding machines. It's a horrible thing. They don't love them or try to create an atmosphere of happiness, they simply force them to produce babies."

"And what is it you think you can do to stop them?" His voice was utterly devoid of expression.

Juliette felt a chill go down her spine. She sensed his sudden stillness. She had been in his mind and there was a ruthless, merciless quality buried deep inside of him that alarmed her. "Someone has to rescue the women. I'm strong. I'm capable of shifting, and I'm not afraid of those bastards. I can protect my sister and cousin. Well, maybe Solange protects me." She turned her head to look up at his face. "They took my mother. She was held in a tiny room, and several men raped her to get her pregnant. It didn't happen immediately so they had her for a long time. It took us two years to find her."

"Juliette." He breathed her name. Her sorrow beat at him, tore at his heart and soul. He nuzzled the top of her head. "I am so sorry." She didn't need to tell him the rest. He saw it in her mind. Her mother had died in childbirth, too long neglected by the men who held her prisoner. The child had died as well, and Juliette felt responsible because it had taken so long to find her mother.

Riordan had been prepared to forbid her to assume the part of a warrior woman, but he couldn't speak, couldn't issue commands even though it might keep her safe. Her pain ran too deep. He understood the need to protect others. He understood honor and responsibility. His fingers crushed her hair in his fist. "Did you find the men who took her? You must know them by scent."

Tears burned behind her eyelids, tears she vowed would never be shed. She refused to spend her time crying. There were very few women capable of shifting and the jaguar males who had banded together were determined to possess them. She was every bit as determined that they would never get their hands on them.

"Jasmine may not be able to shift on command, but even the small ability she has places her in danger. She has other gifts to aid her, but she couldn't fight against the males if they captured her. I live with Jasmine and my cousin. Solange is my mother's sister's daughter and my mother raised her after my aunt was killed when several males tried to capture us. She fought them off, giving my mother time to escape with the three of us girls."

"So now you and your sister and cousin live in fear of these men coming after you. Why did you stay in the jungle where there is danger?"

"Why do you hunt the vampire?" she fired back. "This is our home. We're not the only women these men are after, but we have skills. After what they did to our mothers, we don't plan to just let them steal and kill other women. We know the way the men think now, and we've successfully taken back several women."

"Juliette, what you do is very dangerous. These males are not right. I have known some of the jaguar race and the men did not commit these crimes against their women. Something is wrong."

"It isn't all the men. It is only a small group, yet they are very powerful because they have banded together." She turned in his arms. "Do you understand why I have to stay with these women? They have no other protection. Jasmine and I feared the males were in league with someone at the new Morrison laboratory. Too many animals on the endangered species list were being captured. We thought the jaguar males were trading animals for help in finding the females. That was one of the reasons we broke into the laboratory."

"Is it possible a vampire has connected with a jaguar male and corrupted him?"

"I think these males have corrupted themselves."

"We will return to your family and make certain they are safe, Juliette. If you care about them, then, of course, I care about them. There is no question this practice must be stopped."

"I tried not to blame the males, I really did. Our species is dying out, but they don't care at all about the females, only that they want the race to go on." She shook her head sadly. "It isn't right. We have a right to our lives."

He kissed her temple, the corner of her mouth. "I understand their desperation. Our species is nearly extinct also." He tipped her chin up so he could capture her mouth. His kiss was gentle, tender. "I bound you to me with no thought of your feelings, Juliette. Perhaps I am as guilty as these males." His arms circled her waist, pulled her onto his lap so that they half floated in the water, her body fitting into the cradle of his hips. "I never thought how selfish that would be. In my culture, life mates are destined and must be together for survival. It is another world now, one where our women, perhaps, are not even from the same species. I should have thought more of what you wished to accomplish in your life and less of what I needed to survive."

Juliette lay back against him, resting her head in the niche of his sternum. His hands cupped her full breasts, taking the weight in his palms, his fingers gently massaging her almost without thought. Pleasure shot through her. She thought she might never want to move again, yet his hands on her body created a molten heat that moved slowly through her bloodstream and licked at her skin.

"I wasn't thinking either, Riordan, only how much I wanted you. I could barely think straight with wanting you. You hadn't bound us together at that point so I'm not so certain I would have said no." She turned over lazily and slid down his body, skin to skin, rubbing along his chest and rib cage, delighting in the differences between men and women. His belly was flat and ridged with muscles. She licked off droplets of water. The rain fell gently, cool drops that seemed to sizzle against her hot skin. She wrapped her arms around his hips, nuzzling his navel lazily. Her teeth nipped his skin.

Riordan felt his body harden in response. Looking down at the clean line of her back, the rounded enticement of her bottom, her legs floating over his in the cool waters of the pool was enough to give any man pleasure. Her mouth wandered over him, tasting and licking. There was nothing inhibited about Juliette. She loved having sex with him, loved his body, and in her mind she let him know. With her body she let him know. It was exciting to have a woman so completely open and natural with him.

"I should have given you the opportunity to at least discuss what it meant, Juliette," he said. His voice was husky. Her mouth was doing delicious things to his body and it was becoming much more difficult to think straight.

"I don't think I wanted to discuss it." She slipped a little lower so she could breathe hot air over his heavy erection. She smiled when she felt his muscles contract and his hands clamp over her arms in reaction. Juliette lifted her chin so she could meet his gaze, reveling in the hunger darkening his eyes. "If I'd thought too much, I wouldn't have been able to have you. And I really, really wanted you." She lowered her head so she could lick along the head of his penis, a slow, leisurely exploration of the shape and texture of his body.

His breath slammed out of his lungs. "I have to admit, I am eternally grateful you want me. I do not think we will ever have enough time to do all the things I have in my mind." Deliberately he let her see his every desire, his every need.

Juliette laughed softly. "It's good we think along the same lines. I would hate to be tied to someone who isn't adventurous. I definitely need adventurous."

It was his turn to yell. The sound ripped from his throat when her mouth engulfed him, took him deep into her throat and began a slow, sensuous foray. *I thought I would find out how you taste. Whether you're hot and spicy and tangy.* Her teasing laughter played over his senses and stroked at his body. He lost time, drifting in the waves of the pool lapping at his body, with her hot mouth and tongue bringing him to a fever pitch. When he could no longer stay still, he moved his hips into her, letting her take charge of the rhythm, set the pace. She teased him to the brink of an orgasm, sucking hard and lavishing attention with her tongue, only to slide her mouth loosely over him, her teeth gentle. *I love to feel what you feel. I love to hear the roar in your head and know I can put it there just by doing this.* Her mouth pulled at him. His hands fisted in her hair, his hips growing more urgent, more frantic in his response. She took him deep, working him until he was so caught in her spell, so far gone with pleasure he couldn't think straight.

"Finish it or let me have you," he managed to hiss out between his teeth.

She complied, her soft, taunting laughter only teasing his senses more. Juliette reveled in her power. He was enormously strong and dangerous, and yet he needed her. *You need fun in your life, Riordan. You really do need me.*

Damn it. He growled it in her mind, his hands bunching in her hair.

Her mouth sent him deliberately over the edge, milking him as her teasing laughter burned in his brain. She was etched in his very bones for all time. He would never be able to go back to what he had been. And he would never be able to be without her. She carried light with her and she made him feel it in the unrelenting darkness that had been his home.

She ducked under the water, pushing away from him. Riordan reached out and caught her, dragging her back. He pushed the wet hair from her face and stared down at her. His miracle. "I do need you," he admitted. If she could be brave and honest and admit what she wanted and needed he could do no less. "You are everything."

7

"I need blood, Juliette. The night is slipping away from us. We must return to your family at full strength. I would love to spend the rest of my days here, making love to you and discovering the secrets of my lifemate, but I must have sustenance to renew my strength." Riordan waded out of the pool and held out his hand to her.

Juliette took her time, her eyes taking her fill of him. "I swore I would never have anything to do with a man. The men I've known have no knowledge of caring." She looked down at the ground. "It's a terrible thing to grow up being ashamed of what you are, knowing you might give birth to a male of the species and no matter what you do, how much you love him, how you raise him, his nature will always prevent him from loving you back."

His fingers settled around her wrist and he drew her to him. "I have lived many years and have found that each species has both strengths and weaknesses. The males of the jaguar race are wanderers, but the ones I encountered cared about their women. They could not settle down and the continual drive to perpetuate their race became their downfall. They would not stay with one female, though I believe many of them tried and were very distressed that they could not." He drew her into his arms to comfort her. "The rain forest here in South America is very large and there are no borders in the jungle. We settled in Brazil, on the edge of the forest, but we travel from country to country to insure the safety of the inhabitants. In our travels we often encounter the males. They are all solitary creatures. We had been instructed by our prince to avoid them if possible, but often we spoke with them. Jaguars, like our species, are on the verge of extinction. They are intelligent and know they contributed to their own extinction, yet they still could not stop what nature dictated." And a part of him felt very much as if they deserved their fate when they refused to treasure their women and children.

"You're saying it's not their fault." Juliette pulled out of his arms, turning her face away from him as she gathered her clothes with shaking hands. She stepped into her jeans and dragged them up over her bare skin, blinking back tears. That was twice she'd nearly cried in front of him. She didn't cry. Not because of a man.

"We are not talking about the rogue males, the ones out of control and doing harm to their women. They should be brought to justice, not allowed to be kidnapping and raping women with the idea of creating baby machines." He took the shirt from her hands and turned her around to face him, tipping up her chin so she had to meet his dark gaze. "I may be rough, Juliette, and I will admit I have long ago forgotten how to be gentle, but I would never harm a woman unless she threatened my life or my people. It is not done."

She framed his face, her palms resting along his shadowed jaw. "You're gentle enough for me." And he was. He moved her like no other man had ever done—or ever could. They had come together in fire, burning hot and out of control, yet then he had stroked tender caresses down her body with a trembling hand, sitting her on his lap, cupping her breasts reverently.

Riordan leaned down to kiss her upturned face, taking his time, lingering over it. His heart found the rhythm of hers. "You are an unexpected gift. I am not a man to throw such things away."

She took her shirt from him and slipped into it.

He reached out to pull the edges of the material together over her generous breasts. "Even in your clothes, you look so sexy I am uncertain whether or not I can keep my hands off of you." He lifted the soft weight of her breast, his fingers sliding over creamy skin. "Your skin is so soft and warm and inviting." He bent down and drew her nipple into the heat of his mouth, unable to resist the temptation.

Juliette closed her eyes, pressing closer to him, wrapping her arms around his head, holding him to her while waves of pleasure coursed through her body, swamped her utterly and completely. She loved the way he indulged himself with her body. She loved that he enjoyed her so much and that he obviously wanted her to feel the same about him. "We're never going to leave this spot if we keep this up," she murmured, wanting to strip off her jeans and wrap her legs firmly around his waist. "I think sex with you is addicting."

"I cannot help myself." His tongue teased her nipple into a hard peak before reluctantly releasing her. "Your body is such a temptation."

Her fingers drifted over his heavy erection. "There you go again, blaming it on me. I see you like this, hard and thick and so in need, and naturally I want to do something about it."

He groaned. "I have no discipline around you." He tugged at the jeans until they were down around her ankles and she could kick them aside. "If I do not get some relief, I doubt I will be able to walk, let alone battle any vampires. What do you intend to do about it?"

She circled his neck with her arms and pulled herself up his body, wrapping her legs tightly around his waist. "I thought I would just take a ride," she whispered and licked his ear with a teasing tongue. Very slowly she settled over his penis, lowering herself with slow deliberation. As he began to push his way through her tight folds she shivered with pleasure. "It's always so perfect with you." She waited to move until he had filled her completely, sinking down onto his shaft so that she was impaled and full and every nerve ending was alive and sizzling with flames.

Riordan didn't wait for her, catching her hips in his hands and helping her with her sensuous ride; long, hard thrusts that went deep inside of her, joining them together. He loved the way her breasts rubbed against his chest, the way she threw her head back, obvious pleasure lighting her face. She purred, just like a cat, deepening the movement, as wild and uninhibited as he was. He was so tuned to her mind now, he could adjust his every movement to better give her pleasure. He knew the moment she wanted him to be slow and deep and he knew when she needed the hard, long strokes that sent fiery friction whipping through both of them.

Night shadows hid them in the small grotto. The wind rustled in the canopy overhead. Bats fluttered above the water, hitting insects just above the surface. Raindrops splattered into the pool. Juliette inhaled the scents of the night, the combined scent of man and woman. Her nails dug into Riordan's shoulders and back as wave after wave of orgasm burst through her. He shared the experience in her mind and the riptide of ecstasy coursing through her sent him over the edge. Juliette, merged so completely with Riordan, felt the pressure start deep in his core and explode through his body with the force of a locomotive. They fed each other passion and heat, a firestorm of pleasure that washed over and through them and left them breathless and clinging to one another.

Juliette fastened her mouth to his—hot, wet, hungry. She tried to crawl inside of him, share the same body, the same mind. Kisses went from greedy lust to slower, calmer, leisurely exploration, to long, lingering enjoyment. She lifted her head and looked into his eyes. They stared at one another for a long time, drinking each other in, falling into the depths of each other's eyes. "I look at you and everything just comes together, Riordan. I don't know why, and I don't think I want to question it too closely. I'm just going to take what fate offered me and grab on with both hands."

"You will never be sorry, Juliette," he promised, raining kisses over her face, her eyes, down her neck and throat. "You will never be sorry."

"I can feel your hunger now, the call inside you. It's a frightening thing. How can you keep it at bay the way you do? If I felt like that, I would be devouring something." She swept back his hair and slowly allowed her legs to drop to the ground. "You have to get some nourishment. I don't mind, Riordan. I'm not in the least bit hungry and the thought of food makes me want to gag, but it's sort of sexy when you take my blood. I think I'm getting a bit kinky." She looked around for her clothes, missing the look of wonderment on his face.

He reached down to snag her blouse from where it had been carelessly tossed aside. He didn't even remember stripping it off of her. "You are a very generous woman, but I think I will refrain from the temptation of your blood." This time he firmly buttoned the blouse. "You know I am going to think of your breasts just waiting behind this very thin barrier. If I am distracted later, you will know why."

Juliette laughed. She couldn't remember being so happy. "That's all right, you go ahead and think about my breasts. I'll be thinking of your very nicely put together anatomy." She yanked her jeans on and deftly braided her hair. "How much time do we have for traveling tonight?"

He glanced at the sky. "A few hours. We should be able to cover many miles. I will have to carry you, and that means I will have to find blood." He glanced down at the terrible marks on his chest. "Carpathians heal in the ground and yet I did not. I need to get back to full strength for the coming battle, and that means I need to find people."

She suddenly went still. "Not my sister or cousin." There was a warning note in her voice.

He grinned at her. "I do not think you have to worry. I would not risk your wrath." He tugged playfully at her braid. "You sound so fierce."

Juliette watched him clothe himself. It was done with a simple wave of his hand as if he'd manufactured the clothes from thin air. His hair was neatly brushed back away from his face and tied with a leather thong. There wasn't a drop of water on him anywhere and his hair was dry. "Oh, that is cheating. Look at me, I look like a drowned rat." She flipped her thick wet braid over her shoulder. "I want to be able to do that."

"You will," he assured. "Come here. We need to get started."

"You aren't going to throw me over your shoulder like you did last time, are you?" she asked suspiciously.

He grinned at her, his teeth very white. "Well, I was thinking about it."

"Refrain. Last time I considered getting sick all over you."

"I am so glad you didn't." Riordan gathered her to him, holding her close, and took to the air, shifting into his favorite form of a bird as he rose. It was easier to fly above the canopy then to try to wind his way through the thick branches and leaves. And he was wary of traps. They were nearing the area where he had first heard the voice of the vampire calling to him for help. He was certain the vampire and his human accomplices were responsible for the net that had nearly claimed him a second time.

Juliette laughed aloud as Riordan raced across the sky. Twice she reached out, trying to touch a cloud, unable to resist. *This is astonishing.* She felt a part of the night sky, the stars and the clouds and even the rain. It was as though she had merged with nature. She expected to feel fear, but she felt elation, joy, completely alive. It was every bit as wonderful as running through the jungle in the form of a jaguar.

Do not ever feel regret, Juliette. You will be able to shift into many forms and effortlessly hold those forms.

I have to tell you something. The smile faded from Juliette's face. Riordan caught the uneasiness rising as he followed the directions in her mind. *We have to move often. We have several homes.*

He waited. It wasn't what she wanted to tell him. She was hesitant, very unlike his bold Juliette. She carefully turned over her words, trying to formulate the best way to get him to understand.

Juliette. You must trust me. Just say what you need to say and trust me to understand.

She could see the canopy far below her. The leaves of the trees were silver-black in the moonlight. The raindrops dazzled her eyes, glittering like diamonds as they fell from the clouds. *We have seen terrible things from the males. Young girls unable to shape-shift beaten and abused. Solange, Jasmine and I vowed never to have anything to do with a man other than the necessities.*

Necessities? She meant sex. Riordan felt his heart pound. Something black and dangerous swirled in his gut. It was ugly and volcanic, and he was ashamed of his reaction. She was telling him something terribly important, not only to her, but to her life, and his first thought had been that the necessity was sex with another man. He despised himself for being so petty. She was a beautiful and sensual woman. Many men would find her attractive, and he should be proud of her. Lifemates trusted one another implicitly. It was impossible to lie to one another or hide anything, and as they grew to know each other better it would be natural to spend more and more time in one another's mind.

I am not such a man, Juliette. At my worst, I would not harm a woman or child. It is abhorrent to me. I had no idea my returning emotions would be so overwhelming and intense, but I know myself well. I would never, I could never hurt you or your sister and cousin.

Juliette leaned into him, felt the tickle of feathers and immediately wanted to be able to join him in the form of a bird. *You don't have to tell me that. I already know you wouldn't ever hurt a woman or I would never be with you. I'm concerned my family won't be very accepting of our relationship.*

I will win them over.

Far below them, near the edge of the rain forest, was a small settlement. Riordan began his descent cautiously, one part of him scanning the area below for signs of the vampire. *Always scan to look for danger before revealing yourself.*

It feels a bit intrusive. You pick up random thoughts. She was studying his ways carefully, trying to learn as much as possible. *I would hate to pick up my sister's thoughts or worse, my cousin's.*

He laughed as he set her gently on the ground, shifting back to his natural form as he planted his feet in the thick vegetation. "You can avoid scanning the thoughts of your family. You will learn to tune things out once you refine the process. Start experimenting now with volume and reading the air. You can feel danger vibrating. If there is a blank spot where what seems natural to you is not there, a vampire is attempting to hide his presence from you."

"Do you always know a vampire is a vampire?"

"Unfortunately, no. If a vampire is skilled, such as a master vampire, he could easily walk up to one of the hunters, greet him in the way of our people and go on his way unscathed."

"How frightening."

"Stay here while I feed. You should be safe for the moment. There is a feel to the forest, as if the animals are in hiding."

Juliette went still. She had been so busy trying to think as a

Carpathian, so wrapped up in Riordan as a man, that she had forgotten the first rule of living in the jungle. She hadn't paid attention to the warning system of the inhabitants. Riordan strode away from her, melting into the shadows so that it was impossible to see him, even when she was looking directly at him.

She lifted her face to the wind. She was jaguar. And her senses were enhanced by ancient Carpathian blood. She could read the forest news. Animals were hiding, lying low and trembling, waiting until a night bird signaled they were once again safe from predators. Juliette turned her head this way and that, on the alert, feeling the vibration of danger moving through the air. Something was wrong. They were a few miles from the laboratory and several miles from her home.

Her heart jumped. "Jasmine." A large predator or a hunting party had passed through the area and frightened the inhabitants. A sudden chill went down her spine. Or a *group* of predators. She was supposed to lead the guards from the Morrison laboratory away from the direction of her home, but Riordan had carried her off instead. Had they found Jasmine's trail? Jasmine might not have been as cautious as she should have, thinking Juliette would be drawing the guards away from her. What if it was worse than the human guards? What if the male jaguars had cut across Jasmine's trail? Solange was on a scouting mission, hunting for any news of missing females. Jasmine had been alone.

Juliette didn't hesitate; she turned and ran, following the small animal trail through the brush. *I think my sister's in trouble.*

I am feeding, near full strength. Wait for me. I will get us to her.

She couldn't wait. She knew it didn't make sense, but she had to do something. Adrenaline was pouring through her body. Fear took hold of her mind. What if Jasmine had been taken the night before and the males had her already for nearly twenty-four hours? *Please God, please God.* She chanted the plea, her chest burning, her throat closing. The more she ran, the more she was certain the jaguars had been on her sister's trail, tracking her.

"Juliette," Riordan caught her in strong arms, in front of her, blocking her way. She hit his chest hard, but his larger frame barely rocked under her assault. "We have to be cautious. And we do not want to ruin any tracks. If they have her, it is better to slow down and find her trail, than to go running around without direction."

"You don't know what they do," she hissed, pulling away from him.

"We will find her and get her back."

She stepped away from him and wrapped her arms around her body, hunching. "You have no idea what she will suffer, and I can never take it back."

He led the way, moving fluidly, so silent not even the leaves rustled. Juliette tried to breathe, to get her brain functioning again. *I couldn't bear it if something happened to Jasmine. It's my fault. I was supposed to draw the guards away. I wasn't here to do it, and she probably left tracks. The males would be able to follow her easily.*

This is not your fault, Juliette. Riordan could smell them now. He didn't want to tell her, but he knew as they approached the small hut covered over with vines and creepers. The structure was difficult to see through all the foliage. He reached for her hand. The door was splintered down the middle, one half cracked and broken out, leaving a large hole.

A terrible cry welled up in Juliette. She couldn't stop it, couldn't repress it. The sound tore through her body, raw and horrible, tearing her throat. It was an agonized cry of pain and heartache and grief. Itwas a cry of revenge, of promise, a vow of absolute retribution.

8

Riordan went through the door first. The stench of terror permeated the room. The pungent odor of large cats was overpowering. A table was overturned. There was a smear of blood on the wall and another on a broken chair.

Juliette pressed her hand to her mouth, choking back a sob. "She's just a child, Riordan. She's just turned twenty." She pushed past Riordan and hurried across the room to the wall. She inhaled deeply, scenting the blood. "This isn't from Jasmine. It's Solange. She was here."

Riordan was examining the room and the forest floor just outside. "She came when they were taking Jasmine and she must have shifted on the run. Can she do that? See, here are her footprints, and here are ripped clothes and claw marks. She did not have time to shed her clothes and shifted with them on. The seams of the material separated and she ripped the rest away from her so she could fight. She was the one who destroyed the door trying to get to your sister. They barred it from the inside and took your sister out the back. One was carrying her. They were in the form of men. See," he crouched beside the tracks. "This one is suddenly heavier, and he's bearing a weight. Jasmine is not struggling."

"She's unconscious," Juliette said. "She would fight them with her last breath. We all watched my mother die. Solange saw them kill her mother and yet she raced in, without hesitation, to try to stop them." She turned back to study the blood. "She isn't hurt too bad."

"One remained behind, a big male, and he shifted into jaguar form. He probably didn't want to harm her when he saw she was female and she shifted on the run. After all, she is probably extremely rare." Riordan followed the tracks. "She got away, into the forest. The big male is after her." He turned back to Juliette. "Which one do we go after?"

"Maybe we should split up. I'll follow Solange. We've fought together before, and I know how she thinks. She'll accept me. You go after Jasmine. You're far stronger and can travel faster. You have a chance of getting to her before they hurt her."

"Dawn will be breaking soon, Juliette. I will have to go to ground. If I do not reach your sister before that time, she will spend another day in torment." Riordan cursed the vulnerability of his heritage. "I cannot walk in the sun." His fingers brushed her cheek. "You will burn, Juliette. Your skin is no longer able to stand intense sunlight and your eyes will burn."

"I don't care about my skin." Juliette pushed past him and studied the ground, the direction the group of men had taken. She tried to think who would need her the most. Riordan was fast; he could get her close to her sister before he would have to get away from the sun. "Jasmine's already been with them for hours. If you don't think you'll have enough time to get to her then I'll have to trust Solange to get away from her attacker alone. We have to find Jasmine fast, Riordan."

Riordan circled her waist with one arm, lifting her. The

surrounding jungle was a blur as he raced through it. She had no idea how he could focus on the tracks, on the small bruised leaves, snapped twigs, and occasional footprint when he moved so quickly. She didn't need to tell him her younger sister was in dire trouble; he could read every worry in her mind. When the males shifted form, they were without clothes. Jasmine was alone and without protection. Juliette could only pray that the males would want to get her as far from help as possible. She tried not to think of her cousin—alone, hurt, running for her life.

I can send for my brothers, but they are hundreds of miles away. They would not be here for several risings.

Solange will fight. They will not take her easily. Even as she thought it, a wave of hope went through her. It was true, Solange was a fighter. She would never surrender, never give up, no matter how injured she was. *I feel as if I'm deserting her, but she has a much better chance than Jasmine.*

From what I have seen of your cousin in your mind, she would want you to go after Jasmine.

Riordan was all too aware of the time slipping away from them. The jaguar males were adept at losing themselves in the forest. They had spread out, weaving through the trees, more cunning now, obviously certain there would be an attempt to follow them.

The wind rose in a sudden rush off the forest floor, carrying a swirling eddy of vegetation, leaves and twigs and petals of flowers in a dark funnel straight toward the sky. The debris burst over them, a cloud of missiles hurled from the ground by unseen hands. Riordan reacted instantly, instinctively swinging his body around in midair to better protect Juliette. Debris embedded in his skin, drove for his heart. He swore in several languages as he raced to get them to earth where he could fight without the burden of Juliette's human form hampering him.

Remove your clothes now and as soon as you feel the ground under your feet, shift and blend into the trees. Hide your true self deep within the animal.

It was the grimness in his voice that had her obeying without hesitation. She couldn't always shift to her other form, certainly not at will in the way he did, or even the way Solange was able to do, but she recognized they were in mortal danger. She managed to wiggle out of her jeans and unbutton her blouse before they were on the ground. She tossed her clothes away from her, willing the change, embracing it.

Riordan moved in her mind, picking up the image, lending his strength. The shifting was slightly different from that of Carpathians, but he was deep in her mind and knew how it worked now so he was able to provide the extra speed. The jaguar sprang into the lower branches of a tree and disappeared entirely into the canopy. Riordan turned to face his enemy.

A shadowy figure exploded out of the ground, erupting directly in front of Riordan, fist slamming into his chest and driving deep. Riordan twisted slightly, taking the pain and letting it go, sweeping with one leg to send his attacker sprawling. There was no sound, and no face. The vampire was nothing more than black smoke dissolving rapidly. It was eerily silent. Not even the insects hummed.

Zacarias. Riordan reached along his private mental path for his older brother. *A master vampire is here, one with powers beyond all imagining. I cannot spot him. I cannot attack him. Should I fall, you must find and protect my lifemate.* Riordan crouched low, restless eyes searching, every sense on full alert. He dug into the forest floor and scooped handfuls of rich soil. He was losing blood fast. The vampire had deliberately weakened him. To preserve his strength, Riordan didn't move, other than to pack his wounds. He heard Juliette's distress in his mind, knew she remained close in hopes of aiding him, but there was no way to fight the unseen.

Riordan felt his brother moving through him, examining the

terrible hole opened in his chest, estimating his strength, searching through his memories to replay the attack. *Get out of there. No lone hunter will take this one down alone.* Even as he sent the command, he was working to repair his younger brother's injury from a distance. Riordan could feel the warmth moving through his body, hear the healing chant in his mind.

He felt the air stir around him and immediately flung himself away from the disturbance, rolling to his left and coming up to face the shadowy figure. Riordan managed to deflect the jagged bolt of lightning before it struck him. The energy slammed into the ground, shaking the earth. He raised his arms and the ground continued to roll and pitch. Great cracks opened up, one rushing toward the insubstantial figure with ominous speed. Riordan felt the exact moment when both Juliette and Zacarias threw their strength in with his. The crack widened and split the ground and the vampire fell into the hole. Riordan sent the bolts of lightning streaking down after him, spear after spear, driving each deep in an effort to score a blind hit.

Riordan staggered as he moved to get away from where the vampire had last seen him. There was stillness now, as if the forest held its breath. Riordan realized the sky was dark due to storm clouds. Dawn was only a matter of minutes away. The vampire had struck fast and ferociously in the hopes of defeating him quickly.

He felt me with you. Zacarias thought it over. *He will not return to fight. He will most likely go to ground for a long period of time or leave our area. Whatever he wished to accomplish here is not worth his life. Whatever brought such a powerful enemy to our lands had to be important.*

I believe he has tainted some of the jaguar males. They have been capturing women and forcing them to mate for the purpose of breeding. Their women all have psychic abilities and are capable of becoming lifemates to our males.

Riordan was certain a powerful vampire would only come to the jungle if it profited him. If the vampire could prevent the Carpathians from finding lifemates, more and more of their males would turn vampire or walk into the sun.

You are thinking this is a very defined conspiracy. Zacarias turned the idea over in his mind. *This must be reported to our brethren in our homeland. I will send Manolito. We will deal with the jaguar males who are abusing their women. You must go to ground quickly, Riordan. Put your lifemate in the ground and stay until you are fully healed. I will begin the hunt for the women.*

The sister of my lifemate has been taken.

You must heal or we will lose both of you. That cannot happen. Without children our race faces extinction, just as the jaguar.

Riordan abruptly broke off contact with his brother, despising the truth, despising the command in his brother's voice. It made them no different than the jaguar males.

"That isn't true." Juliette was at his side, pushing him onto the ground while she examined the blood-soaked pack in his chest. She pressed him to lie flat while she gathered more rich soil and healing herbs and mixed them with his saliva. "I learn fast. This ugly little recipe was in your mind while you were trying to do it yourself."

"It is true, Juliette. We need women desperately, and we need them to give birth to female children." He couldn't stop looking at her, bending over him with her beautiful feminine body. She was naked, crouched beside him, anxiety on her face, her incredible breasts swaying with every movement. He felt as if he were in a dream. She couldn't possibly be real. Women like Juliette didn't exist in his world.

"Riordan." She said his name sharply. "You're fading on me. Don't you dare pass out. Let me pack this tight and then I'll provide you with blood." She looked around nervously. "Are you certain he's gone? I never saw him. I couldn't help you because I never got a clear glimpse of him."

"It is dawn." Riordan sounded far away. He lifted his hand and touched her breast, barely skimming the soft skin to confirm that she was real. "He had no choice but to go to ground."

"Riordan, take my blood."

He shook his head. "You will be left weak and dizzy with no one to protect you."

She ignored the hand cupping her breast, massaging her flesh with gentle fingers. She caught his face and forced him to look at her. "Do as I tell you and take my blood. You can't die, and you will if you don't have blood. I need you to help me get Jasmine back. I want you to live for me. Forget everything else, Riordan."

"I cannot protect you while I lie beneath the earth these long hours."

"I can protect myself. Please take my blood, Riordan." She was beginning to feel desperate.

There was a faint stirring in her mind. Another voice swirled there for a time, whispering with the same accent, far away and distant as if it was difficult to find the exact path. And then it was suddenly clear. *I am Zacarias. He will never willingly put you in more danger by weakening you. I will aid you, but you must remember, should anything happen to you while he rests beneath the earth, he will rise vampire and I will be forced to destroy him. You must stay alive.*

"Somebody ought to lay out the rules ahead of time," Juliette muttered under her breath, but gave the mental nod to Riordan's brother. She couldn't bear the idea of losing Riordan, and she could clearly see he was going to be stubborn and combative if she persisted without help.

She knew the exact moment Zacarias struck, taking hold of Riordan and forcing him to bite deep into Juliette's wrist. Even though he was under strong compulsion, she felt Riordan striving to protect her, swirling his tongue over her skin to lessen the pain. A surge of anger went through him briefly at what Juliette and Zacarias were doing, but his temper died a quick death. Juliette went her own way when she felt justified. If Riordan wanted to spend a lifetime with her, he had better get used to who she was.

Riordan pulled away from Zacarias's control the moment the blood gave him enough strength. He took only enough from Juliette to aid his healing before closing the wound with his tongue. He brushed his thumb over the pinpricks. "I want to spend several lifetimes with you, and I know exactly who you are, Juliette." He loved every inch of her, loved looking at her with her bare feminine curves, but time was slipping away and he was far weaker than he should be.

He fashioned jeans and a blouse for her, a soft lightweight material that wouldn't cling so much in the high humidity. "You must protect your eyes as best you can. I made the shirt long-sleeved to protect your skin. Try to stay under cover as much as possible. I know you will continue to track Jasmine, but do not put yourself in danger until I can aid you. It will not help your sister to have you killed or captured."

She pulled on the clothes, a little shaky from the blood loss and the terrible fear that welled up each time she looked at the shocking hole in his chest. "I'll be careful." She ran her fingers through his hair. "Do what you have to do. I'll see you as soon as the sun sets."

Riordan glanced around him, his fingers suddenly shackling her wrist, halting all movement. Uneasiness was beginning to creep into his mind. Scanning didn't connect with enemies, human or otherwise in the area. It would be impossible for a vampire to stand the rising of the sun. Although most Carpathians could take the early morning hours, Riordan was severely injured and the light was already affecting his body. He rolled over to stare up into the canopy, unable to shake the sudden alarm coursing through his body. The leaves rustled and swayed with the mild wind. Every kind of plant climbed the trunks of the trees and twisted around branches, creating a jungle of foliage. The wind touched the leaves, the smallest of brushes, but it was enough to reveal turquoise eyes, gleaming like rare gems, glittering down at them.

The jaguar sprang, its stocky, compact body hurtling through the air, claws extended, eyes focused on its prey. Riordan shoved Juliette hard enough to send her sprawling and dissolved into mist, so that the cat hit the ground where he had been. The cat whirled, using its flexible spine, swiping with large claws at empty space.

"Solange! No!" Juliette rushed to grab the cat, running her hands through the soft fur, looking for damage. There were several lacerations, a series of ragged, gaping wounds where a cat had obviously raked her side. "You're hurt, these are deep." She turned to look for Riordan, felt his fingertips brush her cheek.

She meant to kill me, Juliette. I feel it in her mind. I must go to ground. She is enraged over the taking of her cousin. You stay safe and do your best to settle her down.

She heard the regret in his voice, the weariness and pain. "Go, Riordan. I'll see you at sunset."

Clothes floated to earth as he streaked away. The jeans were for someone with longer legs and a smaller waist. The shirt would cover Solange's well-endowed body. It had been easy enough to catch her exact proportions from Juliette's memories.

"He's gone, Solange. Tell me what happened."

Solange shifted to her natural form, remaining crouched on the ground, facing Juliette. "They already had her before I reached the house. I couldn't stop them, I'm sorry. I'm so sorry." She shook back her heavy fall of dark hair. "One stayed behind to try to give the others a head start. Once he realized I was female, and capable of shifting fast, with a more pure bloodline, I had a very real advantage. He didn't want to hurt me." Blood was dripping from the wounds in her side. "He did this before he realized what I was. I'm afraid it puts Jasmine in more trouble. They'll guard her much more carefully."

Juliette hugged Solange. "We'll find her and take her back."

"Who was that man?"

"Not one of them. He is Carpathian. Riordan. You heard Mom talk about them before." She couldn't help the defensive note in her voice.

"He's still a man, and they can't be trusted, Juliette. What does he want us for? Isn't the Carpathian race in the same trouble as the jaguar race?" Solange took the clothes from Juliette's hands and knotted them together before tying them around her neck. "They need babies to keep their race alive."

"They at least respect women and want them to be happy, Solange. All men are not responsible for what a few have done. And there is some suspicion that the jaguar males have come into contact with a master vampire. I saw one, and if that is so, I felt how evil he was. The males may very well have been influenced by him."

"It matters little to me why they do what they do. They cannot have Jasmine," Solange said. "Get rid of the clothes and let's get out of here." She studied Juliette as her cousin stripped. "You're very pale." There was suspicion in her voice.

"I don't want to argue with you, Solange. Let's find Jasmine before we do anything else."

"We don't argue," Solange objected. "At least we didn't before you took up with a man." She studied her cousin's pale body. "A man who takes blood from others."

Juliette ignored the implication. "Is the jaguar still on your trail?"

"I doubled back and led him near the laboratory just to see if he would ask for assistance. A bunch of men are sifting through what's left of the building. It completely collapsed. Did the Carpathian have something to do with that?"

Juliette nodded. "I found him there, chained in a cell, and got him free. He was in bad shape. They'd tortured him."

Solange swore. "I suppose that makes me like him more. At least he knows a little bit of what our women go through."

9

"The sun is burning my eyes," Juliette said, pressing her fingertips to her face. "No matter what I do they weep. My skin feels like it's blistering."

"It is. Shift, Juliette, hurry before you're a mass of blisters. We'll talk about this later." Solange looked at her closely. "You can tell me what that man has done after we get Jasmine back."

"Tell me whether or not the jaguar male went near the humans," Juliette encouraged as she tied her own clothes in knots and looped them around her neck.

"He did. He spoke briefly with them, although he didn't reveal his body to them. He was able to half shift. *Half* of his body human and the other half jaguar. I can't do that. None of us can."

"You come from the purest bloodline we know of," Juliette pointed out. "Mom referred to you as a princess once."

Solange made a face. "Somehow I don't consider myself very lucky. I wouldn't want to be the princess of the jaguar people." She glanced around her. "Are you ready? We have to get out of here. Those men have had Jasmine far too long." She was already shifting, fur bursting through her skin, rippling over her face while her muzzle elongated to accommodate teeth.

Juliette closed her burning eyes and reached for Riordan. *Tell me you are safe.*

I am deep in the arms of the earth. Let me help you shift. He sensed how tired she was, how weak. He stifled the need to keep her with him. Greater than his own need, there was hers. She had to find her sister, and he understood that. He didn't like it, but he understood it.

Juliette called up her large cat, concentrating on the shifting of muscle and bone. She felt Riordan moving within her, lending her power and strength when he didn't have it to give. A part of her wanted to weep when she felt his pain. She feared the coming separation from him, but she had to find Jasmine.

The change took her rapidly. Juliette touched muzzles with Solange and they turned together and raced off into the darkened interior. Using the jaguar's highly acute sense of smell they found Jasmine's trail immediately and hurried after her. They took to the overhead highway, the tangle of branches high up in the canopy that allowed them to travel fast and in secret.

Birds took to the air, shrieked warnings at their passing, but neither jaguar paid any attention, and after a moment the birds settled back into the tops of the trees, ignoring them. The forest had stirred to life, insects humming, frogs croaking and deer barking to warn of the larger predators.

Juliette knew the exact moment when Riordan succumbed to the climbing sun and his heart stopped beating. The breath went out of her lungs, her heart stuttered in reaction, and she was suddenly and utterly alone—bereaved, grief-stricken. The jaguar stumbled, nearly tumbling from the branches. Claws dug into bark, scattering leaves and twigs and sending the birds once more shrieking. Solange turned sharply to growl a warning for stealth. They did not want to alert any of the males that might be guarding the back-trail.

The heavy canopy protected her from the sun, but Juliette still felt the rays piercing her skin through the thick fur. Her eyes wept continually, burning in the light. None of it mattered—not her grief, not her discomfort. Not the separation from her other half. She focused on her beloved sister. Jasmine was all that mattered. Juliette followed Solange.

The trail grew warmer in early afternoon. The pungent odor of the jaguar males was easier to follow. They were taking turns, hurrying through the forest, four in jaguar form and one in human form carrying Jasmine.

In spite of her determination, Juliette found she was having trouble keeping up with Solange. Her body, even in the form of the jaguar, demanded she sleep and worse, wanted to shift back into her human form. She'd always had trouble holding her animal shape for long periods of time. She had never gone from early dawn to early afternoon and it was nearly impossible to continue.

Solange stopped abruptly, her animal form suddenly stiffening. Juliette caught the scent of fear, of violence, of sexual predation. She lost her jaguar self, gagging, choking, catching the branch of the tree for support to keep from falling. Solange shifted into her human shape, holding Juliette as she was violently ill.

For a few minutes, Juliette's head roared with protest, with rage. She pounded at the bark of the trees until her fists were bruised and bleeding, weeping uncontrollably. "She fought them. She fought them, and I wasn't here. How could they do such a thing to her?"

Solange wept silently, the anger in her deep and firm and enduring. "We will get her back, Juliette. Be strong. You have to be strong for her. We can't let this slow us down. They wanted her docile and shocked. This was to show domination. This was to strip her of dignity and hope. But she knows we'll come. She knows we'll never stop until we have her back or we're dead." Solange brushed the hair from Juliette's eyes. "I see the sun is hurting you, that your body needs rest, but you haven't given in to it. You haven't stopped no matter what the cost to you. Jasmine knows what we're like. She will count on that and she will endure."

Juliette allowed her cousin to hold her, to comfort her for a brief moment. "We have to hurry, Solange. They can't do this to her a second time."

Neither woman wanted to think about their mothers, but it was inevitable. "Can you hold the jaguar form?" Solange asked.

Juliette nodded. "I don't know how long, but I'll do my best. Do you have any weapons stashed in this area?"

"About a mile from here. I think we're close to one of our caches. Clothes, food, drinking water, meds and knives. They have to stop soon. They're big males and they'll want to rest."

Juliette reached for her other form. It was easier not to think about Jasmine and what the males had done to her. She didn't want to see the smears of blood on the ground and the signs of struggle. It only weakened her. Her fury needed to burn bright and strong, and vengeful.

She struggled through the next couple of hours, pushing her body when it desperately needed sleep. Her eyes streamed every step of the way, but this time she was uncertain if it was the affects of the sun, or the grief raging in her. She knew by the way Solange carried her body that she felt the same intense emotions, a mixture of rage and sorrow that might never go away. She tried not to think of the girl Jasmine had been, her pixie smile and gentle kindnesses. Solange and Juliette burned with passion, hot and fiery with strong emotions. Jasmine was sweet and steady and irresistible.

Juliette felt a scream of denial welling up and just managed to choke it down as Solange veered from their path to indicate where the cache of weapons and food was stored. In human form, they dressed, strapping on knives with the same ease they dragged on clothes.

"They're close," Solange said, her voice very low. "I feel them. We're downwind of them." She drank water from the bottle stored with her supplies. It was brackish from age, but it was wet. She passed it to Juliette. "Are you up for this? It won't be easy."

Their eyes met. Juliette nodded. "We will succeed, there is no other alternative."

Solange took back the water bottle. "They outnumber us and they're strong, incredibly strong. I've heard Carpathians can perform incredible feats. Obviously if the man can become mist when under attack, it's true. Can he aid us, even from beneath the ground?"

Juliette reached for Riordan eagerly. Her mind had continually tuned itself to his, needing to touch him, compounding her sorrow when she couldn't. This time she was demanding, her call to him edged with need.

Juliette? His voice was faint and far away, but it was there, and relief swept through her heart and soul.

She replayed the events of the day in her mind. He went very still, withdrawing, but not before she felt the impact of his black, dark rage. It boiled up, dangerous and deadly and far more lethal than her own. She should have been frightened, but she was comforted by his anger on her sister's behalf.

When he managed to get his anger under control, Riordan reached for her. The connection was much stronger. *These males are dangerous, perhaps their behavior is tainted by the vampire, perhaps they are a group of deviants who have banded together. They must be stopped, but two women against such odds is ludicrous and you know it. It will not help your sister if you are dead.*

We have no choice but to go in after her now, Riordan. We cannot subject her to more of their violence. Please understand I have no other choice. Can you help?

It is two hours until the setting of the sun. I can rise early. Give me another hour. He wanted to claw his way through the earth to get to her, but his body lay leaden.

Solange will scout them, but if they are raping her, we cannot sit back while they brutalize her. You can't ask that of us.

He swore softly. *I should have converted you immediately and you would be fully under my protection.* It was far too late to correct his mistake now. He was locked beneath the earth, and she was in terrible danger. He switched tactics, feeling her slight withdrawal. He didn't dare lose their connection. *Zacarias, awaken. I need your help. Manolito, we need you.*

Juliette held her breath, waiting. She knew Riordan was powerful, and she had already experienced his eldest brother's tremendous abilities. Hope surged through her.

Manolito is traveling to the Carpathian Mountains. Zacarias answered his call. *I will feed you my strength when needed. Warn the women that should your lifemate fall, so will you, and in such a way that they cannot conceive of the monster that will be unleashed.*

She understood more than they realized. She was already adept at reading Riordan's memories. She honestly didn't know whether or not she would have bound Riordan to her and converted him immediately if she were the one that could be consumed by the madness of the vampire. Juliette sent him as much reassurance as she could. *Th ank you, Riordan. Please thank your brother.*

She turned to her cousin. "They are with us, Solange."

Solange handed her back the water bottle. "I'll trust your man if you do. Stay here and wait for the signal. I'll see what we're up against. That should give you another few minutes to rest."

"We go back-to-back, Solange, like we always do. If Jasmine is safe, we stall until Riordan is able to rise. If not, hopefully they can help us." Already she noted the storm clouds floating above them, helping block the sun and protect her eyes. The wind shifted completely, bringing the strong scent of the jaguar male to them. Juliette turned and pushed her way through the shrubbery, careful to keep from making noise. Solange had already melted away, lost in the forest of orchids and fungi and fern. Few could surpass Solange's ability to blend into the forest and remain unseen. Juliette had complete faith in her cousin. She moved into position, a distance from the small encampment.

The jaguars were using a small cave, man-made, dug into the side of the embankment. The opening was a mere slit between two boulders. Solange worked her way in a circle around the area, knowing there had to be a back entrance. The jaguars would never risk being trapped in the cave. The wind shifted as she moved, always in front of her, giving her the exact location of the sentries. A jaguar male, obviously trusting in the forest warning system, rested in the tree branches to the left of the cave, sleeping in the late afternoon, tired from the two-day rush through the forest. The second guard crouched in human form near a large group of ferns. Solange was certain it was the bolt-hole for emergencies. She made her way back to Juliette to confer.

The two lay side by side in the grasses. Solange pressed her mouth to Juliette's ear. "I couldn't hear anything in the cave. I think they're resting. I'm fairly certain I can get close enough to the guard in his human form to kill him, but neither of us is going to be able to do much with the jaguar. He's big and he's a fighter." She touched her side. "He's fast too."

"We don't stand much of a chance inside," Juliette pointed out. "With the one up in the tree, I counted five. We're not going to win against five fully grown jaguars."

"Four," Solange said firmly. "After I take out the guard. You're right though, we have to draw the others out of the cave to have any chance at all."

"I can do that," Juliette said with confidence.

No! Riordan's harsh command was sharp. She heard the echo of Zacarias's protest. *Wait as long as possible.*

"Riordan wants us to wait, Solange," Juliette reported uneasily. She had no idea how her cousin would react. "He will try to rise before sunset to help us."

Solange nodded slowly. "I guess it makes sense, Juliette. We don't have to like it, but we don't have much chance against five males."

"I want to get closer, just to make certain they aren't touching her," Juliette said.

"I'll go. I can be invisible." A small, humorless smile tugged at Solange's mouth. "Well, not like your Carpathian, but I manage."

"You have a gift," Juliette acknowledged.

Solange began to circle back around toward the rear entrance, presuming Jasmine was being held as deep in the cave as possible. Once the jaguar in the tree stirred, yawned, his mouth gaping open to show sharp teeth. Solange sank into the bushes, going completely still. Juliette slid a knife into her palm. The jaguar stretched, looked around and sniffed the air, testing with his tongue and sensitive whiskers. The wind carried the scent of the women away from him. The jaguar dropped his head back onto his leg and closed his eyes.

Juliette let her breath out slowly. Solange waited a few more minutes before continuing to creep forward again. Juliette strained to watch her cousin's process. The fronds of a fern swayed slightly, in tune with the wind. Juliette couldn't understand how Riordan and Zacarias had the strength to guide the wind and follow Solange's progress. She could almost feel Riordan moving through her, attempting to get the layout of the battlefield through her eyes. He was waiting, much like a coiled snake, waiting for that moment when he could explode into the sky and come to her. Riordan's concern was comforting, and she sent him her appreciation.

Juliette's first warning was the way the human guard at the back entrance suddenly turned his head toward the cave with an evil smile. He walked a few steps and peered into the collection of shrubbery, his hand absently rubbing his crotch. She saw Solange move in behind him. A scream, a mixture of anger, terror and pain came from the interior of the cave. It was choked off abruptly. *I have no choice, Riordan.* It was her only apology for whatever might happen. Using higher ground, she ran to the entrance of the cave, catching a brief glimpse of Solange and the guard, the man falling to the ground, the bloodstained knife in Solange's hand. Riordan was calm. He didn't protest, he simply waited, watching the events unfold through her eyes. Juliette could feel the presence of his elder brother. They coiled in her waiting their moment.

Stay to the side, hold the blade edge up. Riordan instructed as she neared the cave's entrance. Juliette didn't argue; she already knew his plan, catching the details in their shared minds. She called out Jasmine's name to let her know she wasn't alone and to draw the men from the cave. She had to trust Solange to watch her back and keep the jaguar off of her. Her arm flashed, faster than she knew how to move, an instinctual, timed movement that brought down the first man rushing from the cavern. Blood soaked the ground, but Juliette couldn't look, didn't dare look. She heard the roar of the jaguar as it leapt from the branches onto Solange.

Juliette turned to help her cousin, sprinting with a burst of speed not her own. Solange shifted on the run, coming together in fury with the heavy male cat, raking and biting, fur and material flying everywhere. Juliette skidded to a halt. She had no chance to help Solange, to try to kill the jaguar with the knife. The two cats rolled over and over in a terrible fury making it impossible to aid her cousin.

Juliette! Riordan was rising. She felt him bursting through soil and leaves to take to the air. At his warning she spun around, knife held low and close to her body, meeting the rush of the jaguar as it burst from the cave. The heavy cat hit her chest hard, driving her backward, the jaguar's foul breath hot in her face. Pain ripped through her as the sharp claws tore through her skin to the bone. She felt Zacarias and Riordan moving in her, the knife plunging into the cat's sides and chest as his teeth drove at her throat. Breathing was difficult, but Riordan forced the air through her burning lungs. She slammed into the ground hard and lay pinned beneath the heavier body. Leaves and twigs soaked red with blood beneath but she couldn't tell whose blood it was. The cat's teeth were embedded in her throat and her arms were leaden, making it impossible to push the heavy body off of her.

Look at Solange. Riordan, so calm it was frightening. There was a command in his voice she couldn't disobey.

Jasmine screamed again, and Juliette's body jerked at the sound.

Look at Solange. Riordan repeated it. He was much closer and gaining in strength as the sun began to set.

Juliette couldn't move her head, so she shifted her gaze to see the male cat clawing Solange viciously. Blood seeped through fur and Solange staggered under the assault. A white haze was forming over Juliette's eyes. She blinked rapidly to clear her vision. Jasmine screamed again. Juliette could hear her weeping.

Stay focused on Solange. Riordan's voice softened. *Hold on for me. Just hold on, Juliette.*

Flames ran over the male jaguar's fur. Bright red and orange flames tipping the ends of the spotted coat and engulfing the animal. The two jaguars rolled on the ground in a terrible frenzy of claws and teeth, but not a single flame touched the female. The male howled and broke away.

10

Riordan erupted out of the sky, a demon with red eyes, his black hair unbound and streaming in the wind. He materialized directly behind the man holding Jasmine as a shield. Juliette actually felt the man's head as if she had grabbed him. Riordan twisted hard. The frightening crack was loud as he snapped the man's neck and dropped him carelessly to the ground.

Jasmine ran to kneel by Solange while Riordan eased the teeth of the jaguar carefully out of Juliette's neck and tossed the heavy body of the cat away as if it were no more than a bothersome branch. Pain engulfed her, rushed through her body now that it was over and he was there. He pressed his hands to the puncture wounds on either side of her throat, clamping down hard to prevent her from bleeding to death.

Juliette began to choke. *Is my sister okay? Solange? I can't see them.*

Riordan glanced over his shoulder toward the two women. Jasmine's face was swollen and black and blue. Her clothes hung in shreds. There was blood smeared on her body, but she was alive and trying desperately to staunch the flow of blood from her cousin's many lacerations. Solange was naked and bloody, lying on the ground, but she was alert, watching Riordan as he bent over Juliette.

They are both alive, Juliette. Lie still for me. He trusted his brother to remain alert for further trouble as he went outside his body and into hers to attempt to heal her from the inside out. Juliette gurgled, choked and coughed up blood.

"Save her. Damn you, I know you can save her," Solange called to him. "Do whatever you have to do." She attempted to rise, pushed feebly at Jasmine, who held her down.

"I have to convert her."

"What does that mean?" Jasmine asked fearfully.

"Who cares," Solange snapped. "Hurry, before it's too late."

Riordan ignored everything and everyone around him. Juliette was slipping away from him. He bent his head to her throat and drank, taking more of her precious fluid for an exchange. Riordan gathered her into his arms, slashed his chest and pressed her mouth to the wound. Deep within Riordan's mind, Zacarias gathered his spirit into a healing ball of energy and moving through Riordan, found the puncture wounds and torn arteries in Juliette's throat and began to repair them from the inside out. He took his time, making no mistakes, closing the gaping holes and removing foreign bacteria from her system.

Juliette felt both men from a distance. Zacarias broke off abruptly as if the connection between them had grown too difficult to maintain. She felt the lack of warmth immediately and shivered. Riordan leaned down and whispered to her, ending the flow of nourishing strength pouring into her body. She tried to lift her hand to his face. He looked so worried. Her hand fluttered next to her thigh but didn't quite make it into the air. Someone was crying. She turned her head toward the sound.

Jasmine sat beside Solange, wiping ineffectually at the bloody wounds and weeping softly. She was barely recognizable with her swollen face. "Is my sister going to live?" Her voice was very soft and shaky. She didn't look at Riordan, but kept her gaze fixed on her cousin.

"Yes, little one," Riordan answered gently. "She will live. I have to take her away for a short time. I would like you and your cousin to go to my ranch where you will be safe until I can bring her back to you."

Jasmine shifted closer to Solange. It was a small movement for protection, but Riordan noted it immediately.

Can you take it away from her? What they did? Can you undo it?

Riordan lifted Juliette and carried her to her sister and cousin. "We can't stay long. I need to get Juliette to a place where she is safe while the conversion takes place and where I can heal her fully." *You know I cannot undo what has been done.*

Solange reached out to take Jasmine's hand. Jasmine twined her fingers through Juliette's. "Together we get through," Solange whispered.

Juliette tried to speak, but her throat was too swollen and raw. *Ask Solange if you can heal her.*

Riordan could feel the waves of distaste and fear coming from both women. They were doing their best to tolerate him and trust him because they loved Juliette. "She wants me to heal your wounds, Solange. I do not think she will leave this place and be calm without me doing so." It was the only leverage he had. If Solange didn't comply he would have no choice but to use his other gifts.

"Get it over with then." Solange never took her eyes from her cousin. "I am not going to your ranch. I'll destroy these bodies so our race remains secret, and Jasmine and I will go to our home at the edge of the rain forest, far from this place. We'll wait there for Juliette's return. Jasmine and Juliette will not be happy being apart." It was a clear warning.

Riordan nodded. "I am fully aware of that." Not wanting to waste any more time on talking, Riordan immediately allowed his physical self to fall away, called his spirit into a strong ball of healing energy and entered Solange. She had many wounds. Most were superficial, but some went bone deep, just as he had found in Juliette. He spent precious time healing from the inside out, shocked at how difficult it was to keep his mind from Juliette and the fact that time was slipping away from him. He was always focused, yet it required tremendous discipline to shutout all thoughts and concentrate on his task.

Solange lay watching him. Her gaze never wavered. Her eyes never blinked. Her hand remained in Jasmine's, but her attention was fixed on Riordan. When his body swayed and the soothing warmth disappeared from inside of her she let out her breath. "Jasmine, he's got to take Juliette now. We have to be strong a little longer."

Jasmine leaned over immediately and kissed Juliette. She didn't look at Riordan when she spoke. "Thank you."

"You two must be safe. If you go to my ranch—"

Solange shook her head. "No, I can't. Please try to understand. I know you've helped us, but we haven't had very good experiences with men and we feel safer alone."

Riordan couldn't help but see the shudder that went through Jasmine. Juliette squeezed her sister's fingers. "I am sorry. I really have to take her to a safer place for the conversion. I do not like leaving the two of you alone and unprotected."

"Thanks to your healing skills, I'm able to protect us." Solange looked around her at the bodies lying on the ground. "Most of our enemies are dead. Take her before we lose her."

Riordan gathered Juliette in his arms but stopped when Jasmine made a soft sound of distress. "What is it, little one?" He used his most gentle voice.

"How long?" Jasmine clung to Juliette as if she couldn't let her go.

"Can you be separated two days? That will give her time to heal enough to be safe rising. Solange knows of my people. Our word is our honor. I give you my word, we will return at once to you, the moment we rise. Juliette would want nothing else."

Jasmine nodded and reluctantly allowed her sister's hand to drop limply from hers. She leaned into Solange for protection. Solange wrapped her arms around Jasmine. "Go now, we can be unselfish enough to let you take her. I'll take care of things here."

Riordan didn't wait for a second invitation. He already felt the first stirrings in Juliette's fragile body, a wave of unease, a ripple of fire. Time was running out. He launched himself skyward, hugging Juliette to him, hearing Jasmine gasp then begin to sob. Glancing down he could see Solange sitting up slowly and gathering her young cousin to her.

I should be with her, with Jasmine.

It should never have happened, Riordan replied grimly. He had no idea how he managed to keep the black anger swirling inside him at bay. He had Juliette's memories now, the intensity of her love for her sister and cousin. The memories of her aunt and her mother dying at the hands of deviant males. His every protective instinct was aroused, and rage lived and breathed inside of him.

Thank you for caring about them. And thank you for what you did for my cousin. I know it was uncomfortable not being accepted.

Fire blossomed in her stomach, spread through her body, engulfing every organ. He shared the pain, shocked at the intensity. He was as unprepared as Juliette for the violence of it. She shivered in his arms, biting back the cry of pain and trying to break the merge between their minds.

Riordan increased his speed. He couldn't make the protection of his ranch, or even get close to his home range, but after centuries living and hunting vampires in South America he was very familiar with their current surroundings. He dropped to earth in the rise of mountains, heading for a deep cave with natural hot springs. The soil was rich with minerals and the cave would be a natural protection against enemies. He could set strong safeguards and know humans and animals were safe from accidental encounters.

It took only minutes to prepare the cavern. Candles sprang to life, casting eerie lights across the shimmering pools. He placed Juliette on a soft bed he'd fashioned of rich soil that cushioned her body in welcoming arms. "I know it hurts, Juliette. I had no idea it was so painful."

We really didn't have much of a choice. Juliette didn't try to speak. Her raw throat wouldn't allow it, and in any case it was too tiring. She could feel the beast in her fighting for life, resisting the change in her body. The jaguar didn't want the reshaping of organs and tissue. Juliette was just too weary and in too much pain to care.

I would have converted you without the attack from the male. He felt compelled to confess it, settling next to her, holding her in his arms, lifting her fingers to his mouth. *I would not have been able to continue without you.* Riordan wasn't certain it was an apology, only that he wanted her to understand his conflicting emotions.

I would have been unable to continue without you, Riordan, so stop beating yourself up. Get my clothes off, I can't stand the weight of them against my skin. The last was said in desperation.

He stripped her clothes away without a thought for the material, shredding it from her body as quickly as possible. Her skin was hot to the touch. Riordan dipped his shirt into the coolest of the pools and bathed her face and wrists.

"I dreamt of you once," he said softly as he squeezed droplets of water over her throat and down the valley between her breasts. "You were laughing. I remembered the sound of your laughter for years afterward. It kept me going at times when I could not find a reason to continue." He pushed the hair from her face. She was sweating. The beads of sweat mixed with tiny beads of blood.

I dreamt of you, too. There was happiness in her voice, the only thing that kept him from crying when a convulsion took hold of her and pain lashed for what seemed an eternity. She gripped his wrist, held on, trying to breathe through it, stay on top of it. When the wave released her she sighed. *I still think you're a dream.*

He had to swallow several times before he could speak. "Even now, with what I'm putting you through?"

Her eyes flashed, a reminder of her passionate nature, the fire contained in her feminine body. *I am jaguar. I have choices, and I make them. I wanted you from the first moment I saw you. As a jaguar, I have no future. With you I do. As a jaguar, there is no happiness, with you there is. I know the difference, Riordan.*

Before she could say more, the next wave hit her, even stronger than the last. The jaguar was not going to let Riordan have her without a fight. Riordan ground his teeth together, trying to take the pain from her, the bursting fire that rushed through her body and seared her insides. She was stoic about it, enduring the pain without a complaint. There wasn't a hint of blame in her mind. When the wave passed she inhaled the scent of the healing candles. *I'm going to be sick.*

It was his only warning and he moved quickly, holding her while her body rid itself of toxins. She was violently ill even as another wave of pain raced through her. Riordan was cursing when it ebbed away.

Wrapping her in his arms, he carried her into the coolest pool, submerging both of them up to their necks. He buried his face against her neck. "Are we going to survive this?"

She smiled. Not physically, but he felt it in his mind. *You are such a baby when it comes to me. I see you all rough and tough when you're scaring everyone around you with your bad-boy image and you fall apart because I'm in pain.* She caught a glimpse of something else and it brought tears to her eyes. *You're falling apart because of what happened to Jasmine. Riordan, it wasn't your fault. How could you think that?*

Before he could answer, the blowtorch blossomed in her stomach and lungs, eating through her until it was so great she convulsed again, her brain shutting off to prevent her from overload. All Riordan could do was hold her, feeling helpless and guilty and angry for not understanding what would occur.

Juliette opened her eyes and looked up at him. *You're crying blood, Riordan. Don't cry for me. I chose this path and I didn't expect my passing from one to the other to be easy. I feel the jaguar fading in strength. I knew from your memories that human women with psychic abilities could be converted, and all the jaguar women, and hopefully the descendents with more diluted blood, are psychic. I had hoped Solange would find a Carpathian to bring her the same happiness, and even, eventually, Jasmine, but I fear the jaguar in Solange is far too strong. It would never let her go.*

Had I not taken you when you saved me from the laboratory, you would have been home to aid your sister. He couldn't say the words aloud to her. He whispered them in her mind. The idea that a male would commit such atrocities against a woman burned like a hole in his belly.

I was not expected back that night, Riordan. Jasmine knew I would draw the human trackers away. Neither of us expected an attack by the jaguars. I didn't even know they were in our part of the forest. I wasn't worried about the males.

He forced air though his lungs, so much rage in him the ground shook. *I know her through you. A younger sister who will remain scarred for life. I wanted to insist she come home with us to the ranch, but I have brought you fully into my world. Who will be with her in the hours when she is alone?*

The next wave was even longer, her thrashing body creating

waves in the pool. Water splashed in agitation. The flames from the candles leapt as if a wind rushed through the cavern. The lights flickered, and the scents mingled to bring healing aroma wafting over the pool.

Juliette's nails dug deep into Riordan's skin. It took a few moments to find her breath again. *She'll always have me. And now you. She's uneasy with your presence, and so is Solange, but they'll get better with time. We'll be more able to watch over them. Two of us with the Carpathian gifts will be able to guard them more carefully.*

He bathed her, taking his time, cleaning her skin thoroughly, his hands lingering in places he sensed soothed her. The water helped to keep her skin cool.

The water helps. And the feel of your hands. When I dreamt of you, I dreamt of your hands touching me. I knew what they'd feel like on my body before you actually touched me physically.

"When did you dream about me? Did I look the same?"

Your hair was flowing in the wind, and you had that same incredible smile. I couldn't see your eyes as clearly because you were touching me and I was feeling rather than looking.

His heart nearly stopped beating. He remembered his dream vividly. He had awakened with a terrible hunger and his body alive with heat. He hardly recognized the sexual urges, he hadn't experienced them in centuries. He heard her in his mind, laughing softly, sensuously, calling to him. She was running just ahead of him, her scent ripe with heat. In his dream he had no choice but to follow her. She was always just out of reach, a tantalizing temptation, leaving in the air behind her a trail of sexual excitement.

We must have been close to one another and I was telegraphing my need. The purer the blood of the jaguar, the more the sexual heats hit us hard. Fortunately, there aren't many of us women left. We stay as far away from the males as possible.

Riordan closed his eyes against the next wave of pain. The

convulsion actually took her out of his arms, so that she nearly sank beneath the agitated water. He cursed his people, even his God, everything he could think of, then began to pray, promising everything he could think of if only her ordeal would be over.

He heard her soft laughter in his mind even before the pain leeched from her body. *You're going to save the world if this stops?*

He rubbed his chin over the top of her head. "I was desperate. It has to be over soon."

No wonder women have all the babies.

"Not you, not if it is anything like this. We will do without babies. I am serious, Juliette. I think I am going to be sick."

Well don't. I'm sick enough for both of us. I'm so tired. I just want to sleep.

He waded out of the pool, bringing her back to the rich, welcoming soil. "I can send you to sleep the moment it is safe to do so." He kissedher eyes closed. Kissed the corners of her mouth. "I love you."

How strange. I love you too.

It took two more intense waves of burning fire and convulsions before the jaguar was gone, the conversion was complete, and he could issue the command for healing sleep. He wrapped his arms and body protectively around hers and wept while the candles burned brightly and the water lapped at the edges of the pool.

11

Riordan paced back and forth, his restless nature showing through his normally calm demeanor. Juliette had been in the house with her sister and cousin for most of the night. Dawn was only a couple of hours away, and he had yet to spend time with her. He understood completely the need to be with her sister after such a trauma, and he tried hard to suppress the selfish part of his nature, but fear was an ugly, clawing thing that kept him on edge. Solange and Jasmine wanted nothing to do with men. Riordan didn't blame them. Jasmine's gentle nature could barely tolerate what had happened to her. She was hanging on to her sanity by a thread. Juliette would help with her healing skills, strengthened by Riordan, but he knew the two women were a tremendous influence on Juliette. She also had a nature that demanded loyalty and responsibility. Jasmine was in pain, was terribly wounded. Juliette might feel she needed to stay with her.

The moment they had risen, he had fed, taken care of her needs and kept his promise to her family, bringing her straight to them. He knew they needed to be alone, and he had been the one to suggest he wait outside, but he couldn't help wanting to protect her from the pain of what Jasmine had gone through. It was difficult in the ensuing hours to keep his mind firmly away from hers to give Juliette and her family complete privacy, but he managed by pacing restlessly back and forth just in front of the small house.

He heard the door and spun around. Juliette was framed there, holding Jasmine and Solange to her, hugging them hard. She emerged with a bright smile on her face and tears in her eyes. It was obvious she had been weeping on and off for hours. Riordan's heart moved in his chest. He opened his arms, and she came into the shelter of his body.

He glanced over her head, nodded when Solange and Jasmine both lifted a tentative hand before closing the door. "I am so sorry I could not be there to comfort you," he whispered, brushing soothing kisses along her temple and down her tearstained cheek. "I wanted to be there for you."

"I know. I carried you with me and leaned on your strength more than once. She needs time, Riordan. Please don't take the way they are personally. They'll come to love you, I know they will."

"They have given me acceptance," he pointed out. "I did not even expect that much, so I am grateful."

"I want to shift into another form and run away for awhile. I want it to be just you and me somewhere beautiful where I can't think about terrible things happening to people I love. Take me away, Riordan. Let's go find our pool. Let's just be together where I can't think anymore."

"Would you like to try a leopard form? I often use it to travel through the forest."

She tugged until he let her loose. "That might be best. I still feel like a cat inside." Being close to Riordan definitely brought cat traits out in her. "Let's try." The thought of losing herself in an animal form was enticing. It had been wearing, all those long hours, holding her baby sister, rocking her, crying with her. She looked up at

Riordan. "In the end, there's no real way to take it back. No way to help her." Juliette looked ashamed for a moment. "I almost asked you if you could remove her memories."

"Not with that large of a trauma. I could perhaps lessen the impact, but it would be in her memories and she might not know why she had reactions to things that were upsetting to her. If you want me to try—"

Juliette shook her head. "Jasmine is strong. She can survive this, maybe better than the rest of us. I've never seen Solange so filled with sorrow. We chose to remain here, moving from place to place because mom told us the males were kidnapping women they suspected of being of jaguar blood and bringing them here. They have no one else, no hope of rescue other than us. So we stayed."

"Now there are others to help, Juliette. I will. My brothers will. My people will."

She smiled at him, for the first time, her heart lightening. "Our people, Riordan. I'm Carpathian now."

He trailed his fingers over her cheek, framed her face with his hands and bent his head to find her mouth with his. His kiss was gentle, loving, tender even. "Absolutely, you are Carpathian."

"So how do I make the change?"

"In much the same way as before. I have the image and structure in my head. Study it, focus on it and reach for it. I will help. With us, we actually have to hold the image in our mind the entire time we stay in the form. You become the jaguar. We are the image of the animal. We have all of its senses and abilities, but we must maintain the outer shell."

She liked the idea. It would occupy her thoughts entirely. And she found she wasn't quite ready to give up the freedom she always felt running in her jaguar form through the heavy canopy. Juliette stretched her arms up to the night sky. "Show me the leopard."

"The leopard is in your mind. Hold its form, Juliette, do not think you can forget it as you did the jaguar," he cautioned.

"With you to remind me, I doubt I would have a chance," she teased, already reaching for the image. It wasn't all that different from her own unique beginnings, but it was complex. As she changed form, so did Riordan. He made it seem easy and natural and fun.

The moment Juliette felt the familiar ropes of muscle, joy spread through her. She turned her head to look at the large cat beside her. He was big and shiny black with darker rosettes covering his body. He looked powerful and muscular and very alluring. She rubbed against him, body to body, a long affectionate signal to play. Whirling, she took off running in the direction of their private grotto.

Riordan, deep inside the body of the leopard, paced just behind her, admiring her sleek lines and beautiful curves. They leapt over fallen logs, rousted rodents from the shrubbery, chased a small squirrel through several trees and splashed through two creeks and up an embankment. Both raked the bark from the trees, Juliette trying to reach higher than the much larger male.

He rubbed his muzzle along her face and neck. His teeth playfully bit at her neck and shoulder. Her fragrance was ripe and enthralling, captivating him until all he could do was think about her. She teased him openly, running away, waiting for him to catch up, crouching temptingly in front of him, only to leap away before he could blanket her.

Riordan was grateful to see the shimmering pool of water waiting for them in the natural rock grotto. The high ferns screened the lush oasis from prying eyes, making it a virtual paradise.

They shifted together, Juliette laughing with glee. "That was so fun." Her gaze drifted boldly, possessively over him. "I see the experience was particularly arousing to you." Juliette stepped close to him, inhaling his scent. Her fingers trailed with tantalizing expertise over his aching erection.

Before he could react, she shifted her palms to his bare chest. "I don't think the change completely took the cat out of me." She ran her hands over his chest, feeling every defined muscle. "I thought I wanted all of it gone, every last bit of that DNA from my body, but I've changed my mind."

Her fingers rubbed over his skin in small, demanding caresses, transmitting a certain urgency. "What part of the cat remained behind?" It was hard to breathe when she was so close to him. When he was already throbbing and mercilessly hard for her touch. For her taste. He closed his eyes briefly. For the feel of her tight hot sheath surrounding his body and milking him dry.

She leaned forward and lapped at his chest, rubbed her body the length of his. "Touch. Touch is very important to cats." Her hand slid down his body, over his belly, wrapped around his thickened penis. Her thumb rubbed the sensitive tip gently. "Like this. Cats love to touch and feel. We like to be stroked." She smiled up at him. "Do you think you can manage a little stroking?"

She didn't give him the chance, kissing his chest, her mouth open and wet, her tongue working along his ribs and her teeth nipping until he thought he might go out of his mind. Riordan stood it as long as he could, with his body growing harder and the pressure building with every touch of her fingers and lips. He tunneled his hands into her hair and pulled her head up to fasten his mouth on hers. He devoured her, kiss after kiss, unable to stop to take a breath, his tongue dueling with hers.

The roaring could have been in his head, maybe it was hers, the roaring was so loud he couldn't tell. His body burned and ached and demanded relief. He kissed his way from her mouth to her throat, laved the valley between her breasts before stopping there, lavishing attention while he brought her body more fully into his.

Juliette twined one leg around him, aligning their bodies so the head of his penis was pressed tightly into her wet, welcoming entrance. "I don't want to wait anymore," she said, tugging at his hair. "I want to feel you inside of me."

He stroked her nipple with his tongue. "When?"

"Right now, this minute."

She tried to impale her body on his, but he moved, his mouth pulling strongly at her breast. With each strong pull a wave of liquid heat pushed over the head of his erection and trickled down the shaft.

"Are you certain?" When she squirmed again, he abandoned all pretense of teasing, caught her bottom in both hands and lifted her up onto him.

She cried out, sliding over him, fitting like the proverbial glove, contracting her muscles around him to hold him to her. She moved with him, meeting him stroke for stroke, urging him to move into her harder and faster. Her breath came in ragged gasps, but pleasure burst through her like a rainbow, beautiful after what seemed like endless darkness. She wanted their ride to be wild and abandoned and to go on forever.

Riordan, so tuned to her, drove into her body, going deeper with each stroke. He urged her hips into the rhythm of his. Juliette went unexpectedly over the edge, her body shuddering with pleasure, the intensity of her orgasm shaking them both. Riordan slowed the pace, heightening her enjoyment, drawing it out so that she had a series of strong orgasms. She moaned softly then cried his name, her nails digging into his shoulder. He allowed himself to go over with her, exploding with passion, riding the wave of pleasure until for the moment he was somewhat sated.

They clung to one another, her head on his shoulder, their arms around each other, as close as they could get. It took a few minutes before they could make their way to the inviting coolness of the pool, slipping into the water.

"I love this place, Riordan. Do you? Do you want to remain here in South America, or do you long to travel back to the place you were born?"

His white teeth flashed, robbing her of breath. It was always so unexpected, her reaction to his genuine smile. "I love this land. It has become my home, Juliette. And I would never take you far from your sister and cousin. You forget I am in your mind and can read your fears."

She grinned at him, looking mischievous, but obviously relieved. "What am I thinking now?"

His entire body tightened. "What you are thinking is anatomically impossible, but we can try variations."

She laughed at him, fully aware of his growing fascination with her. She hoped it would continue to grow for all eternity.

"It is obsession, not fascination," he pointed out.

She turned over to lie floating on her back, drifting with the small waves, staring up at the stars glittering over her head. "I'd like to think that somewhere out there is a man for Solange and another one for Jasmine. Good men." She turned her head to look at him as he paced slowly beside her.

Riordan scooped her up in his arms, unable to bear the melancholy in her voice. He wrapped her up tightly, holding her against his body, wanting to protect her from everything evil in the world.

Juliette brushed back his hair to look into his eyes. "Someone like you, capable of loving them no matter what. Someone capable of understanding what our lives have been like and the trauma they've been through. Do you think that will ever happen for them?"

"It really will come out right," he whispered, burying kisses in her hair. "Everything will be all right."

"I almost feel as if it will never be right again," she said and buried her face against his shoulder.

"They have us, Juliette. It will not happen overnight, but we can help them rebuild their lives. They are my family now, too. And they are under the protection of the Carpathian people."

She turned her mouth blindly to his, nearly sinking them beneath the lapping water. He responded, kissing her over and over again. His hands stroked her hair. "It will be all right, Juliette. I promise you, and I take my promises very seriously." He rested his cheek on the top of her wet hair, nuzzling her, making every effort to console and comfort her.

Juliette snuggled deeper against his body, tightening her hold onhim. "I know as long as I have you with me, I'll be happy. With the twoof us working together, I can only believe that the people I love will findhappiness too. I'm not afraid of our life."

He lifted her chin and took possession of her mouth with his. Th eystill had a few hours until they absolutely had to go to ground and hewas determined to make the most of his time.

DARK SECRET

For my sister, Bobbie King,
and for Cassandra and Donna Kennedy-Hutton.

Because no vampire has ever met
an honest-to-God cowgirl before.

ACKNOWLEDGMENTS

Special thanks to Cheryl Wilson and Manda Clarke as always, I would never have managed without you. And to Maria Atkinson for her help with the Portuguese language.

Prologue

"Come on, Colby," Sheriff Ben Lassiter yelled, feeling like a fool running alongside the tractor. "You have to be reasonable. Get off that damn thing and listen to me for once in your life. You're being stubborn!"

The ancient tractor bounced along in the gathering dusk, shooting up clouds of powdery dirt to spray over Ben's immaculate sheriff 's uniform. Colby waited until he was totally out of breath and at a complete disadvantage before she stopped the tractor and sat staring moodily out over the field. Very slowly she pulled off her leather work gloves. "I'm getting tired of these visits, Ben. Just whose side are you on, anyway? You know me. You knew my father. The Chevez family don't belong here and they certainly don't have the right to try to force me to turnover my brother and sister to them."

Ben swiped at the dirt covering him, gritting his teeth against his frustration. He took several deep breaths before he answered her. "I didn't say it was right, Colby, but the Chevez family have the De La Cruz brothers on their side, which means a lot of money and power. You can't just ignore them. They aren't going to go away. You have to talk to them or they're going to take you to court. People like the

De La Cruz brothers don't lose in court." He raised his hands to grasp her small waist before she could jump off the tractor by herself. Resisting the urge to shake some sense into her, he lifted her down easily, retaining possession for a moment. "You have to do this, Colby. I mean it, honey, I can't protect you from these people. Don't put it off any longer."

Colby pushed away from him, a small gesture of impatience, swinging her head so her disheveled hair spilled out from under her hat, hiding the sudden sheen of tears swimming in her eyes. Ben quickly looked away, pretending not to notice. A man would have to kill for her if she cried, and anyone witnessing her tears would be very likely to take the brunt of her anger.

"Fine." Colby began moving across the field at a fast pace. "I presume you have the entire lot of them camped on my porch?"

"I knew Ginny and Paul were gone tonight." Ben had ensured his sister-in-law invited Colby's sister and brother over for homemade ice cream.

"Like that was hard to see through." Colby tossed the words sarcastically over her shoulder at him. She had known Ben since kindergarten. She was certain he persisted in thinking of her as a wild, untamed little girl, not quite bright, when she was perfectly capable of running a ranch all by her little lonesome and had been doing so for some time. She wanted to box his thick skull.

"Colby, don't go in there like a powder keg. These people aren't the type to be pushed around." Ben easily kept pace with her.

"Pushed around?" She stopped so abruptly that he had to rock back on his heels to keep from running her over. "*They're* trying to push *me* around. How dare they come here acting so arrogant I want to sic the dog on them! *Men!*" She glared at him. "And another thing, Ben. Instead of kissing up to Mr. Moneybags and his entourage, you might consider what is going on out here. All my equipment keeps disappearing and some little gremlin is messing with the machinery. That's your job, isn't it?—not escorting the rich and infamous around." She began moving again, her small feminine body radiating fury.

"Colby, you and I both know it's a bunch of kids playing pranks. Probably friends of Paul," Ben said, trying to soothe her.

"Pranks? I don't think stealing is a prank. And what about my missing person's report? Have you even tried to find Pete for me?"

Ben raked a hand through his hair in sheer desperation. "Pete Jessup is probably off on a binge. For all you know that old man stole your things to pay for his alcohol."

Colby stopped again, and this time Ben did run into her and had to catch her shoulders to keep from knocking her flat. She slapped his hands away, a fine outrage smoldering in her. "Pete Jessup quit drinking when my father died, you turncoat! He's been invaluable around here."

"Colby," Ben said, his voice persuasive and gentle, "the truth is you took in that homeless old coot out of the goodness of your heart. I doubt if he did more than eat your food every day. He's a broken-down cowboy, a drifter. He's just taken off somewhere. He'll turn up eventually."

"You would say that," she sniffed, truly aggravated with him. "It's just like you to let the disappearance of an old man and sneak thieves go by the wayside so you can mix with some rich idiots who are here to try to *steal* my brother and sister."

"Colby, come on, they proved they're relatives and they claim they have the children's best interests at heart. The least you can do is listen to them."

"You probably agree with them, don't you? Paul and Ginny are *not* better off with that group. You don't know anything about it, or them. Paul would end up just like them, so arrogant no one could stand him, and poor little Ginny would grow up thinking she was a second-class citizen because she's female. They can all go straight to hell for all I care!"

Although it was early evening and still relatively light, the sky suddenly darkened as ominous black clouds boiled up out of nowhere. A cold wind arrived on the wings of the dark mass, tugging sharply at Colby's clothes. A shiver of apprehension blew straight down her spine. For a moment something touched her mind. She felt it, felt the struggle for entrance.

"What is it?"

Colby could see Ben was clearly uneasy as he turned in a slow circle to scan the surrounding area. He had his hand on his gun, unsure what was stalking them or where the threat was coming from, but he obviously felt it as well.

Colby stayed very quiet, not moving a muscle, like a small fawn caught in a hunter's sights. She immediately sensed she was in mortal danger. It wasn't hostile toward Ben, but she could feel the malevolence directed at her. Whatever it was struck directly at her mind, seeking entrance. She took a deep slow breath and let it out, forcing her mind to stay blank, thinking of a wall—high, impregnable—a fortress nothing could enter. She focused completely on the wall, keeping it strong, impenetrable.

The thing seemed to withdraw for a moment, puzzled perhaps by her strength, but then it struck again, a hard spearlike thrust that seemed to pierce her skull and drive right for her brain. Colby uttered a soft cry of pain and dropped to one knee, holding her head even while she forced herself to breathe evenly and calmly. Her mind was strong, invincible, with a wall so thick and high no one would ever break it down. Whatever malevolent thing was after her would not be allowed to breach her defenses.

She became aware, after a few minutes, of Ben's large hand on her shoulder. He was bending over her solicitously. "Colby, what is it?"

Cautiously she lifted her head. The presence was gone. "My

head, Ben. I have the headache from hell." She did, too; it wasn't a lie. She'd never experienced anything quite like the attack. She actually felt sick to her stomach, and she wasn't certain she could walk. Whatever it had been was strong and terrifying.

Ben took her elbow and helped her to her feet. She was trembling—he could feel the continuous shivering beneath his hand—so he held onto her. Colby didn't pull away from him like she normally would have and that worried him. "You want me to call an ambulance?"

Her emerald green eyes laughed at him even as they mirrored her pain. "Are you crazy? I have a headache, Ben. The mere thought of contact with the Chevez family gives me major headaches."

"Your brother and sister are both members of the Chevez family, Colby. You would have been too if the adoption had gone through."

Colby ducked her head, his words hitting her dead center in her heart. Armando Chevez had never adopted her. He had confessed his reasons on his deathbed, hanging his head in shame, tears swimming in his eyes while she held his hand. He had wanted his grandfather to relent, to accept him back into the family. Due to the circumstances of Colby's birth, Armando had known if he adopted her, his grandfather in Brazil would never allow him to come back to the family. It had been too late, then, to push the paperwork through. Armando Chevez was ashamed that he had betrayed her unconditional love for him for a family who had never answered a dying man's letter. Colby had remained loyal and loving, nursing him, reading to him, comforting him right up until the day he died. And she still remained loyal to him. It didn't matter that he had died before the adoption—Armando Chevez wasn't her biological father, but he was her father all the same. In her heart, where it counted.

The way the Chevez family hated her had never mattered to her, but she loved Armando with every fiber of her being. She loved him with the same fierceness with which she loved her brother and sister. As far as she was concerned, the Chevez family didn't deserve Armando and his children. And the two De La Cruz brothers, guardians and bullies for the Chevez family, could go straight back to whatever hell had spawned them. They were directly responsible for Armando's grandfather's bitter hatred of her. *She* wasn't good enough to be a member of the Chevez family. Neither was her beloved mother. Armando's grandfather had pronounced they would never be accepted into his illustrious family and his reasons had been abundantly clear. Colby's mother had never married her father, there was no name on Colby's birth certificate, and Armando's grandfather would never accept an Anglo harlot and her bastard into his pureblood family.

As she and Ben moved around the vegetable garden toward the ranch house, Colby slowed her pace, turning her mind inward for a moment to focus her strength of will on control. It was important to stay calm and relaxed and to breathe naturally. She tilted her chin and walked with her head up to meet the all-powerful De La Cruz brothers and the Chevez family members who had come to steal her brother and sister and their ranch.

They were gathered together on her small porch. Juan and Julio Chevez resembled Armando so much Colby had to blink back unexpected burning tears. She had to remember this was the family who had so cruelly rejected her mother because she had given birth to Colby out of wedlock. This was the same family who had callously ignored her beloved stepfather's pleas and allowed him to die without so much as a word from them. Worst of all, they were here to take Paul and Ginny away and to confiscate the ranch, their father's last legacy.

Ben saw her lift her chin and he sighed heavily. He had known Colby nearly all of her life. She had a stubborn streak a mile wide. If these men underestimated her because she was young and beautiful, because she looked small and fragile, they were in for a big surprise.

Colby could move mountains if she set her mind to it. He had never seen anyone so determined, with such strength of will. Who else could have nursed a dying man and run a huge ranch with only the help of an old broken-down cowhand and two kids?

Colby walked right up to the two men, her slender shoulders straight, her small frame as tall as she could make it. "What can I do for you gentlemen?" Her voice was polite, distant, as she gestured toward the chairs on the porch rather than inviting them into her home. "I looked very carefully over the papers you sent and I believe I already gave you my answer. Ginny and Paul are United States citizens. This ranch is their legacy, entrusted to me to preserve for them. That is a legal document. If you wish to dispute it, you can take me to court. I have no intention of turning my brother and sister over to complete strangers."

A man stirred back in the shadows. Her gaze jumped to his face, her heart pounding. It was strange she hadn't noticed him immediately. He seemed blurred, a part of the gathering darkness. As he stepped under the porch light, she could see he was tall and muscular, very imposing. His face held a harsh sensuality, his eyes black and cold. His hair was long, pulled to the back of his neck and somehow secured there. Every warning sense shrieked at her. He held up his hand, effectively silencing Juan Chevez before he could speak. That imperious gesture, stopping the proud, very wealthy Brazilian, set her heart pounding. She had a feeling he could hear it. The brothers moved aside as he glided silently forward. The parting of the Red Sea, Colby thought a little hysterically. Was there a touch of fear in the eyes of the Chevez brothers?

Colby stood her ground, trembling, afraid her rubbery legs might not hold her up. This man scared her. There was an edge of cruelty to his mouth and she had never seen such cold eyes, as if he had no soul. She forced herself to stand, not to look at Ben for assurance. Clearly this man could take a life and never think twice about it.

That made her all the more determined to keep her brother and sister with her. If the Chevez family used him for protection, what did that say about them? She stared up at him defiantly. He bent closer, his black eyes staring directly into her green ones. At once she felt a magnetic pull. She recognized that touch from the mental attack on her in the field. Alarmed, she jerked back, twisting away from him to focus on Ben's scuffed boots.

This man had psychic abilities just like her!

"I am Nicolas De La Cruz." He said his name softly, his voice as mesmerizing as his eyes. "I wish you to hear these men out. They have come a long way to see you. The children are of their blood."

The way he said "blood" sent a shiver running through her body. He didn't raise his voice at all. He sounded perfectly calm and reasonable. His voice was a powerful, hypnotic weapon and she recognized it as such. If he used it in a court of law on the judge, could she combat it? She didn't honestly know. Even she was somewhat susceptible. Her head was pounding. She pressed a hand to her temples. He was exerting subtle pressure on her to do as he bid her.

Colby knew she wouldn't be able to resist the relentless force for long. Her head felt as if it might shatter. Pride was one thing, foolishness completely another. "I am going to have to ask you gentlemen to leave. Unfortunately, this is a bad time for me. I'm afraid I'm ill." Pressing a hand to her pounding head, she turned to Ben. "Would you please escort them out of here for me and I will try to schedule another meeting when I'm feeling better? I'm sorry."

She jerked open the door to her home and fled inside to the safety of her sanctuary. Nicolas De La Cruz would be a powerful enemy. The pounding in her head from fighting off his mental attack was making her physically sick. She buried her face against her quilt and breathed deeply, waiting until she felt the steady pressure slowly retreating. She lay there a long time, terrified for her brother and sister, terrified for herself.

1

The huge chestnut snorted, his eyes rolling wildly in his head. "Hang on to him, Paul," Colby quickly warned her brother. The horse was sidestepping nervously, jerking his head, stiffening his legs.

"I can't, sis," Paul cried out as with a surge of savagery the animal swung around, breaking the boy's precarious hold. Paul scrambled to safety, his anxious eyes on his sister's slender figure.

The chestnut was crow-hopping, whirling, slamming into the fence with a resounding crash that shook the posts and the ground itself. Paul winced, his olive skin going pale beneath the dark tan. Colby was smashed up against the fence twice more before she hit the ground and rolled to safety beneath the rails.

"Are you all right, Colby?" Paul demanded anxiously, flinging himself on his knees beside her in the powdered dirt.

Colby groaned and rolled over to stare up at the darkening sky, a humorless smile curving her soft mouth. "What a stupid way to make a living," she told Paul absently. "How many times has that worthless animal thrown me?" She sat up, pushing at the damp tendrils escaping from her thick red-gold braid. The back of her hand left a streak of dirt across her forehead.

"Today or altogether?" Paul teased, then hastily wiped the grin from his face when she turned the full power of her eyes on him. "Six," he answered solemnly.

Gingerly she stood up, swiping at the layer of dust on her worn, faded Levi's. Ruefully she examined her tattered shirt. "Who owns this beast anyway? Whoever it is had better be someone I like."

Carefully Paul brushed dust off her hat, avoiding her gaze. Unless a horse was being trained for rodeo riding, Colby allowed Paul to handle all the details. Worst possible luck. "De La Cruz," he muttered apprehensively. At sixteen he was taller than his sister. Lean, tanned, already with the muscles of a horseman, Paul was unusually strong for his age. His face held the stamp of someone much older. He held out the weathered flat-brimmed hat almost as an offering of atonement to his sister.

There was a small silence while the wind seemed to hold its breath. Even the chestnut stopped snorting and reefing while Colby stared in horror at her brother. "Are we talking about the same De La Cruz who came to this ranch and *insulted* me? The same one who demanded we pack up our things and leave our father's ranch because I'm a woman and you're a child? That De La Cruz? The De La Cruz who *ordered* me to turn you and Ginny over to the Chevez family *and* gave me a whale of a headache with his insulting domineering disgusting male chauvinistic behavior?" Colby's soft husky voice was nearly velvet, the delicate perfection of her face utterly still. Only her large eyes betrayed her mood. "Tell me we aren't talking about *that* De La Cruz, Paulo. Lie to me so I don't commit murder." Her brilliant eyes were fairly shooting sparks.

"Well," he hedged, "it was Juan Chavez who brought the horses over, sixteen of them. We had to take them, Colby. He's paying top dollar and we need the money. You said yourself Clinton Daniels was pushing us about the mortgage."

"Not their money," Colby snapped impatiently. "*Never* their money. It's conscience money, for their sins. We'll find other ways to pay the mortgage." She shook her head to clear it of the anger welling unexpectedly out of nowhere. Slamming her hat against her denim-clad thigh, she muttered unladylike things under her breath. "Juan had no right to offer you the horses behind my back." She glanced at her brother's miserable face and instantly the anger evaporated as if it had never been.

She reached out to shove her hand affectionately through his jet black hair. "It isn't your fault. I should have expected something like this and warned you. Ever since that family showed up, that De La Cruz person has been nothing but trouble. I wrote the letter to the Chevez family for Dad nearly three years ago. Isn't it a blooming miracle they're finally getting around to answering it?" Colby swung around to face the chestnut, watching it carefully with wary eyes. "This horse is probably their way of getting rid of me so they can have you. With me out of the way they might have a chance at taking you and Ginny with them back to their South American hellhole. *And* robbing you of your inheritance while they're at it."

Colby was short and slender with soft full curves, large deep green eyes fringed with lacy dark lashes, and an abundance of long silky hair. Shapely arms deceptively hid strong muscles. White scars marred the deep tan on her arms and on her small hands, showing the years of labor. Paul, watching the dimple melt into the corner of her mouth, felt a surge of pride. He knew how she hated her scars, her hands, yet they were so much a part of her. Unorthodox, free, untamable, so natural, there was no one like Colby.

"They live on a multi-million-dollar ranch," Paul pointed out. "Posh. Probably a swimming pool, no work. Beautiful women.

Sounds like a tough life to me. Maybe it's a conspiracy and I'm in on it."

"Are you telling me you can be bribed?"

He shrugged his wiry shoulders, winking at her with a little mischievous grin. "If the price is right you never know." He tried to waggle his eyebrows and failed. "You don't have to worry, Colby," Paul offered suddenly, "I don't think Mr. De La Cruz knew Juan brought the horses to us. In any case"—he shrugged pragmatically—"money's money."

"So it is, my boy." Colby sighed.

At seventeen Colby had shouldered sole responsibility for the ranch, her eleven-year-old brother, and six-year-old sister after a freak small plane accident had left their mother dead and Armando paralyzed. She had done so without a murmur of protest. Two years after the accident, her stepfather had insisted Colby write to his family in Brazil and ask them to come out quickly. He had known he was dying and he had put aside his pride to ask for help for his children. No one had answered, and their beloved father had died surrounded by his children, but without his brothers and sisters. Now, at sixteen, Paul could appreciate what these last five years had cost Colby. He did his best to take some of the load from her, knowing, for the first time in his life, what it was like to really worry about someone else. Each time Colby was thrown from a horse, he found his heart beating overtime.

Colby never complained, but he could see the signs of strain, the weariness growing in her. "You want to take a break? The sun's down," he suggested hopefully. No doubt Colby was bruised from head to toe. His eagle eyes noticed she was cradling her left arm.

"Sorry, hon." Colby shook her red head regretfully. "I can't let this one get the idea he's boss. Let's get back to it." Without a trace of fear she entered the corral and caught the reins of the huge animal.

Paul watched her as he'd done a thousand times in the past, her small slender figure, fragile looking beside a half wild horse, yet totally confident. She had built such a reputation for herself as a trainer, many of the top rodeo riders brought their newest acquisitions to her from all over the United States. Normally, she spent weeks, months, gentling them patiently. She had a special affinity for animals, horses in particular. Colby's methods were usually harder on her than the horses. It was when she had to break them fast, like now, that Paul worried the most.

Their ranch was small, mainly for horses—the few cattle and acres of hay were for their own personal use. It was a hard life, but a good one. Their father, Armando Chevez, had come to this country when he was buying horses for his wealthy family in Brazil, looking for new bloodlines for the enormous ranches they had in South America. He had met and married Virginia Jansen, Colby's mother. Their match was not looked upon fondly by his family and he had been virtually disinherited. Colby never told her father she had found the letter from the Chevez patriarch stating he was to leave the "promiscuous, money-hungry American woman with her bastard daughter" and return home at once or he would be considered as if dead by the entire family. Colby had no idea who her birth father was and could care less. She loved Armando Chevez and thought of him as her true father. He had loved her and protected and cared for her as if she was his own blood. Paulo and Ginny were her family and she guarded them fiercely. She was determined they would have the ranch when they came of age, just as Armando Chevez had planned. It was the least Colby could do for him.

It had been a long afternoon and seemed an even longer evening. Paul was clenching his teeth and swearing softly under his breath as again and again the big chestnut broke his grip on the bridle and Colby was sent crashing to the ground or into the fence with bone-jarring force.

Ginny arrived and placed a picnic basket filled with a thermos of lemonade and cold fried chicken on the ground, then sat down outside the corral waiting patiently, one fist jammed into her mouth, her large brown eyes, round with anxiety, fixed on her sister.

Colby tightened her hold on the reins, her delicate features set with determination. Ducking her head she wiped the thin trickle of blood at the corner of her mouth onto her sleeve. Beneath her she could feel the powerful muscles of the horse begin to bunch, to stiffen. Paul took a step forward, his hand clenched so tight on the bridle his knuckles were white. The animal's huge head attempted to drop. Colby fought it up expertly. Even as the struggle took place Paul marveled at Colby's control. Then the horse once again broke free of Paul's grip and threw itself from side to side, rearing, bucking, whirling, and crow-hopping.

Ginny leapt to her feet, clutching the railing as she stared in awe at the expertise with which Colby anticipated the chestnut's every move. Twice Paul was certain the horse was going to fling himself over backward. But Colby was determined to remain in control, her entire being concentrated on the horse.

Rafael De La Cruz parked his truck near a cliff overlooking the entire valley. Behind him the mountains rose steeply, covered thickly in pine and fir. The woman nestled beside him touched him with a scarlet-tipped fingernail, very reminiscent of a bloody talon. He stared at it a moment then leaned over her abruptly, dispassionately, and pushed her hair away from the pulse beating strongly in her neck. He tried to recall what her name was, someone who was thought important in the small world he inhabited at the moment, but no one to stir his interest. All that mattered to him was the steady sound of her heartbeat calling to him.

She was prey like all the rest of them. Healthy. Strong. A woman who wanted to sleep with someone rich and powerful. There were so many of them, women who were drawn to the De La Cruz brothers like moths to flames. She tilted her head at him and he immediately captured her gaze, mesmerizing her. It was almost more trouble than it was worth.

Rafael sank his fangs deep into her neck and he fed. He drank his fill, all the while fighting down the beast threatening to rise, demanding the kill, whispering of ultimate power, whispering of emotion, of *feeling*. Just to feel once again, for one microsecond, it would be worth it. The woman was nothing, useless to him other than as prey. Easy to control, easy to kill. She slumped against him, and the movement snapped him out of the enthrallment of the beast. He closed the tiny pinpricks, healing the wound with a sweep of his tongue. He stared at her for a time, then contemptuously pushed her away from him so that she slumped across the seat. She was like all the rest. Willing to sell herself to the highest bidder. To sleep with a virtual stranger because of his wealth and power. Dressed in low-cut, revealing apparel to attract men to them. So many of them, like cattle. She had lured a predator, thinking herself the temptress, thinking she was luring him into her sexual web. He slid out of the cab into the night air. Rafael paced along the top of the cliff, his sensual features stamped with a hard, ruthless confidence. He was used to instant obedience, used to manipulating the mind of his human prey.

Rafael and Nicolas wanted to go home, to South America, and the Amazon rain forest. Back to their world, back to their ranch where they ruled and their word was law. Back to the neighboring jungle where they could shape-shift whenever they wanted without fear of being seen. Back where life was uncomplicated. But they had one small job to do before they could return, persuading a human female to do as the Chevez family wanted.

Rafael and Nicolas, answering the call of their prince hundreds of years earlier, hunted the vampire in South America. It was little enough to give back to their dying race. They wanted to go back to the country that had been their home and way of life for hundreds of years. It was far more difficult for them to remain for long in this unfamiliar country. But the Chevez family, which had faithfully served the De La Cruz family for centuries, needed their help now, and they were honor-bound to provide it. The problem was one small human female.

Nicolas had gone to her and ordered her compliance, "pushing" at her mind with a hard command, but to his surprise and displeasure, it had not worked. She became even more stubborn, refusing to talk with any member of their family. In all the centuries of their existence, such a thing had never happened. All humans could be controlled, could be manipulated. It was Rafael's job now, even if it meant taking her blood to force compliance. When the brothers wanted something, anything, they got it. She would not stand in their way. For a moment a muscle jerked along his shadowed jaw. One way or another, they would get what they wanted.

He sighed as he stared up at the stars. There was nothing to ease the unrelenting merciless nights. He fed. He existed. He fought the vampire. He went through the motions of everyday life, yet he felt nothing but hunger. Insatiable hunger. The whispering call of power to kill. To be able to feel. What would it be like to sink his teeth deep into human flesh and drain his prey, to *feel* something, *anything,* for a few moments. He glanced back toward the woman in the truck, temptation whispering insidiously.

Rafael! Nicolas's voice was a sharp reprimand. *Shall I come to you?*

Rafael shook his head, denying that ever-present enticement. *I will not give in this night.*

Rafael swept his gaze across the dusky sky, noting the bats dipping, performing their evening ballet. The wind brought him untold information. He was uneasy, his senses telling him a vampire could be close, but he was unable to ferret the undead from its lair, if, in fact, it was in the area. It had probably gone to ground the instant

Nicolas and Rafael had shown up and was waiting for them to leave before rising.

The wind carried the distant sound of voices. Alarmed. Soft. A beautiful cadence that touched something deep inside him. He heard the voice, a melodious voice, yet he couldn't understand the words. He stepped closer to the edge of the cliff. Something caught at the corner of his eye and he looked at the scene below him, his burning gaze fixed on horse and rider. He stared down at the small woman on the large horse in a kind of mind-numbing shock. It was nearly seventeen hundred years since Rafael had seen color or felt emotion. Now, in the blink of an eye, staring at the drama unfolding in the small corral, the horse and rider locked in battle, everything changed.

He saw her bright hair, a flame of color. He saw the faded blue of her jeans and the pale rose of her shirt. He saw the horse, a burnished red, tossing its head, whirling and bucking. Time seemed to slow down so that every detail was etched in his mind. The way the leaves on the trees glittered with a silvery sheen, the colors of earth and hay. He saw the silvery tones to the water as it shimmered from a distant pond. The breath slammed out of his lungs and he stood quite still, a part of the mountain he was standing on, frozen for the first time in all of his existence.

Behind him, the woman in the truck stirred, but she didn't matter. She was waking, drowsy, certain they had made love and that she had been overwhelmed by his attentions. The teenage boy and young girl near the corral didn't matter. His brothers waiting at home on their ranch in Brazil, Nicolas waiting here in this crowded country, the Chevez family, none of them mattered. Only that single rider.

Colby Jansen. Instinctively he knew the rider was Colby. The defiant one. Fire and ice like the mountains she lived amongst. The mountains she loved and clung to so fiercely. He studied her, his gaze black and hungry. He didn't move for several moments, his mind filled with chaos, emotions crowding in fast and furious. Emotions stored somewhere for hundreds of years poured through him like burning lava, forcing him to sort them out at an outrageous pace.

He had four brothers and all of them were telepathic, could touch each other at will. Rafael reached out, on the common path his brothers used, to share the colors, the unfamiliar raging in his body, the rising tide of hunger. Nicolas had no experience with such a thing. *She can only be your lifemate,* he responded.

She is human, not Carpathian.

It is said there are some who can be converted. Riordan's lifemate was not Carpathian.

The emotion and sexual hunger rising together were overwhelming, a fireball streaking through his gut, burning his blood, sharpening his appetites. He stretched, reminiscent of a large jungle cat. Beneath the thin silk of his shirt, ropes of muscles contracted. Colby Jansen belonged to him and no other. He wanted no other near her, not the Chevez family and not Nicolas who had seen her first. He felt the beast in him rising, fast and ferocious, at the thought of her with another male, mortal or immortal. Rafael stood very still, forcing himself under control. Dangerous at any time, he recognized he would be even more so in the state he was in. *It is most uncomfortable, Nicolas. I doubt I can stand for other males to be in close proximity to her. I have never felt such emotions. Never felt such jealousy or fear.*

It was a warning and both brothers recognized it as such. There was a small silence. *I will leave here, Rafael, and go to the high mountains to the east. The hacienda is empty and I will wait for you to sort this out.*

As always Nicolas was calm and serene, a quiet confident sanity that stirred others in the direction he wanted them to go. Nicolas didn't express his opinion that often, but when he did, his brothers listened to him. He was a dark, dangerous fighter, proven many times over. The brothers were connected and had stayed close down the long centuries, relying on one another for the memories that kept their code of honor intact. Relying on one another to keep the insidious whispering of the power of the kill at bay. *Obrigado.*

Rafael's fingers curled into tight fists until his knuckles turned white as he watched the drama unfolding below the bluff . This woman, small and fragile—*human*—insisted on doing dangerous, bone-breaking work. There were limits to a man's endurance when he had emotions. He found that he could not take watching her on the back of the pitching, bucking animal.

She went down hard, her body small and fragile, the huge chestnut powerful and dangerous, the pounding hooves inches from her. Rafael stopped breathing, his heart stilled. Colby rolled free, said something to her brother, who caught the horse's bridle. Instantly she was back in the saddle. Rafael had had enough.

It was Ginny who first noticed the intruders, the new four-wheel-drive truck, sleek and gleaming, as it roared up the dirt road. The driver parked the vehicle on the grassy knoll a few yards from the series of corrals. The two occupants stared out the windows at the struggle between horse and rider.

Ginny's low alarmed cry spun Paul around. Every vestige of color drained from his face, leaving him pale and strained. Instinctively he climbed over the railing and put his tall body in front of his younger sister, one hand wrapping around her wrist protectively.

The driver was out of the car, crossing the dirt road, moving with fluid grace, power and coordination combined. A rippling of catlike muscle lent the stranger a predatory appearance. He looked a hard, cold, dangerous man. Tall. Broad shouldered, with sinewy muscles beneath a thin silk shirt. He had thick wavy black hair, long and drawn back at the nape of his neck. Harsh implacable features were strong and sensual. He looked elegant and tough at the same time. This had to be Rafael De La Cruz. They had met Nicolas, and he was intimidating enough, but this man seemed to ooze menace from his every pore.

Rafael vaulted the fence with all the ease of a jungle cat, clearing the top rail by several inches. He caught at the snorting, bucking horse, dragging its head around and commanding obedience with an authority that even the animal seemed to recognize.

Shocked, Paul could only stare. Lord only knew what Colby would do. Paul had a sinking feeling she might throw a punch at the stranger and Paul couldn't see himself winning a fist fight with the man when he was forced to defend his sister. He could see the stranger was the type of male who would hit sparks off of Colby.

The chestnut was acting like a lamb now and when Rafael stepped back to give her room, Colby expertly put the horse through its paces. His dark features a mask of indifference, Rafael circled Colby's waist with one arm, lifting her bodily from the saddle. He was enormously strong and he practically tossed her to the ground.

Ginny clutched at Paul, gasping aloud. How dare he do such a thing! Appalled, she glanced at the woman watching with an air of annoyance and feigned boredom from the pickup. To humiliate Colby like that!

The moment the arm spanned her waist, Colby felt an unexpected connection. A heat from him seeped through the pores of her skin and spread throughout her bloodstream. Color stained Colby's face as she pulled free of his hold. Her chin went up, emerald eyes sparkling dangerously. "Thank you, Mr ...?" Her voice was velvet with exaggerated patience. She knew very well this had to be the *other* obnoxious De La Cruz brother. Who else? This was what she needed tonight. More misery!

He bowed slightly from the waist, a curiously courtly gesture. "De La Cruz. Rafael De La Cruz at your service. I believe you met my brother Nicolas and, of course, Juan and Julio Chevez. You, undoubtedly, are Colby Jansen."

Taking the hat Paul handed to her, she slapped it against her leg to remove the dust. Her eyes slid over Rafael's imposing figure once, then returned to his broad shoulders before she seemed to dismiss him. "To what do we owe this honor?" Even Paul had to wince at the honey dripping sarcastically in her voice. "I thought your brother and I covered everything needed in our last *friendly* discussion."

His ice-cold black eyes moved broodingly over her face, rested on her lush mouth, on the thin trickle of blood at the corner of her lips. His gut clenched hotly, and for a moment desire flared in his eyes. "Did you think we would give up so easily?" His voice whispered over her skin, soft, hypnotic, mesmerizing. Colby actually felt him touching her, his fingertips trailing over her skin so that little flames seemed to dance through her, yet his hands were at his sides.

She shook off the effects of his voice and eyes by concentrating on the woman in the cab of the pickup. "Is your lady friend ill?"

At her words the woman lifted her head and glared at Colby. She pushed open the door of the cab and shifted so she could carefully turn on the seat, showing off long legs in spiked heels. She was a tall willowy blonde with white skin and perfect makeup. In her cool lavender dress she looked like a fashion model. She didn't bother to hide the contempt she felt as she approached, her eyes sliding over Colby, taking in her faded dusty jeans, torn shirt, dirt-streaked face, and wild braided hair.

Colby, all too aware of the contrast in their appearances, the scars on her hands and arms from bites and wicked hooves, lifted a hand to her unruly hair. Before she could attempt to tidy it Rafael caught her wrist, easily pulling her arm down, his expression harsh.

Electricity arced between them, jumping from his skin to hers and back again. That slow burn was back, heating, thickening her blood. For a moment their eyes locked, clashed, a terrible sexual hunger leaping between them, devouring them. Colby's chin went up in that familiar challenging way her brother and sister recognized. She pulled her hand away from him, not liking the way her body seemed to have a mind of its own around him.

"Louise Everett," the woman introduced herself, laying a possessive hand on Rafael's forearm. "You know my brother, Sean, and his wife, Joclyn. The De La Cruzes, their servants, and I are all staying on Sean's ranch." She made it sound as if she had arrived with the De La Cruz family. "When they heard Rafael and I were coming over to see you they asked me to deliver a message to you." She stared for a moment disdainfully at the dirt on Colby's forehead. "Joclyn would like her daughter to have riding lessons." She examined her long fingernails for damage. "Although it looks to me as if that horse has thrown you more than once. I want my dreadfully crippled little niece learning from someone qualified, someone competent."

Paul's deep breath was audible. Colby was a professional. The best. Her reputation for training horses was known throughout the States. He wanted the snobs gone before he lost his temper and did something foolish. He took an aggressive step forward, his hands curling into fists. He didn't care if De La Cruz was a dangerous man and could beat him to a bloody pulp, no one was going to put Colby in such a position and get away with it, not as long as he was around. And that crack about the De La Cruzes' servants—the woman meant the Chevez brothers. Paul was a Chevez, so was Ginny. Did that mean if the family succeeded in taking them to Brazil, they would be servants instead of ranch owners? Out of the corner of his eye he caught sight of Ginny. She was glaring as angrily as he was.

"There's been some mistake." Colby's voice was, if anything, softer than usual. She crossed to the thermos of lemonade more, Paul was certain, to keep from punching De La Cruz than anything else. She had that look in her eyes Paul knew very well. "I don't give riding lessons, Ms. Everett. I don't have time for anything like that." Her green eyes slashed at Rafael's hard features. "Evidently Mr. De La Cruz has so many *servants* running his ranch for him he's forgotten what hard work actually entails." *Crippled little niece.* The words echoed in her mind so that she wanted to clap her hands over her ears and drown out the sound, the image of the poor child obviously unloved by her aunt.

Rafael's icy black eyes seemed to smolder but the rugged features remained impassive. He moved then, *glided*, a ripple of muscle and sinew, no more. She blinked and he was beside Colby, crowding her close, leaning down to remove the thin trickle of blood at the corner of her mouth with a brush of his thumb. Her heart jumped at his touch. Her body actually ached for his. It was damned maddening and Colby wanted it to stop. She recognized that he would be dominant sexually. It was bred into his very blood and bones. He would demand everything from his woman, *own* her, possess her, until there would be no going back—ever. And she hated that she was so susceptible to his dark sensuality when she prided herself on independence.

"Louise misunderstood the message," he said softly, his black eyes unblinking on Colby's face. Burning. Devouring. *Hungry.* He seemed to be looking right into her soul. She had the uncomfortable feeling he might actually be reading her thoughts. She watched as he raised his hand to his mouth and touched the pad of his thumb to his tongue almost as if he was savoring the taste of her.

Her entire body clenched. She found herself staring almost helplessly at him. The idea should have repelled her, but he was sinfully sexy, and she was mesmerized by him, the way he moved, the way his eyes were so hungry as his gaze drifted over her face. He had the ability to make a woman feel as if she was the *only* woman on earth. The only one he saw. He also made her feel as if he would take her, throw her over his shoulder and stride off with her if she defied him. It was unsettling—and, God help her, exhilarating.

"Colby." Ginny caught at her sister's hand, suddenly afraid for her. The stranger was looking at her older sister as if she belonged to him, as if he might be a wicked sorcerer bent on casting a spell on her.

Colby shook off the sexual web Rafael was weaving, silently cursing. This man was truly dangerous. He would *own* a woman, make her a sexual slave with no thought but to please him. He was an erotic temptation no woman could ever afford to succumb to. They had sent the first brother to order her to turn over the ranch and the children to the Chevez family and when that didn't work, they obviously sent the first string in to deal with her. She lifted her chin in challenge. "What message exactly were you supposed to deliver?"

"Joclyn would appreciate you meeting her later this evening at the saloon." The voice was so beautiful she ached to hear more. She forced her hands to stay at her sides instead of pressing them to her ears. "I believe she wanted to do you the courtesy of speaking to you herself."

Colby found herself clutching at Ginny's hand for solace. Rafael De La Cruz was capable of casting spells, a dark sorcerer weaving black magic, and she was highly susceptible. She wanted him gone before she fell into the depths of his black eyes. He was leaning so close to her she could smell his masculine scent. Outdoors. Sexual. Definitely male. "It seems to be very important to her."

"I'm very busy this time of year," Colby said a little desperately. She couldn't look away from him, not for a moment. His eyes were so hungry, so needy, so demanding. And damn him, her body actually ached for his. *Crippled little niece.* She couldn't let the image go.

"Then I will have to stay and convince you," he said, his accent very much in evidence. Everything in him, every cell, his heart and soul, his brain, even the buried demon roared at him to chain her to his side. He could do it, just take her. There was no one capable of stopping him. He was used to nothing, no one opposing his will. Certainly not a little slip of a woman. A human woman.

"Eight o'clock then," she said impatiently, trying not to look as frightened as she felt. No one had ever made her feel as confused and edgy as he did. There was something possessive in his eyes, something that seemed to claim her. She had never been truly afraid of anyone before. "If you'll excuse me, I've got to get back to work." He was the enemy. Closely associated with a family who hadn't wanted her or her mother. Someone who would consider her brother and sister servants in a land they knew nothing of. She had to remember that. She had to remember how hard their father had fought to give his children a legacy of their own. Rafael De La Cruz had that Latin charm she'd heard so much about but had never experienced. The man was lethal. Deliberately Colby looked at Louise. She was obviously drowsy and purring like a domesticated cat. She looked very much as if the two had just made love. Louise was stroking his arm and looking up at him with a singularly rapt expression on her face, one that turned Colby's stomach.

Rafael gestured imperiously toward the pickup, and Louise sent him a smile, her face lighting up at his attention, and she obediently went to the truck. The motion set Colby's teeth on edge. *Why didn't you just snap your fingers?* The De La Cruz brothers had a way of acting as if women were inferior to them and it irritated the hell out of her. That wasn't altogether true. It was more like *every* man or woman, every human being on earth, was considered inferior to them.

Rafael turned his head and looked at her almost as if he could read her thoughts. For a moment she froze, almost afraid to move.

She had never seen eyes so hard or cold. If his eyes were a mirror to his soul, this man was truly a monster. He made no move to follow Louise; instead his gaze swept over Colby's slender figure, his merciless features devoid of expression. "Why do you persist in this nonsense? This is work for a man, not one such as you. It is obvious you have spent most of the afternoon on the ground."

"It's none of your business, De La Cruz." Colby's pretense at good manners was thrown to the wind. Colby had no idea why she felt so threatened but she had the impression she was caught in the crosshairs of a powerful scope.

"I believe that is one of my horses you are breaking. How did you get him?" He asked it softly, as if he could not be bothered becoming disturbed by their disagreement.

"Like a thief in the night I crept into your corrals and made off with a number of them," she mocked sarcastically. "Try not to be more of a jerk than you can help. Juan Chevez sent over sixteen head. It must have been a conscience thing."

"The Chevez family has suffered greatly over this misunderstanding," he replied patiently. "They wish for nothing more than to heal the breach in their family. As I consider their family a part of mine and under my protection, it is of equal importance to me." His black gaze didn't blink once as it bored into her green eyes. She felt *hunted*. More than once she'd had to track cougar after her horses, and they had looked at her with just that same focused stare.

"Go back to Brazil, Mr. De La Cruz, and take your family with you. That will go a long way toward healing the breach."

His teeth flashed, very white, his smile wolfish. For no reason at all it made Colby shiver. She went to move away from him, to give herself breathing room, a delicate feminine retreat, but he glided with her like a jungle cat stalking prey. His hand curled around the nape of her neck, his fingers almost gentle, yet she felt his immense strength, knew she couldn't break his grip, knew he could snap her neck in an instant if he chose. A shiver of apprehension raced down her spine. She stilled beneath his hand, her gaze jumping to his face. His black eyes were suddenly hungry, a dark intense hunger that robbed her of her breath while he stared almost fascinated at her pulse.

Why had she thought his eyes flat and hard and icy cold? Now they were burning with so much emotion, alive with need and hunger and an intensity that scorched her all the way to her very soul.

You are not going to get away from me, pequena. No matter how far you run, no matter how much you fight, none of it will matter.

The words shimmered in her mind, shimmered between them, yet Colby had no idea whether they were real or not. He hadn't spoken; he was only looking at her with his smoldering black eyes.

She paled visibly, suddenly very, very afraid. Of herself. Of him. Of the dark promise of passion in his eloquent eyes.

"You aren't welcome here, De La Cruz," Paul burst out, his face bright red beneath his tan. He took a step toward the larger man, his fists clenched, but Ginny caught at his arm and held on to him like a pit bull. "Let go of my sister right now."

Rafael swung his head slowly around, his gaze reluctantly leaving Colby's face so that he could look at Paul. The boy noticed at once that Rafael's black eyes never blinked. Not once. For a moment Paul couldn't think or move. He stood frozen in place, his heart pounding. Rafael smiled at him then, no humor, just a flash of white teeth and then he was striding for his pickup truck.

They watched him move, mesmerized by his fluid grace. No one spoke until the truck had been swallowed up in a cloud of dust, then Paul flung himself onto the grass. "I must have been out of my mind! Why didn't you gag me? He could have killed me with his little finger."

Ginny laughed nervously. "Fortunately I saved your life by holding you back."

"For which I thank you from the bottom of my heart," Paul said, staring up at the darkening evening sky.

Colby flung herself on the ground beside her brother, dragging Ginny down beside her. They clung together laughing at their audacity, slightly hysterical with relief. Colby was the first to sober up. "Pride is going to cost us big bucks this time. With Daniels pressing us on the balloon payment for the mortgage, I'm afraid this is a serious setback. I've only got two months to come up with the payment and he's told me in no uncertain terms he won't give me an extension."

"He didn't say we have to give the horses back," Ginny pointed out pragmatically. "Just keep them and bill him for the work."

"We'll sue if he doesn't pay," Paul burst out indignantly. "You've worked hard on those horses and they've been eating our supplies. De La Cruz couldn't find anyone better here in the States, or Brazil for that matter. He can't expect to get your services for nothing."

"That's probably how they got rich in the first place," Colby said snidely, then was immediately ashamed of herself. She thankfully accepted a piece of fried chicken from practical Ginny. "Blast that man for coming over here! Although, to be strictly honest, I never would have accepted those horses had I known they were his."

Paul grinned at her unrepentantly. "That's why I didn't tell you."

Colby turned the full power of her emerald gaze on her brother. "That's not something you should be admitting to me. Rafael De La Cruz is worse than his brother and I never thought that was possible." She touched the nape of her neck where the warmth of his touch seemed to linger.

"I wish they'd all leave," Ginny stated clearly. She looked at Colby with frightened eyes. "Can they really take me away from you, to another country? I don't want to go with them." She sounded young and forlorn.

Colby immediately circled Ginny's shoulders with her arm. "Why would you ask such a thing, Ginny?" She glanced at Paul with a slight frown. "Did you hear that somewhere?"

"It wasn't me," Paul defended, "it was Clinton Daniels. We saw him at the grocery store and he told Ginny the Chevez family was going to take the two of us to Brazil and you couldn't stop them. He said you'd never win custody in a court of law and the De La Cruz family had political pull and too much money to fight. With the De La Cruz family backing the Chevez family you didn't have a prayer of keeping us."

Colby counted silently to ten, listening to her heart pound out a strange, irregular beat. For a moment she could scarcely breathe, scarcely think. If she lost her brother and sister she would have nothing. No one.

Pequena? The word was a soft inquiry in her mind. A gentle soothing caress of reassurance. She heard it clearly, as if Rafael De La Cruz was standing beside her, his mouth against her ear. Worse, she felt his fingers trail down her face, *touching* her skin, touching the inside of her until she felt her body react in a purely sensual way.

Colby was shocked and frightened by the way his voice seemed familiar and right. Intimate. By the way her body tightened and heated in response. She managed to smile her reassurance at Ginny even while she tried to build the wall in her mind to keep Rafael out. "Clinton Daniels always seems to find the time to gossip about everyone, doesn't he? I think that man needs a full-time job to keep him occupied." She hugged Ginny to her. "You are a legal citizen of this country, honey. The courts aren't just going to turn you over to someone you don't even know. It will never come to that. Daniels was just trying to get a rise out of you. These people will go back to Brazil and everything will be back to normal." They had to go back to Brazil and Rafael had to go back with them. Soon. Immediately.

"Yeah," Paul added, digging at his sister's ribs, "the normal thing, hard work, more hard work, working from early morning until late at night. Getting up in the middle of the night and working more."

"Don't we all wish you did that," Colby teased. "Seriously, you two, forget this problem with the De La Cruz brothers. They don't like me any more than I like them. Those men are positively archaic. I can see them as some kind of dungeon masters in the fourteenth century, where women were owned by their fathers and husbands."

"Really?" Ginny looked dreamy for a minute. "I picture them as kings in a castle, great lords or something like that. They're good-looking."

Colby wrinkled her nose. "Do you think? I hadn't noticed." She managed to keep a straight face for all of three seconds before she dissolved into gales of laughter along with her younger sister while Paul looked on in complete exasperated disgust.

2

Ginny knocked on Colby's bedroom door a few minutes after she heard the shower shut off. Colby had put in so much time with the cattle and out in the garden and the hay field that Ginny was afraid she might have forgotten the appointment with Joclyn Everett.

Colby was towel-drying her long hair and smiled at Ginny as she peeked through the door. "Got everything set up for barrel racing?"

Eagerly Ginny bounded into the small bedroom, seating herself on the bed. "Did you send in my entry fee for the Red bluff Rodeo?" she asked hopefully.

"I told you when you were twelve you could travel a bit. The local rodeo's enough until then."

"There's an eleven-year-old girl barrel racing already," Ginny protested. "She's making enough money for her college education." Shrewdly she pulled out a magazine and read quickly from the article, determined to prove her point.

"Shelve it, chickadee, I'm tired and in a hurry. As it is I'm going to be very late meeting with Mrs. Everett. What do you think? Should we take on the daughter?"

"I wouldn't mind if she was nice," Ginny admitted. "It would be cool to have a friend. Maybe sometimes I could go to her house. Paul told me Mr. Everett is really just a business associate of the De La Cruz family; they aren't like really close friends or anything. Maybe if I was friends with Mr. Everett's daughter and Mr. De La Cruz wants to do business with him, he'll start being nicer to you."

Colby didn't want Rafael De La Cruz to be nice to her. She didn't want him near her. "Don't count on it, honey." Colby grinned impishly. "I have this strong feeling the De La Cruz brothers would rather give up their business ties with Everett in a minute than be nice to me. They don't like independent women." It was strange how Colby thought Nicolas was so cold, the coldest man she had ever met, yet she found Rafael just the opposite, a seething cauldron of dangerous emotions, intense and darkly erotic. Rafael De La Cruz was a truly sensual man and he scared the hell out of her. If she never saw him again, it would be too soon.

Ginny scowled darkly. "You aren't ever serious, Colby," she reprimanded.

"I wouldn't say that." Colby pulled on a long-sleeved cotton shirt to cover the white marks marring her tanned skin.

"Did you notice how good-looking Rafael was? He's a hunk," Ginny pointed out solemnly. "His brother is a hunk too. And they're stinking rich, Colby. You're missing a great chance."

Snorting inelegantly, Colby stamped her foot down into her worn boots. "Have you ever noticed the type of women who flock around those men?" Throwing her hips forward, shoulders back, she batted her eyelashes. "Dawling," she purred, mimicking Louise's voice perfectly, "you're just soooo strong! My little old heart just flutters whenever I lay eyes on you." Dramatically clutching her heart, Colby fell onto her bed.

Ginny, giggling, gave up her matchmaking. "All right, all right," she surrendered. "But it wouldn't be bad having a niece or nephew to play with. I'll be an old lady by the time Paul gets roped."

"So I'm to be the sacrifice. No thank you, young lady." Colby wrinkled her nose. "I'm perfectly happy being an old maid. Gotta get out of here or I'll never get there in time." She glanced down at her watch. "It's already past time."

Ginny clutched at her hand, eyes serious. "I really would like to have a friend, Colby. I get lonesome in the summertime. We're so far from everybody . . . " She trailed off, hating to complain when Colby worked so hard.

Colby gave her a quick hug. "I know, honey. Paul and I get so busy we forget you're here by yourself doing all the cooking and cleaning. I'll see what I can do."

"Thanks." Ginny hugged her tightly. "You look great tonight. Is Joe going to be there?" There was a hopeful note in her voice.

"Joe? Joe Vargas? Ginny, don't you dare try to saddle that poor man with me. He'd be lost." Laughing, Colby caught up her purse and hurried out to the pickup truck.

Paul was there to open the rusty, dented door. "Drive carefully, Colby, the tires are completely bald," he cautioned. "Gone. Totally worn out."

"Everything is," she commented as again and again she tried to coax the truck into starting. When it finally turned over they both cheered. "Good old truck, still hanging in there." She patted the dash in appreciation and, waving at Paul and Ginny, took off in a cloud of dust. Bouncing high with every rut and hole, springs protesting, she cranked up the radio and happily sang all the way into town.

She found a parking space in the side lot and slid out of the battered cab. It was pushing close to nine. Chances were good Joclyn Everett would think she'd been stood up. Colby was simply too tired to care. With a sigh and a hasty prayer De La Cruz wouldn't be in the bar with his multitude of female groupies, Colby pushed open the door. It wasn't hard to spot Joclyn in spite of the crowd. Her simple white dress shouted money, her makeup and hair were perfection. In a group of cowhands she stuck out like a sore thumb and she was looking distinctly uncomfortable. Colby could imagine the hard time she'd been given, the joshing, the come-ons, the snide catty remarks only women make to one another. Colby made up for it the only way she knew how. "Joclyn!" She waved across the room. "I was hoping you'd wait for me. Joe, get out of my way, will you?" she added as a tall dark-haired man swept her up in a bear hug.

"Ah, Colby, when are you going to marry me?" he complained, kissing her soundly as he held her dangling with her feet several inches from the floor.

She slugged him good-naturedly. "One of these times I'm going to drag a preacher in here and you'll head for the hills." As he put her down, she wiped at her mouth with the back of her hand. "And stop kissing me in public."

"You want to go somewhere more private?" he offered, waggling his eyebrows.

Everyone in the bar laughed at Joe's antics and greeted her as she pushed past the cowhand to weave her way through the mass of people. "Sorry I'm so late." Colby flung herself into a chair.

"I was afraid you weren't coming after Louise admitted how rude she'd been," Joclyn ventured, looking more uncomfortable than ever.

"Colby!" Another man swept off his hat as he dropped into the chair beside her. "You're a hard woman to track down."

"Hi, Lance. This is Joclyn Everett, Sean's wife. Joclyn, Lance Ryker. Lance, we're in the middle of a business discussion, or," Colby corrected with a rueful grin, "at the beginning."

"I bought Diablo—I finally swung the deal. You promised me you'd help me train him." His words tumbled out. "I made the deal based on that promise."

"When will he be here?" Colby inquired with a small, apologetic smile at Joclyn.

"A month or so. I'll want you to take him to your ranch."

"Sure, give me a call. Paul makes the appointments so if I'm not around leave a message with him or with Ginny."

"Thanks, Colby." Lance leaned over to kiss her cheek before nodding at Joclyn as he left.

"You know everyone," Joclyn commented.

"It's a small town and this particular group is all ranch. I grew up with most of them," Colby explained, smiling her thanks at the waitress who was putting a tall glass in front of her.

Joclyn laughed softly. "I ordered a beer because I was certain you'd drink beer but I can see I made another mistake."

"Seven-Up. Sometimes I get really brave and have them put orange juice in it." Colby laughed. "They all give me a bad time about it."

Joclyn's dark eyes were suddenly serious. "I know you felt it was an insult for Rafael to ask you to teach my daughter to ride. And then I found out it wasn't Rafael who asked, it was Louise in her usual endearing manner. Please don't apologize—I understand. You work very hard, and you take a great deal of pride in what you do. Rafael didn't want us to ask you. He said you would be far too busy."

"More likely he made a few cracks about me trying to fill a man's boots," Colby said. "He's a male chauvinist."

Joclyn didn't bother to deny it. There was something very cold about the De La Cruz brothers that bothered her, but she wasn't about to discuss her husband's business associates. "I had to ask you anyway. Since my husband and I moved here, all I've heard is 'Colby's the best tracker, the best trainer, guide, anything to do with horses.' They say you have a gift."

Colby's grin was positively devilish. "I hope all this has been said in the presence of the De La Cruz brothers, especially Rafael."

"Invariably," Joclyn laughed.

Colby wanted to be strictly fair and give the devil his due. "I did hear that Rafael and his brother, Nicolas, were excellent with horses."

Joclyn nodded slowly, thoughtfully. "That's true, I've seen them. They keep odd hours for ranchers, though. They're night owls. I think they live pretty well in Brazil. But I watched Rafael walk right up to a severely injured horse and calm it with a touch of his hands. It was amazing." She shook her head as if to clear the memory. "But they aren't very good with people. At least not with children. I don't think either one of them has even looked at my daughter. Maybe her physical disability puts them off. Some people are like that. Tanya was struck by a car two years ago and must use braces to walk. The children at the school she was attending were very cruel and she's become withdrawn from us and quiet."

Joclyn fiddled with her glass, avoiding Colby's disconcerting steady gaze. "I know it would take a great deal of time, time you'd be using to train horses. We're willing to pay you whatever you would normally get for training a horse; that way you wouldn't lose anything." She was speaking very quickly, afraid of Colby's reaction. "It's so important to her, the first thing she's expressed interest in ..."

"Wait a minute, hold up." Colby reached out to pat Joclyn's hand soothingly, her natural compassion for the little girl already aroused. "It's not a question of money so much as time. She would need to work at her own pace, not feel rushed by my time schedule. Perhaps Ginny could help us. She's been riding horses since she was two. I could start the lesson, then let Ginny take over and just oversee it a bit. What about you? Do you ride?"

Joclyn ducked her head, flushing. "I'm terrified of horses," she admitted. "I'm a total city girl. When Sean suggested we move out here and buy a ranch I nearly died of fright. But I didn't like Tanya being in a boarding school and we traveled so much we had no choice. At least it was an opportunity for us to be together."

"I've never really known any other way of life," Colby mused. "My earliest memories are of my father putting me in front of him on his horse and riding all over the ranch. It's amazing to think all these years I've taken it for granted. I'd be lost in a city."

"And I'm lost here," Joclyn attempted a little laugh that didn't fool either of them.

"Don't worry, I wouldn't throw you on the back of just any horse. I have a couple of wonderful, very steady animals. You may as well take lessons with Tanya; that is, if Tanya would like to ride once she actually meets me." Colby made her commitment, trying not to think about what Paul was going to say.

"It's all she's talked about, learning to ride, I mean." The relief on Joclyn's face was so apparent Colby had to look away. As she did so, she encountered a pair of coal black eyes, an eyebrow raised in a kind of mocking male amusement.

At once her heart slammed hard against her chest and her mouth went dry. She could actually hear her heart pounding overloud in alarm. "Why didn't you tell me he was here?" Colby couldn't look away from those unblinking eyes. She had seen many predators, both bear and mountain lion. Rafael De La Cruz had the same uncanny stare. Her internal warning system had failed to let her know he was watching her, yet now it had kicked in and was work-ing overtime so that every nerve ending was shrieking in trepidation.

"Rafael? I'm sorry, Colby, I know it must be difficult for you when you feel as if the Chevez family is trying to take your brother and sister away, but Sean has to entertain them somehow. They are business associates. Rafael insisted he come along tonight and Sean didn't have a good enough reason to deny his request."

With tremendous willpower, Colby tore her gaze from Rafael's mesmerizing one. He could hypnotize the entire room with his glittering black eyes, she decided as she stood up and shoved ineffectually at the unruly hair spilling around her face. "Three o'clock on Wednesday sound okay?" Even her voice was shaking. Colby knew when to cut her losses and run. Rafael De La Cruz was more than she could handle.

"Thank you, Colby." Joclyn was sincere, intuitively not attempting to detain her any longer. Whatever was between Colby and Rafael put Colby visibly on edge.

Colby had made it nearly to the door when Rafael's vise like fingers circled her upper arm. He had moved with all the silence and stealth of a hunter, swiftly, unerringly, bringing his prey to ground. "Dance or a scene, you have your choice." His voice whispered over her skin like a velvet glove, tempting, taunting, a sinful male enticement when his words were so at odds with the seduction of his voice. He didn't care if she struggled, if every man in the bar leapt to her defense; he was not going to relinquish his hold on her. She knew it instinctively. People—her friends—would get hurt if they tried to interfere.

There was an edge to Rafael tonight, a distinct warning in the very way he held her. His body was as hard as a rock, his skin hot. There was raw possession in the depths of his eyes, in the enormous strength of his arms. Colby was used to men who were ranchers, strong men who thought nothing of tossing hay bales around. Rafael De La Cruz was deceptive in his looks. Long and lean, steel ran through his blood and bones. As soon as Colby felt the heat of his chest through the thin silk of his shirt where her cheek brushed his body, she knew dancing with him was a big mistake. Her heart gave a crazy lurch and she stiffened, tried to hold herself away from him.

Rafael simply pulled her that much closer, so close she could feel the warmth of his breath against her temple. Felt the hard, thick thrust of his arousal pressed against her. Honestly. Casually. As if it didn't matter in the least that she knew the urgency of his body's demand for hers. His fingers curled around her wrist, held her hand tight against his heart. "Shhh," he cautioned, his accent very deep, his voice so husky her entire body trembled with need. "You would not want these men to rush to your rescue."

"They would, too." She forced the words out of her mouth. For one terrible moment she thought her vocal cords were paralyzed. He was too potent up close like this. She had never seen such a sensual man. But it was more than his good looks. More than his raw sex appeal. There was a dangerous untamed aura clinging to him. She smelled it on him, felt it up close to him. Like an animal, a wild marauder. He was very dangerous, not only to her, but also to others. The knowledge was deep inside her, elemental, certain. She didn't know where it came from, but she trusted her instincts.

He leaned his dark head toward hers while the music beat through their bodies and rushed through their bloodstream. "What if I told you I could read your mind?" He whispered the words, his lips against the pulse beating so frantically in her neck. Little flames began licking along her neck and shoulder.

Colby closed her eyes. The music surrounded them, encasing them like satin sheets so that she burned with need. They burned together, she felt it in his body. Dancing with him was a kind of sexual torment. She could hear her blood pounding in her ears and her body felt molten with liquid fire. "I would have to call you a liar, Mr. De La Cruz. If there is one thing I know for certain, you can't read my mind." And for that she was eternally grateful. Because she wanted him with every cell in her body. She wanted to feel that perfectly sculpted mouth crushing hers, his hands moving over her, needing her, possessing her.

Rafael held her close, his body painful in its new demands. This woman was the one who belonged to him. He would have her. He had never denied himself a single thing he wanted in centuries of living. Nothing, no one, had aroused his interest in well over a thousand years, longer even. Now his every waking moment was occupied with thoughts of her. Torment. Pure and simply she was torment. Colby Jansen was his and no one would take her from him. Not now, not ever.

What she said was true. And it was shocking. He could read minds easily, yet hers was partially closed to him. *And she knew it was.* The fact maddened him, sent temper drifting through his bloodstream to mingle with the sexual hunger and lust rising so acutely. He would have her. *All* of her, no matter the cost. He would keep her for his own, make love to her when he chose. Feed his hunger, possess her. Own her. She would obey him and she would *never* close her mind to his once he unlocked her secrets.

Rafael bent even closer to the temptation of her satin skin. When he inhaled her scent, she smelled of spring and forest. The high mountains. Colby was different, far different from any other human he had met. An intriguing puzzle he would enjoy working out. He would take his time, feel his way through the unfamiliar situation. If it became necessary, he would simply take her and go to his homeland. Rafael's family ruled there; no one would attempt to interfere. Either way, she would not escape him.

Colby made the mistake of looking up at his sensual, handsome features. There was a ruthless set to his jaw, a merciless stamp to his mouth. At that moment his eyes were flat and hard and cold. She shivered and immediately he pulled her even closer so that her soft body was imprinted against the hardness of his. "I can't breathe." She meant it to come out sarcastically, but her voice betrayed her, a whisper of sound, husky, breathless, fearful.

Rafael guided her expertly through the traffic of drunken cowboys on the dance floor, straight into the deeper shadows. His dark head bent closer until his mouth rested against her tempting pulse.

Their bodies were swaying together to the music, a dark erotic tango they shared together. He inhaled deeply, taking her scent into his lungs, his body and soul, so he would know her anywhere, find her anywhere. Deep inside him the demon raised its head and roared for supremacy. She could sate his ever-present hunger. She stopped the emptiness, the cold gray world, she could quench the firestorm burning out of control in his blood. He *would* have her at any cost. She *belonged* to him.

"You can breathe, *querida.*" His voice was soft, gentle even when his arms were like steel bands. "You are afraid to take me inside your body, afraid of my possession, but you will come to accept it." His accent was thick, sexy, a temptation, and no one had ever tempted her before. She gave a small gasp at his choice of words, but the pad of his thumb brushed a caress over her lower lip, effectively halting her protest. His mind was working on the secret of hers. What protected her from his invasion? It wouldn't protect her forever. If he took her blood, he would have her. She would never escape him. "You will not, you know, not ever." He said it aloud, as if she might read his thoughts, testing her, even as he bent his head to her neck.

She felt his teeth tease her pulse, scraping back and forth, nibbling, caressing. Her entire body clenched in response. Her womb throbbed and ached. Her breasts swelled, nipples tightening into hard peaks. Gasping in sheer shock at her own response, Colby tilted her head to look up at him. His face was dark with desire, his eyes smoky with a raw intense hunger now. He had the look of a natural born predator. He didn't try to hide it, or soften it, he simply stared into her horrified gaze. She had the strange sensation of falling again, of moving toward him, embracing him, *asking* him into her mind and soul.

"Let go of me!" She hissed the words between her small clenched teeth, suddenly terrified in a room filled with people. A room filled with tough cowhands, every one of whom would fight for her protection. Deep down, where it counted, Colby knew they wouldn't win against him. No one would defeat him. Not alone or together. No one would be able to save her from him if he decided to forcibly take her. Rafael De La Cruz was truly a dangerous man under that very thin veneer of civilization. The knowledge was there, strong in her mind.

He held her for another long moment, savoring the feel of her body pressed so close to his. Her eyes were beautiful, sparkling with a hint of temper, but mostly fear. "You think to escape me, *pequena,* but there is no chance for you. You may as well accept it as you accept the air you breathe into your lungs. And I don't like you saying no to me. No one says no to me, least of all you."

It wasn't even what he said that disturbed her, it was the *way* he said it, the sound of his voice, sexy, husky, heavily accented. It was the intensity in his black eyes as they moved so possessively over her face.

"You'd better get used to it, then. Go back to your home, Mr. De La Cruz. You can't have my brother and sister and you certainly won't get them by trying to seduce me," Colby said insultingly, her words muffled by the thin silk of his shirt.

He let her go, his soft laughter a mocking male amusement that filled her ears with a kind of menace, with a promise. She lifted her chin at him, her expression defiant as she turned on the heel of her worn boots and stalked across the crowded floor. Halfway to the door, Joe caught her up in his bear grip. Joe, the perpetual clown. She'd known him all of her life. Easygoing Joe. Safe Joe. Joe didn't move the earth or shatter mountains with one touch. She went into the safety of his arms, allowing him his dance, acutely aware of a pair of mocking eyes following them around the dance floor. She didn't talk, she couldn't, so shaken was she by her encounter with Rafael. She just wanted to snuggle with someone familiar and safe.

Never once did those black eyes leave her face. They had gone back to hiding all emotion. Ice cold. Hard. Flat. The direct, focused gaze of a hunter locked on its prey. There was something very dangerous in those eyes as they touched on Joe's face. She shivered, suddenly afraid for the great bear of a man who had always been her friend. She pulled out of his arms, driven by fear. Colby tried to appear as normal as possible as she stood on tiptoe to kiss Joe's cheek before slipping outside into open air.

Crossing the parking lot to the sanctuary of her beat-up pickup truck, Colby swore under her breath, lots of unladylike things the cowhands had taught her at an early age. It was impossible—she had seen Rafael on the other side of the bar when she went out the door—but he was there, lounging against the hood of her truck. He looked lazy and contented, not a mass of nerves like she was. His long legs were stretched out and crossed at the ankles, his clothes were impeccable, black jeans and black silk shirt, his arms folded across his powerful chest.

"Do you know what harassment is?" Nobody should look that good. Nobody. It wasn't fair. Colby didn't fall all over herself staring at good-looking cowboys; she was a busy woman, she didn't have time to faint at their feet. Besides, she was the independent bossy type, according to Paul, and every man within a hundred-mile radius was afraid of her sharp tongue. "I don't know about your country, but in mine, it is against the law."

"And you have much faith in these laws?" His voice was very quiet, a mild question, gentle almost, but she heard the edge of humor.

"I suppose you're above the law," she snapped, yanking open the door to her truck. It wasn't going to start; she knew it wouldn't. It never started first time out.

He moved then, a ripple of muscle, but he was standing beside her, crowding her body with his superior height, the heat from his skin causing her bloodstream to catch fire. He seemed to glide across the ground, as silent as any cat, his attention fixed on her with the same intensity as a jungle beast hunting night prey.

"We have a code of honor my family lives by. That is the law that binds me." He touched her hair with his fingertips, drew strands of fine silk into his palm almost as if he were mesmerized. "Have you ever felt your hair? Really felt it? It is truly beautiful."

She stood there, afraid to move or speak, her body restless with unfamiliar demands. As hard as she could, she gripped the door of the truck, needing something solid. "I have to get home to my brother and sister." Colby wasn't entirely certain, at that moment, whether she was asking his permission or not. He was that potent, that powerful.

His perfectly straight white teeth flashed. There in the darkness he seemed a lord of the night. His realm. Invincible.

"Miss?" The voice was soft, but it pulled Colby out of her mesmerized state. She spun around to see a young woman standing hesitantly near them. "Do you need help?"

Colby recognized her as the new waitress, only because she was a stranger in a small town filled with people Colby knew very well. She didn't once look at Rafael, even when there was a small surge of power and Colby knew he was influencing the woman to walk away.

Rafael reached out and settled his fingers around Colby's arm. *You wouldn't want anyone to get hurt.*

The woman turned her head then and focused wholly on Rafael. "You could try to hurt me," she said, as if he'd spoken aloud to her, "but you'd get more than you bargained for. If you try to hurt her, I'll find a way to make you pay."

Colby looked at the woman's face. She was young, but her eyes were old. A startling green, almost sea green, deep and fathomless. "Thank you," Colby said, meaning it. "I can handle him. He's from Brazil where women fall at his feet all the time. It's shocking to him that I don't. I'm Colby Jansen, by the way."

Rafael's fingers tightened on Colby, but he was watching the other woman with a dark, disturbing look. Colby was suddenly frightened for her.

"Maybe I'll see you around, Colby," the woman said. She turned and walked slowly away without giving out her name.

"She heard you," Colby said. "When you spoke, telepathically, she heard you. In my life, you and your brother were the first people I ever met who were like me. Now there's this woman. Isn't that such a strange coincidence?"

"I don't believe in coincidence," Rafael said. His hand slid from her arm as he stared after the other woman.

Colby felt a sharp tug of jealousy. It was unreasonable, stupid— it possibly bordered on insane and plain made her mad at herself. She wanted away from Rafael De La Cruz more than anything. She ducked into the cab, clutching the steering wheel for support. The truck *would* start. *Absolutely* would start. She took a deep breath and turned the key. The starter made its usual grinding protest. She stared hard at it, determined that it would start. Nothing defied Colby Jansen in this mood. The engine turned over and she revved it carefully, a swift, triumphant smile crossing her face. She couldn't help but glance at him smugly as she backed out of the lot and headed home.

Rafael watched thoughtfully as the old rickety pickup disappeared around the corner. The sudden surge of power vibrating in the air as she started the engine had been impossible to miss. Had she known what she was doing? Colby Jensen was unique among humans. She possessed qualities, talents he had not expected. There had been rumors that his family was not completely isolated. He had heard, although none of them had ever really believed until Riordan had found his lifemate, that there were human women possessing certain rare gifts that deemed them lifemates to the males of his race. Colby not only was telepathic, but she could do a variety of other things as well. And who was the mystery woman who would have challenged his authority over Colby? Friend or enemy?

Rafael and his four brothers were immortal. From their home in the Carpathian Mountains, they had gone willingly to South America when it was a wild, lawless land plagued by vampires, far from their homeland and their kin. The ancestors of the present-day Chevez family had eventually been chosen to run their vast estates during the daylight hours. In exchange, the De La Cruz brothers provided protection and wealth for those members of the Chevez family who remained loyal to them. In the intervening years, Rafael had certainly hunted countless vampires, males of his race who had deliberately chosen the darkness and had become wholly evil.

He glanced around the parking lot, blurred his image so that the few stragglers wouldn't see him, and, with the ease of long practice, launched himself skyward. Shape-shifting on the wing, he circled once and then flew across the night sky. Colby Jansen was unlike anything he had ever experienced. It was the first time in his long life he could remember being uncertain how to proceed. Emotions were new and raw, colors were vivid and blinding, his body was alive and crawled with relentless sexual hunger. It was amazing to be in her company, to have her in his world. He wanted to spend every moment with her, yet he could not control her as he did everything and everybody in his realm of existence. *But I will.* He sent that thought winging ahead of him into the night. A promise. A need. A vow.

Colby hung on grimly to the steering wheel, her mind in total chaos. Something was very, very wrong with Rafael De La Cruz. He certainly was the epitome of the Latin charmer. He could knock off a woman's socks at fifty paces. Everything about him screamed sin and sex. She muttered unladylike imprecations under her breath.

She was a practical woman, certainly not someone easily swayed by physical attraction. This man was turning on the charm to get his way. He wanted Paul and Ginny and with them, their ranch. He was ruthless enough to use any method possible to get what he wanted.

Colby groaned aloud. She certainly showed him she was totally susceptible to his sex appeal. She'd acted just like every other female in a hundred-mile radius, throwing herself at him. She glanced in the mirror to see if her face was shiny crimson with shame. For a split second she saw eyes staring back at her. Inky black. Unblinking. Icy cold. The eyes of a merciless hunter. In the depths of those staring eyes were wicked red flames flickering and growing. The gaze was fixed on her; she was prey, helpless and weak in the face of such relentless strength.

Colby's heart slammed hard and loud. She nearly cranked the wheel to the side of the road as she twisted around to look behind her seat into the bed of the pickup. There was nothing there. She had seen those red flames before, felt the shiver of fear, of apprehension. A wind was whipping up out of the mountains, hitting her face through the open window, an ominous portent of things to come.

Resolutely she pressed the gas pedal down, bumping along, the springs on the seat squeaking in tune to the radio she had blasting. As hard as she tried, Colby couldn't stop herself from continually checking the rearview mirror for those merciless eyes. She had enough to worry about without seeing things. So many little things had gone wrong on the ranch lately—Pete's disappearance when she needed an extra hand so desperately, the balloon payment due on the mortgage, and the South American group showing up out of nowhere demanding the children. She swept a hand through her hair, shoving it away from her face. The wind blew the silken strands right back at her.

Something was terribly wrong at the ranch. She knew it, she *felt* it, but how could she make Ben understand she just knew things? Like the plane crash. She had known the moment it was in trouble. She had known the moment her mother died. She had been the one to find the wreckage, knowing her beloved stepfather was clinging to life and waiting for her. How could she explain how she knew things? How could she explain to anyone the things she could do?

For a moment wild emotion welled up out of nowhere, blindsiding her, unexpected when she was so careful to be controlled. She felt tears burning in her eyes, her throat tight, her chest like stone. Loneliness hit her hard. She was so alone, so lonely. There was no one with whom she could ever share who and what she was. Colby fought desperately to control the burning in her chest. She didn't dare lose control, wouldn't lose control. It could be dangerous, very, very dangerous.

The dirt road leading to her ranch loomed up, the gate closed and locked. She glanced around the lonely area just once, ensuring she was completely alone. Slowing the truck, Colby leaned out the window and stared intently at the padlock and heavy chain wrapped around the gate. It trembled once, then fell open. The gate swung inward, clearing the path for her. With her ragged fingernail she tapped a rhythm out on the rusted door as she pulled the truck forward. She leaned out of the window to concentrate on locking the gate behind her, thankful she had certain useful talents. It came in handy in the rain and on nights she was just too tired to pretend she was normal.

The wind washed over her again and she felt eyes on her. The scent of a hunter. Something, someone, was out in the darkness and it had turned its attention to her. Perhaps it was the disturbance of power in the air when she used her strange talents that drew unwanted attention in her direction. Colby only knew something was very wrong, and evil stalked her family. She was the only protection Paul and Ginny had. She loved them and she would guard them fiercely. From anyone. *Anything*.

With a sigh she drove the rest of the distance to the ranch house. Ginny's dog, King, a border collie, rushed out barking a greeting. She rested her head against the steering wheel for a moment, trying to absorb the vibrations in the night sky. What was out there, close, watching her ranch, marking her family? Why couldn't she isolate the direction it was coming from? She knew something was watching, yet she couldn't pinpoint the trouble. Colby knew things. She knew the cow in the barn was going to give birth soon and it wasn't going to be an easy birth. She knew when it was going to rain and just how long she had to get the hay out of the fields.

Patting the dog, she made her way to the porch. Paul was waiting for her, on the porch swing. His long, lanky frame was stretched out, his hat pulled low over his eyes. His arms were folded across his chest. Colby stood there looking down at him, love for him welling up inside of her. He was an amazing brother. He looked so young and vulnerable when he was asleep. Colby touched his shoulder gently.

Paul woke with a start. "I was just resting my eyes," he said, his grin lighting his face as he pushed back his hat with his thumb. He had seen the gesture in a western movie and had copied it ever since. He had been about seven and Colby didn't have the heart to remind him of its origins. In any case she found it endearing.

"Joclyn Everett is a very nice woman, Paul. I've met her husband, of course, many times, but never her. What do you think of them?"

His sigh was audible in the silence of the night. "What I think is that you told this woman you would take on her kid for riding lessons even though you are totally swamped. That's what I think, Colby."

Colby rubbed her forehead, avoiding his eyes. "Well, the girl is Ginny's age and Ginny gets very lonely."

"Colby, you can't do it. You're running yourself into the ground already. Don't you think I know you're staying up half the night? You can't take on any more."

"They're offering good money, Paulo, and Ginny needs a friend. I thought I could spend a short period each lesson with the girl and then let Ginny take over. It shouldn't really take that much time."

Paul groaned aloud. "You really are crazy, Colby, but there's never any good arguing with you." He held open the door. "I checked the stock, made the rounds so you can hit the sack."

She flashed him a quick smile. "Thanks, Paul. I am tired tonight." She leaned over to kiss his cheek. "I appreciate it, I really do."

"I'd give you a lecture," he said, "but I kind of like Sean Everett. Since he's a neighbor, we might as well become friends with him." Colby burst out laughing, the sound soft and quite catching. Paul found himself with a big smile on his face.

"You're only saying that because you want another victim to rope into fixing our broken-down equipment."

"Are you accusing me of having an ulterior motive?" He did his best to look innocent.

Colby signaled King toward the barn. Usually the collie slept curled up on the floor of Ginny's bedroom, but Colby had been so troubled lately, she had taken to using him as a night guard. Paul watched her signal the dog, a frown on his face. "You really are worried, aren't you, Colby?"

She shrugged casually. "I just think it's better to be safe than sorry, Paulo. Ben says he thinks a bunch of kids are playing pranks."

Paul snorted his denial. "Ben always blames teenagers. What's up with that?"

Colby laughed again, filling the house with the sound of her warmth. "You should have seen him as a teenager. He was the bad boy of the school. He just thinks everyone is like he was."

Paul shook his head and opened the door to his bedroom. "I can't imagine him as a teenager. He doesn't even know how to smile. Goodnight, Colby, you need to actually go to bed."

She raised an eyebrow even as she hid her amusement of his authoritative tone. "Good night, Paul."

3

Colby sighed and threw back the covers. For a moment her hand lingered on the beautiful handmade quilt covering her bed. Her mother had sent away to Paris for the comforter. A very famous but elusive designer had made it. She remembered very vividly her need to have the quilt after she'd seen it advertised in a magazine. Colby had known it was something special, almost as if it possessed a power of its own. Her mother and stepfather had given it to her for her tenth birthday and Colby prized it above every other possession she had. Along with the rare beauty and unique feeling of comfort and safety it gave her, the quilt was a symbol of her parents' love for her.

She stretched languidly and wandered across the hardwood floor to her open window. The wind blew the thin lace curtains inward. She was wearing a pair of drawstring pajama bottoms and a small spaghetti-strapped top. Colby slowly unbraided her long hair as she stared out the window into the night. She loved the mountains at night, always mystical and mysterious. A veil of thin white fog shrouded the high ridges. She was surrounded by the giants, her ranch snuggled into a deep valley. She stretched out her arms to the high mountain range, lifting her face toward the shining half-moon crescent.

Colby was worried about so many things she couldn't sleep. She was exhausted and yet determined to be up at four-thirty. She leaned against the windowsill, staring up at the stars. She didn't tell Paul, but after feeding the stock, she intended to take her horse into the hills and look for old Pete. She had been making sweeps of the ranch over the last three days, getting up extra early and devoting as much time as she could spare to look for signs of him. Despite what Ben said, Colby didn't believe that Pete had simply drifted away or that he had gone on a drinking binge.

Pete was in his late seventies, his body riddled with arthritis from his rodeo days. He had a home with Colby, a warm bed, a roof, good food, and the ranch work to make him feel useful. He was a man who knew the meaning of the word *loyalty*. She was certain he would never leave the ranch, especially when he knew Colby was in danger of losing their home. He would never desert her. Pete just wouldn't do that. Colby was afraid he was sick or hurt somewhere on the property.

In the large oak tree across the yard from her window, a bird flapped its wings, drawing her attention. The bird had a round facial disk with a very pronounced ruff. It wasn't an owl but it was large. Very large. The unusual bird could easily weigh in at twenty pounds. She stared at it, and it stared right back. She could see its eyes, round and shiny black. She was familiar with the birds on her ranch and she had never seen one like this. If she didn't know better, she would think it was a harpy eagle. Colby leaned all the way out of the windowsill, concentrating on the bird.

She watched it closely as she tuned her mind to the path of the raptor. The beak was wicked looking, curved and sharp, the talons enormous where they curled around the thick branch of the tree. It had a keen intelligence shining in its eyes. Colby's breath caught in her throat, her heart beating in sudden excitement. Harpy eagles lived in the Amazon rain forest, flying gracefully, agilely through the trees. They were unquestionably the world's most formidable bird, capable of taking monkeys, snakes, even sloth as prey. It couldn't possibly be, yet the more she studied it, the more she was certain. What in the world was an endangered eagle from South America doing in the Cascade Mountains?

Colby continued to stare at the creature, keeping eye contact, whispering softly, more in her mind than with her voice. She often lured all kinds of animals to her, whispering to horses, sheep, and cattle, drawing wildlife to her when she was alone. She called to the bird, shocked at its size. It was really quite beautiful. Wild. Untamed. Powerful. She was afraid it must have been injured in some way to travel so far from its native territory.

Deep within the body of the bird, Rafael De La Cruz smiled. Colby had taken the bait. She was calling the bird to her, using a mental path unfamiliar to him, but the trail of power led straight back to her mind and gave him the opening he needed. The key to unlock her memories, to take control. She would never willingly invite him into her home, yet she was inviting the bird. Once invited inside, he would have even more control of Colby. In the body of the large eagle, he spread his enormous wings and stepped off the branch of the tree. He saw her face, startled by his sudden movement, drinking in the beauty of the harpy eagle in flight. Circling high, he spiraled down in a lazy show and landed on her windowsill, talons digging deep into the wood. Slowly, majestically, the eagle folded his wings.

Colby looked beautiful in the moonlight. In the faint silvery light she looked a young pagan goddess offering up a sacrifice, a homage to the high peaks. Her skin was soft looking, gleaming at him with an invitation to touch. Inside the body of the bird, his gut clenched hotly. His need was a fever in his blood. Dark and out of control when he needed restraint the most. Her innocence shook him, yet it drew him. She was his. Made for him. Exclusively for him. Only Colby Jansen could rid him of the dark shadows in his soul.

Colby stared at the bird, entranced. It was a little frightening to have the raptor so close to her. She wasn't altogether certain she was safe. Very carefully she took two steps backward, the sound of her heart loud in her ears. It was an amazing bird, huge and very intimidating. Colby forced her mind to be calm as she examined it. It didn't appear to be injured in any way. She didn't get the impression it was hungry or hurt. It was staring at her as intently as she was staring at it.

Rafael watched as Colby's tongue moistened her full lower lip. The action tightened his body even more and turned his bloodstream to a molten heat. He could not control his reaction to her. He was very much aware it made him more dangerous than he had ever been. He needed to be in control at all times. He didn't want to risk harming her. She was temptation itself, standing there with her bare feet, looking young and beautiful and slightly afraid. He felt his heart turn over, his every protective instinct welling up. He hadn't known he had protective instincts. She was doing things to him so fast he couldn't adjust.

Rafael was determined to have her under his command. He wanted her to himself, away from others where he could slowly and carefully work out what he wanted to do with her. He would have her. He would imprison her, he decided; it was the only way she would be his, under his care, under his dominion. There was a fierce need in him, hungry and growing each moment, to chain her to his side.

Colby could feel her heart pounding hard, but it was more out of excitement than fear. She should be afraid, the bird was a true raptor, but it was magnificent. She worked harder at finding the path to its brain, sending waves of reassurance, trying to keep it calm. It hopped from the window sill onto the hardwood floor, still keeping its eyes fixed on her face.

It had black eyes! Round, shiny, very intelligent black eyes. She stared at it for fully two minutes. That wasn't normal, she was certain. Very slowly, so she wouldn't startle the creature, she backed across the room to her bookshelf. Still looking at the bird, she slid her fingers over her books until she found the one she wanted. It slipped off the shelf into her waiting hand, the pages already turning to the very entry her mind was seeking. Strangely, the bird was observing her just as intently, an intelligence in its gaze as it watched the pages of the book open without her hand. She brought the book in front of her and glanced down to look at the photograph of the harpy eagle. The eyes were round and shining with intelligence, but they were not black. The eyes in the picture were a bright amber with a black pupil. She let out her breath slowly. Something *was* wrong with her bird.

You aren't blind, though, are you? She sent the words, images to the creature. It was watching her too closely to be blind.

It stirred then, almost in triumph. Colby's heart jumped in response. For one moment she felt threatened in some undefined way. She thought she caught a fleeting expression in the eagle's eyes and then it hopped back onto the windowsill and launched itself skyward. For such a large bird, it amazed her how perfectly silent it was. It circled for a moment, climbing higher and higher until it was a mere speck. She watched it until it was gone.

Colby felt inexplicably lonely as she climbed back into her bed. Her fingers plucked at the quilt, seeking comfort. The book lay on the bed beside her. She tapped on the cover with her fingers before waving it back to the shelf. Telekinesis was a very handy talent. She had discovered it at an early age. She had often set her toys dancing around her room when she was alone. Once, she had shown her mother, proud of her ability. Her mother had seemed delighted, yet

Colby could read the worry in her mind. She learned at a young age she was "different" and people didn't tolerate differences very well. She stared at the open window sadly. *I am so alone.* She sent the heartfelt cry winging into the night.

She had other things she could do. Not nice things. Things her mother cautioned her over many times. Colby was older now and knew control was very necessary. She never had taken a drink of alcohol in her life and never would. She couldn't afford to allow some of her unusual gifts to erupt unbidden.

She sighed and turned her face into the pillow. It would have been nice to have someone to talk with. To be herself with. Just once. Just one time, to be who and what she was, instead of so afraid of betraying herself. She missed her mother. Tears were welling up out of nowhere and Colby hated that.

Querida, why are you so sad this night? The voice was heavily accented, musical, a whisper of enticement. She heard it as clearly as if the words were spoken aloud.

Colby stiffened, butterflies fluttering in her stomach. She opened her eyes, searching the shadows of her room. It appeared empty at first, but then she felt a hand brush a lingering caress over her face, the fingertips trailing over her skin as it removed silken strands of hair from her forehead. She sat up, pushing at the shadowy figure bending over her. The broad chest was real and very solid. How could she have missed his presence?

"What the hell are you doing in my bedroom?" She hissed the words very quietly, afraid if Paul heard he would rush in with a gun.

You called me to you. Deliberately Rafael used the more intimate method of telepathic communication, determined to strengthen their bond. *I heard your call. Felt your tears. Why are you so sad this night?*

He was too real and solid in the confines of her small bedroom. His masculine scent clung to the corners, his voice brushed over her skin, at her insides like black velvet. It wasn't just his words, it was literally the sound of his voice. A seduction, an intimacy stolen in the night. He washed over her and into her so that she was at a loss. No one had ever made her feel so aware of her body, so feminine, or so blatantly sexual.

She blinked to keep him in focus. He seemed substantial to the touch, yet in the dark room, his shadowy figure blurred as if he was a part of the night itself. *Not real.* Colby had the good sense to be afraid. It was so dreamlike she dug her nails into her palm to ensure she was awake. "How did you get in here?" The moment she spoke aloud, she wished she hadn't. Her voice was husky, sexy, not entirely hers. *An invitation.* Her heart thundered out a fast rhythm. The heat of his body crowding so close to hers warmed her skin despite the coolness of the wind. She should have been furious, going for the gun herself; instead, she was mesmerized by him, by his overpowering sexuality.

His hand curled around the nape of her neck. Possessively. As if he had the right to her. Her body went pliant, soft in reaction. In her entire life, she had never responded so sexually to anyone. She ached for him until it seemed to be a craving she couldn't control. Colby sat there helplessly, trapped in the depths of his black eyes. She was falling forward, his captive, forever his prisoner. In that moment she was willing to be his prisoner. His dark head bent very slowly, relentlessly to hers. She could see the impossible length of his lashes, his sinfully sexy lips, the bluish shadow on his jaw. Her body was heavy and aching and demanding things she knew very little about. He was so out of her league. A man like Rafael would consume her, use her up, make her his so completely there could never be another. She should have screamed for Paul and his gun.

Instead she closed her eyes and allowed his mouth to take possession of hers. Beneath her the bed lurched and rocked as if the ground beneath it had moved. She was swept onto a tidal wave of pure feeling, into a sensual world beyond her comprehension. Her body no longer belonged to her, but to him. Colors whirled and danced and the room spun. And she was alive. It wasn't simply her body burning for his, but her mind, craving, reaching out for his, her soul crying out to his. She felt a curious shifting deep inside, a merging, two ragged halves sealing perfectly. She felt his arms tighten like two steel bands, a wildness growing in him. She realized he was not only gaining possession of her, but control as well. She was losing herself, wanting to merge deeply with him, wanting to be whatever he needed, do whatever he wanted.

Rafael lost himself in her sweetness. She was heat and honey, melting into him, twining around his heart until he knew he would never be complete without her. His mouth moved to the corner of hers, along her chin to her vulnerable throat. She was aching for him, burning as he was. Her pulse beckoned to him. She thought him an erotic dream and he fed the haze in her mind, fed the illusion of a dream to her, even while his body pulsed with need and excitement. He allowed his hunger to deepen as he forced her body back against the mattress. She struggled for just a moment, a thought of resistance. He took it ruthlessly from her mind, kissing her until she was pliant. His mouth was merciless onhers, demanding kisses, taking her response rather than asking for it. He stretched her arms above her head and pinned her wrists together to hold her captive beneath him.

Colby Jansen possessed a mind with a complex guard, one he needed to bridge in order to claim her for his own. He had succeeded in being voluntarily invited into her home. He had succeeded in finding the path to her mind. Now he was going to take what he needed to unlock the door keeping her from him. Nothing would stop him. Not the boy sleeping so restlessly in the next room. Not even Colby herself, half shaken by her unfamiliar needs and desires.

Colby was wrapped in his body so tightly she was unsure where she left off and he started. His mouth burned a trail of fire along her throat to her neck. She felt the nip of his strong teeth, the swirling caress of his tongue. A rush of liquid heat beckoned him and she was helpless to stop it. She turned her head, wanting his mouth, wanting him to kiss her again, but he held her easily, his black eyes drifting possessively over her face. The dark needs there made her shiver. There was such a sexual hunger, a merciless passion in his heavy-lidded eyes. Heart thudding wildly, she thought to fight him. Before she could move, he bent his head with deliberate slowness to her slender neck again. At once she felt a fiery pain, a white-hot blaze streaking through her bloodstream so that she moaned, so that her body rippled with pleasure, with a need so intense she wanted to cry.

Rafael tightened his hold on her, locking her to him while he took the essence of her life into him for all time, for his keeping. He wanted her, wanted to take her body, possess her fully. It wasn't simply wanting. He *needed*. It was an urgent demand as elemental as the earth and sky. He needed her. His hand slid under the thin material of her top to cup the weight of her breast in his palm. Her blood flowed into him like nectar and he allowed himself to indulge in her exquisite beauty, the taste and scent of her. The feel of her soft skin next to his.

His body hardened with a savage, unfamiliar need. At once his sexual appetite grew, erotic desires pouring into his mind, into his cells, flooding him with images of taking her in every way possible, of having her whenever, wherever he wanted. He had never thought about the things he would need or want from a woman, but she roused dark passions and an edgy hunger in him.

Rafael had never needed anything or anyone in his life. He had dedicated his life to guarding mortals from the demonic vampires. He had the memories of his love for his brothers. He had vague memories of his homeland. He had his honor. He fed. He existed. His brothers were just like him. But he was unlocking Colby Jansen's mind and it astonished him. Shocked him. She was all about love and compassion. Her thoughts were mainly of others, her need to serve and help them. Where he wanted his own way in all things, where he believed others inferior to him, she was light and goodness. She made him ashamed of his predatory nature.

Colby was no longer certain she was dreaming. She could never have conjured up a fantasy as erotic as Rafael De La Cruz. He was holding her submissive, a dominant sexual being that was both rough and tender. He demanded her response, took her response, rather than coaxed it. And she seemed helpless to stop the tidal wave of passion he unleashed in her.

She began to struggle, afraid of losing who and what she was. He seemed to be slipping into her mind and wrapping himself deep inside her so that she was afraid she would never again be free. He was enormously strong and the more her body moved against his, the more vise like his grip became. He didn't hurt her, but he refused to allow her to get away. She tried surfacing from the dream, afraid of the way her body responded to his, even when he was being roughly dominant, but she couldn't manage to wake and save herself. And a part of her knew she would be saving herself.

Rafael lifted his head slowly, his black eyes burning with fierce possession. He bent his head to catch the twin beads of blood running toward the slope of her breast. His tongue swirled over the mark he had deliberately left. A brand. His brand of ownership. The healing agent in his saliva closed the tiny pinpricks. His arms held her easily, his strength enormous. She was very small, and surprisingly strong for her size, yet her struggles were nothing to him. Sheer nonsense, barely registering.

He caught her chin firmly and forced her deep green eyes to meet his. Even as he did so, his mind tuned itself to the path of hers, thrusting sharp and deep, taking command. *You will take what I offer.* He gave the order as he used a lengthening fingernail to open his own chest. Pressing her mouth to the dark liquid that would bind them together, Rafael ruthlessly forced her to swallow. He closed his eyes as her mouth moved against him, her body so like hot satin he could scarcely contain himself. A groan escaped, and his hands moved over her skin exploring the soft creamy curves.

So lost in his own needs and desires, Rafael almost missed the movement of the young girl in the room across the hall. Nightmares were intruding, and she was calling out, thrashing on her bed, tears running down her face. His body was so hard and taut with desperate need heal most didn't hear the intrusion.

Shockingly, Colby stirred, right through the dark haze of her strange, terrifying dream. She began to fight the fog, sensing Ginny's troubled sleep. Rafael cursed eloquently under his breath as he closed the wound on his chest with his own saliva. Gently, almost tenderly he laid Colby back on the pillows. She was very pale, her red hair spilling around her like a fiery halo. He had given her enough of his ancient, powerful blood for an exchange, but not enough to replace the volume she had lost. Unable to stop himself, he bent his dark head to the swell of her creamy, round breast. Her heart thundered beneath his roving mouth as he wantonly marked her a second time. He had never ached so much, needed so much in all of his existence.

With a sigh of regret, he melted into the shadows, waving his hand to quiet the child's dreams and send Colby into a deeper sleep. Bending, he brushed a kiss on her forehead even as he stroked a caress over his mark on her neck and the second one on the swell of her breast with a fingertip in great satisfaction. Without another sound he dissolved into mist, an insubstantial fine vapor. He poured through the window out into the night air. As he streamed toward the trees the droplets connected to form the large harpy eagle. He landed on the branch of the oak tree and stared thoughtfully at the house.

Colby tried to surface to go to her sister, but Ginny had quieted under Rafael's command, so Colby subsided, giving in to her need for sleep.

"Colby." The frightened sound of Ginny's voice pushed through the uneasy dream Colby was caught in. Her body was leaden, her mouth dry. Strangely her breasts ached and were sore. She tried hard to rouse herself, when all she really wanted to do was sleep. "Colby, wake up now." Ginny was shaking her shoulder, her young voice very frightened.

"I'm awake," Colby muttered thickly, surfacing, prying open her eyelids. "What is it, honey, are you sick?" She glanced past Ginny to see Paul standing against the wall watching her. "What is it?" she asked again.

"Your alarm was going off for so long, I got up to see what was wrong and then I couldn't wake you up," Ginny said tearfully. "I shook you and shook you."

"She woke me up." Paul made it an accusation, but there was fear in his voice.

Colby forced her body to move, sitting up, sweeping back the wealth of hair tumbling around her face. "I'm sorry. I guess I'm more tired than I thought. I set the alarm for four-thirty so I could do a few extra things."

"I *knew* you were getting up early!" Ginny pounced on that. "You can't do that all the time, Colby. You need to sleep like everyone else."

"*I* need to sleep," Paul corrected. "Speaking of which, I'm going back to bed. Colby, if Ginny spent all this time waking you up, don't you think maybe that means you shouldn't get up?" He sounded very superior.

"Probably," Colby admitted, wanting to crawl under the covers. Her body was not cooperating, feeling heavy and cumbersome, her eyes wanting to close. She was so thirsty her mouth was dry. There was a faint coppery taste on her tongue. "I think I'm beginning to believe that I'm the totally unbalanced crackpot the Chevez family and the De La Cruz brothers think I am." She absently raised a hand to push her palm against the pulse throbbing in her neck.

"Well, you are," Paul stated, giving his brotherly opinion.

"For that you get to feed all the horses while I exercise Domino. He gets hard to handle if I don't ride him every day. I want to put in sometime checking fences and if you do the feeding, I can take some extra time." She yawned inelegantly.

Paul scowled at her. "You ought to get rid of that horse. He's really dangerous. Even Joe Vargas says so, everybody does."

Ginny caught her sister's hand. "Is that true, Colby? Is Domino dangerous? Is he a man-killer like they say he is?"

Colby's head went up, the drowsy look suddenly gone from her face, leaving her green eyes blazing at her younger brother. "Did you tell her that?"

Paul had the grace to look ashamed. "Joe told me Domino killed a man, and Ginny overheard the conversation. You know Joe, he has a thing for you. He was worried."

"Domino was mistreated, Ginny," Colby explained quietly. "You can see the scars on him. He can be difficult in certain situations, but I can handle him. I really can. I don't overestimate my abilities."

"I'm sorry, Colby." Paul was quick to get the apology out. "I should never have allowed Ginny to hear that."

"I'm not a baby." Ginny tossed her blue-black hair, chin going up, a small replica of Colby. "You don't need to hide anything from me. I'm not stupid, either, Paul Chevez. Working with any horse can be dangerous if you don't know what you're doing. Colby does," she added staunchly. "No one does it better."

"There speaks the unprejudiced voice," Colby laughed softly, ruffling Ginny's hair tenderly. "Honey, later on today, if you have the time, you can start setting up the north paddock for barrel racing. Janna Wilson's bringing her horse, Roman, in on Thursday. He's in a slump and she can't afford that with Regina breathing down her neck for first place all the time. Janna wants the world championship this year."

"Sure." Ginny was excited. Janna Wilson was a barrel racer out of Oklahoma, the leading female money winner halfway into the season and Ginny's heroine. Ginny was determined to barrel race professionally in the not-too-distant future.

"Go back to bed, you two," Colby advised. "It will be sunup soon enough."

"You don't have to tell me twice," Paul said gratefully. "And, Colby, you really are nuts to be getting up now. Come on, Ginny, it's embarrassing enough to have one crazy sister, I don't want to admit to having two of them."

Colby was laughing as she stumbled her way sleepily to the shower and drenched herself with hot water, hoping to clear the cobwebs. She actually felt weak and listless. It was no wonder after such bizarre dreams. Rafael De La Cruz sneaking into her bedroom, kissing her … his hands touching her breasts, her body. Instantly heat swept through her, her breasts aching with need. Colby groaned and closed her eyes against the humiliation of such an erotic dream and its aftermath. She allowed the water to cascade directly onto her face, hoping to wash the scent of him from her body, his taste from her mouth, the feel of his hard strength against her skin. *You're probably the devil in disguise.*

She wiped at the fog on the mirror then wished she hadn't when she saw herself. She was so pale her eyes looked enormous, vividly green. As she pulled the thick mass of red hair back to braid, she noticed the strange mark on the side of her neck. It looked like a strawberry, or a teenager's hickey. When she stood on her toes and examined it closer, she thought there were two tiny pinpricks in the center of it. It burned, not painfully, but intimately, so that she covered the mark with her palm as if to hold it close to her. She had no idea what it was, but it made her uneasy after her strange dream. As she stared at her reflection, she caught sight of the second mark. Her breath caught in her throat and her heart began to pound. The mark was on the swell of her breast, a vivid red standing out starkly against her white skin. How had it gotten there? It was no insect bite. Worse, as she looked at her hand, pressed tightly against her neck, there were faint smudges on her wrists that looked suspiciously like fingerprints. She snatched her hand down, breath catching in her throat. He *couldn't* have been in her room.

Had she really allowed Rafael into her bedroom? Kissing her. Touching her. She forced herself to look at the all too real marks. A brand on her skin. Was it his brand of possession? She groaned aloud, her face flaming crimson. She preferred to believe it was an erotic dream. She shook her head and dressed hastily, unwilling to think too much about what seemed like a hazy dream.

Domino was a large horse, and always restless when she saddled him. She worked quickly, her movements deft and reassuring. All the while she crooned endearments to him. She took Domino up the narrow trail leading into the mountains. He was difficult to handle; she could never sit back, relax, and enjoy the ride. Domino had more tricks than most rodeo broncs. The narrow trail made it almost impossible to bolt, effectively eliminating one of his favorite bad habits.

Colby had literally pulled the rifle from his previous owner's hands, saving Domino's life. Half crazed with pain and fear from the ugly beatings he had received, the horse had lashed out at anything and everything that came near it. She still couldn't remember exactly what she'd said or done to convince the owner to sell her the horse, or even how she had managed to load him for transport in his terrible condition.

It had taken three years of patient love, hundreds of hours spent sitting on a fence rail talking soothing nonsense. He looked for her eagerly now, thrusting his head toward her, trumpeting a welcome when he saw her. But to ride him ... Colby shook her head, smiling to herself. Riding him was never easy, but it was exactly what she needed. It would keep her mind away from Rafael De La Cruz.

Forty-five minutes up into the mountains she dismounted, preferring to lead Domino and enjoy the tranquility of her surroundings while she looked for signs of Pete. The Cascades were seven hundred miles in length, stretching from California through Oregon and Washington into Canada. The range had been born of fire then carved of ice. Along with a chain of volcanoes, the mountain range boasted heavy forests, a multitude of waterfalls and cataracts along with miles of snowfields. The Columbia River literally cut the mountain range in half. Guarded by three towering volcanoes, white-water rapids ripped through its steep rocky gorge with dizzying speed. Lava cliffs, lakes, streams, lush evergreen forests, the Cascades were unequaled in beauty or potential ferocity.

Colby stood on the edge of the cliff, not looking down but up the sheer mountain wall rising above her. Commanding respect, these mountains were the very foundation of legends. Thousands of miles of untamed wilderness, rarely did man penetrate the deep forbidding forests, the treacherous canyons, the slopes rising mile after mile. Horror stories were repeated around campfires of the howling which reverberated from the interior, of the legendary Bigfoot carrying off intruders, never to be seen again.

Colby gave a small sigh and bent to pick a wildflower struggling valiantly to survive among the boulders. She loved the stillness of the mountains; she could sit for hours just absorbing the feeling. That didn't for a moment mean she allowed herself to be careless. Even Colby, who was familiar with more miles of mountains than almost anyone in the area, didn't become complacent. Having a ranch nestled in a small valley on the fringes of the rising mountains, she was all too aware of mysterious unexplained happenings. A smell rising out of nowhere, off ensive, noxious. The strange silences even the insects respected. So many times one felt watched, an eerie feeling occupied by the sensation of skin crawling.

Most of the ranches were farther down the mountain, several thousand feet down from the Chevez ranch. Clinton Daniels's property bordered Colby's to the south, but only Sean Everett's twenty thousand acres stretched beyond Colby's property, with the state land behind him. Everett had wrangled with the state over most of the land, buying up the rest from small-time ranchers. Like Colby, he seemed to prefer the mountains, leading a fairly self-sufficient existence. His fleet of vehicles, not to mention the small Piper and helicopter, made her green with envy.

The Everett hands who lived in the ranch's comfortable cabins with their families stayed mainly to themselves although she knew all of them by name and could call a few of them friends. They seemed to work hard. Everett's ranch had definitely prospered, his cattle remaining fat even through the harsh winters. Some of his hands, most of whom had never worked on a ranch until Sean had given them a home, were becoming interested in rodeo competition.

Colby smiled to herself as she gathered up Domino's reins. She spent a great deal of her time doing business with men, earning her reputation as a reliable and shrewd rancher with an exceptional talent with horses. It had given her a quiet confidence in herself, a joy of life. She was one of those lucky people who accepted her way of life and simply lived it to the best of her ability.

She swung easily into the saddle, liking the familiar creak of leather. Pulling her hat to a better angle to shade her eyes from the sun's rising rays, she turned her mount toward the farthest corner of her property. The fence had been sagging for some time and, unlike Colby, the cattle favored this rugged, remote area. Perhaps Pete had come here to repair the fence. She rubbed her eyes several times. The sun wasn't high, yet her eyes felt sore, unduly sensitive to the light.

As Domino picked his way carefully over the loose rocks, his hooves the only sound in the utter stillness, Colby alternated between anxiously scanning the ground for tracks and scowling nervously up at the jutting remorseless mountains. The unrelenting steep rock guarded the series of dark, forbidding caves winding into the very bowels of the mountain. She disliked this section of property intensely, avoiding it with every excuse possible. There was a sense of evil, a dark somber dread as if the land were alive, waiting patiently, relentlessly to reclaim her. She was never able to approach it without her heart rate doubling, her stomach churning, and a terrible sense of foreboding overtaking her, a leftover bogey from her childhood. She would never forget being trapped in the old abandoned mine shaft, a primitive affair, a hundred years old with rotting timbers. It had all come crashing down, smothering her nine-year-old cries, nearly suffocating her. She had been buried alive, trapped in the damp rotting earth for eleven hours and twenty-two minutes. It had been an eternity. Even with her special gifts, she had not been strong enough to move the mounds of earth and rock by herself. She had waited alone and frightened in the terrible darkness for her stepfather to rescue her.

Something had moved in the dark bowels of the caves, something not human. She had seen red flames in glowing eyes and smelled dead flesh. The thing had taunted her, its voice gravelly, skin stretched taut across its skull. She had seen jagged teeth stained with blood and long, razor-sharp talons for fingernails. Her parents had sworn to her over and over, when she woke screaming in the night, that it had been her imagination. Colby still had a difficult time believing she could have conjured up the hideous creature.

Armando Chevez had closed up the mines and she hadn't gone exploring there, feeling the place was like a giant spider web waiting for her return. It was only after Armando had been paralyzed in the plane crash that Colby had gone back to declare the mines unsafe and totally off -limits to Paul and Ginny. She refused to allow Paul to patrol this section of fence line, doing it herself or letting Pete take the job.

The fence was on the ground, strands of barbwire wrapped around a fallen post. She could see a leather glove caught in the wire. She dismounted quickly and hurried over to the glove. The three ranches joined together at this point. Everett's property climbed steeply behind hers, erupting into dense, thick forest running wild. Daniels's property off to her south gradually sloped into gentle, grassy hills. He had dotted the area with a series of small shacks and old machinery. His dump, she thought a little wryly, a nice eyesore to add to the ambience of the place.

She carefully worked the glove free of the barbwire and held it up to examine it. The sound of a rock dropping abruptly spun her around just as Domino threw his head up, ears forward, snorting. Colby stepped closer to her horse, smoothly drawing her rifle from its scabbard. She turned, her heart in her throat. Several yards away a man was standing, holding his horse, as startled as she was.

Slowly she relaxed when she recognized the foreman of Clinton Daniels's ranch. "You do turn up in the oddest places, Tony," she greeted. "Thanks for taking ten years off my life."

He continued toward her, his dark gaze touching the glove in her hand, then resting briefly on the rifle she held. "I didn't expect to find you out here either. The fence has to be lying on the ground before *you'd* repair it."

She mounted Domino smoothly, not liking to appear so small around Tony. She pushed back her hat, shrugging indifferently at the accusation. She had never liked Tony Harris. She had known him for years, long before Daniels had hired him. He had a mean streak in him. His reputation for brawling was legendary, almost as much as his notoriety with women. She had never understood his fatal charm, was appalled by the number of women who suffered physically, mentally, and emotionally, yet like moths to a flame always went back for more. He made her flesh crawl.

Colby tucked the glove into her belt and raised her eyebrow at Tony. "You want to tell me what you're doing on my property?" She made herself smile, although the way his eyes were running over her body made her all too aware of his isolation.

He grinned nastily. "Maybe I was looking for you. The ice princess. The little virgin sacrificing herself for the kiddies. We all want to know who will melt your heart." He laughed loudly, the sound coarse in the stillness of the silent mountains.

"Not you, Tony," she assured him coolly. "You're way too wicked for my taste."

"You mean I'm too much of a man," he countered, swaggering a little as he crowded closer to her horse.

Colby raised an eyebrow at him. "I hear they're looking for stand-up comedians at the Wayside Saloon. Why don't you check it out?"

"I just might do that." He was right in front of her, close enough for her to read the thoughts lurking behind his too handsome face. "I've always wanted to have you to myself, just for a couple of hours," he said softly, as if thinking aloud. "You're always sitting up on that pedestal; it'd be kind of nice to have you groveling at my feet."

Colby laughed openly at him. "You have a vivid imagination, Tony. It's a wonderful fantasy, but I'll have to pass. I've got too much work to do. Which reminds me, just what are you doing on my property? Not looking for stray calves, are you?"

"Are you accusing me of something?" he snapped, instantly angry, taking another threatening step toward her.

Domino moved restlessly, not liking the man's close proximity. Colby casually turned the horse sideways, resting the rifle naturally across her body, the barrel low, but unmistakably centered on Harris's large frame.

"Hey, Tony, you drive those cattle back yet?" A voice bellowed the question from the rocks nearby.

Colby kept her eyes on Harris. She didn't recognize the voice, but Harris looked triumphant, more malevolent than ever. "Sure did, but Miss Jansen isn't nearly as grateful as she should be. Maybe she needs a lesson in how to treat a man properly."

The second man, a total stranger, dark, with a day's growth of beard and shrewd assessing eyes, scrambled from the rocks and into her line of vision. His eyes were red-rimmed and streamed constantly. He shoved dark glasses on, but not before she saw his expression. Where Tony Harris annoyed her, this man frightened her. Harris was a bully; this man was truly evil. Daniels had himself a wonderful crew. Most likely they were stealing him blind. "So you were returning my cattle," she said thoughtfully.

"That's right, Colby, those little critters of yours just don't want to stay put." Tony took another step closer to Colby, watching her carefully with hot eyes.

"What the hell is taking so long?" Daniels strode up to the fallen fence, glaring at his foreman. "Get back to work, Harris. It shouldn't have taken the two of you all this time to return a couple of steers. And you could have fixed the fence." He dismissed the two men with a wave of his hand, ignoring Harris's surly grumbling and the other man's mocking insolence. "Sorry, Colby, it didn't occur to me they wouldn't fix the fence." For the first time he seemed to notice the rifle. "They weren't giving you any trouble, were they?"

Colby faced him across the fallen fence. Smooth. Charming. A shark. Clinton Daniels had deliberately used her stepfather's terrible accident for his own gain. The hospital bills were piling up and Colby had taken out a loan using the family ranch as collateral, the terms nearly impossible to meet. A blur of movement caught her eye. Up on the ridge one of Everett's somber, silent workers stood beside Juan Chevez, surveying the scene below. The worker lifted a hand at her, still watching from his vantage point.

Colby burst out laughing. "It's a regular convention out here. I thought I was all alone, but we've got enough people out here to have a party."

Daniels was scowling up at the two silent men. "I don't think it's so funny, Colby. There's something strange about Everett's hands. Every last one of them is an ex-con. It makes me nervous to know they sit up there watching everything we do."

"They just want to be left alone."

"It isn't safe for you riding around alone out here." Daniels cast another fierce glance up at the two men. "And those foreigners are a strange bunch too. I think they're up to something."

Colby gathered up the reins as Domino sidestepped nervously. "Thanks for returning my cattle, Clinton. I'm sorry about the fence. I'll get some materials out here as soon as possible and we won't have the problem anymore."

"You might want to hold off a couple of months, save yourself time and expense," he told her suavely.

Colby's chin went up. "You don't have to worry, I'll have your money for you."

"Colby"—he shook his head, clucking his tongue at her—"I understand you went to the bank and they turned you down. How do you expect . . . "

"They turned me down because of you, Daniels. Don't think I don't know that. And it's none of your business how I come up with the money. You'll get it."

He reached out and caught her reins, preventing her from moving. "You're being stubborn, Colby. Let the Chevezes take the kids away. Marry me. You'll still have your ranch, it will all work out. You shouldn't be running yourself into the ground. Look at you, you're pale and tired. You have dark circles under your eyes. And you've lost weight. Let me take care of you."

She backed Domino away from Daniels. "No one is taking my brother and sister anywhere. Now if you'll excuse me, I have work to do." Abruptly she turned the horse, urging him back over the rocks as she thrust the rifle into the scabbard. Automatically her eyes were on the ground, picking up signs, noting Tony Harris's mount needed a new shoe on his left rear foot. It took a few minutes before she realized she hadn't seen any fresh cattle tracks accompanying Tony's mount.

One last time she looked up at the high, craggy peaks, feeling the familiar curling in the pit of her stomach. She was already running behind time on her chores. As she started back toward the ranch, she caught sight of a vulture circling lazily in the sky. She watched its path, turning Domino so she could pick her way through the larger boulders along the steep cliffs. As she rounded a particularly steep rock face, she saw more of the large birds. They were gathered together near the base of one of the cliffs.

At once she felt a terrible dread, her body stiffening. Domino began to dance nervously, Colby's body language communicating instantly to the animal. She bit at her lower lip, made a long sweep, scanning the area to ensure this time she really was alone.

Colby approached on foot, not trusting Domino's reaction with the birds and the odor. She kept her rifle with her, but used her handgun, firing into the air to frighten off the vultures and to alert the Everett riders she needed their help.

She circled the area, careful not to disturb anything, looking for tracks to tell her what had happened. She knew before she ever reached the body that it was Pete. He had been dead for days. It looked as if he had been on the ledge up above and had slipped and fallen. The back of his head must have hit the small boulder near where he lay. There was blood on the rock and plenty of it staining the shirt across his shoulders.

Colby saw the broken pieces of a whiskey bottle scattered around. She closed her eyes, suddenly tired, her throat choking on unshed tears. For a brief moment she rested her hand on Pete's arm. Immediately she snatched it away, backing away from the body, looking around her, very, very afraid.

She felt it, the instant she touched him: she knew it had been no accident, knew Pete had been murdered. She didn't know who or why, only that someone had killed him. The aftermath of violence was still haunting the ground, the rocks, especially the body. Colby examined the area carefully, wanting to read the messages the earth might give her, yet she didn't want to disturb the crime scene.

She moved away from the body, back to Domino, and buried her face against the animal. For once he remained steady, unmoving, as if he knew he was consoling her with his presence.

Colby? Her name shimmered in her mind. Warmth seeped into the coldness of her body. *Pequena, I feel your pain. I cannot come to you. Share it with me. Let me help you.*

The words were there, velvet soft. Real. She heard them. Knew Rafael's voice. Felt his presence. She also felt the tremendous effort he was making to reach her across what must have been a great distance. It should have shocked her, but she was accepting. She was different. He was different. For the first time in years she wanted to throw herself into someone's arms in a storm of weeping. She didn't even mind that he called her "little one."

4

"This doesn't look good, Colby," Ben said as he walked over to where she was sitting on a large, round boulder. "I'm sorry, honey, I know you loved that old man. I should have listened to you." He put his hand on her slender shoulder, an awkward attempt at comforting her.

"It isn't your fault, Ben. He must have already been dead when I reported him missing." Colby rubbed her pounding temples as she looked up at the sheriff. "It wasn't an accident, was it?"

Ben sighed heavily. Colby had always been as transparent as glass. He could see her grief, the heaviness in her as if the weight of the world was on her shoulders. "We're treating it like a homicide until we know different. I took pictures of the scene; we've finished that finally. I know it's been a long morning for you, but we had to get this done before we could move the body."

"I can read the signs, Ben. He didn't fall off that cliff. He was hit from behind. The blood splatters aren't consistent with a fall. And his body isn't beat up enough. His knees hit the dirt first, like his legs went out from under him." A sob welled up out of nowhere and she looked away from him, pressed a hand to her soft, trembling mouth.

Ben swore softly. "It looks bad. You and the kids need to be careful, Colby. I don't know what's going on, but I don't like it."

Ignoring his outstretched hand, Colby jumped down from the rock and paced away from him, swiping at the tears running unchecked down her face. "Who would do something like this to him, Ben? He was in his seventies. He couldn't hurt a fly. He didn't have any money. Why would someone do this?"

"Go home, honey, let me take care of this. You need to be with the kids." Ben was suppressing his own anger. This hit far too close to home. Someone had murdered Pete, there was no denying the fact. Ben had examined every inch of the cliff. Someone had been up there all right, and they'd started a small rockslide to make it look as if Pete had slipped over the edge, but he lay right where he had been killed. Ben would have staked his reputation on it. Colby was a good tracker and she was right about Pete going to his knees before he fell backward.

Ben had examined the old man's fingernails. There wasn't a speck of dirt to indicate Pete had clawed at the mountainside if he had slipped. And the patterns of blood splatters just weren't consistent with Pete falling and hitting his head. The body had been torn up by the birds, which didn't help the crime scene, but Ben had found other disturbing lacerations on Pete's body that he hadn't discussed with Colby. There were teeth marks—human bite marks—as if someone had tried to cannibalize the body after Pete was dead. He was certain the bites were made after death. It was bizarre and terrifying when they rarely had major crime in their area. Colby had to have seen those disturbing bites, but he wasn't going to force her to admit it. Ben swore again as he glanced at Colby's small figure. "Go home, honey. I'll call you when I know more."

Colby nodded, suddenly shivering. What had Tony Harris and the other ranch hand really been doing on her property? What were Everett's rider and one of the Chevez brothers doing so far from the homestead? Had one of her neighbors actually murdered Pete? Who would benefit from such brutality? She shoved a hand through her hair, dreading telling Ginny and Paul.

"Colby, you can't do anything more for him. Go on home. You're just torturing yourself by sticking around." Ben was adamant. "It will be a few days before the body is released. I promise I'll call you and help with the arrangements. In the meantime, stick close to the house—no more riding around in the middle of nowhere by yourself."

Colby nodded slowly, turning heavily, her shoulders slumping in defeat. Ben was right, she couldn't bring Pete back and there was no sense in putting off telling the kids. Paul probably already knew; he had a scanner. He would have seen the sheriff and his crew coming onto the ranch. She swung into the saddle and resolutely started home.

Deep beneath the earth, locked in the rich soil, Rafael lay helpless to comfort her. The blood tie ensured he could touch her mind and know her thoughts at will. She needed him, needed him to hold her, to comfort her. She was trying to be very brave for her brother and sister. She was weeping. Deep within her heart, in her soul, she was weeping. Her sorrow was so strong it had penetrated his rejuvenating sleep, waking him to share her suffering. His chest hurt, the weight of her anguish pressing like a heavy stone into his heart. He ached for her, ached to hold her, comfort her.

It was a singular experience for him to feel for another being. *Real emotion.* He had forgotten the feeling. It humbled him to think of her and her lone fight to keep her word to her stepfather. She was alone and afraid. She was fighting an unseen enemy. She didn't know what they wanted, or why they were attacking her, but she was valiantly ready to defend her ranch and her beloved brother and sister. Rafael concentrated on keeping the link open between them.

Her mind was complex. It had natural safeguards, barriers he was still working to break through. But she was the one. His lifemate. Her blood called to his. Her soul cried out to his.

Rafael shared her heart and soul. His duty was to see to her health and happiness above all other things. Above his own happiness. He was beginning to understand what that meant. Trapped by the high price of his immortality, he lay waiting, needing to be with her, helpless to comfort her. Right now it mattered more that he comfort her, than that he possess her. He needed to hold her safe in his arms. He learned many hard lessons while he lay in the ground. And he learned each of the lessons from his unknowing lifemate.

She spoke softly, lovingly to her brother and sister, a world of confidence in her voice when deep inside her mind Rafael could hear her frightened screams. She took time with each of them, answering questions, reassuring them, endlessly patient when she knew she had a long list of chores that had to be accomplished before nightfall regardless of the tragedy. Through it all she continually asked herself if she could have found Pete sooner, if she could have somehow saved his life.

She worked hard, one task at a time, treating each job the same whether the chore was difficult or easy, whether she enjoyed it or hated it. She was quick and efficient and always thinking ahead, mentally checking off the list. To Rafael it was the longest, most difficult period of his life. He lay helpless, trapped in the earth, his body weak, his great strength drained, while somewhere above him Colby, exhausted from lack of sleep and his taking of her blood, worked the afternoon away.

She had to use her unique talents to start the old tractor and keep it running as she worked one of the fields. It was draining to use mental powers to keep machinery working. Her head was pounding as she went from the field to the corral of restless horses.

Her young brother joined her to help hold the wildly bucking horses.

Rafael went back and forth between absolute admiration for her and a slow burning rage. She was a woman. Young. Vulnerable. Why was she alone and unprotected? Why was she working at a job that demanded so much, both physically and mentally? He felt every bone-wrenching fall as she hit the ground. Every jarring crash against the fence. It was dangerous. Incredibly dangerous. It would stop. He would never allow her to continue when he could make her life so much easier. He bided his time, waiting for the setting of the sun.

Colby was beyond exhaustion, stumbling in the waning light through the barn to stare with a grim frown at the tack. Most of it needed cleaning or mending. Paul's job. Probably passed on to Ginny some time ago and long forgotten. Someone had to do the mending soon or it was going to go downhill like everything else on the ranch.

"Downhill," she murmured aloud, leaning one hip against the doorjamb. "Downhill fast." The entire ranch was going downhill fast and she couldn't keep up with all the work. She was one person and there was just so much time. She hadn't been hungry all day and had skipped her meals, using the time to make up for the hours she had spent with Pete's body. She seemed to be terribly thirsty all day, yet she wasn't hungry at all and the thought of food sickened her.

For a moment she listened to the sound of young voices laughing, coming from the porch. She was tempted to call them to help her, but they sounded so innocent and young she didn't have the heart after such a terrible day. The kids were grieving for Pete, and if they could find a few moments to laugh together, she wasn't about to take that away from them. Pete's death was there in her mind, tearing at her, and she crushed down the sudden overwhelming urge to join them. To feel young and carefree for one moment, however brief again.

With a little sigh she moved through the large barn to the tiny room at the far end. It was very dark in the tack room with no window to allow the last rays of light in. The weight of the world seemed to be on her shoulders and she found she was walking stooped over. Annoyed at giving in to feeling sorry for herself, Colby straightened her shoulders resolutely, taking a step toward the light switch.

A hand shot past her head, flicking the switch, illuminating the small tack room. Colby gasped, turned quickly to face the intruder, although her body already knew exactly who was there. Rafael. She had closed the door behind her and she had been positive no one was in the small room when she entered.

"What are you doing sneaking around in my barn?" she demanded, desperately hoping he couldn't hear the frantic pounding of her heart. For some reason the mark on the side of her neck began to throb and burn. Defensively she placed her hand over it as she looked up at him.

He was unbelievably intimidating. Large, muscular, his broad shoulders filling the small room until there was only Rafael. More than that, he exuded a dark sexual snare she couldn't quite break free of. His eyes were filled with dark promise, full of need and hunger. For a moment that hot gaze rested thoughtfully on her palm covering his brand on her neck. A slow smile softened the edge of cruelty to his mouth, his black eyes dwelling on the pulse beating frantically in the vulnerable hollow of her throat.

"I am honing my skills," he said very softly, gently, almost teasingly, so as not to frighten her. "You look a wild thing, on the verge of flight." She tilted her chin, a gesture he found himself unconsciously watching for.

"Which skills?" Colby asked suspiciously. She was trembling so hard she put her hands behind her back so he wouldn't see when he seemed to notice every little thing about her. Colby twisted her fingers together to hold them still. It was annoying to act like the proverbial country bumpkin any time he was close to her.

Rafael took a step forward, gliding easily over the straw-strewn floor. Colby had the impression of a giant jungle cat stalking her, silent on any surface. His black eyes burned possessively over her small, slender figure. She actually shrank back against the wall, staring almost helplessly up at him. Just seeing him made her want to burst into tears. She couldn't fight his steely authority. Not now. Not tonight. He was overpowering and she just wasn't in any condition emotionally to stand up to him.

"Mr. De La Cruz," she said, trying to find her voice, "I've had a particularly rough day today. I really don't want to do battle with you."

She intended to sound firm; he read that in her mind. Instead she sounded so infinitely weary his heart turned over. He wanted to gather her into his arms and shelter her by his heart. "I heard," he replied in his most soothing voice. "I do not intend to fight with you, *querida.*"

His eyes were no longer ice cold and hard, but smoldering with such a dark intensity she felt as if he was actually physically touching her when he directed his gaze to her. His accent twisted its way right into her senses, embedding deep so that she was breathing him into her lungs. It was terrifying the way her body reacted to him. To his looks. To the sound of his voice. "Which skills exactly?" she persisted, needing words to destroy the disturbing electricity building up in the small space of the room. It seemed to be arcing and crackling between them, jumping from his skin to hers.

He really seemed to be touching her, his strong fingers caressing her skin. His hands hung loosely, innocently at his sides. The sensation was so real she found herself blushing wildly. "Your sneak-ing-up-on-women skills?" She tried a severe frown. Already her traitorous mouth was dry. She rubbed her palms down the sides of her faded jeans, touched a piece of straw with the toe of her boot to studiously avoid looking at him. It would have been a great time for an earthquake, the earth opening and swallowing her.

His laughter was soft, inviting. He moved a step closer, very deliberately forcing Colby to backpedal hastily. "So far you are the only woman I have ever had to sneak up on." Colby backed right up until she was nearly against the wall. Rafael reached out with a casual hand and pulled her away from the metal hooks to safety.

"Did you have anything in particular you wanted or did you just come over here to irritate me?" She scowled at him, doing her best to look intimidating. She could readily believe he never had to sneak upon women. Any woman. They probably just threw them-selves at him.

His smile widened, revealing amazingly white teeth. "Is that what you think I do, *pequena*, irritate you?" He leaned closer still, resting one hand on the wall beside her head, effectively imprison-ing her. "I would not have described your reaction to me quite so."

Colby held her breath as his heavily muscled frame brushed tan-talizingly close to her smaller one. Her legs felt weak, her breasts ached, every nerve ending leapt to life, tingling with awareness. The heat of his body was astounding. She thought the room tempera-ture might have shot up a few hundred degrees.

His hand gathered up tack from its storage place on the wall. Colby could have sworn he laughed softly as he turned to sit on a bale of hay, but when he looked up, Rafael's expressionless mask revealed no emotion whatsoever. "Are you going to stand there, or are you going to help me?" he asked, patting the hay beside him.

She stared at him as if he had grown two heads. His hands were busy on the leather, his fingers sure and deft. She watched him, counting the beats of her heart. Finally, reluctantly, Colby took the two steps bringing her to his side. "You're going to help me with the tack? What's the catch, De La Cruz?"

"I think it would be a good time to start calling me Rafael," he said quietly.

Colby hesitated a moment then sat down, careful to avoid touching his body. Even so, she could feel the heat radiating out to her. Body heat. "Rafael, then," she repeated with a sigh, "what's the catch?" She caught the bridle he dropped in her lap, desperate to do something to distract her attention from him.

"Is that your philosophy on life?" he replied mildly. "There always has to be a catch? A most interesting way to live. It is an American tradition?"

She reprimanded him with one look from under her long lashes. "You know very well there is no such thing. It's occurred to me more than once over the years that there's a price tag on almost everything."

His black eyebrow shot up. "Including simple friendship?"

She didn't look at him as she worked the leather, her fingers sure and quick. "I don't think you know what *simple* means. What is it you want from me, De La Cruz?"

"Is it so difficult to use my name?" he asked softly, the sound of his voice washing over her, brushing at her insides and causing a melting sensation in the region of her stomach.

"I don't believe in fraternizing with the enemy." She glanced at his perfectly chiseled features and just as quickly looked away. "You are the enemy, Rafael." Deliberately she used his name to prove she wasn't afraid of him. It was a mistake. It created a further intimacy between them in the small room. "You want my sister and brother. You want the ranch." Her eyes suddenly locked with his. "Mostly you want to go home and I'm in your way." She stared intently at him as if seeking something beyond what he was telling her.

Rafael felt the sudden surge of power in the room. It was strong and focused. He knew immediately she was reaching for the information in his mind, seeking answers to the sudden change in him. Joy surged through him, but he kept his triumph buried deep. He reached casually for the next piece of equipment, his arm deliberately brushing her body. "That was true a couple of days ago. It no longer is so."

"What has changed?" There was a wealth of skepticism in her voice.

"I met you." He said it softly, meaning it. Everything had changed. He was going home, but he was taking her with him. Nothing else mattered to him, he *would* have her, whatever it took. He should just take her. He had enough power to kidnap her, get her to his home territory, yet his very feelings for her prevented him from doing so. She looked sad, weary. He wanted to sweep her into his arms, close against his body, and comfort her. Rafael was a vampire hunter, a man of swift decisions and action. After more than a thousand years of living, he found himself in new territory. "I am very sorry about your friend. Sean tells me you were very good to the man. I am sorry, I do not know his name."

"Pete. Pete Jessup." Her throat constricted, but she fought her way through the emotion and continued. "He was a very good friend to me. I'm not sure I can run the ranch without him. He couldn't always do the work, but he gave me very valuable advice. Everyone thought he was a charity case, but Pete knew so much about running a ranch; he'd worked on ranches all of his life and he was willing to teach me." He had provided companionship to her as well as advice.

She hung up the bridle she had been working on and found another ragged piece to avoid looking at him. She was embarrassed and slightly ashamed she had come out with such private information. Rafael De La Cruz was dangerous to her. In such close proximity she could feel his need to comfort her, to protect her, and that was dangerous to her peace of mind.

"You are a woman, Colby, you should not have to run a ranch." He said it so quietly, so gently, the words almost didn't register.

For a moment she sat there beside him until the words sank into her brain. Rafael felt it again, the swift surge of power, filling the room until the walls were nearly bulging outward in an effort to contain it. Colby struggled for control of her temper. She shoved a hand through her thick hair, taking several deep breaths while she battled with herself. "I think it would be best if you left, Rafael," she finally suggested. "I appreciate the attempt at friendship, but we are never going to be friends."

His black eyes glittered at her, fathomless, holding a thousand secrets. "I think we will learn to be very good friends." His smile was frankly sexy, his teeth very white. "It will be necessary for you to lose the chip on your shoulder first."

In spite of everything, the terrible day, her worries over the ranch, even who he was, Colby found herself wanting to smile at his choice of words. Both her brother and Ben Lassiter often accused her of exactly the same thing. "I do not have a chip on my shoulder." When his black eyes continued to stare steadily at her she shrugged. "Okay, maybe a small one where you're concerned. I don't like you."

He leaned close to her so that his thigh rubbed against hers. "Do you flatter all men, or am I the only one so privileged?"

"I'm sorry, that was rather rude. I'm usually not rude." She rubbed her forehead. "At least I don't think I am. Okay, maybe I am sometimes. What are you doing here?"

"I am courting you." He sounded very old-fashioned.

Her vivid green eyes jumped to his face. "Courting me? Whatever for?"

He turned the power of his black eyes on her face. Mesmerizing. Hypnotic. Sexier-than-sin eyes. "Why do men usually court women, Colby? I think you can work it out for yourself." His voice was velvet soft and slightly husky, the accent giving him a tremendous advantage.

Colby could feel her skin burn. Little flames seemed to be licking along every nerve ending. She sent him a quick reprimand from under her long lashes. "I think you are so used to women falling all over you that you can't stand it when one doesn't. I'm a practical person, Rafael. Men like you do not court women like me."

His black gaze slid over her from head to toe like a whisper of velvet, leaving her skin on fire and slow color creeping into her face. "See, right there, that's what I'm talking about," she accused. "You've spent your life seducing women, and I just think of men as friends, colleagues. You wouldn't know how to relate to a woman as a friend. And I wouldn't know what to do with one who wanted to seduce me."

His teeth were whiter than ever, his smile slightly mocking. "I do not think you quite understand the situation you find yourself in, *pequena*. I am *courting* you as a man would his bride, not looking for a mistress to spend a few nights in my bed. You do not have to know what to do with seduction. I have enough knowledge for both of us."

The breath rushed right out of her lungs and she gaped at him, silently appalled. For a moment she could only stare at him. "Do you even hear yourself when you spout this nonsense?" She leapt up to put a couple of feet between them so she wouldn't wring his neck with the bridle. "Is that supposed to be a compliment, that you would choose me to be your bride and not your mistress? How many mistresses do you have exactly? Is there a set number after you're married or do you just wing it?"

She looked so beautiful she robbed him of breath. There was a steel thread running through her small soft body, a fierce pride, hard-earned. He looked at her and saw himself through her eyes.

What had he done with his life? She knew nothing of him other than the image they had so carefully cultivated of powerful, rich playboys.

Who did he love? Members of the Chevez family had lived with him for centuries, running his affairs during the daylight hours; his own brothers, loved only through dim memories—he felt it now, that intense, protective emotion; but Colby had seen him cold, uncaring. She had seen he had little interest in others. People were thought of in the same vein as his cattle, his property. It was necessary to protect them, but it was his duty, a matter of honor, nothing more. Women were to be seduced, fodder, really, easy prey for a man as alluring and as seductive as Rafael. Colby Jansen was looking at him as if he were a rather useless ladies' man. She thought him handsome, sexy, but rather cold and cruel. Useless. There was the slightest curl of contempt in her mind when he managed to slip past her guard. A Latin lover. She thought his life one of endless parties and women. Rafael's long fingers tightened on the old leather.

Colby knew what it was like to love fiercely, passionately, protectively. She worked hard without complaining, without thought for anything but those she cared about. Rafael found he wanted desperately to be one of those few she counted as her own. Taking her to his lands and claiming her would not earn him her genuine love. She was his lifemate, and her body had all the responses to him of a lifemate, but her heart and mind viewed him as a rather useless individual. He found he didn't like her assessment of him at all and, more importantly, that her opinion mattered to him.

Rafael and his brothers had been sent from the Carpathian Mountains in times of turbulent war and massacres. It had been long after they had lost their ability to see in color, to feel all emotion, but they had served their prince to the best of their abilities in keeping with their rigid code of honor. It was all they had left to them in a gray, barren world of endless existence. But through the long, long centuries, memories dimmed and more and more the darkness had crept up on them.

Colby's eyes suddenly flashed fire at him. "And have you forgotten my rather unfortunate parentage? As I recall, I was the reason the Chevez family could not find it in their so-called hearts to accept Armando back into the family fold. I believe I am illegitimate. A De La Cruz shouldn't associate with someone like me, let alone court me. It might ruin your good name."

His black eyes went from a sheer black intensity to icy cold so fast she shivered. "Where would you get an idea like that?" His voice was very soft, yet carried a wealth of menace. He didn't move, but all at once he was far too close, looming over her.

Colby stood her ground, but suddenly it seemed to be shifting out from under her. "I read the letter. The letter from the family patriarch ordering Armando to get rid of my mother and me before I brought disgrace to the name of De La Cruz. It was in my mother's drawer. I found it after she died."

He stared at her a long moment hearing the hurt she tried so hard to hide. *Feeling* her hurt. "Ah, I see. That does explain quite a bit. Just to set the record straight, my brothers and I have our own strange reputations; we do not much care what others say of us or anyone else." He waved a graceful, dismissing hand and Colby had to believe him. He was too casual, too arrogant and sure of himself to worry about what another might say gossiping. "Old Chevez was a man much taken with his position in the community. He believed if he brought disgrace to us we would retaliate against his family in some way. It was not so."

Rafael sighed. "We did not intervene when we should have," he admitted heavily. He ached inside her, for that young girl who had found a letter written by a proud old man who didn't understand the ways of the new world.

She could have sworn there was a fleeting tenderness in his expression when he looked at her. "Somehow I don't think that old man would have listened to you," Colby conceded, slightly ashamed of herself. "Maybe your father, but certainly not you."

He had forgotten for a moment to be careful about time sequences. He was always pointing it out to his brothers, to be cautious about talking of things in the past as if they had all been present and had lived it. He chose his words, his voice very soft.

"I am sorry your *família* was hurt by the pompous attitude of an unbending man. When he died, and Armando's brothers discovered the letter, they would not rest until they had come in person in an attempt to right this terrible wrong. To their credit, they did not know Armando had married and had children. They didn't know his wife was killed in a plane crash or that he was injured so severely. Had they known, or had my brothers or I known, we would have come at once." That was true. The De La Cruzes considered Armando a member of their family. Had they been informed of his need, they would have come in full force.

They should have known, should have cared enough to monitor him from a distance. Rafael would have to live with that knowledge.

"That makes me feel much better, but I'm still not letting perfect strangers run off with my brother and sister." Even to her own ears she sounded defiant.

"You did not really read the entire letter the lawyer sent you, did you?" he asked gently, his black gaze on her face.

She shrugged carelessly and lifted her chin. "I read as much as I needed to and skimmed the rest of it. The ranch is in my name; it belonged to my mother. Did the Chevez family know that? It has been in my mother's family for a hundred years. I am not going to hand it over to them. Armando recovered all the acres lost over the years and managed to turn a run-down property into a thriving business. It is his legacy to his children and I intend to hold it for them. I loved him. He deserved better than he got."

Rafael nodded slowly, his eyes never leaving her face. "So did you, *querida*. The Chevez family wanted you to accompany Ginny and Paul. They are relatives, Colby, and they are not responsible for the terrible tragedy their *avô* precipitated upon the *família*. They are doing their best to make amends." There was the gentlest of reproofs in his voice. "They do not need this ranch, as they are wealthy in their own right. Each of them has property and they manage our lands as well."

Colby swept a hand through her hair. "I'm tired and it's been a rotten day. I will admit you've helped me enormously and you took my mind off Pete's death, but I really think you should go, Rafael." She had reached a point where she was aware of nothing else in the room but his well-muscled masculine body. Her blood seemed to surge and pound with heat and fire. Her entire body was restless and unfamiliar. She didn't want to know this side of him. Not the kind and gentle side. It was so much easier to resist him if he had a heart of ice.

He had come to her in her dark hour while she was alone and tired and vulnerable. He had offered his help with his melodic voice. His voice alone could soothe the heaviest heart. She didn't want to like him or the Chevez family. That would mean she would have to be fair and reasonable.

Rafael could sense the weariness in her. Her body was sore and tired, muscles aching. She had been up so early, searching for her lost friend, and the day had dragged on endlessly. She was hanging on by her fingertips, wanting to crumple somewhere safe where no one could see her. He stood up slowly and carefully replaced each piece of tack back in its original place on the wall.

When he turned his head to look at her, Colby stopped breathing. His eyes were black and hungry. Alive with raw need. She stared at him rather helplessly, frozen to the spot like a hypnotized rabbit. Unable to move. She had never seen eyes so alive, so hot and hungry with an intensity that frightened even as it drew her like a magnet. How had she ever thought him cold? Rafael reached out slowly, shackled her wrist, and drew her slowly, relentlessly, to his side.

At once it was there, the electricity, sparking and crackling, sizzling hot. She barely came up to his chest and had to tilt her head, as close as she was to him. He merely bent down, his black gaze never leaving her small, pale face as he came closer and closer. She could see his long thick eyelashes, his seductive mouth. Her heart began to pound a rather frantic rhythm, matched the exact same beat as his. His hand slid up her back in a long slow caress. She watched his mouth coming closer to hers.

"I can't do this," she whispered softly, even as she moved closer to his beckoning heat. He was fire; she was ice, like the looming mountains surrounding them. Two halves of the same whole. "I can't do this," she repeated more for herself than for him. A last attempt at self-preservation. Her body was melting against his, boneless and pliant like so much hot silk when she needed to remain aloof, the ice princess, as some of the cowboys labeled her.

I need to do this. The words shimmered in her mind, shimmered between them, in his heart and soul, in hers. He needed it more than the air they were breathing, more than the blood that gave him life. *You need to do this.* Rafael's palm curled around the nape of her neck. His fingers were warm and strong and firm, dragging her inexorably, relentlessly closer to him. He brought her across the last scant inches separating them. *I need this.* Stark, raw truth. She didn't trust him, the rake, the playboy. Worse, she saw him as the man trying to seduce her to get her brother and sister and the ranch. It hurt, the image she had of him uppermost in her mind, it hurt more than he cared to admit, yet at that moment it didn't matter to either one of them.

There was a difference between wanting something and desperately needing it. Rafael needed the feel of her silken mouth and her soft, pliant body. He fastened his mouth to hers, a melding of hot velvet and even hotter silk. Whatever it was that was between them seemed far stronger than either of them. A molten heat thickened their blood and set their hearts pounding frantically. The earth seemed to shift beneath their feet and he gathered her even closer, protectively, possessively against him.

She felt small and fragile to him, yet a living, breathing flame. His every good intention seemed to go right up in a fire raging so hot it seemed to sweep aside his very sanity. His mouth moved over hers, dominating, exploring, whisking them both into a world of raw sexuality. He fed on her sweetness, wanted to devour her, taking her into his own body and locking her in his soul for all time. She had a passionate nature and she gave herself up to the sheer erotic pleasure.

His hands moved over her body possessively, needing to take in every inch of her skin. He swept aside the neckline of her shirt so that his mouth could blaze a trail of fire along her neck, lingering for a moment to swirl his tongue over the temptation of her pulse. His hand moved up her narrow rib cage beneath the thin material to cup her lace-covered breast even while his mouth found the ripe offering.

His mouth was hot and moist right through the lace, his tongue coaxing her nipple to a hard peak, the lace scraping erotically along with his teeth, teasing, driving her wild so that her body was pulsating with a terrible need. She circled his head with her arms, tears close, as the waves of sensation rippled through her. Stark pleasure, hot need, a drenching liquid response she couldn't prevent. It was shocking to Colby and totally unexpected. And unacceptable. She made a sound like a frightened animal, shocked that in his arms she was no longer a thinking person. He could so easily sweep aside her beliefs. She didn't even know if she liked him.

"Rafael." Her voice ached with need. Came out breathless and sexy, not at all as she intended. "Stop." She managed to get the word out. One word. Her body didn't want him to stop, she wanted him to go on and on forever, to set aside the warnings of her brain and just take her up into the flames. She had never experienced such total pleasure, had no idea anything or anyone could make her feel like he did.

"You do not want me to stop." He whispered it, a sinful temptation against her breasts, the warmth of his mouth enticing her.

God help her she didn't want him to stop, not ever. Colby summoned her strength and pushed at him. "I *need* you to stop. I can't do this." She caught her shirt, pulling it down to cover her full aching breasts. Tears glittered, turning her eyes to a deep emerald. "I'm sorry, I don't know what got into me. I've never done this. You have to go." She could never face him again. Never.

"Colby." He said her name very softly. His voice seemed to start a fire in the pit of her stomach, the flames spreading rapidly. It terrified her. Totally terrified her.

Colby stepped back away from him and turned and ran as if Rafael was the devil himself. She raced across the yard to the safety of her porch. He listened to her speaking to her brother and sister. Rafael stood in the shadows and watched as they went inside. He stood alone in the darkness. Alone. As he had always been alone. Inside that house was color and life, emotions, passion. Inside that house was life. His world. He stood in the dark where demons belonged, uncertain if he could control the darkness gathering inside him, spreading rapidly. She was hurting inside, a raw aching wound, unsure of herself. And he knew he couldn't leave her that way.

5

Rafael waited until the house was quiet. He couldn't tear himself away from Colby. Though hunger beat furiously at him, demanding fulfillment, he refused to heed its call. He would feed later. He could not leave Colby. He found he had less and less control around her. He wanted her, his body raging for release, needing her desperately, needing to complete the ritual to make her wholly his. It was the only way to chain the beast inside of him. It was growing stronger, roaring for release continually. He felt himself close to the edge of madness and knew he was nearly falling over that precipice. He felt it in his every waking moment. And his brother felt it as well. Nicolas monitored him closely, lending him strength when the beast gripped him hard.

One by one the lights shining through the windows went out. He heard the soft murmured words of good night and he felt lonelier and edgier than ever. When he was certain the residents of the house were asleep, he glided across the yard and gained entrance to the house through Colby's open window.

Nearly insubstantial, Rafael floated across the hardwood floor silently, a dark shadow in the night. Colby was sleeping deeply, her long hair spread out on her pillow, skeins of flaming red-gold silk. One hand was curled into a fist and the other was flung out as if reaching for something. He bent over her, his hot gaze resting on his mark on her neck. He eased his weight onto the bed, his hands finding her beneath the covers even as he deliberately fed her erotic dreams, wanting to arouse her, prepare her body, for she was an innocent. *Wake, meu a lindo amor, I need you to be with me this night.*

Colby stirred immediately, drowsy, lashes fluttering, not quite awake. She looked sexy, a temptress. "Are you here again? I've got to stop dreaming about you."

You cannot help yourself when you know you are mine alone. The words shimmered in her mind so that the sound of his voice wouldn't disturb her further. She shook her head, a faint smile greeting him. She looked so beautiful he bent to kiss her. Colby's skin was incredibly soft and he couldn't resist touching her. Rafael stretched out beside her, slowly, lazily, an unhurried movement. He had all night with her. At once he felt the hidden power of the comforter covering her. His fingers found the symbols and he traced them carefully. They were safeguards, Carpathian safeguards woven into the patterns on the quilt. Where had she acquired such a thing? It was a work of art, rare and precious like the woman it guarded.

Rafael turned on his side, studying Colby. He needed to spend every moment in her company while he could. She was a ray of light in his dark world, sunshine and laughter. He had long ago forgotten even his memories of such things, yet now he clung to the light in her. He didn't know if he had ever felt gentle or tender toward another, yet he felt something close to those things each time he looked at her.

She murmured his name softly, her breath warm against his neck. Rafael's body hardened and thickened even more, until he groaned softly, a protest against the urgent demand he couldn't quite control. He dragged her into his arms and lowered his head to the pillow close to hers. Only her thin pajamas separated him from her soft skin and the haven of her body. *I want you, querida. I want you almost as much as I need you.* He was aching for her, the words that would bind them together for all eternity in his head, on his tongue, so that he tasted them with every breath he drew.

A smile curved her soft mouth, an invitation. Her body moved restlessly against his. He needed her. There was nothing else in his life. He needed her. With an oath, he wrapped his arms tighter and nuzzled the thin material covering her body up out of his way to expose her breasts to the cool night air. To his hot, burning gaze. She was so beautiful and so vulnerable.

I need to touch you, meu lindo amor, just for a few minutes, allow me to touch you. His voice ached with his need. Ached with his hunger. A velvet soft seduction.

Her eyes opened, emerald green, slumberous, sensual, meeting his black hungry gaze with her own dark passion. Without a word, she turned in to him, slipped her arms around him, her body pliant with surrender.

Colby had no real idea if she was awake or asleep, in the middle of an erotic dream or fantasy, but she couldn't turn away from the desperation burning in those eyes. In her dreams, she could have anyone she wanted, do anything she wanted, she wasn't bound by her responsibilities. She wanted him. Wanted the feel of his skin next to her skin. Wanted his mouth on hers, his hands on her. She had wanted him almost from the first moment she had seen him, and in her dreams she didn't have to be afraid that he would control her.

Rafael's breath caught in his throat at the sight of her lying beside him, her top pushed up exposing her perfectly formed breasts. His hand looked dark against her white skin, his palm on her bare midriff , his fingers splayed wide. She looked delicate, almost fragile, while in contrast his bones and muscles were so much larger. Yet in her own way, Colby was tremendously strong.

The ritual binding words, imprinted in him long before his birth, burned in his mind while his body was on fire, painful and uncomfortable. In the room across the hall, the little girl stirred. His hand closed over Colby's breast possessively. His mind sought Ginny's. She was opening her window stealthily, sticking her head out to whistle for the dog. Ginny had nightmares of her parents' deaths, of something happening to Colby. Rafael heard the dog enter the room and immediately sent it a command so that it would stay on the child's bed, giving her comfort, but would not detect his presence in the home. Nothing could stop this. Nothing. His mind and body were clamoring for Colby and he knew he couldn't stop. He shielded both Paul and Ginny from waking, sending them into a deep sleep.

He bent his head to the warmth of Colby's skin, his tongue swirling over her breast, indulging his ravenous hunger for her. He felt her response, the way her body tightened and clenched, the way her blood heated and pooled. His hands moved over her slowly, inch by slow inch, pushing her clothing aside so that he had access to her body. He wanted to know every inch of her, wanted to touch her, taste her, inhale her. His mouth was hot and needy as he lowered his head to take possession of her breast. He suckled there, his hand sliding along her ribs, across her flat stomach to linger for a few moments, brushing his fingers over her skin, tracing the faint outline of a birthmark there. It was intriguing enough to warrant a quick foray with his tongue, before he returned to her breast while his hand drifted lower to find the tight thatch of curls at the junction of her legs. She was moist and hot as he pushed his palm against her. At once her hips arced against him in response.

Colby had dreams of her dark lover, arousing her body, his hands exploring every inch of her, his mouth hot and needy, suckling at her breasts, stroking and caressing until she wanted to beg him for release. His mouth was everywhere, kissing and caressing, knowing her body even more intimately than she knew it. She burned for him, needed him, needed his body buried deep inside hers. She opened her eyes again to look at him. Real. Solid. He was naked, his body strong, his muscles rippling with power. His long black hair swept across her aching sensitive breasts, as his tongue swirled around her belly button. She caught at him with both hands.

"What are you doing?" She whispered the words, her body on fire. "And why am I letting you?" Fear thudded in her heart and mind. She'd never felt so needy, so painfully aroused. She should be screaming, but she couldn't quite shake off the veil covering her mind.

He smiled against her flat stomach. "I am courting you." His teeth nipped along the curve of her hip, found the strange birth-mark, and scraped at it with small bites. "Persuading you." His tongue eased the ache. His hands opened her thighs wider, stroking, caressing. His finger found the hot core of her, wet with liquid fire, scorching and tight as he slowly inserted his finger deeper and deeper into her body. "I want my body buried in your body. Is that what you want, *querida?* Do you want me the same way I want you?" Her delicate muscles clenched around him. Hot. Fiery. Moist with need. Watching her face, he withdrew his finger, carefully inserted two, stretching her a little more, inch by inch. "Tell me you want me, Colby. I need to hear you say it." He *needed* to hear her say it because he had to be with her, share her body, share her skin and blood and bones.

Colby shook her head, tormented beyond all reasoning. Yes, she wanted him, every cell in her body needed him. Her body was wound so tight, the pressure unbearable so that she didn't think she'd survive without him. But he was demanding everything from her. Not a part of her—*everything*.

And you will give me everything. It was a growl. A command.

"No." She said the word even as he pressed his fingers deeper, even as her body tightened and threatened to shatter into a million fragments, she struggled to keep who and what she was intact.

Rafael could feel her body's response. She wanted him. She moved restlessly, her head turning from side to side on the pillow, a soft sound escaping from her throat. She tried to protest again. He felt it welling up in her as she struggled away from the rising need. He withdrew his fingers and replaced them with his mouth, his tongue probing deep. She cried out, startled, her body rippling with life, fragmenting, imploding, so that she was shocked at the intensity of the waves of pleasure rocking her. She tried to wrench away, the pleasure shattering her, but he clamped his arm over her hips and held her still, drinking her in. He refused to stop, pushing her further, wanting her need to rise in direct proportion to his own voracious hunger.

Colby struggled against the pulse after pulse of sensation tormenting her body, carrying her away when she needed to be anchored. She thrashed beneath him, unable to tamp down the fire racing through her body enough to breathe. She couldn't catch her breath, couldn't think clearly. Fear clutched at her. The sheet knotted in her fists and she tried to pull away from the assault his mouth was making, his tongue flicking and teasing until her nerves were screaming for release.

"You have to stop," she gasped. Colby was completely losing herself in the firestorm of pleasure rushing through her. He was taking her over. She couldn't get away from his mouth and tongue. Her body just kept winding tighter and tighter, burning hotter and hotter until she knew she would explode. Worse, lust was rising, sharp and deadly, the need so strong it terrified her.

She couldn't hold a single thought, not even to save herself. The pleasure was bordering on pain, the pressure building and building.

She never wanted him to stop, she wanted to shatter into a million pieces.

She wanted to be whatever he needed, go wherever he led. A low cry of terror escaped her as his tongue picked up the rhythm and pulsed deeper into her body. He was ravenous, driving her over the edge ruthlessly as her body twisted and bucked beneath him. Not once, but twice, three times, until one orgasm ran into the other and her mind dissolved and her body blew apart.

He rose above her, shoving her thighs apart to accommodate him, opening her fully to him. His erection was thick and heavy and intimidating, his eyes like flint as he pressed into her slick entrance. She could feel him there, stretching her, just waiting, when her entire body tensed, frustrated, pulsing and throbbing with need. She had the mad desire to impale herself on him, but he held her hips still with hard hands. His expression was raw hunger, his mouth a merciless slash. "Are you going to say no to me again, Colby? Are you going to deny me what is truly mine?" His voice was rough, harsh, his temper swirling over both of them.

She gave a small tormented cry. Was he giving her one last chance to save herself? How could she say no when she needed him now, when everything in her had to have him deep inside her body?

"Are you?" he insisted.

Colby shook her head. She couldn't speak, couldn't breathe, her body on fire, fear flowing like lava through her veins at the thought of what was to come. He was shattering her and reconstructing her, so that she would always crave him, always need him. A part of her recognized it, but she couldn't stop the dark hunger he was arousing in her.

Never again. It was a decree, bit out between his clenched teeth.

Rafael thrust hard, driving deep into her in one hard stroke, knowing she was too innocent for what he was doing, but unable to stop himself. He had centuries of hunger in him, a dark, ravenous hunger that spilled out of him, erupting into a fever of frenzied pounding. She was hot and tight and gripped him with a fire that nearly drove him mad.

"It's too much. It's too much," Colby cried out, desperately trying to push him off of her. He was going to kill her, driving her body so high, the sensations so electric she was losing herself completely.

He caught her wrists in a vise, pinned them to the bed on either side of her head, his mouth taking hers, tongue driving deep as his hips thrust harder, deeper, wanting more, taking more.

The call was on him now, wild and primitive, a need as old as time to seal them together for all eternity. His lifemate. His other half. The words beat at him, rising from his soul as he buried himself deeply into her hot fiery sheath with the world going up in flames and spinning out of control. She was making little gasping sounds and he could feel her muscles tightening, clenching as he switched into a pounding tempo that only fed his voracious hunger.

The need to taste her grew stronger and stronger, more demanding until his mouth left hers, moved down to the warmth of her neck, traced an erotic path lower to scrape his teeth over the tempting beat of her heart. His body clenched, drenched in sweat and his heart thundered and pounded. The demon roared for release, urging him on. He was trembling with such need he thought his entire body might explode in spontaneous combustion. With a groan, Rafael gave in, sinking his teeth deep.

Colby moaned aloud as white-hot whips of lightning seemed to dance through her body. He calmed her, his mind now firmly in hers. Rafael held her still, possessively, while he indulged his appetite, and his body plunged deeply, wildly into hers. She tasted like hot spice and warm honey. He never wanted to stop; the terrible hunger that had haunted him for centuries was, for the first time, satiated by her. Colby. The blood in his veins. His life. His world.

The demon roared for more, for all of it, insisting he stake his claim. For a heartbeat of time the ritual words welled up, desperate to spill out. It was instinct, something deep within him urging him onward, instructing him in the ritual. At once tiny sparks leapt around him, colors of deep blue and silver, little stars rising from the comforter to leap around him in glittering reprimand. The words beat at him needing to be said, demanding he claim her, but Rafael hesitated, the little stars dazzling his eyes. He would be below ground and she would be running the ranch in the daylight, unable to touch him when her heart and soul, her mind, urged her to do so. She would be in hell, driven to the point of insanity while he slept deep beneath the ground.

Rafael immediately swept his tongue across the pinpricks on her breast and lifted his head, breathing heavily, his teeth clenched as he fought for control. He uttered his command softly to her, holding the enthrallment now. He lowered his body until her mouth was nearly against his chest, wanting her to take enough blood for a true exchange. He slashed a wound across his chest and pressed her mouth to the gash to replenish what he had taken, holding the back of her head so she couldn't escape, his body pinning hers beneath him. The moment her lips moved against his skin, he shuddered and her body tightened, an endless spiral gripping her, gripping him. Little jackhammers seemed to be tripping in his head. Fire consumed his blood. He drove into her harder and faster, his body slick with sweat, with pleasure.

With a small curse he clenched his teeth to prevent the words from slipping through as he stopped her from feeding. He closed the wound on his chest, bent to take possession of her mouth, releasing her from the enthrallment so that his mouth could dominate hers, sweeping every trace of his taste from the silken interior. He surged deeper into her, harder, moving like a piston, claiming her body when he couldn't take her as his species demanded.

Colby began to fight him, an instinctive, almost mindless battle against the pleasure so intense she felt she might not live through it. She didn't understand how her body could be so out of control, hips rising to desperately meet his, gasping sobs pleading with him. For what? For more? Always more. He was taking her apart with pleasure. She could feel her body tighten around his, her muscles clenching until she felt a scream welling up. The orgasm burst over her, endless, mindless, wiping her away so there was no Colby without Rafael. She felt him swell even thicker, until his hands gripped her hips hard and he thrust harshly into the tight, slick folds, over and over, sending her tumbling into another orgasm as he erupted deep into her body.

Rafael lay over her, his veins singing with excitement, with exaltation. He might be sated for the moment, but he wanted more. He would live and breathe to have her again and again, to feel her body coming apart around his. He buried his face in the warmth of her neck, feeling her body shudder, feeling the aftershocks tighten her muscles around him. She was breathing hard, her heart racing. He braced himself with his arms and lifted his body carefully from hers. The way her slick heat poured over him as he emerged from her sent his blood pounding all over again.

Colby touched her tongue tentatively to her swollen lips. Her breasts ached. She was sore between her thighs. She couldn't look at him. Couldn't look away from him. She had no idea having sex could be like that, a pleasure so deep it actually bordered on pain. A hunger so strong it bordered on insanity.

His fingertips brushed her face, her neck, trailed over her breasts. Her nipples tightened, and between her legs she felt an instant throbbing response. Colby turned her face away from him. "What have you done?" She whispered it, grateful for the darkness. "What have you done to me?" Tears burned behind her eyelids. She would never be free of his sexual web. Colby, who had always been free, always been in charge, would be forever addicted to the things this man could do to her body. And that terrified her.

His tongue rasped over the underside of her breast, dipped into her belly button, and traced her birthmark once again in a leisurely foray. He kept his body firmly over hers. She was exhausted and sore, but Colby might try anything. He could feel her fear, alive and breathing in the room with him. "I told you that you were mine."

"I don't understand this." There were tears in her voice. "How did you get here? How did I let this happen?"

He lifted his head, lazy façade gone. "Do not cry." *Deus*. If she did that, she'd take him apart. He gentled his voice. "Tell me why you fear me so much."

"How can you ask me that? I'm naked in my own bedroom with you and you just crawled through my body as if you owned it. You take control of me somehow. I can't get away from you." She wasn't fighting him. She was lying beneath him like a sacrifice, an offering. She couldn't even manage to summon the energy to do battle because she knew it wouldn't matter. She would never win. Rafael was too powerful and he owned her body and maybe even her soul. "You don't have any idea what you've done to me, do you?"

The despair in her voice raked at him, clawed at his gut. Rafael touched her mind. Colby had thoughts of waiting for the right man. She wanted her first time to be with someone she loved. She had visions of a tender, romantic union.

His hands framed her face. "I know that I was rough, *pequena*. But I am the right man for you. I felt your pleasure. You were drowning in pleasure." And she had been. Was she disappointed because he was so rough sexually? Damn it, he made absolutely certain he had given her pleasure. Why would she dream of some tame man who would never satisfy her the way he could? If he bent his head and took her breast in his mouth, she would shiver with need. Hunger would flare instantly. He knew it. Why didn't she? Who was this other man she wanted? Rafael could feel the fangs aching to explode but he fought back the urge, struggling to understand. Her sorrow beat at him. Was it so impossible for her to love him? She loved Paul and Ginny. She had loved her stepfather. She even loved Ben. He was beginning to detest Ben.

"I was drowning," she said, her voice quiet. "You've taken me over without my consent, Rafael. I have no pride, no way out. You left me with nothing."

He had been prepared for anger, but not this quiet hopelessness. Colby was a fighter. He could turn anger to sexual need. He had no idea what to do with her as she lay staring up at the ceiling, her heart so heavy he ached inside.

As a young Carpathian he had thought often of what his lifemate would be like. Later, he'd dreamed of having a woman of his own. As the endless centuries passed, he despaired of ever having one. Colby was an unexpected and treasured gift and yet she didn't feel what he felt. She was supposed to love him. Supposed to want him. A part of him stirred with anger, the animal in him that demanded a mate. The man tried to workout what was wrong. She belonged to him. They had shared unbelievable mind-numbing sex, their bodies so compatible, he couldn't imagine anything better. He was already eager for more, yet she was far away from him in her mind. She believed he might own her body, but was determined he would never touch her heart. He had no way to combat that.

What was he doing wrong? "I do not understand what you are telling me. We merged. I felt it. I know you felt it. How could that mean I left you with nothing?"

Colby wanted to turn away from him. She wanted to be left alone to figure out what she was going to do. There was no running away. No pretending it hadn't happened or that it wouldn't happen again. "I have no choice. You left me no choice."

Her sorrow beat at him. He would have preferred her anger.

He could only nod in agreement. Of course he left her no choice. There was no choice for either of them. She was born for him. "You do not object to my touch."

"Of course I object to your touch." Anger was beginning to smolder in the pit of her stomach. It darkened her eyes and little sparks leapt around the comforter.

Heat flared instantly, his jaw tightening. "You lie both to yourself and to me." His hand slid possessively over her breast, tugged at her nipple. He bent his head, watching her face, watching the helpless desire in her gaze, felt her body arc into his mouth. Deliberately he slid his hand between her legs to find her damp. He lifted his head to look at her. "Your body does not lie."

She slapped his face as hard as she could. She didn't have a good angle or a lot of room for movement, but the sound was loud in the room. "What you did to me was the same as rape. I don't care how much you lie to yourself, but it was. And you can do it again and again, but unless you have my consent, *which you don't,* it is rape when you touch me. I despise you. I despise what you can do to me. I don't want it. I don't even like you, let alone want you touching my body."

Anger was hot and ugly, churning in his gut, welling up like a fountain that she dared to defy him, dared to strike him, worst of all, dared to call him a rapist. Next to vampire, it was the worst condemnation he could think of. He slammed her wrists to the sheets, rising above her, his mouth coming down hard on hers. He meant it as a punishment, but the moment he touched her, the moment his tongue swept inside her mouth, he also swept inside her mind.

There was such pain. She was desolated. She didn't like him, didn't trust him. She had no tender feelings of being his lifemate as he had for her. Shocked, Rafael pulled away from her and sat up, pushing his fingers through his hair. She meant it. She wasn't lying to him. Her body responded, but it was only her body. He had aroused her, knowing she was inexperienced, thinking she wouldn't be uncomfortable when they came together. He had not wanted their first time together to be painful to her, but she hadn't wanted it at all. She hadn't wanted *him* at all. He pressed his fingertips to his temples.

What had he done? Lifemates were meant to be together for all eternity. Her reactions made no sense to him. He thought of her every moment of his existence. She wanted him out of her life.

Rafael. You are weeping.

Nicolas's voice moved through him, making him aware of the burning in his chest. Rafael touched his cheek and found a blood-red tear. He didn't weep. He was a man. A Carpathian. A hunter of the vampire. *I understand none of this. It is her pain I feel. I have taken something precious from her.*

Her virginity belonged to you. Nicolas was pragmatic about it. *She has no choice but to accept you. Convert her, bring her home, and she will eventually come around.*

Rafael winced. It hadn't been the taking of her virginity, it had been the taking of her right to choose. He swept both hands through his hair. Was he so close to becoming a monster that he already behaved as one? *Is that it, Nicolas? Are we both so close to turning that we cannot behave in an honorable fashion? If that is the case, we no longer belong on this earth.*

Colby rolled away from him, her back to him. Her body throbbed and burned and she felt sick with wanting him. How was she going to get through the rest of the night? The rest of her life? She could taste him in her mouth. Feel him in her skin. She ached for him between her thighs. She may not want him, but she *needed* him the way an addict did a drug. The terrible pressure in her body would never go away without him. It wouldn't matter what man she turned to, Rafael's possession of her would haunt her every relationship. She burned. There was no other word for it. She lay there crying, tears running down her face, despising him, despising herself, but she wanted him buried deep in her body, hard and hot and taking her beyond anyplace she could go herself. He had made her his whore, pure and simple.

"You are not my whore." Rafael was appalled that the thought had come into her mind. "Where do these thoughts come from?" He laid his hand gently on the small of her back, fingers splayed wide. "I'm sorry, Colby. I did not understand what you were telling me. I did not think beyond my need for you." He was sorry for the pain he caused, for taking her without permission, but try as he might, he couldn't be sorry for possessing her. He ached inside. He wanted to find a way to fix his mistake, but without knowing *why* she wasn't responding to him other than physically, he had no way of doing so. He wanted more than her physical love. She was his lifemate and she was supposed to love him wholly.

His palm, meant to comfort, burned a hole through her back. Sent electricity sizzling through her bloodstream. Her body ached for his. She buried her face in the coolness of her pillow with a soft, desperate cry of protest.

"Colby," he coaxed softly, "look at me."

"I can't. I can't stop crying. Go away." Her words were mu ed.

"You know it is impossible for me to leave you like this. You need me. Let me help you." He swept her hair from the nape of her neck and brushed a kiss there. He couldn't leave, not when she was in tears and her body was screaming for his. Every instinct he possessed demanded he see to her needs. He kissed his way down her spine to the small of her back. "Let me take care of you."

"I can never look at you again. After tonight, I never want to see you again." Colby turned over, her eyes swimming with tears. "I mean it. I'll never be able to face you if I have to have you do this." She *needed* him. She was terrified to let him touch her. The moment he did, she would be lost. She knew that. She was certain of it.

Rafael didn't wait for her to fully make up her mind. He was already damned either way. If he left her frustrated sexually she would hate him and if he satisfied her she would hate him. His body was already hard and hot and making demands of its own.

"Colby, I am not a gentle man." It was the only way he could warn her. He couldn't find the emotion, even when he wanted it, not when it came to sex. He was dominant and passionate and demanded she follow his lead. He trailed his hand from her lips to her breasts, making her shiver with response.

"There's a bit of news I wouldn't have known," she whispered and closed her eyes as he bent to take her peaked nipple in his mouth.

At once he lifted his head to pin her with his gaze. "Do not look away from me. You have to know that this is not just me taking you, *querida*. Not without your consent." Her sorrow was killing him. He ached inside. It was a terrible feeling, claws raking his heart and lungs from the inside out. He touched a tear on her lashes, brought it to his mouth.

Even that was sensual. Everything about him, his eyes, his mouth, his smoldering expression. He didn't have to touch her to make her body come alive. "You're taking all my pride, Rafael," she said.

He despised the sadness in her voice. He heard his own cry, deep in his mind, a cry of pain and sorrow as his despair merged with hers. "You accused me of something vile, *meu amor*. For me, you are the only woman I will ever have in my life. I thought it was a mutual feeling between us." The shock still rocked him.

All the while he talked, his hands moved possessively over her. Large, strong hands that cupped her breasts and teased her nipples. That swirled small circles across her stomach and slid between her thighs. Colby gave in because there was no other choice. She was desperate for his body. If he didn't assuage the terrible hunger building inside of her, she didn't know what she was going to do.

"How can you make me feel this way, Rafael? I'm so afraid, but it's worse without you."

He kissed her throat, his hair sliding over her sensitized skin making her shudder with pleasure. "You do not ever have to be without me, Colby. Lifemate is forever. Tonight, be in my world with my laws. I can do no other than to see to your every happiness. Your health and needs and desires will be forever mine." He kissed his way down the valley between her breasts. "My world was one of darkness until you gave me back life. I know absolutely you are everything to me. You will always be everything. I may command you in bed"—he swirled his tongue around her beloved belly button—"but you command me in all other things."

His voice was a soft seduction in itself. "I can take you places no other man can take you and always I will keep you safe. No man could want you more. No man could ever desire you or need you the way that I do. I am as much a prisoner as you feel you are. The need to be with you is as deep and as elemental as your need to be with me. Find a way to love me a little, Colby."

His tongue stroked and swirled, moved over her skin, his teeth scraping, adding a small bite of pain that only seemed to enhance her pleasure. His hands shaped her body, the pads of his fingers finding every sensitive spot so that she jumped and writhed beneath him, flaming to life. Her blood rushed with a kind of liquid fire. She couldn't find the strength to do more than lie there while he examined every inch of her, tasted every inch, learned a very thorough, intimate knowledge of her body. Tears burned in her eyes for the ache in his voice. There was honesty, even purity in his tone. He meant the things he said. His words, his absolute assurance, frightened her, but it drew her to him, closer to the fire. She tried to hold on to thought, to understand, but his hands and his mouth were destroying her so it was impossible to keep a single thought.

Heat seared through her body, flames danced over her skin, licking every inch of her until she was crying out again and again. His name. For him. Needing him. She crushed his silken hair in her fists, his face a sensual etching above her. He was everywhere. Around her, on her, and, God help her, she wanted him in her. She caught at his hips as he pressed tightly against her and she felt his invasion. Slow this time. Stretching her with incredible fire. He watched her face, watched as she took him into her body, as he pushed through her tight folds, deeper and deeper into her. She was mesmerized by the expression on his face, the harsh sensuality. The raw passion. He sank into her until he was lodged so tightly she felt too full, too stretched.

She couldn't help the way her muscles tightened around him. The action heightened her pleasure, but he gasped and gripped her hips. "You are so tight, Colby. Feel what I am feeling when I take you like this." He merged his mind with hers, and she felt his raging fire. Felt his need for her submission, the need of soft skin sliding against his hard body. The small cries he wrung from her added to what amounted to ecstasy.

He reared back, plunged hard. Colby heard his name echoing through her mind. She screamed it, not aloud, but more intimately.

"More. Give me more," he commanded and began to drive into her.

She had no choice but to obey. Her body had a will of its own, arching her hips, tightening her muscles so that she pulsed around him. His arm caught her hips and held her down while he thrust roughly into her, sending shockwaves through her body. The tension spread, grew, the heat building and building and never relenting. He was merciless, even when she pleaded for release, even when she begged him. Every frenzied thrust wound her body tighter and tighter until she felt the strange hazing in her mind. She wouldn't live through this tormented pleasure.

"Rafael." He was her only refuge in the storm of lust and hunger. She couldn't take it, couldn't survive it. The sensations took her body over and built a raging inferno in her. Her body tightened around his, the orgasm ripping through her, over her, tearing up through her body until she screamed with the release of it. It lasted an eternity, holding her in its thrall, breaking over her like waves as she felt him empty himself, filling her with his hot release.

Tears burned behind her eyes. She jammed her fist into her mouth to keep from screaming aloud. It was bad enough that he'd heard her in her mind.

"Again, Colby, say my name. Know who I am. Know whose body is buried deep inside your body." He whispered the words against the swell of her breast.

"I know who you are," she said.

"And you know I am not some vile rapist. I belong here, inside you, right here in your heart and mind, in your body. I am not ever going to give you up. Look at me, *meu amor*, know I am telling you the truth. I will never give you up. You have to come to terms with the fact that we belong together."

His eyes burned fiercely, a dark reminder he was a predator she had taken into her home, her body, her life. She sighed, her body rocking over and over, little aftershocks she couldn't control. The things he said didn't make sense, yet she felt their rightness. He believed she felt as he did when he'd entered her room. He was driven to possess her by some law of his people she had no real knowledge of.

"Rafael." She murmured his name, her body so exhausted she could barely think. "I don't understand any of this. I don't know why you believe these things or why they feel right to my body. I'll try, though. That's all I can promise. I'll try to understand. But not tonight. I'm so tired." She turned her head away from him, drifting as he slowly allowed their bodies to separate. She felt his mouth at her breast, his hands cupping her bottom. Each strong pull as he suckled sent more shock waves dancing through her body, but this time she was too worn out to do more than lay quietly, drifting off to sleep as he kissed his way back up her body before allowing their bodies to separate. Strangely, she might have protested had she had the energy. Instead she snuggled close to the protection of his body and slept.

Rafael lay beside her until the gray light was creeping through the bedroom window and he knew he could wait no longer to hunt prey. Reluctantly he slipped from her bed, arranging her exhausted body in a much more comfortable position. He wrapped her protective quilt close around her. Rafael bent once more to her neck, wanting his mark fresh on her, a brand for the rest of the world to see. For her to see. His ancient blood would flow hotly in her veins calling for him, his scent would cling to her. The mind meld between them would be stronger than ever. He would know where she was every moment. There was nowhere she could go that he would not find her.

To prevent dishonoring himself by sealing them together before he had worked out the safety of her brother and sister, Rafael left her to hunt prey. He must feed soon if he had any hope of maintaining self-control. He would seek the ground as early as possible to prevent going back to her and forcibly taking her for his own.

The moment he stepped outside and inhaled the night, he felt the disturbance. It was subtle. A small feeding of power into the air. A seeking. It was so light he couldn't get a fix on the direction, but he felt the taint of evil. At once he reached for his brother.

A vampire, Nicolas. A powerful, ancient one. It is nearly dawn yet he has not gone to ground and he knows we are near him. His power is subtle, one I cannot get a direction on for the hunt.

Your woman draws him. You must turn her and take her back to our home.

There was weariness in Nicolas's voice, as if his fight with the darkness was becoming too much, lasting too long, and he was slowly succumbing.

You have been using your strength to keep me from the darkness, Rafael guessed.

You are so close. She is not helping by fighting you. Take the woman and let us leave this place and go back to where we belong. I will hunt the vampire while you secure the woman.

Rafael turned the offer over in his mind. With every kill, the darkness stained their souls, took them over until there was nothing left of who and what they stood for. Nicolas was too empty, too long without solace. Rafael had an anchor. If he took possession of Colby, tied her to him for all eternity, he could safely hunt the vampire and rid the area of the danger. Nicolas and he would both be safe from the danger of embracing the life of the undead.

I will hunt this one, Nicolas. He is strong and in hiding, but I have his scent and he will not escape the justice of our people. He is not acting normal. There are no kills, no unexplained deaths. The murdered man was killed by a human, not a vampire. And I met a woman of psychic talent, a strong telepath. She knew what I was. Something is happening here I do not understand.

I will come if you need me.

Rafael wanted Nicolas far from the danger of a hunt. *I will call should I need assistance.* He broke the connection to his brother and moved swiftly away from the ranch, feeling for the vampire, for a blank spot that would give away the lair of the undead. Evil was in his nostrils, the stench foul and unclean, but he could not pursue what permeated the air. There was no direction. Nothing at all to define a trail. There was only the certain knowledge that a powerful vampire was in the area. Everyone was in danger.

He found sustenance in the small town, drinking his fill to replenish his strength. He would need much in the coming days. And he would need all his courage to face Colby after he changed her life for all time.

6

Colby stirred restlessly, a sound slipping in and out of her dreams like a persistent alarm. It took a moment to fight her way to the surface, her head throbbing, a faint coppery taste in her mouth. Her body was unfamiliar, heavy, sore and aching, thoroughly used. But she knew immediately what had roused her from her sex-induced slumber. Her instincts shrieked at her as she woke abruptly. A high-pitched scream, far off, echoed disturbingly by a resounding crash had her sitting up, throwing off the covers, and dragging on her discarded pajamas. "Paul! Ginny!" She was running, her bare feet slapping softly on the wood of the floor.

Her ability to hear and smell seemed ten times magnified. She felt dizzy and shaky, her mouth dry. Sheer terror gripped her. Tearing open the front door, she paused on the porch, staring with horror at the raging inferno that was her stable. "Paul! The horses!" Her agonized cry lent wings to her brother so that he nearly beat her across the uneven ground.

The smoke was already thick in the yard, the flames shooting into the sky, sparks flying in all directions. Colby, sobbing in fear, driven by the panicked screams of the horses, seized the metal bar locking the stable door with her bare hands. She heard her own agonized scream, felt the echo of Rafael's voice in her mind, but the pain didn't matter, the horses did. Flames were licking hungrily along the doorjamb, dancing across the roof, raging up the walls. The sprinkler system seemed powerless against such an inferno. What had happened to the fire alarm? "Ginny, get back, don't come near this!" She made it a sharp order as her younger sister came running up.

"Colby! No!" Paul caught at her arm, preventing her from entering the hellish inferno of smoke and flames. The heat on their faces and skin was nearly unbearable.

She swung around, trying to be calm. There was no way to take a deep, calming breath without drawing the thick smoke into her lungs. "Ginny, call nine-one-one, then Sean Everett." The Everett spread was the closest neighboring ranch. "Paul, keep water on this entrance, but stay back. I mean it. The stable is going to come down any minute. Don't you dare come in, no matter what happens. That's an order." She turned and rushed to the very entrance of the burning building.

"No!" Paul screamed it, but Colby had already disappeared, greedy smoke whirling around her like a huge black cape, swallowing her into the gaping maw.

She focused on the doors to the stalls, trying to get her mind to work, to open them. The doors refused to budge under the pressure. She didn't know if it was her desperation, the screaming of the animals keeping her from focusing properly, but she had no choice but to go all the way inside.

Nineteen. She had nineteen horses in the stalls. Colby forced her numb mind to concentrate. Her eyes were stinging from the smoke and the fire roared in her ears. In the choking black smoke, thick and dangerous, it was impossible to see anything at all. The heat was intense, the noise loud and frightening. The horses were beyond reason, dangerous, desperate animals.

Colby felt her way to the long row of stalls. One by one, she swung the stall gates open, trying to hold her breath, eyes streaming. Her lungs burned and she coughed horribly. She was becoming disoriented. Domino loomed up, eyes rolling wildly. Colby was choking too much to soothe him. He reared up, his slashing hooves inches from her face. Colby lurched back, tripped, and fell. Domino thundered past her, narrowly missing stepping on her. His back left hoof slashed a wound into her thigh as he ran.

The air close to the ground was somewhat better and her painfully aching lungs gulped at it. She managed to get her shaky legs under her and, pushing herself up, propelled herself forward. Waving her arms, hollering hoarsely, Colby ran at the panic-stricken horses. Whirling, they rushed at the entrance. The open doorway was burning too, but not with the same intensity as the walls. Colby stumbled after them, falling to the ground coughing and retching.

Hard hands caught her, bit into her waist, pulled her from the entrance and into safe arms. Rafael dragged her free of the smoke and flames. He smelled the blood on her from the painful gash on her thigh and something ugly and demonic deep within him lifted its head and roared for vengeance.

Part of the roof caved in and somewhere deep within the raging inferno an animal screamed in agony so intense there was a dead silence in the yard. Colby was the first to react, wrenching herself from Rafael's grasp, running straight toward the flaming entrance to the stables. "Paul, the rifle!"

Without preamble, Rafael caught her up as he shouted an order to the men in the yard. He put her on the porch and stared down into her terrified eyes. "Stay right here. Do not move, do you hear me?" Rafael caught the rifle thrown to him by Juan Chevez and disappeared into the leaping flames greedily devouring the stable.

Paul knelt beside Colby. She looked dazed, in shock. He couldn't help but admire Rafael's efficiency—helicopters for transportation, men seeing to the frightened, wounded animals. It was obvious that it was Rafael directing the well-coordinated operation. He had picked the rifle out of the air with one hand and calmly entered a rapidly disintegrating building.

A shot rang out, and the pitiful cries ceased abruptly. Aware he had been holding his breath, Paul let it out slowly, bending solicitously over Colby, who was leaning back against the porch post. Her face was streaked with black smoke and tears. There was a bruise high up on her forehead, and several on her ribs, he guessed from the state of her top, probably from the horses knocking into her. Her pajama bottoms were torn and singed. Blood smeared her leg high up on her thigh. Both palms were an ugly mass of blisters. She was struggling to breathe with the terrible smoke already deep in her lungs. Clumsily Paul tried to comfort her, circling her slender shoulders with his arm.

Then Rafael was there, bending over them, lifting Colby into his arms with exquisite care. "See to your younger sister," he commanded Paul softly. "She is very frightened. I will take care of Colby." He signaled to Sean Everett's foreman, directing the crews toward saving the barn. Colby lay in his arms dazed, unable to take in the enormity of what had happened. He carried her a safe distance from the smoke and activity, putting her down in the grass to examine her injuries. Shielding her from any prying eyes with his body, Rafael tipped up her black-smeared face to study the bruise. "I am sorry, *pequena*. I could not save the horse, nor allow it to suffer." Even as he spoke he laid his hand over the laceration on her thigh. Strangely the throbbing and burning ceased immediately. His hand glided, feather light, across her throat, touched her pounding temples. Then his palm moved to the bruise on her head. "I came the moment I heard you awaken."

"I can't believe this is happening," Colby whispered hoarsely, afraid to cry, afraid if she did she might never stop.

Rafael brushed back her hair with gentle fingers. She had a few minor burns, the bump, and the gash, but it was her hands where she had grasped the metal bar that concerned him. He murmured to her softly as he raised her hands to the healing warmth of his mouth. His tongue swirled in a sensuous motion, ensuring the healing agent bathed every blister and burn mark. Where it should have stung, she felt a tingling warmth that only soothed. She wanted to crawl inside of him and hide where it was safe.

"I have to help," she said, trying to draw her hands away from him. She could barely breathe, the smoke trapped deep in her lungs. Her chest burned and she was gasping for clean air.

Rafael signaled to Juan Chevez to watch the sparks coming off the fire, leaping toward the main house. He knew the Chevez brothers were worried about him, as he should have gone to ground in the early morning light. He could take the morning hours if necessary, but his strength was slowly waning and he would eventually succumb to the limitations of his species. The sun was already burning his skin, turning him to a mass of blisters, and his eyes were streaming in the light. Rafael kept the clouds overhead to help shield him, but the sun was taking its toll. The Chevez brothers knew he had very little time before his body would turn to lead and he would be completely vulnerable.

Rafael leaned toward Colby. "Look at me, *querida*, you must really look at me this time." His black eyes were magnetic, impossible to ignore, and Colby stared rather helplessly, knowing she was falling into the dark pools but unable to summon up the strength to stop herself. Rafael took possession of her mouth, breathing into her body, pushing out the black tarry smoke attempting to choke the air out of her. His hands glided over her body, touching the bruises on her ribs, even as he veiled their presence from any prying eyes.

He lifted his head reluctantly, his black gaze still holding her captive. Focusing in the way of his people, concentrating until he separated his spirit from his body, until he was pure energy, he entered her body to aid him in pushing out the smoke and heal the gash and burns. He held her in his thrall until he was certain every injury had been treated and there was no danger of infection. No danger to her lungs. Slowly, reluctantly, he released her. Already, with his mind, he was directing the various crew chiefs and those arriving as the call went out for more help.

"We have this under control, Colby," he murmured softly. "I do not want to turn around and find you are placing yourself in danger. Going into the stable was brave but very foolish. Do not ever do such a thing again. I cannot tolerate such a danger to you."

She clung to him for just one more moment, appreciating his hard strength and air of complete confidence. She didn't have to know her own feelings to admire his efficient manner and total authority. The man certainly knew how to get things done.

The next couple of hours were a nightmare, Colby and Paul treating the burns on the terrified horses while the men fought to keep the fire from spreading to her house and the other outbuildings. Sometimes she would look up to find Rafael looking at her with his intense black gaze. He seemed to be everywhere, a machine working tirelessly throughout the long early morning hours.

At last, as the fire was reduced to glowing embers and tails of smoke and the animals had all been cared for, Paul and Ginny went to her for comfort—for answers. In her tattered, singed pajamas and with smoke-blackened face, Colby surveyed the destruction. "How could this have happened?" She groaned softly in despair. "We had no chance of saving the stables. The fire was everywhere, completely out of control. No alarms went off, the sprinklers didn't work." She shook her head, unable to believe it.

Colby was devastated. Fourteen of the horses housed in the

stable, including the one Rafael had put down, didn't belong to her. She was boarding and training them. They were priceless to their owners, bred for specific purposes. Now they were traumatized and burned, covered with cuts and bruises and suffering from smoke inhalation, and Colby would be held responsible for their injuries.

Paul put his arm around her, a clumsy gesture of support even as his eyes went automatically to the one person who seemed in control of the chaotic situation. Rafael and the Chevez brothers had fought long and hard along with Sean Everett's ranch hands and the forestry department to keep the entire ranch from going up in flames. Paul didn't want his uncles to drag him off to a foreign country away from the home he loved and he was deeply afraid of Rafael De La Cruz, but he couldn't deny that without them they would have lost everything.

Rafael read the desperate plea in Paul's young face and immediately said something to the small group of men he was talking with, easily excusing himself. He took Colby's arm, guiding her very gently across the yard and up the stairs to the porch of the ranch house. Pushing her gently but firmly into the swing, he poured her a glass of water from the pitcher Ginny had thoughtfully kept filled for the men fighting the fire. Colby looked dazed.

She stared up at him helplessly, confused and afraid. "How could the smoke alarms not work? There are several—how could *all* of them malfunction?" she murmured. "And the sprinklers. I just had the sprinklers checked. How could the entire stable go up that fast? I don't understand."

"We will find out, *meu amor.*" Rafael was gentle as he took a cup of hot, sweet tea from Ginny and pressed it into Colby's hands. "You are in shock, *pequena*, I want you to drink this. It will help." He raked a hand through his hair. "It looks as if it was started with kerosene. Do you store kerosene here?"

"In the stable?" Colby said incredulously. Restlessly she jumped to her feet. Pushing past Rafael's larger frame, she entered the kitchen. "I'd never keep kerosene in the stable. You must really think I'm an idiot."

She was so fragile, so close to tears. Rafael was in her mind, reading the jumble of emotions, the horror of what had happened, the fears of facing the future and her frantic attempts at putting the pieces together to discover what could have happened. He followed her patiently, a silent jungle cat stalking after her. "That is not what I asked you, *querida*. I am telling you I think this fire was set. I think the fire captain also believes this to be the case. Do you have insurance?"

Colby went very still, half turning to face him. "Is that what you think? That I would burn down my own stables with horses still inside for insurance money? Is that what you're suggesting?" She waved a hand to encompass the yard filled with her neighbors. "Is that what everyone thinks? That I would be capable of harming animals for my own monetary gain?"

Her green eyes began to smolder dangerously. "Or maybe that's what you and the Chevez brothers want everyone to believe. That I would be capable of such an atrocity. That would certainly help your case, if I were to be thrown in jail, wouldn't it? No one would stand in your way to get the kids."

"Enough." He said the word very quietly through clenched white teeth. His black eyes were ice cold again, his mouth a merciless slash. He looked quite cruel and ruthless so that she backed away from him, her heart pounding out her sudden fear. "You are very upset and you do not know what you are saying. It is better to stay quiet than throw out groundless accusations. You are scaring your sister, Colby."

Ashamed at her loss of control, Colby shook her head and stared out the window to avoid his penetrating stare. She had no way of knowing Rafael had already discovered the key to her mind and was well aware she was incapable of such a treacherous action as starting a fire in her own stable filled with live animals.

Rafael hunkered down beside Ginny, his tone very gentle. "It is going to be all right, *menininha*. No one would ever believe such a thing of Colby. Do not look so frightened."

"Are we going to lose the ranch?" Ginny burst out anxiously. "Are you going to take us away from Colby and turn our ranch over to that horrible man?" Tears were making a path through the smoke on her small face.

Rafael looked at the child and his heart turned over. It was a singular experience to see a human through the eyes of love. Connected as he was with Colby's mind, he felt tremendous emotion for the little girl and her fears.

"No, darling." Colby's voice was extraordinarily gentle. "Don't worry, Ginny, we've seen worse times and come through. You and Paul are alive and unhurt, that's all that really matters." Even in her distress, she was reassuring.

"Which horrible man, Ginny?" Rafael asked, his black gaze seeking and finding the child with a firm compulsion to answer him.

"Everything is just fine," Colby interrupted, sounding weary even to her own ears. She reached for Ginny in an attempt to break the lock Rafael's gaze had on her.

Rafael glided without appearing to move, keeping his body inserted between Colby and Ginny. The little girl looked up at him trustingly. "He wants to take our ranch away. He is always coming here and telling Colby to give him money." She leaned closer confidentially. "He wants to marry her. I heard him say we wouldn't lose the ranch if she cooperated with him."

"Ginny!" Colby spoke much more sharply than she intended, humiliated all over again. Rafael De La Cruz was the last person who needed to know their business. For a moment she covered her face with her hands. She'd slept with him. *Slept with him.* That wasn't even the right words for what they'd done together. A virtual stranger, she let him touch her, *devour* her. She had taken him inside her body. She felt naked and vulnerable and slowly lowered her hands to meet his black eyes. He had possessed her, marked her, and she had been so eager for his body, his touch. She would have done anything for him. God, she had *begged* him. Screamed his name over and over in her mind. What was wrong with her?

Rafael released the child from his thrall, his gaze thoughtful as it rested on Colby's face. Her eyes were alive with pride, but he was a shadow in her mind and he could read her humiliation and fear. He circled her fragile wrist with his strong grip, careful to keep his enormous strength leashed. "Who is this man and what does he have to holdover your head to threaten you in such a manner?" He said it softly, his teeth very white and almost wolfish. He was very much aware of time slipping away from him. He had pushed his endurance far beyond normal in order to be with Colby.

"It isn't your business." Colby attempted to twist free, feeling foolish when he didn't appear to notice. "I'm too upset to cope with an interrogation right now," she murmured rebelliously, fighting back tears. It didn't help her state of mind to notice that her various injuries hadn't been hurting since Rafael had attended to her earlier.

Rafael's breath came out in a slow hiss. "You will answer me, Colby." It was a command, his voice so low, so laced with velvet, she felt it rather than heard it. For all of that, it was sheer menace. His glittering black eyes did not blink once.

"All right then." Goaded beyond endurance, her usual control shattered into fragments, Colby glared at him. "I made a huge mistake when my father was ill. We needed money. Everyone knew he was sick, the bank wouldn't loan us anything. I couldn't keep up with the ranch work because he needed me with him. There were so many bills. The kids needed clothes for school." Her chin was up, belligerently. "I was only nineteen, no one would take the chance of loaning me the money and the bank wouldn't go for another mortgage on the ranch because of the hospital bills and my father's paralysis. It was fairly common knowledge." She jerked at her wrist again. "I hate this, telling you this."

She didn't have to tell him, he could "see" the memories in her mind. She had loved Armando Chevez with the same fierce loyalty and passion she gave the children. To Colby, Armando Chevez had been her father, blood or no. Grief-stricken when her mother had died, she had still taken on the daunting task of caring for her paralyzed father, two children, and the enormous ranch. She had been very frightened, with nowhere to turn and everyone depending on her.

Rafael ached for her, his eyes burning with unfamiliar emotion. He tugged on her wrist until her resisting body was close to the protective shelter of his. He needed to comfort her even more than she needed the comfort. Colby wrenched herself free and jerked open the door to the kitchen. He moved with her like a dance partner, graceful, fluid, sheer energy. He made no sound on the tiled floor.

Colby looked at him, feeling trapped and very vulnerable. "I borrowed the money from a neighbor. I knew what he was like, but we needed it. I sent the letter to the Chevez family first, they were our last hope, but there was no reply. I went to Clinton Daniels and I borrowed the money we needed to keep going." When he continued to look at her she shrugged. "I wasn't stupid—I knew he wanted the ranch, and I knew he was responsible for the bank turning me down. I also knew he would give us time if he thought he might have a chance with me." Her green eyes wavered, shame creeping into them. "I took the money and I've managed to come up with the payments every month since then, but we have a balloon payment due. Unless I can sell off part of our land quickly, we'll lose the ranch. Unfortunately it isn't so easy when the ranch is part of a trust."

Paul had followed them into the kitchen on the pretense of pouring himself a cup of coffee. Colby had to have been shattered by the events of the morning to reveal such personal details to a man she didn't even know. She had to be in shock. He spun around, ready to set the record straight. "She makes it sound like she was selling herself. All she did was keep us going when our *family* didn't bother to even contact us after my dad died. She's worked hard to pull us out of debt, done more than any two men could have done! She's got nothing to be ashamed of!"

"I realize your sister is as stubborn as a mule," Rafael said grimly, "but I thought better of you, boy. You should have told me or your uncles this immediately instead of allowing your sister to run herself into the ground." The voice was very low, but there was a whiplash in it.

"Don't you dare talk to him like that!" Colby came to life, her green eyes blazing. She radiated fury, her fists actually clenched at her sides. She even took a step toward Rafael.

He felt the surge of power vibrating in the air. It was so strong several pots hanging on hooks swayed, clinking together so that she glanced at them in alarm. Her skin paled beneath the layer of soot and she immediately took a deep breath to calm herself.

Amusement warmed Rafael's eyes. "Think twice, *pequena*, before you launch yourself at me. If you hurt me, how am I going to sign the check?"

"You'll loan us the money?" Paul gasped eagerly.

"No way, Paul, absolutely not." Colby was outraged at the idea. "I'm not selling my soul to the devil, not even to keep the ranch. Not for any price!" She would feel like a prostitute, and how could she explain that to Paul or Ginny?

"You do not have a scrap of manners." Rafael's low voice was suddenly steel encased in velvet. A muscle jerked along his jaw. "The truth is you already made a deal with the devil and whether you like it or not, you need help."

Her chin lifted at him, green eyes alive with pride. "Not from you or the Chevez family. You had your chance to help us and you let our father die alone."

Warning bells went off in Paul's brain. Colby was quite capable of attempting to throw De La Cruz out on his ear. They couldn't afford to make an enemy of Rafael. "Hang on, Colby, I'd like to hear the man out. What kind of terms are you offering?"

Colby glared at her brother. "Whatever the terms are, we can't afford them. Paul, haven't you learned by my mistakes?"

"I want to hear them," Paul insisted stubbornly, proving he could be just like his older sister when the situation called for it. "You think I don't know you get about four hours of sleep a night? Look at you, Colby, you're getting skinny."

"Thank you very much," she snapped, humiliated all over again. "If you two will excuse me I've got to shower." Colby brushed past Rafael, her slender body stiff with disapproval. She couldn't look at him when she said "shower," when Rafael's attention was suddenly on her body. She could feel the weight of his gaze on her, could remember how his mouth felt. *Rafael's hands had been all over her, inside her. His mouth, his tongue, his body. She had called out his name, begged him, pleaded for more of his possession. Over and over. She had burned for him all night. She burned for him still.*

The hot water stung her hands and the small burns she hadn't noticed before on her arms and legs. She turned her face up to let the water wash unwanted tears from her face. She was exhausted, the morning was already half gone, and her chores were waiting. Everything was waiting. She washed the smoke from her hair, all the while trembling uncontrollably. Why had she told De La Cruz about the mortgage? It was just one more weapon in a growing arsenal he could use against her. And what had he said? Someone set the fire? With the horses inside the stable, someone had deliberately set the fire?

She dried herself slowly, turning it over in her mind. It was a difficult thing to believe, yet she doubted Rafael would lie about it. Obviously if arson was suspected, there would be a full-scale investigation. She would be the number one prime suspect. Everyone knew she needed money. Colby groaned softly and pulled on a clean pair of faded Levi's. Why would someone want to burn down her stable? The insurance money wouldn't cover her full losses, let alone be much good to anyone else.

Had she done it? Colby sank slowly onto her bed. *Could she have done it?* Could she have inadvertently started the fire without knowing it? Was it possible? She had been in the stable earlier in the evening with Rafael. She remembered the surge of power rushing through her body like a fireball. The strength of it had filled the room. *She had burned for him all night long. So much power and energy.* Colby pressed a trembling hand to her mouth.

Now you are truly being silly, querida, you could not have done this. Had your powers started the fire, it would have been spontaneous combustion, not kerosene soaked into the walls. This was deliberate. I know what monsters are, Colby, and you are not one. Come out here and rescue me from these children. They are afraid and trying to be very brave for you. They need reassurance from you.

Colby sat up, finding her reflection in the mirror. Her eyes were enormous, vivid green with shock. Rafael De La Cruz had tremendous talent. She could no longer deny they had a connection. A strong connection. She couldn't pretend that she wasn't hearing him speaking to her, mind to mind. She couldn't pretend that every single time he came near to her, even in a crisis, her body reacted to his. Suddenly, in the mirror, her eyes widened in shock. *He could read her thoughts. He wasn't simply talking to her, he was responding to her thoughts. And he wasn't even in the same room with her!*

Colby sat very still, afraid to move. She could hear her heart beating loudly in the small confines of her bedroom. It was then that she realized she was hearing far more than her heart. She could hear the men in the yard, their conversations, the restless continual stomping of the horses. She could hear insects buzzing. Worse, she could hear whispers from the firemen near the stables. She pressed her hands to her ears, suddenly afraid she was losing her mind.

She felt him this time, a stirring of a shadow in her mind. Warmth flooding her, comfort, a soothing tranquility he was projecting. *It is a gift like any other. Work with it for a few moments. You can control the volume with your mind, Colby. It is nothing to fear. Turn it down until you are comfortable.*

Why is this happening? The question shimmered in her mind, a plea for help in the insanity of her world. Not just the hearing. Everything she was feeling. Even her attraction to him was bizarre. She didn't trust it. It was too violent, too passionate, when she didn't even like him. She also was touching his mind and felt his terrible weariness. The need of his body to cease all movement. His skin burned painfully and his eyes stung as if hot needles were pushing into them. *What is happening to you? Why are you in so much pain?* She was suddenly very, very frightened *for* him.

"Colby?" Paul knocked hesitantly. "Are you all right?" He pushed the door open wide enough to stick his head in.

Looking at his young, worried face, the naked concern for her, Colby felt her strength and resolve flowing back stronger than ever. "I'm getting there, Paulo," she reassured him softly, "how 'bout you?" *Answer me.* She might scream if she didn't know that Rafael was going to be all right. Had he been burned?

"I think it will hit me tonight or tomorrow. I'm still in shock." Paul walked across her floor to push the hair back from her forehead. "You have bruises everywhere." He indicated her denim-clad thigh. "Was the cut bad? There was a lot of blood," he pointed out in a clumsy attempt to show his love.

I am fine. It is good that you care.

"I'm tough, Paul, and I've been kicked by horses and hit the ground a lot harder than that. What about Ginny? How is she doing?" Rafael was right, if she concentrated, Colby could turn the volume down on her hearing and the assault on her senses lessened. She couldn't stop thinking of him, couldn't prevent her mind from trying to tune itself to his.

"Ginny has food and drink prepared for the troops," Paul said. He cleared his throat. "I think you'd better come on out here. The fire captain wants to talk to you. Sean Everett found some things you should know about. There are kerosene containers, blackened, inside the stable."

Colby nodded and silently followed her brother back to the kitchen.

She took a deep breath to stay firmly in control. "Someone did set it, then." She said the words aloud to test them. It was such an impossible thing to believe. "Who would do such a thing?"

Sean shook his head. "I don't know, Colby, but the alarm system was dismantled completely and the sprinklers were tampered with. Whoever did it was very professional, very thorough. We were lucky to save the barn and outbuildings."

There was a long silence while Colby digested the implication of his words. Lifting her head, she looked around the room at the circle of grim-faced men, at Paul's pale features and little Ginny huddled uncertainly in a corner. Rafael stood tall beside her, his body protectively shielding the young girl from the eyes of the men in the room.

Instantly ashamed of herself, Colby gathered Ginny to her and brushed her sister's grimy forehead with a reassuring kiss. "I think there's been enough excitement for you, honey," she said firmly. "Thank you for all your help, the coffee and food for everybody. I would never have thought of it. Take a shower and crawl back into bed for a few hours. It's going to take a lot of hard work to repair everything." Colby glanced up at Rafael. *Thank you for looking after her.*

At once she felt the brush of fingers on her face, the smallest of caresses, yet Rafael hadn't moved, hadn't physically touched her. She could see the fatigue etched on his face. His eyes were covered with thick black glasses, the lenses so dark she couldn't see through them. Colby could still feel how tired and drained, how much pain he was in, although she felt him throw up a barrier so she couldn't feel his actual pain. She could see the Chevez brothers were concerned for him. They stood in a tight knot in front of the window, anxiety on their faces as they watched Rafael.

"What can we do?" Ginny was pleading. "We won't lose the ranch."

"No, little chickadee." Colby's gaze jumped to meet Rafael's above the little girl's head. "We won't lose our home. Skip off now, I'll be right in to tuck you in."

Reassured, Ginny went down the hall toward her bedroom. Paul couldn't be sent off to bed, insulated from bad news or shocks. Highly intelligent, he showed his sense of responsibility in nearly everything he did.

"Colby," Ben began, holding up a hand to stop her before she could speak. "No one thinks you set the fire. I've known you all of your life. You might burn down your own stable if you were mad enough, but not for insurance money and not with horses in it. Someone did it, though. Who could benefit?"

"Do you have any enemies?" Rafael asked quietly.

Her green gaze jumped to his face, her chin lifting belligerently. *Not until recently.* Rafael had spent the night with her on the ranch.

He had not been there when she woke up. The thought came unbidden, unwanted.

Be very careful of saying things you cannot take back, meu amor. Do not poison your brother's mind against his uncles or against me. You know better.

Part of her felt she might be losing her mind. "Not to my knowledge."

Sean rubbed the bridge of his nose thoughtfully. "You've corralled ninety percent of the training business around here. Anyone wanting to work with horses is out of luck."

"Most ranchers break and train their own horses. In any case, most of the ranches are cattle ranches. I don't see how I could be stepping on toes taking in horses to board or train. I've been doing it for years."

"What about this man Daniels Ginny was telling me about?" Rafael straightened from where he was leaning casually against the sink, a fluid motion of sheer grace and power. "Does he stand to gain the ranch?"

"Clinton Daniels may be the biggest creep in the world, but he's a wealthy man. He doesn't care whether he has this ranch or not. I wish it was that simple."

Julio Chevez cleared his throat. "Don Rafael, the sun has risen and you have been up all night. Perhaps Juan and I should stay here and oversee things while you return with Senhor Everett in the helicopter," he suggested.

Colby looked at him, for the first time really noticing the resemblance to his brother, Armando Chevez. She also realized he was nervous, very nervous, and it had something to do with Rafael De La Cruz. She studied the Chevez brothers. They were handsome men as Armando had been, as Paul would surely be. They were obviously wealthy in their own right, and very educated. They both were watching Rafael carefully, and both of them were definitely tense.

Rafael reached out in front of everyone, his palm curling possessively around the nape of her neck. "You may let it be known that
this woman and these children are under my protection. Should any
harm befall them, I will take a hand in the hunt for the person
responsible." He spoke the words almost formally, as if it was a
ritual she didn't understand. But if she didn't, the Chevez brothers
did. They looked at one another uneasily and one made the sign of
the cross, even as they nodded their acknowledgment of his words.

Rafael bent closer to her. "*Querida*, I will see to the legal papers
and return as soon as possible. You must try to eat something." Even
through his dark lenses she could feel his penetrating, mesmerizing
gaze. As tired as she was, Colby was afraid of falling forward and
drowning in Rafael's strong personality. Without turning his head,
Rafael added softly, "Paul, instruct Ginny to make vegetable soup
and insist Colby eat it. None of you must wander too far from home
in my absence. Juan and Julio will assist you with your work today."

Colby tried to shake her head. "That won't be necessary."

His thumb moved over her pulse in a long slow caress that sent
her blood pounding. "It is necessary, *meu lindo amor,* as I can do no
other than protect my own." Abruptly he released her, his black
gaze finding and pinning the Chevez brothers. "You will walk with
me to the helicopter." Rafael had circled the burn site, studying it
with more than human senses. The taint of the undead was there,
but the vampire had not been the one to start the fire. He may have
been the will behind it, but he had not done the actual work. Rafael
had no way of picking up the scent of the arsonist as too many volunteers had shown up to fight the fire. The men, who come from
the various ranches and the town, had been everywhere. He could
only wait for the next time, and Rafael was certain there would be
a next time. He might be helpless, locked in the ground, but he
would see to it that Colby was protected while he slept.

Paul's eyebrow shot up as he watched the group of men walking toward the helicopter, Sean talking earnestly to the fire captain, Rafael and the Chevez brothers a distance apart. Rafael had his arm draped affectionately around Julio's shoulders, but he obviously was giving them orders. "Protect my own? What does that mean, Colby?"

She had turned up the volume of her hearing again, finding it a useful tool now. "Shhh, just a minute." She could hear the captain reassuring Sean Everett he was certain Colby hadn't set the fire and thanking them for their help. But she couldn't hear a thing Rafael was saying to the Chevez brothers. And strangely, she couldn't hear what they said to him. But they were talking about Paul and Ginny and her. She was very certain of that. "Do you trust him, Paul, enough to put the ranch into his hands? Because if we borrow that money from him, that's exactly what we're doing."

Rafael De La Cruz removed the dark glasses and turned his head to look straight at her with glittering merciless eyes. She shivered and moved closer to her brother for protection. The helicopter was very loud, yet she knew he heard her question to Paul. Colby lifted her chin at him, pretending not to be intimidated. But she was. The Chevez brothers were not servants. They were wealthy businessmen, proud, strong men. They knew cattle and obviously worked their ranch. Yet they had exhibited signs of something very close to fear when speaking to Rafael. Who was he to have such an effect on them?

"If he comes back with the terms he stated to me, there's no problem," Paul said. "He didn't say we would have to go back to some other country; it was a straight-up loan. Of course, you'll have to go over everything carefully, I just don't see we have much choice."

"You're right, Paulo, it's just that everything is so awful. And he isn't a man who gives you something for nothing." *She had lain with him, her hands on his body while he took possession of her over and over.*

"I don't trust him." *His hands had been all over her, his body buried deep inside of hers.* "Even if he lends us the money for the mortgage, where are we going to get a new stable? All of the horses are a mess, their owners are going to be upset, and rightly so. And Shorty— what am I going to tell him? Butane was his up-and-coming hope for calf roping. Now he's dead. Shorty won't be so understanding that the fire was deliberately set." She was rambling and she knew it. Normally she would have shielded Paul from her fears, but she needed to talk, to think aloud. To keep her mind away from the shocking night she had spent with a virtual stranger. To keep from thinking someone hated them enough to burn down a stable filled with horses. To keep from dwelling on Pete's violent murder.

"Like you always tell us: one thing at a time," he reminded her. "We got through Mom dying. And we got through Dad being con-fined to bed. And then we made it through when he died. We can do this too, Colby. You're just tired."

The morning sun shone bright, holding the dark at bay for another day. She smiled a little at that, knowing ranch life contin-ued no matter what the drama. Animals had to be fed and watered. The world didn't stop turning because Colby Jansen was weary and depressed. Not even because her little corner of the world was tee-tering on the brink of disaster.

She watched the helicopter lift off until it was a small speck in the distance, then turned to stare at the smoldering ruins of her stable. It was almost too much to comprehend. Slowly Colby sank onto the porch swing, drawing her knees up, resting her arms on her legs. Who could hate them so much? Who could have done such a thing? First Pete and now this. Groaning softly she buried her face into her hands. She had to have a stable. A bank loan? If they bor-rowed the money from Rafael and the existing loan was cleared up . . .?

Paul laid a hand on her slender shoulder. "Stop sitting out here staring at it, you'll go crazy. Come in and get something to eat, or at least sleep for an hour or two. Rafael left those two men, my ..." He trailed off.

"Uncles," she inserted firmly. "We may as well take the time to get to know them." Her voice softened. "They do look a lot like Dad." And Rafael was gone. From her sight. Gone. Her body ached, was sore in places she hadn't known about, reminding her continually of his possession. Her heart pounded a drumbeat in her ears, in her throat. Grief welled up, a tight pressure in her chest. She wanted to believe it was grief over the burned stable, over the loss of an animal, but she feared it was her separation from Rafael De La Cruz.

7

Paul rubbed a hand over his face and looked at the black streaks left behind on his fingers. "I'm going to shower first. If I'm going to spend time with relatives, I'd rather do it looking halfway decent. You know how Dad was about details."

"Never forget the little things." They both repeated the creed together, then laughed. The sound was astonishing in the midst of the smoky smell of their ruined stable. "Don't worry so much." Paul leaned down and unexpectedly gave her a kiss on the top of her head. "We'll beat this just like we do everything."

Colby watched him disappear into the house, her heart filled with love for him. He didn't realize the implications of both incidents on the ranch. All the small annoying things like disappearing tools could be put down to petty larceny or misplaced implements. The broken gate and downed fences might have been because they were old. She could write things off as coincidence. But Pete's murder and someone burning their stable to the ground could not be written off that easily. Somehow they were connected. And that meant that Paul and Ginny could be in danger.

She moved down the steps, her gaze on the brothers from Brazil.

They were talking quietly to each other, still some distance away. Without Rafael's protection she could hear them clearly and she unashamedly eavesdropped. These men had come thousands of miles to claim Paul and Ginny, to take possession of the ranch. They did not believe a woman should be running such a business. She knew nothing about them, and only God knew whether they were capable of the terrible atrocities committed on her property. Both spoke in Portuguese, but Colby had learned the language from her stepfather.

It was the one called Juan who spoke. "I have never seen him like this before. Not with anyone else. Nicolas and Rafael never tolerate being away from our homeland long. And he thanked me for my help. He put his arm around my shoulders. I do not recall a single instance when he did such a thing in my lifetime."

"He did the same to me," Julio answered. "Something is different here and I think it is Colby. It is not right, Juan. They need the freedom of the rain forest, away from so many people. Nicolas has gone to the hacienda to be alone, but Rafael will not leave now." Julio's voice betrayed his worry.

"I do not know what is happening, but he is different here. He is not so cold, yet he is more dangerous. And I think it is Colby also. There will be blood and death if this is not resolved. We must be vigilant day and night now," Juan added.

Colby paused on the steps, her fingers wrapped tightly around the railing until her knuckles turned white. Blood and death? Were they referring to Rafael? Was he so capable of bringing about blood and death that they were obviously worried? She let her breath out slowly. Rafael was cursed with unexpected talents just as she had been. The special gifts weren't always easy to control, especially when surrounded by too many people. Emotions played a tremendous part. She had "done things" before, when she was much younger. She had been upset and started fires more than once just by staring angrily at something too long. She had been responsible for the terrible landslide that had blocked the entrance to the mine and trapped her for so many hours. There had been accidents, mistakes, and they were truly frightening.

Colby could understand why Rafael didn't want to be around people and why he preferred the freedom of the wilds. The continual bombardment of smells and sounds on heightened senses was difficult and wearing. She loved the mountains and needed the solace of them. His brother, Nicolas, must have the same talents. Both of them seemed remarkably cold and ruthless when she'd first met them. She didn't like Nicolas, yet Rafael . . . She walked over to inspect the horses. Her heart did a funny little flip. Heat moved through her body. She wouldn't make up her mind about him yet.

She thought of the way his eyes looked at her with such intense hunger. He hadn't seemed cold then. And there was the way he had been with Ginny. Gentle and caring. Protective even. Rafael had healing abilities. He had worked on the animals after she had. His hands had been quick and sure, the horses calm around him as he whispered to them. But then again, Rafael could look as cold as ice, as intimidating as a jungle cat stalking prey.

Colby examined the horses again. The burns looked better and the horses were less restless. All of them still showed signs of trauma, shaking, sweating even, but none of them showed signs of smoke inhalation. She spent an hour with them, seeing to the wounds and soothing them. The danger of infection was high and she made a mental note to call the vet out a second time just to make certain they were all doing well. The animals were used to her and trusted her. It was obvious they were comforted by her presence.

Colby was aware of the Chevez brothers working at feeding and watering the animals. They were hard workers, not sitting on the porch sullenly because they had been ordered to stay and watch over the children. They seemed powerful in their own right, yet they did what Rafael commanded. Why would they choose to do what he said? Was it of their own free will? Were they afraid of him?

Colby went to the corral to saddle one of her working horses. She did it with the ease of long practice, but she was so tired, she would have used telekinesis if the Chevez brothers hadn't been so closely observing her. Juan wandered over to lean his weight casually against the gate. Up close he looked so much like Armando she was afraid if she looked at him she might cry. She was becoming altogether too emotional. It wasn't safe.

"What can I do for you?" She didn't let her eyes meet his.

"Which horse shall I use?" He asked it gently.

His accent and voice were very like her stepfather's. She looked away from him over the back of her horse to the shadowy foothills. They were dark even with the sun shining. "Are you planning on following me?"

"*Sim, senhorita*—yes. It might not be safe to go riding. Don Rafael has said you are under his protection. This is no small thing. In any case, my brother's *família* is my *família*. I wish to see to your safety."

Colby thought about arguing but one glance at his set features told her it wouldn't make any difference, he would simply follow her. Besides, she was curious. She gestured toward a paint. "He's a steady horse, and there's a saddle in the barn you can use." It had been her father's saddle, but she didn't tell him that. She hadn't thought about all the tack they had lost, including Ginny's custom-made saddle. Ginny hadn't said a word. How would Colby ever replace that saddle?

Colby pushed away the need to explode with pain and sorrow. *Who had done this?* Rafael had been in the tack room with her. And King, Ginny's dog. Why hadn't he barked? She had sent him to the barn to sleep. She had seen him earlier in the morning watching the fire fighters. *He hadn't barked when Rafael had come to visit her.* She distinctly remembered that. Cautiously she pulled her hat lower over her eyes and took a quick look at Julio. Presumably he was staying to look after the children. Did she trust him?

While Juan was saddling the paint, she swung down and hurried across the yard back into the house. Paul and Ginny had gone back to bed and were asleep, King curled up on Ginny's bed. Colby issued a firm command to the dog to guard them. The border collie was well trained and she knew it would alert them should Julio come near the house. At the last minute she strapped on the holster she often used when riding the fences. Sometimes cattle stepped in ground squirrel holes and broke a leg, other times rattlesnakes bit them. She needed to carry the gun for emergencies. Catching up her rifle she hurried back to her horse. This time Juan was ready and in the saddle. He looked born to ride, easy, natural, a fluid rider. He raised his eyebrow when he saw her rifle but said nothing.

"My brother was an excellent horseman," he said, easily reading the sorrow in her eyes when she watched the way he moved in the saddle. "Even as a young man he could outride most of us."

Colby looked away from him quickly, swallowing the lump in her throat. "He used to put me in front of him when I was just a toddler and we'd ride all over the ranch together. He taught me to ride."

"You perform the same ritual as he always did before mounting your horse." Juan smiled in memory. "We used to tease him over it. He always patted the horse's neck and ran his hand along the chest and front legs, patted a second time, then swung on, most of the time without even using the stirrups."

Colby felt the memory rising, vivid and painful. Armando had been an amazing horseman and he loved the animals. He'd instilled that same love in Colby. "He was incredible with the horses," she said. "I've never seen anyone better."

"He would want his children to know his *família*," Juan said, his voice gentle.

Colby leaned down to open a gate. "What did you expect, that I would just turn my brother and sister over to you? Perfect strangers? Is it so wrong of me not to allow strangers to drag my family off to a foreign country? Tell me, would you have done so?"

Juan pushed his hat farther back on his head. "No, *senhorita*, I would never give my *família* over to those I did not know. Armando wrote to us on his deathbed to come for his children. *All* of his children. It was his dying wish that you would come to us. My brother made it abundantly clear that he considered you his daughter and his heir. We came for all of you."

"You came five years too late. I wrote to your family when the accident occurred and no one responded. And three years ago I wrote the letter again when he was on his deathbed. There wasn't a single sentence in it about me." Her green eyes touched his face, skittered away. She wished there had been something in the letter, but she had written it word for word as Armando had dictated it to her. She didn't want Juan to see her disappointment over not being adopted by Armando, or the anger she felt at Juan's lying, reflected on her transparent face.

The sun was beginning to make its way through the thick bank of clouds shrouding the mountains and, for some reason, Colby's eyes were ultrasensitive. The light stabbed at her so that she pulled the brim of her hat lower to shadow her face. Even so, her eyes hurt, burning in the morning sun.

Juan swung the gate closed after them. "Armando must have added to the letter. His hand was shaky and we would not have known but for his crest."

"He couldn't have. He could hardly move at the end." Colby said it stiffly, not looking at him. Her stepfather had asked her to leave the letter on his nightstand so he could look it over in case there was something more to be said. The next morning, the letter was folded neatly and Colby had inserted it into the envelope and sent it off. She wanted Juan to be telling the truth, but she was afraid if Armando hadn't included her it would break her heart, and if he had, she might cry a river of tears.

"Did you ever know Armando to tell you a lie?" Juan asked it quietly while the leather of their saddles creaked and the horses' hooves chinked against rock. A melody she found soothing, one she remembered from her childhood with her stepfather.

Colby shook her head mutely.

"I would not dishonor my brother's memory by telling you a lie either."

Colby rode for a few minutes in silence, turning the information over in her mind. "That's why your grandfather refused to answer him, isn't it?" she guessed shrewdly. "He didn't have me put it in the letter myself, because he didn't want me to know your family rejected him because of me."

"Do not mistake that it was *a família.*"

She looked at him then, her green eyes alive with a fierce pride. "The De La Cruz family, then? They didn't want me to ruin their spotless reputation with my lack of a name?"

Juan sighed softly. "The De La Cruz brothers are not interested in such things. They do not concern themselves with the lives of others. This is solely the responsibility of my *avô*. He did not tell my father or any of us of Armando's letters. Had he done so, we would have come at once. I cannot tell you how much sorrow this has caused our *família.*"

"Armando was happy with my mother," Colby told him, leading the way through a narrow canyon that emptied out into the flats where most of her cattle were spread out. She rode straight to the small barn where the hay was stored and urged her mount inside. The sun was really bothering her eyes now, and the shadows of the barn provided some relief. She must have suffered some damage in the fire without realizing it. Even her skin seemed ultrasensitive, burning fiercely wherever the sunlight touched her.

Juan followed her, silently cursing his grandfather's snobbery. "I am certain it is so. He would never have stayed in another country away from his *família* had he not found something better."

Colby dismounted, the movement swift and fluid despite the fact that she was short. She moved efficiently, with no wasted motion. Juan had to admire her abilities as she began to toss the flakes of hay. "Where does the De La Cruz family fit into all this?" Colby asked it with studied casualness.

There was a small telling silence. Colby knew the man was choosing his words carefully as he worked beside her. "Their *família* is ancient, as is ours. The two families have been intertwined for hundreds of years. Who knows how far back it goes? We look after their estates, and they look after us. We have existed that way for so long we have become one *família.*"

"But you have your own money and lands."

"That is true, but our families have a symbiotic relationship. What is good for De La Cruz is good for us. They have special abilities and we aid them in other areas."

He was telling her something, yet nothing at all. For some unknown reason, something in his voice sent a shiver down Colby's spine. "What are they like?"

"There are five De La Cruz brothers. The others are all much like Rafael and Nicolas." Juan paused for a moment. "Do you do this work by yourself every day?"

There was a hint of censure in his voice, although she could tell he tried to keep it out. "My brother helps me and I had a man, Pete Jessup, working for me."

Juan leaned on his pitchfork. "The man found dead." He made

the sign of the cross reverently. "That was not a good place for you to be riding by yourself."

Colby shrugged carelessly. "I do it all the time. Someone has to."

He shook his head. "It is not safe. That is not a good place. It felt . . ." He made the sign of the cross a second time. "It felt evil to me. I do not think those men would have allowed you to leave had Senhor Everett's rider and I not been there watching."

"I could have handled them," Colby said, not certain she was telling the truth.

"This cannot continue. The things you do are too dangerous."

She shoved a hand impatiently through her hair. "Fortunately for me, I don't have to answer to anyone." There was sheer defiance in her voice and an open challenge. "I run this ranch, Mr. Chevez. That means I have to ride everywhere and work like a man."

"But you are not a man," Juan pointed out patiently. "Don Rafael will not allow this to continue. He is a man who will have his way and it is not good to oppose him. If he decrees otherwise, do not attempt to defy him."

Colby stopped working and looked directly at him for the first time. Her green eyes blazed at him. "Rafael De La Cruz may be a big man where you are, but here, on my ranch, in my little corner of the world, his opinion means this." She snapped her fingers. "He doesn't rule me or my brother or sister."

Juan shook his head slowly. "You do not know Don Rafael, *sen-horita;* he is not like other men. You are Armando's daughter and therefore *minha sobrinha,* my niece. You do not wish to claim the relationship, but I must look after you the way he wanted us to. I do not want you to test this man."

Did she hear the faint sound of fear in his voice again? "Why should you worry? Rafael De La Cruz has nothing to do with me. Hopefully he will be gone very soon." As soon as the words left her mouth, fear almost amounting to terror gripped her. The thought was unbearable. It was more than grief, an inconsolable grief. The mark on her neck throbbed and burned in protest.

"Don Rafael is a very influential and powerful man. He is not like other men." Juan was obviously searching for the right words. "The De La Cruz brothers are not as we are. They are formidable opponents and make harsh, unrelenting enemies."

Colby kept her smiles to herself. Obviously Juan knew Rafael and his brothers were gifted with unique talents, which she had begun to discover through her own touch of those gifts. He did not want to betray a confidence, yet he was attempting to warn her. She found it rather sweet. "I doubt that I could do anything to make Rafael notice me enough to make him my enemy. I've seen him in action. Quite the ladies' man." Even saying the words seemed to hurt, but Colby didn't want to examine too closely why that might be.

"You mistake him, Colby," Juan said. "Don Rafael is a man of honor. And there is something different about him since he has shown interest in you. I saw him with the little one. He was very gentle with her and protective. Don Rafael has never shown much interest in children. He has rescued them when it was necessary, but as a matter of duty, not the way he was with your sister. I have never seen this unusual behavior in him. And he is different with me, more open in his emotions."

She didn't want to think too much about Rafael. She rubbed her eyes and could tell they were beginning to swell severely. Tears were streaming unchecked down her face now and she couldn't stop them. "I think the fire somehow hurt my eyes," she murmured by way of explanation. "If you go home, Rafael would go home too. I had the impression both brothers were anxious to leave here immediately."

Juan looked at her closely, his eyes dwelling on the strange mark on her neck. "I am afraid it is too late for that," he said ominously.

He looked very alarmed, his gaze remaining on the blemish, all at once speculative.

Colby sighed heavily and, to keep from self-consciously covering the mark like an embarrassed teenager, added another flake of hay to the feeders. "Just say it straight out, Mr. Chevez. You can't have it both ways, you know. One minute you can't be implying I'm a good influence on him and the next that he might in some way be trying to harm me. If there's some reason you think I'm in danger from Rafael De La Cruz, you may as well tell me." Her gaze settled on his face. "I'm not afraid of him." That was a terrible lie, but she persisted, trying to force Juan into admission. "Has he threatened me in some way? You don't think he was responsible for what happened to the stable, do you?" She would have looked at him challengingly but her eyes were far too swollen. And she was tired. Her arms and legs felt leaden. She wanted to lie down in the hay and go to sleep.

"Don Rafael would never do such a thing." Juan sounded horrified at the mere suggestion. But he didn't look horrified; he looked worried. "I think we should go back to the house; you are unwell."

A protest began in her mind, but she did feel terrible, the skin on her face and forearms already burning fiercely. Her eyes felt like redhot needles were poking into them. Even within the shelter of the barn, she felt the light poised to attack. Worse, she was constantly thinking of Rafael. He was invading her mind to the point of driving out every practical thought she had. No matter how strong her will was, she couldn't seem to stop from thinking of him, needing to see him. Colby had never considered herself a woman who would need a man so much she pined for him, yet she wanted desperately to hear his voice, to touch him, to see for herself he was alive and well.

"Please, *senhorita*, the sun is burning your skin. I am most concerned, perhaps I can take you back to the house." Juan had already made up his mind to take her back. He could see she was in trouble and he was being as polite as possible. If anything happened to her, Rafael would hold him responsible. He was very worried. Colby's skin was blistering in the sun, and her eyes were very sensitive to the light. Very much like what happened to the De La Cruz brothers. Juan had never seen the phenomenon in a human. Now he was really alarmed and wanted to talk with Julio.

"I should check on the kids," Colby capitulated, "and get the vet out again to check on the horses." She longed for the relief of the coolness of the ranch house. She wanted to gather Ginny and Paul into her arms and have everything return to normal once again. More than all of that, she needed desperately to see Rafael, to touch him. To know that he was alive. *Where are you?*

Rafael lay locked deep within the earth. Around him the rejuvenating soil offered a soothing comfort to the terrible burns over his arms and face where the unrelenting sun had beaten down on him. He had not been able to leave Colby until he was certain the danger to her was past, so he had stayed far longer in the morning hours than he had ever managed before. His eyes, even lying in the earth, burned and wept from the sunlight. Even obscured by the heavy cloud cover, he had paid a high price to be with her.

Why had the vampire's scent been near the stable, yet the cause of the fire human? Was the vampire using a puppet—a human servant—to destroy Colby? Nicolas was right, he had no choice but to bring her fully into his world where he could protect her at all times.

On that thought came another much more disagreeable one. It was difficult to lie helplessly in the ground while Colby was facing danger without his protection. How would she feel if she lay beside him deep within the earth and little Ginny was in danger or in need? His heart gave a strange lurch. The issue was far more complex than he had first considered. It would be much simpler if he only thought of himself, his own needs and desires. A savage fury seemed to burn through his soul. Colby would wither away beneath the earth, her gentle compassionate soul devastated at a separation between her and her younger siblings. She loved them as if they were her own children. A fierce, protective love, with every fiber of her being. The way he wanted her to love him.

His swearing was eloquent, the words echoing harshly in his mind. He had brought her partially into his world without a thought for what it would mean to her and her life. Her dreams. For what was important to her. She was uncomfortable without him, restless, and the sun was beginning to climb high. Colby was an independent woman, she wasn't even certain she liked him. She was confused by her inability to keep from wanting him, her need to touch his mind, to know he was safe. Rafael could only lie helpless beneath the ground knowing he had contributed to Colby's distress. No, it was more than that; he was directly responsible for her distress.

He had gone to ground near Colby's ranch house, better to feel the first vibrations of danger to her. He had felt so close to her the night before, lying beside her on the bed, listening to her breathing. She was so beautiful. Not just her body, but her heart and soul. She seemed to shine from the inside out. Not one of the firefighters who knew her, not one of the ranchers, had entertained the idea that she could have set the fire for the insurance money. There was something about Colby that just drew people like a magnet. And made them believe in her.

He lay with his body a dead weight, unable to move a muscle as he contemplated the problems he was facing. He didn't want Colby above ground where he couldn't protect her. He wanted to be with her. Not wanted, he *needed* to be with her. He would not go through another day unable to sleep the healing sleep of his people, *terrified* of losing her. He wouldn't do it. He would complete the ritual and drag her kicking and screaming into his world. Consequences be damned. She belonged with him. Was made for him, his other half. He had a right to her. Once in Brazil he could make amends, win her love. She would be locked to him for all time. Eternity. She wouldn't be able to leave him and she would have to learn to accept her fate.

Rafael tried to force his mind away from her in an attempt to close himself off and regain his enormous strength. He could hear her heart beating. He could feel her above the earth, her heart seeking the reassurance of his. He could feel her mind tuning itself in an attempt to find his. He had succeeded in making two blood exchanges. She was already partially in his world. Alarm hit him hard. Her skin would be sensitive to the sun, her eyes would water and burn.

Colby was used to being out in the harsh sunlight, she wouldn't think to protect herself. He made a concentrated effort and touched her, mind to mind, partially to alleviate her distress and partially to relieve his own. At once he felt her pain, the burning of her skin and eyes. She was hungry, yet she was having trouble eating. She needed to touch him often and she was terribly confused by the unfamiliar need. A low sound escaped, a groan of despair. How could he have been so selfish? He had thought only of his needs, his desires. He hadn't stopped to think of the consequences to her. Colby would suffer terribly this day and it was through his own selfishness. In that moment, he hated himself.

Rafael knew he had no choice now, he had to take her back to Brazil with him where he could adequately protect her, yet she wouldn't be happy without Ginny and Paul. *He could never make her happy without her younger siblings.* The thought crept unbidden into his mind and stayed there. A thorn. The truth. He heard her then, the soft cry of her heart to his. *Where are you?* It took tremendous strength and willpower for him to overcome the paralysis and lethargy of his kind at the hour with the sun climbing high. He reached for her with his heart and mind. *Colby?* The lightest of touches. An inquiry.

Colby tried to fight against the terrible pain in her eyes, plus the blinding headache that was so relentless she felt her head gripped in a vise. Her eyes were streaming and swollen and hurting so bad she kept them closed most of the time against the onslaught of the sun. Her forearms were red and small blisters were actually forming. Colby was a redhead, but her skin had long since become accustomed to the sun. She couldn't believe she was so sensitive. She urged her mount to pick up speed and covered her eyes with one hand, nearly unable to guide the animal. Juan reached out and took the reins in silence, leading her back to the ranch house.

She heard the sound of a voice stirring softly in her mind, a flutter of butterfly wings brushing against the walls of her mind. Rafael. His voice was unbelievably mesmerizing and her heart latched onto it immediately. Why had she been so afraid that something terrible had happened to him? It had been a stone weighing her down, crushing her until she could barely think straight.

Rafael! She couldn't keep the relief out of her voice or mind.

I am resting. I will come to you this evening. Sleep and allow Juan and Julio to aid Paul with the work this day. He slipped a slight "push" into his voice, but already his strength was gone, ebbing away from him into her mind.

Colby knew something was wrong with him, she could feel it, his need for rest, for healing. *You're hurt. I can feel pain in your mind.*

It is your pain.

Don't lie to me.

Lifemates do not lie to one another. I feel your pain as my own. He gave a small sigh. *The sun took its toll on me as well. I heal quickly. You must sleep, querida.*

Colby tried to probe his mind further to assess his injuries, but it was impossible. She gave up, the task too difficult in the face of her waning strength. *I think we both need sleep, Rafael.* She was shocked at how easy it was becoming to communicate with him. How right it felt. As if they did belong together, two halves of the same whole. *You've brainwashed me.*

The terrible pressure in her chest weighing her down was gone and all at once she felt much happier. Her eyes were too painful to open, her skin was burning, and the stable was gone, yet she was inexplicably happy just to hear his voice. Knowing he was reading her thoughts and probably feeling smug, she directed one last message to him. *How sickening of me.*

Although Colby went into the barn to get out of the sun, she found she couldn't open her eyes even in the darkened interior. She managed to dismount, but was forced to cling blindly to her horse until Juan steadied the animal, holding the reins. "You go on in, I'll see to the horse."

"Colby!" Paul raced into the barn, seeing his sister stagger as she dismounted. "What happened?" He glared at his uncle as he wrapped his arm around her smaller figure. "What did you do to her?" His voice was filled with belligerence and suspicion.

"Paul . . . " Colby's voice was a gentle warning. "My eyes hurt. I can't see very well. I must have damaged them in the fire earlier. Your uncle was just trying to help me." She leaned into him, relying on him together into the house. "Don't be rude." She buried her face into his shirt, stumbling blindly against him across the yard to the ranch house. She didn't dare open her eyes. Now that she was home her eyes seemed to hurt even more.

Ginny rushed to her side. "What happened? You're sunburned,

Colby, it's really bad." At once she soaked a towel in cold water and pressed it into her sister's hands.

Colby held the cool towel to her swollen eyes. She sank into a chair. "I can't believe how much this hurts. I've never been so glad to be home."

"I can drive you into town to the doctor," Paul offered.

Colby took a deep breath and shook her head. "I think I just want to lie down for an hour or so." She felt exhausted, the need to sleep so strong in her she was afraid she might succumb right there in the kitchen. She rubbed at her pounding temples. "I have so much to do."

"I called the vet," Ginny volunteered; "he's coming out again this afternoon. The chickens are fed and the garden is watered. The fire marshal has someone coming to investigate the fire. Paul made all the calls to the owners of the horses. Well, except Shorty." Ginny hesitated a moment, glancing up at her brother. Colby was never sick. She'd been injured on many occasions but she rarely had gone to bed during the day, not even after a long difficult calving. "Oh, and I called Tanya Everett and asked if she and her mother could come over this evening instead of this afternoon." She ducked her head, her eyes skittering away from Paul's. "I was going to cancel altogether, but she sounded so lonely and I thought maybe I could ride with her in the corral. If you want me to put her off, I will, Colby."

"No, of course not, chickadee." Colby pressed the cooling cloth closer, desperately trying to take the heat from her skin and eyes. "I'm so tired, I really need to rest for a couple of hours. Will you wake me later?"

"Come on." Paul helped her up and led her down the hall to her room. "Don't worry about anything, I can take care of it."

Colby removed the cloth from her eyes to peer at her brother. The light shining through the window hit her with alarming radiance. Immediately she squeezed her eyes shut tight again and hid in the damp, soothing cloth. "Pull the curtain closed, Paulo."

He obeyed her, pulling the heavy drapes across the opening to darken the room. "Are you sure I shouldn't take you to the doctor, Colby? Maybe your eyes were burned in the fire." He sounded very young and scared.

"I think they're just sensitive, Paul, and I'm so tired." She lay on her bed, reaching her hand blindly toward him. "I need to talk to you about Juan and Julio Chevez. They're here to help you and I think you should be respectful as they are our father's brothers. On the other hand, with all the strange things happening around here, I think you should keep an eye on them. I mean it, Paul. Just make sure you and Ginny are safe." She wiggled uncomfortably until Paul reached out to unstrap her side holster.

Colby could still smell Rafael on her sheets and pillow. She wanted to press her face into the cotton and inhale.

"I don't think wearing a gun to bed is in fashion this year. Where'd you leave your rifle?" Paul asked abruptly. His sister looked very fragile all of a sudden.

"In the scabbard. I think Juan was unsaddling the horse. Get it back in the gun rack, Paul, and be sure to unload it."

Ginny bustled in, pushing Paul aside with her small hip. "I've brought some aloe vera. Just lay there and let me smear it on you." She glanced worriedly up at Paul. "She's so tired all the time, Paul. Do you think she's sick? She didn't eat all day yesterday or this morning. She didn't even have a cup of tea."

A smile flirted with the corners of Colby's mouth. "I am here, Ginny. You don't need to talk about me in the third person."

"You know Colby," Paul said decisively, not wanting Ginny to worry, "she's been getting up a couple of hours early to go hunt for . . ." He trailed off, aware Pete Jessup was a dangerous subject. "Just keep an eye on her, Ginny, and stay in the house with her.

Keep King with you too." He spoke gruffly, suddenly feeling the tremendous responsibility for his two sisters.

Ginny rolled her eyes as he swaggered out, Colby's holster in his hands. "Big mistake, Colby, giving that dork power. Next thing you know he'll be impossible to live with." She gathered up Colby's hair, surprised Colby didn't move at all. Ginny bent closer. Colby had already fallen asleep. Ginny sat on the edge of the bed staring intently at her sister, her fingers automatically plaiting the thick strands into one loose braid. There was something different about Colby. It was so subtle Ginny couldn't figure out exactly what it was. Despite the terrible sunburn, Colby *looked* different, more ... everything. Ginny felt comforted sitting beside Colby, but she wished her sister hadn't gone to sleep so quickly. She needed to talk to her.

Ginny leaned very close. "It's all my fault, Colby. I wish you could hear me." She whispered the words against her sister's neck, against the strange mark branding her skin. "I did it, Colby."

Colby lay perfectly still, her breathing even and regular, looking like an angel in her sleep. A tear leaked out of Ginny's eye and trickled down her cheek until it dropped onto Colby's neck, onto the distinctive mark. At once Colby moved, her hand reaching out until she found Ginny's. "You could never have done such a thing." Her voice was soft and drowsy. There was a faint smile in the tone.

"I didn't *start* it," Ginny admitted, sniffing a little. "But I called King in. I waited until you were asleep and I called him into my room and shut the door. I *hate* sleeping without him. I still have nightmares about Mom and Dad dying. About you dying. I don't want anything to happen to you. Not ever."

Colby made a tremendous effort to stir. She had never felt so tired, her body so leaden she felt weighted down. She managed to lace her fingers even tighter through Ginny's fingers. "Baby, why would that make you responsible? You probably saved his life. Whoever started that fire didn't think about the horses locked inside. They wouldn't have hesitated at killing our dog if he had tried to alert us." Because she was so tired, Colby wasn't censoring her words as she ordinarily might have.

"I shouldn't have called him in—then Shorty's horse wouldn't have been killed." Ginny buried her face deeper into Colby's neck so that the mark throbbed like a heartbeat.

Colby roused herself further, slipping her arm around Ginny. "Don't be so scared, honey, we aren't going to lose our home. No one will separate us. I love you and Paul. This was not your fault."

"Mom and Dad went away." Ginny choked back a flood of tears.

"I know, sweetheart. Dad tried to stay with us as long as he could. I know it was hard on you, but no one is going to separate us."

"What if those people take you to court and make us go to Brazil with them?" Ginny's little body was shaking.

Colby drew the comforter over her, surrounding both of them with its warmth and soothing properties. "I don't think they will, Ginny. But if they did, I don't think they'd win. And if they did somehow manage to win, well, I talked to Juan today. He's your uncle, Dad's brother, and he said they wanted me to go along. I would never let them take you without going along as well."

"You could marry Rafael De La Cruz," Ginny said suddenly. "If you did they would never be able to separate us because he's the boss."

Alarm spread through Colby, her body tightening. The thought of being married to Rafael De La Cruz was daunting. He would rule her absolutely. She could see it in the stamp of arrogance on his face, the heat in his heavy-lidded smoldering eyes. She had no way of combating his hold over her. Colby still hadn't opened her eyes and didn't want to. "Has he been talking to you?"

"Only this morning in the kitchen when everyone was looking at me and I was so scared. He was nice to me. He talked about Dad, and when Dad was little, and he said you weren't hurt very bad and not to worry, things had a way of working out. He said you were beautiful." Ginny clutched tightly at Colby's hand. "He made me feel safe and stood in front of me when I was crying so no one could see me."

"That was very nice of him. Rafael seemed to be everywhere this morning. Fighting the fire, healing the horses, helping me, and now I hear he was looking out for you." Colby's voice sounded far away as if she was sliding back to sleep. She turned her face into the coolness of the pillow, inhaled Rafael's scent, and covered the mark on her neck with her palm, holding it like a caress against her skin.

"He said it wasn't my fault and to talk to you about it," Ginny persisted.

"He was right, baby, it wasn't your fault. I'm glad you called the dog last night. From now on if you need King you just go ahead and call him in every night. Ginny? I'm really tired, honey, I need to sleep."

"Do you like him?"

"Like who?" Colby asked, drifting further into a dream.

"Rafael. Do you like him?"

Colby smiled again. "No." Her voice was soft and sensuous.

Ginny snuggled closer, a pleased smile on her face. "Yes, you do, I can tell by your voice."

8

The sun was slow in sinking behind the mountain, and dark ominous clouds began to float across the sky. The sky seemed alive with orange and red hues, as if the entire heavens were on fire. Deep below the earth a single heart began to beat and Rafael awoke, his eyes snapping open, his first breath releasing in a long slow hiss of fury. Somewhere above him Colby's distress had awakened him from his rejuvenating slumber. She was fighting back tears, her mind chaotic and fearful.

Rafael scanned the area to ensure he was completely alone before he burst through the surface, dirt spewing into the air like a geyser. He rose high into the air, shape-shifting as he did so, choosing the familiar form of the strong and powerful harpy eagle. Spreading his wings, he climbed even higher, grateful for the thickening cloud cover guarding his sensitive eyes. He soared above the ranch, inspecting the region closely, looking for potential trouble.

The ranch seemed quiet enough, yet he knew Juan had found a steer, horribly mutilated, the animal killed quite recently. It had been a brutal, savage act, and the steer had been left in the water hole. He had taken the information from Colby's mind. He read

Paul's mind as the boy stood in the shadows of the porch watching the bloodred sunset and talking with his sister. In the body of the bird, Rafael flew higher and higher, unashamedly listening to every word of the conversation taking place below him, his sharp eyes taking in every movement on the ground, seeking to find hidden danger to his lifemate.

"Were you with Juan when he found the steer?" Colby persisted. "How long was he out of your sight?" She was still fighting the effects of sleep, making a concentrated effort to be alert and listen to every detail of the distressing news.

"The fence was down near the field, Colby," Paul said, his young voice weary. "I told Juan I could handle it by myself. They're fast workers, and they know what they're doing. I wanted you to be able to sleep. I thought if we split up we'd get more work done. I know you told me to keep an eye on both of them, but I worked with them most of the day and I . . . " He trailed off. "I'm sorry, Colby."

She reached out to pull his hat lower over his eyes, a loving gesture meant to reassure him. "But you liked them," she finished for him. "I don't really think Juan killed the steer, Paul. It wouldn't be sensible to kill a steer, drag it into the water hole, and then 'find' it just so we could take it back out. The animal would have to be there for a while to foul the water hole. My guess is, whoever did this had that as their intention and Juan stumbled upon it too soon."

"But he might have done it."

Colby sighed. "Maybe. Did you look for tracks? Did you take a look at his clothes? His knife?"

Paul's face colored slightly. "I should have. He didn't leave it in the water. He pulled the carcass out before he came after me." Paul *did* like his uncles, both of them. They were hard workers and knowledgeable. They treated him like an equal, and they reminded him of his father. Paul was beginning to feel affection and a great deal of respect for both of his uncles and he wanted them to feel the same way about him. He hadn't searched for evidence or tracks because it hadn't occurred to him either one of them could be responsible, but now he was confused.

Colby nodded. "We both would have gotten a carcass out of the water. We can hardly fault him for that." She shook her head. "I'm very worried; someone is definitely trying to shut us down. We're operating on a thin financial margin as it is." She glanced around her to ensure Ginny wasn't close by and lowered her voice another notch. "You aren't a little kid anymore, Paul. I don't know who we can trust and who we should be afraid of. But someone murdered Pete. It wasn't an accident. He didn't have money, there was no reason to try to rob him, someone burned down our stable, and now they've killed one of our steers and left it in a water hole deliberately to foul it."

"What did Ben say?" Paul took off his hat and raked a hand through his hair.

"I called him, of course, and he should be arriving any minute. The Everetts are coming for a riding lesson too." When Paul snickered, Colby glared at him. "I expect you to be on your best behavior. This means a lot to Ginny, she wants a friend. We both forget how hard it is for her. You can visit your friends, but she's stuck out here."

Paul kicked at a rock. "Yeah, I have so many chances to visit friends, Colby. I work from sunup to sundown."

"I know you do." Colby looked away from him, struggling not to cry. She couldn't remember a single day in her life for the last five years that she hadn't worked from sunup until sundown and often through the night as well. "What did the vet say about the horses?"

"You did a fantastic job. You and De La Cruz. Watch them carefully for infection, and mainly the scars will be emotional, not physical. They're traumatized and will need work." He looked at her. "Your job, Colby, you're the one good with horses. Did you notice how they reacted to De La Cruz? They were calm around him and he seemed to really know what he was doing. His lawyer called, by the way." His voice had turned very casual. He tried not to notice how Colby stiffened. "He drew up papers for a loan and is sending them by way of Sean Everett for us to look over. De La Cruz will be here later this evening."

"He's probably out entertaining the tall blonde he likes to play with," Colby said. She needed to keep her perspective with Rafael. He was a ladies' man. Just because he made her feel things she'd never felt before, just because he whispered beautiful things in the night didn't mean he wasn't saying and doing the same things to other women. Colby was fairly certain she was going to wake up one morning soon with a head full of gray hair just worrying about everything.

You certainly have strange ideas.

Colby's fingers curled around the porch railing at the whisper of intimacy in her mind. She looked around her carefully, feeling he was close. Her body ached. Her breasts were suddenly sore. At the sound of his sinfully sexy voice her blood began to heat. *Go away. I don't want to talk to you right now.* That was a blatant lie, but she didn't want to face him, face the night with the memory of his body buried deep within hers. Face the accusations she made in the middle of his helping her or the fact that she was going to take his money to bail out their ranch.

Yes, you do. I am in your mind. Why do you never seek to enter my mind?

Beneath her long lashes Colby glanced guiltily at her brother. She couldn't help herself. She was drawn to Rafael in spite of every fear she had. In spite of the fact that he was there to take away her family. She had hidden her strange, unique talents for so long and there was always the fear of discovery. There was always an empty place inside of her. There was such loneliness in the middle of the night that sometimes Colby would stare up at the stars and wish she could just disappear. And the work. The endless work. Rafael held her in strong arms. He took charge and directed everyone in a crisis. His strength alone was a seductive lure. And his body ...

I think whatever is in your mind would scare me. Did you do something to me to make me need so much sleep? She blushed at the thought of it, of the dark erotic dream she couldn't seem to stop replaying during the day or while she slept any more than she could stop the way her body ached and needed him in an unfamiliar way.

Rafael's voice held warmth and laughter, complete male satisfaction. He was nearly purring. *We did a lot of things to make you need to sleep.*

She could feel the flush spreading up her neck and into her face. She should have known better than to open the subject with him. It was humiliating to talk to him or face him, thinking of the things she'd let him do to her, yet when she was alone, she thought of his body and the way he could make her feel continually.

"Aren't you going to ask me what Mr. De La Cruz said about the terms of the loan?" Paul burst out, unable to contain himself any longer. His sister's attention seemed far away, she had a peculiar, almost dreamy look on her face. Colby looked startled, as if she'd forgotten he was there. She even blushed. "Well? It could save the ranch, Colby."

She touched the toe of her boot to the head of a nail on the steps. "We could lose everything, Paul. Rafael De La Cruz came to the United States for one purpose. They might be buying horses and doing business here and there, but they came to bring you and Ginny back to Brazil with them. Men like De La Cruz get what they want one way or the other. You do business with them and you'll lose every time." She closed her eyes, feeling his hands moving over her body. She'd allowed him to seduce her. Was she a complete idiot?

You are not being very polite, meu amor. Rafael sounded more amused than ever, not in the least perturbed by her assessment.

Isn't it the truth? You're going to take what you want and no one can stand in your way. Her chest was suddenly tight.

That is true, querida, and you know exactly what I want.

Did she? Colby didn't feel as if she knew much of anything.

"So what's the worst that can happen, Colby?" Paul demanded. "He would get our ranch, right? He's at least family of sorts. If we let Clinton Daniels take it away from us, we'll never get it back. You know that. If one of them had to have it, which would be better?"

Her green eyes suddenly, shrewdly, lifted to his face. "Juan or Julio Chevez told you that, didn't they?"

Paul shrugged, feeling uncomfortable. "Does it matter who thought of it? It's true." He looked down the road, to where the border collie was barking furiously. "The Everetts are coming."

"Did you wonder why your uncles didn't offer a loan when they have enough money to do it? They're rich too, Paul," Colby pointed out. "Why would they let Rafael loan us the money instead of doing it themselves?" *Why didn't they?*

Because they do not dare cross me, pequena. And neither should you. Rafael spoke the words almost complacently. *They know better than to interfere in my business.*

Colby was silent for a moment thinking that through. A shiver had gone down her spine and she resisted a desire to rub warmth into her arms. *I would think this family would be Chevez business, not yours.*

Ah, that was so at one time, but then you are my business now.

Rafael was near, she sensed him close by, but she didn't see him in the truck approaching the yard. Paul stepped off the porch to avoid answering her, heading for the hay fields so he wouldn't get trapped into giving riding lessons to a greenhorn. Colby watched him go across the yard, her heart heavy just looking at him. He was too young to bear the burden of the ranch, their financial woes, and the knowledge that someone was trying to destroy them.

So are you. The words shimmered in her mind, warm breath teased the back of her neck, and two strong arms circled her waist possessively from behind her.

Colby nearly jumped out of her skin, but he was holding her close to him, his body protective and aggressive at the same time. The backs of his hands deliberately brushed the underside of her breasts. She could feel the hard thick length of his erection pressed tightly against her. Imprisoned against his hard strength, she inhaled his masculine scent with her heightened senses. He smelled of the mountains, wild, untamed. "We are having company, I see. And I wanted you all to myself." He whispered the words wickedly against skin. His mouth skimmed over the nape of her neck, found his brand, his teeth teasing and scraping gently.

"Don't you dare! I look like a teenager as it is. If Paul sees this . . ."Colby turned her head to glare at him. "I have a few things to say to you about your behavior." Except she couldn't remember what she wanted to say, terrible words that would drive him away. She wanted the heat and fire of his body, his hands on her, his mouth on her. His body buried deep inside of hers. She found herself blushing, avoiding his gaze.

"Just how old are you?" he asked suddenly. "You look like a teenager to me." His eyes were devouring her face, black and intense, with that hunger that only seemed to be present when he looked at her. He smoldered with sensuality, his gaze devouring her. She could almost feel the electricity crackling between them. Hot flames licked at her skin and deep inside, her blood went thick.

Colby should have moved. If she had any sense of self-preservation left, if her brain was working, she would have run. Instead she stayed in his arms, letting his mouth blaze a path of flames along her neck to her collarbone. He touched her forearm gently, brought it up to his mouth. She felt the velvet rasping of his tongue against her skin. Instead of hurting the burns, it felt soothing.

"What are you doing?" *Besides setting me on fire. Why do I let you do this to me? Have you hypnotized me?* Part of her felt the familiar despair that she couldn't control her reaction to him, but another part flared with excitement, in anticipation.

I am healing you, pequena, you have burned yourself. You must wear very dark glasses to protect your eyes when the sun is out. And cover your skin. Try to find a way to stay out of direct sunlight. Deliberately he used the much more intimate method of communication as his mouth moved over her skin, his healing saliva taking away the pain of her burns. He turned her around and kissed her eyelids, lingering to make certain he had done a thorough job of healing her.

For a moment, Colby allowed herself to melt into the strength and shelter of his body. His voice was chanting in another language, not Portuguese, but something far older, the words beautiful and soothing. She could hear the chant in her mind rather than with her ears. "Why did I burn today in the sun?" He knew. With their minds merged together, she caught shadows and echoes of his thoughts. His memories. None of it made sense to her. *I live on a ranch, I can't exactly stay out of the sun!*

The truck was pulling into the yard and right behind it was Ben's sheriff's vehicle, a four-wheel drive needed to travel the roads into the ranches. Colby pulled away from the warmth of Rafael's body, standing straight to face the visitors. Rafael laughed, his breath stirring tendrils of her hair at the nape of her neck. Deliberately he caught her to him, fastening his mouth to hers, welding them together, so that for a moment she melted into his body. He took his time, his tongue mating with hers, his hands hot, while little flames licked at their bodies. Her thick hair was crushed in his hand while he kept command of her mouth. Slowly, he lifted his head, his black gaze flaring with a dark intensity that arced like lightning through her body.

Colby blinked hard and tried to recover, then glared at him and stepped away, off the porch, but he moved easily beside her, his hand resting possessively on the small of her back. His palm burned like fire and between her thighs, her body throbbed and pleaded for him. She knew exactly what he was doing, staking a claim on her in front of the people in her world. And he was letting her know there was nothing she could do about it.

Joclyn was watching them, speculation in her gaze. Sean had an open grin on his face, but Ben's expression looked like a thunder-cloud as he slammed the door to his Jeep. Colby was very aware of his disapproval while she was talking to Joclyn and her little girl. Rafael didn't help, talking easily with Sean, discussing the fire, acting as if he belonged. He seemed to take every opportunity to touch her, caressing her hair, sliding his fingers along the nape of her neck until she thought Ben would shoot somebody.

Glaring at Rafael and moving away from him didn't seem to help much. She could hear his soft mocking laughter in her mind. She was forced to acknowledge him, even when she was determined not to fall into his trap. *Will you stop!* She narrowed her eyes at him in warning.

Rafael looked at her in mock innocence. *I am not doing anything.*

Colby turned her attention to Tanya, Joclyn's daughter, as Ginny came running over and wound her arm around Colby for support. Rafael put his hand on the child's shoulder with an encouraging smile and Ginny smiled up at him gratefully, obviously mesmerized by him.

I'm going to throw something at you. Colby tried not to laugh at the situation, but for the first time in her life, she felt like she was shar-ing something with someone else. Like she belonged. Was a part of someone else. It didn't seem to matter that her brain screamed a million warnings at her, she was enjoying his attention. It was a new experience for her.

"I'm on a tight schedule, Colby," Ben snapped, bringing her

attention back to him. "If you can spare me enough time to tell me what's going on around here." He sounded accusing.

Rafael immediately circled Ginny's shoulders with his arm. She looked about to cry. "Go ahead, Colby, report to the official. Ginny and I can handle this, right, Ginny?" His voice was low and intimate, welding them all together as if they were one family. He sounded supremely confident in Ginny. "You know me, Tanya. Ginny and I will start the lesson and when Colby is finished with her business, she will join us. Is that acceptable to you?" He turned on a high-powered smile.

Colby shook her head watching Rafael. He was definitely creating the impression he belonged, he was a part of their family. Ben caught her arm rather roughly, dragging her attention back to him. She glanced up at him, startled, like someone waking up, coming out of a dream.

A low warning growl shimmered in the air, so that the horses stirred restlessly and the adults looked around carefully. They all heard it; most of them thought it might have been Ginny's dog, who was sitting regarding them all with an inquiring eye at the sudden attention. Colby knew better. She tucked her hair behind her ear and surreptitiously glanced in warning at Rafael. "Come up to the porch, Ben. Can I get you some coffee?"

He waited all of five steps before he exploded. "You want to tell me what the hell that was all about?"

Her eyebrow shot up. "What are you talking about?"

"Before you deny the little scene on the porch, Colby, you might take a look in the mirror at your neck. You've been all over that man."

Colby bit at her lip to keep from laughing. If she didn't laugh, she might cry. Her behavior with Rafael was completely out of character. She knew it and so did Ben. "Why are you blaming me? It just so happens he was all over me," she corrected. So maybe she wasn't the most beautiful woman in town, did that mean that Rafael couldn't possibly be attracted to her? "Some men are attracted to me, as strange as the concept might seem, Ben. I don't *always* have to attack them."

"This is so like you, choosing the wrong man. A man like Rafael De La Cruz will eat you up and spit you out! You're playing with fire. You can't do that with someone like him. Damn it, Colby, why don't you settle down with a decent man like Joe Vargas?"

"Joe Vargas! Sheesh! What is it with everyone and poor Joe? He would *hate* being married to me."

"Everyone in their right mind would hate being married to you." He dragged her onto the porch, deeper into the shadows, his fingers circling her upper arms to give her a little shake. "Is this about money? What are you up to?"

"Ben, let go, you're hurting me." Colby pried at the fingers circling her arm. "You always forget how blasted strong you are."

"Let her go now." The voice was very soft, very menacing. A whip of malevolence, a dark promise of retaliation. Colby had never heard anything like it before. Rafael had somehow covered the distance between them, completely across the wide expanse of yard, and was blending into the shadows so that his large frame scarcely could be seen, yet his black eyes were nearly glowing in the dark with unbelievable menace.

A shiver of fear ran down her spine and her hand went protectively to her throat. Rafael looked merciless, ruthless, every inch the predator.

In that moment he didn't look wholly human. There was an animal quality about him, feral, dangerous, untamed.

Ben dropped his arms and would have stepped away from her, his hand sliding to his gun as his instincts took over, but Colby stayed firmly between the two men. "I've known Ben since I was about three years old, Rafael. He's like a brother to me. He would never hurt me, *never.* I'm sure this looked like he was getting rough, but it isn't like that at all. He was just, well . . . " She floundered for a moment, her heart pounding in her throat. The feeling of menace, of *death* was so strong she actually felt terrified for a moment. Terrified for Ben.

Rafael was the first to move, his arm snaking out, fingers circling her wrist to draw her very gently to him. "Then I must apologize as I do not understand the relationships of men and women in other countries." His arms circled her slender body, brought her right up against him protectively. *Shhh, meu amor, your heart is beating far too fast. Listen to the rhythm of mine.*

Ben stood there in silence watching the other man as he bent possessively over Colby. There was a protective posture to his body as he held Colby, his hands gentle, despite his tremendous strength. Rafael exuded power and menace, the arrogance of one long used to commanding others with complete authority. He looked like a man who always got his way and Ben could clearly see Rafael De La Cruz wanted Colby Jansen. De La Cruz was a man, not a boy, and Colby looked young and vulnerable beside him. She seemed a bit frightened and very confused as if she found herself in a situation she was unprepared for. And Ben knew Colby, knew she would never be prepared for a man such as Rafael De La Cruz.

"I would never hurt Colby," Ben said calmly. "We're old friends and I guess I'm used to rough-housing with her a bit."

Rafael smiled, showing gleaming white teeth. There was no humor in the smile, rather a subtle warning. "Perhaps she is becoming too old for such things." His voice was softer than ever and it sent Colby's pulse racing all over again. He sounded deadly.

Colby took a deep breath and let it out, determined to take back control of the situation. "Thank you for worrying about me, Rafael, but as you can see, I'm perfectly fine. I really have quite a bit to discuss with Ben, so if you would excuse us . . . "

Rafael bowed low with a courtly old-world elegance long since gone from the modern world. All the time his gaze never left Ben's face, the black depths of his eyes ice cold. Ben watched as the man bent to brush a kiss on the top of Colby's silken hair before gliding away, back across the yard to the Everetts and Ginny.

Ben stared down at Colby, his features set and sober. "You are nuts to think you can control him. He's dangerous, Colby. He would have torn my heart out with his bare hands. You should know better than to get involved with someone like that."

Colby stood there looking up at him rather helplessly. She didn't know if she *was* involved with Rafael. Everything in her life seemed as if it was spinning out of control when she was anywhere near Rafael. She shook her head and dropped into the porch swing, her knees suddenly rubbery. "I don't know what's happening to me, or to the ranch, the world is so upside down right now, Ben."

It was the first time he had ever heard her sound so lost. At once he hunkered down beside the swing, his hand on her knee to comfort her. "Listen to me, honey. You don't need to sell your soul here. I've got money if you need it. A little saved up, nothing big." He took a deep breath, his face manfully expressionless as he made the ultimate sacrifice. "And hell, if you need me to marry you, I guess we could do that too."

Colby stared at him for all of five seconds before she flung her arms around his neck and hugged him close, laughing softly. "What would I do without you, Ben?"

Rafael heard the entire conversation, his blood surging with such power through his body he held himself utterly still, afraid the demon would break loose. His brother stirred in his mind, questioning the fury pouring through him. Rafael stared at the hand touching Colby's knee, watched as she flung herself into the other man's arms, heard her softlaughter, the camaraderie of a man and woman who had known one another a long time.

He felt the demon raising its head, the roaring, the bestial reaction beneath the thin veneer of civility he had worked so hard at achieving.

Fangs exploded in his mouth and his eyes burned savagely. A red haze seemed to consume his brain.

Call out to her. It was Nicolas. Calm. Commanding. The voice of reason when the dark call of his nature was consuming him. *Rafael.* Deliberately Nicolas used his brother's name to call him back from the edge of disaster. *Call out to her now.*

The beast could see his rival embracing his lifemate. He had not bound them together for fear she would be uncomfortable, now the beast had a firm hold on him.

Call out to her. It was the cool wind of reason moving through his mind. Rafael latched on to the ribbon of sanity his brother provided.

Colby. Move away from him immediately. For me. Do this for me.

The normally soft voice was a menace in her mind. More dangerous than any wild animal she had ever encountered. The threat was there, just like the time she had come upon a large mountain lion in its prime just after it had made a kill. She sensed his fear that she might not listen to him, that she wouldn't see the danger, but Colby was far more adept at reading wild things than he gave her credit for. And she chose that moment to touch his mind.

Colby pulled away from Ben and leapt to her feet, pacing away from him quickly, her mind working on two levels. She wanted to appear normal to Ben, yet she shared the swirling cauldron of dark violent emotions with Rafael. "You would hate being married to me and you know it." She crossed her arms and tried to keep from shivering. Somewhere out in the gathering darkness was something powerful and menacing. It crouched very close, watching them with the unblinking eyes of a tiger. "I'd drive you crazy, Ben, and you know it. But it was very sweet of you to offer. I'm sure you earned your way into heaven tonight."

Ben stood up slowly, trying not to look like he'd dodged a bullet. "You know I'd do it, if you needed me to. Just don't do anything desperate, Colby."

She walked down the steps of the porch and glanced around the yard casually. She *felt* the danger like a living, breathing entity. *What is it, Rafael? Do you feel it too?* Was it Rafael? Or was he simply tuned into the danger? Was Rafael threatening her?

I could never harm you, querida, never. There is no danger to you or yours,

I would know. You are simply feeling me being a jealous man. The voice was his usual calm. She saw him then, standing by the corral as if nothing had happened, talking quietly with Sean and Joclyn as Ginny led Tanya's horse around in a wide circle.

Jealous? That was jealous? Colby stared at him for a long time. He looked completely normal, a handsome, charming foreigner who was very magnetic. Was she going completely insane? What did she think? That he was more than a man? He had power the same way she had power; it was easy enough to lose control. She understood that better than anyone could. Yet she had caught a glimpse of a raging beast, not human, something far more dangerous.

You can project that much danger when you are simply jealous? And not for a very good reason, I might add. She had to ask him. She didn't know if she wanted him to lie or to tell her the truth. But she had to ask him.

When we are alone and I can hold you in my arms we will talk. The words were spoken like a soft caress, running across her bare skin so that she touched her own arm. Astonished, she looked down. The blisters and redness were gone. Her skin was smooth and unblemished from the sun. He had healed her terrible sunburn.

"Are you going to talk to me or stare at that foreigner all night?" Ben demanded, coming up behind her. "I thought you had another problem out here." He sounded almost belligerent and Colby turned back to face him.

"You know, Ben, I don't think I'll understand men in a million years. They aren't at all logical like they try to brainwash women into thinking they are." Colby turned away from him to stare up at the darkening sky. "Paul is over in the hay field. I haven't checked on the problem yet, Ben. Juan Chevez was the one who found the steer and Paul saw it. He can take you out there, but it's getting dark very fast. I don't know if you have time."

"I'm getting worried about you and the kids out here by yourselves. I'm making time, Colby, I'm not going to let anything happen to you."

She smiled at him over her shoulder, her hair falling in a bright cascade down her back. She looked so beautiful Ben was slightly shocked. She looked almost ethereal, hauntingly sexy and a little mysterious. He had considered her a younger sister almost all of his life. Ben's feelings about Colby were very mixed, and he didn't want to see her in this light. They weren't suited at all. He had never noticed her looking alluring and sexy before, not once in all their years together.

Ben glanced over at the dark stranger and caught the man looking at him. Rafael didn't look away, his smoldering eyes odd in the waning light. They reminded Ben of a cat's eyes, more suited to night vision than day. The eyes didn't blink and Ben looked away, not liking that intent, hair-raising stare. Rafael De La Cruz was making it perfectly clear that Colby was off -limits to any other man. Ben didn't trust him, sensing something violent and dangerous seething below that calm exterior. And De La Cruz seemed a playboy type, easily acquiring women and just as fast tossing them aside. Colby was not made for a one-night stand. She was a woman who would give herself completely to someone she loved. Ben didn't want it to be a man like De La Cruz.

He shoved his hat on his head. "I'll find Paul and talk with Chevez, but, Colby, you keep the kids close and don't go wandering off by yourself."

"I have a ranch to run, Ben," she said quietly. "I'm not going to let someone scare me off ."

"You said Juan Chevez found the steer. What was he doing riding your ranch?" Ben sounded casual, but Colby wasn't in the least bit fooled, she had known him far too long.

"After the fire, Rafael didn't want us to be alone here. He couldn't stay with us so he asked Juan and Julio to help us out." She looked down at her hands, ashamed to admit her weakness to him. "It was a good thing they stayed. I was sick this afternoon and slept most of the day away."

"So De La Cruz *ordered* them to stay."

"They wanted to stay, Ben. They are Paul and Ginny's uncles, after all. They are concerned for their welfare."

He turned his faded blue eyes on her. "Are you trying to make me believe that Colby Jansen is not in the least suspicious about this setup? That these people show up out of the blue claiming your brother and sister and wanting the ranch to hold for them? That they just happen to be business associates and are staying with your neighbor Sean Everett whose entire crew just happens to be ex-cons? And that just about the same time they arrive, all kinds of 'accidents' begin happening on your ranch? This is all coincidence, Colby? And now Juan Chevez finds a dead steer mutilated while he is 'watching over you' on De La Cruz's orders. It seems a bit far-fetched to me."

"Didn't we have this conversation before, and *I* was the one saying these things to you? You told me I was stubborn and to get over it. You told me I was talking through my hat when I tried to point out to you that the things going wrong on the ranch weren't accidents."

"Yeah, well, Pete's death was no accident, Colby, and it was no accident that Chevez and Everett's riders were up on the bluff. Or that Clinton Daniels and that scum Harris were out there either, along with that new hand of his, Ernie Carter. Now that's a real winner there. What the hell were you doing riding out there alone?"

"Ben"—she laid a placating hand on his arm—"you aren't suggesting *everyone* is conspiring against me, are you?"

Ben felt the weight of those peculiar eyes staring at him malevolently. He didn't look up to see; he knew instinctively they had De La Cruz's full attention and he knew it was because he had raised his voice to Colby and she was touching him. "I think you're in great danger, Colby, and not just of losing the ranch. That's what I think and you'd better take me damn seriously."

"I will, Ben," Colby conceded with a little sigh. "I'm worried too. I don't know what to think, but I don't want anything to happen to Paul or Ginny. I promise to be careful." When he continued looking at her she sighed again. "Very, very careful."

"And not trust anybody too much," he prompted.

"And I won't trust anybody too much," she added obediently.

Ben walked off toward the hay field, and she watched him until his large frame disappeared around the side of the large barn. She stared at the barn, puzzled. It would have made more sense for the arsonist to burn down the barn. It was located farther away from the house and it didn't have built-in sprinklers. The barn would have gone up fast with the hay in it. Why hadn't they chosen the barn?

"Colby!" Ginny called out, her voice betraying annoyance. She desperately wanted to make a good impression. Tanya was very nice and she wanted Colby to pay her lots of attention so she would want to comeback.

Colby hurried over, ignoring Rafael's hot gaze and concentrating totally on Joclyn and Tanya. She was aware of Rafael watching her intently the entire time she gave instructions, but she forced herself to keep from looking at him. She wanted to look at him. She even needed to look at him. She could feel her mind continually reaching for his. She had felt the sensation before; now she recognized it. And he often touched her mind. Like a shadow. Almost for reassurance. The moment he touched her she could relax again, breathe. She smiled at Joclyn and talked normally. She hugged Ginny often, going through the motions of being interested and excited by her chatter. She lavished attention on Tanya, but all the while she was intensely aware of Rafael. Waiting. Watching.

Sean handed Rafael an envelope through the truck's open window just before they left, promising Ginny they would return in a couple of days. Colby watched Rafael casually tuck it into his shirt pocket. She really looked at him then, allowing herself the luxury. His clothes were immaculate, despite the fact that he had been checking the burns on the horses in the corral and helping with the riding lesson. It seemed as if even the dirt and dust of the ranch didn't dare cling to him the way it did everyone else. And he always smelled so good too.

Rafael met her gaze over the top of Ginny's head and smiled at her. He could rob her of her breath without doing much at all. Colby ducked her head and began walking with Ginny up to the house. "So, what did you think, chickadee, did you like Tanya?"

"She's really nice, Colby," Ginny said enthusiastically. "Paul should have at least come over to be introduced."

"Really?" Colby's eyebrow shot up. "Did you think so? I thought he might say something awful and mortify us—you know Paul."

Ginny thought it over, then shook her head. "Girls think he's cute. He's been talking to quite a few of them on the phone and they always call him first. He never calls them. At night when you're working he's on the phone in the kitchen."

"Your brother talks on the phone to girls while your sister is working?"

Rafael asked quietly. There was no real expression in his voice, it was soft and calm like always, yet it held a wealth of menace.

Colby glanced at him, wondering how he could do that, not raise his voice or change his inflection, yet sound so frightening. "Paul is very young, Rafael. He's only sixteen."

"And when Armando was in the accident and left you to run the ranch *and* nurse him, you were what? Seventeen?" His black eyes moved broodingly over her face.

She took the back porch steps very fast, suddenly angry with him. "Paul helps out a lot, Rafael, and in any case, it isn't your business."

He glided along beside her in his silent way, irritating her even more. His hand reached the door to the kitchen at the exact same time as hers did. Colby jerked her hand away when his fingers brushed hers. "Do you think coddling that boy is going to make a man out of him, Colby? Ultimately, he has to run the ranch. It was your father's dream to keep the ranch for the kids, but he wouldn't want you running yourself into the ground."

Colby was all too aware of Ginny's wide eyes staring from one to the other of them, suddenly very grown-up. "It was my dream too." Colby sounded defiant even to her own ears. She stalked across the room to the refrigerator and stared inside.

Rafael's smile was very gentle. He put a hand on her shoulder. *I have been in your mind, pequena. I did not see such a memory.*

He had been in her body too. The unspoken words shimmered in the air. She whirled around and glared at him. "Then you darn well weren't looking for it," she snapped, hating that she knew what was in his pocket and that she would have no choice but to accept his handout. She was going to take his money and she had slept with him. "I wanted the ranch too. I did. I do."

The memory is not there, querida, and you, more than I, know it is true. It was never there, no such memory, because you had no such desire or dream.

9

"**B**en's in a darn foul mood," Paul greeted as he bounded through the kitchen door much like a half-grown puppy. He went straight to the sink and washed his hands. Colby was death on cleanliness. "I've gotta tell you, I was glad to see him go. Why's he so bent out of shape? What'd you say to him, Colby?"

She spun around, glaring at him. "Say to him?" she echoed very softly. "And why would you think *I* said something to him? Ben is a *man.*" She made it sound like a dirty word. "That should tell you everything right there."

Paul whistled very low under his breath. "Anyone call for me?" he asked hopefully. No one messed with Colby when she was in a man-bashing state. Someone or something had set her off and he was hoping it hadn't been him.

"No, but I was hoping you'd leave Ben out there to get lost."

Paul's eyebrows shot up at Colby's mood and then he glanced from his sister to Rafael speculatively. "So, I'm guessing you brought the loan papers. Has Colby seen them yet?" It was a good guess on his part after seeing the expression on his sister's face.

Rafael extracted the papers and handed them to Colby. "No, not yet. Perhaps she could look these over while we get better acquainted." He gestured toward the living room, herding Paul and Ginny in front of him to give Colby more privacy.

Colby froze, the sound of her heart loud in her ears. "Wait!" She sounded totally panic-stricken. She felt totally panic-stricken. She actually put out her hand to stop her brother and sister from leaving the room alone with Rafael.

Rafael turned to look at her, his black eyes moving over her face with hard authority as she backed away from him. "What is it, *meu amor?*" He spoke gently, his voice like a velvet caress, but she shivered all the same. He was smoldering. *Smoldering.* She could feel the volcano swirling inside him as linked as they were. His eyes were on her, bleak and cold, yet burning with a terrible intensity. Fire and ice. There it was again. The paradox. She didn't understand him. She didn't understand herself. But first and foremost, despite what she might need or want or feel, she had to know that Ginny and Paul were safe from all harm. Rafael was a shadow in her mind and saw her fear.

"Colby?" There was a wealth of concern in Paul's voice. "What is it?"

Be very careful what you say to the boy, pequena; I do not want him to fear me unnecessarily as you seem to fear me. The words purred in her mind, a soothing menace.

Colby's hand went to her throat, a protective gesture, moved around to cover the mark throbbing so frantically on her neck. *Are you driving me insane? I feel like I don't know what's real and what isn't anymore. I'm different. I know I'm different.* She was crying out the words, needing his comfort even as she was trying to drive him away with her accusations.

We will be alone soon enough, Colby, there is no need for all this fear. You and the children are under my protection. That is no small thing. If you do not believe in me, then believe in Armando. He sent for the family. They are men of honor. If they believed I would harm you, do you think they would allow such a thing?

I don't know. They're very loyal to you. She didn't know. She honestly didn't. How could she be so attracted to someone she didn't even trust? How could she allow him to do the things he'd done to her body and still crave more? It didn't make sense to her. And the Chevez brothers feared him. She sensed the uneasiness in them whenever the conversation turned to Rafael. He was much more than a man with unique talents such as Colby had. He was far more powerful. And there was a darkness inside of him she often caught glimpses of. As much as she was drawn to Rafael, she was also equally repelled, her sense of self-preservation kicking in strongly. He was taking her over, bit by bit, cell by cell. Her heart. Her lungs. It felt as if she couldn't breathe without him. No one else looked at her with that burning hungry gaze. No one touched her with such command, such need. He was dominant in every way and something in her she couldn't control responded to him, needed him, *craved* him, even when she wasn't certain of who or what he was.

"Go over the papers, Colby." Rafael sounded tender. "We will be in the other room. Ginny is interested in vegetarian soup recipes and I am quite good in that particular area."

Colby stared at Rafael, almost afraid to make a decision. *You won't . . .* She couldn't actually form an accusation. What if he had directed their minds to do something harmful? Could he have done that?

His black eyes ignited with anger for a moment. *Yes, I could have, but I did not.* He turned on his heel and stalked out of the room.

Paul slipped his arm around Ginny's shoulders. "I'm not going to pretend I know what's going on between you two, but he offered us a huge loan for practically nothing, Colby, and if we don't get money soon we're going to lose the ranch."

Colby shrugged. "Well, maybe you're being altogether too

trusting, Paul. You ought to know by now you don't get something for nothing. It never works that way."

"Maybe so, Colby, but then again you're the one who trusted Daniels enough to take the loan," Paul snapped at her.

Colby winced as though he'd struck her. To her shock, her eyes actually brimmed with tears. Ginny ran to her, circling her waist with protective arms, glaring openly at her brother.

"Do not let me hear you speak to your sister again like that, Paul." Rafael's large frame filled the doorway. He always seemed to materialize out of nowhere, moving unseen and silently to appear and take over. He looked directly at the teenager. "You are too old to yell out accusations when you do not have all the facts. Colby deserves far more respect from you." There was a lash in the quiet strength of his voice. "Think before you speak, boy. I am quite capable of introducing you to the concept of manners." Rafael stepped back in invitation to allow Paul to precedehim, his gaze steely.

Paul looked defiant for a moment, his face slowly turning red. Ginny moved first, hurrying quickly past Rafael into the other room, pausing just long enough to give her brother one indignant look. Colby, for once, didn't help Paul, staring down at the scuffed toes of her boots as if she couldn't bear to look at him. As if he had hurt her so deeply with his accusation that she couldn't face him or anyone else.

"Colby." He said her name softly, already sorry for lashing out at her. He wasn't even sure why he did it, only that he didn't like the way Rafael was looking at Colby, or the way she was looking back at him.

She shook her head without looking up. Paul followed Ginny into the living room. Colby unfolded the papers reluctantly and spread the offending document onto the kitchen table. It was strictly businesslike, legal and very fair. She could find no fault with it. Rafael had left her no way out, no logical reason to refuse him.

The sum was for the amount of money she needed to pay off Daniels and enough to rebuild and even add new equipment. Colby didn't have the kind of cash Daniels or De La Cruz had and she never would.

"Are you planning on scowling at it all day or shall we sign it and get it over with?" Rafael broke into her thoughts, leaning against the doorframe, his arms folded across his chest.

She glanced at him, a slight frown on her face. "I'm reading it over, looking for hidden traps."

"It is not going to work, you know," he said, his voice low.

"What isn't going to work?" she retorted.

"Trying to start a fight with me. It will not run me off. You think to make me go back to my homeland. Do you not realize yet that it is too late for that?"

Colby pushed a hand through her hair and regarded him with serious eyes. "I know we need to have a talk, Rafael."

He indicated the papers with a graceful wave of his hand. "Is it really so hard to decide? Would you have rather I turned my back on you and the children? It is only money. I would have given it to you, but you would not have taken it. Money means nothing to me, it never has." He sighed, his black gaze fastened on her very expressive face. "You hate the fact that I offered the money, but really, *querida*, you had me either way. If I had not offered it, what kind of a man would I have been?" There was no note of censure in his voice, he simply was stating a fact.

Colby was instantly ashamed. It was true. She totally resented him either way. And she didn't trust his motives. Rafael extracted a gold pen from his pocket and held it out to her, his dark eyes eloquent. Colby shook her head at the folly of what she was doing, but she took the pen. Her fingers brushed his, sent a frisson of awareness down her spine. He could do that, but was it simple chemistry? Colby didn't know why she was so attracted to him. She thought he was cold, yet he sometimes burned with such intensity she melted around him. Which was the real Rafael? She thought him selfish and arrogant, yet he was first on the ranch helping nonstop in a crisis. He had sheltered Ginny in the midst of the crisis in spite of the fact that he had been in extreme discomfort. And he was offering the money at more than reasonable terms so they could keep the ranch. Had she been that wrong about him?

No, pequena, you were not so wrong about me. The words brushed in her mind almost tenderly.

Colby glanced up at him, startled. It was disconcerting to have him reading her every thought. "I guess we do need to talk. You need to explain to me just what is going on between us, because I don't know what it is." She wasn't going to be put off. He had promised to talk with her and she meant to hold him to it.

"Do you really believe I have something to do with the problems on this ranch?" Rafael stirred for the first time, a lazy, casual move very reminiscent of a jungle cat as he straightened and moved toward her, immediately filling the entire kitchen with his presence.

The phone rang shrilly. They could hear Paul and Ginny both racing to answer it. Colby pushed open the screen door. She needed the night air, the wide-open spaces. She didn't turn her head and she didn't hear Rafael walking, but she felt him moving right behind her.

As they walked across the yard, his hand brushed hers. At once her heart went crazy, pounding wildly before she could prevent it. She glanced up at him from under long lashes, surreptitiously putting her hand behind her back. "Why did you come here, Rafael? Why are you here at all? You don't belong here, do you?"

"My brothers and I rarely travel. We prefer to stay near the rain forest." He glanced up at the looming mountain range shadowing the ranch. "We need the wilds. Even together we have always been solitary."

His voice was very quiet, almost hypnotic. Colby found her gaze on the mountains also. Everything seemed so much more intense. Vivid colors in the night, the breeze bringing scents and sounds to her she had never experienced before. She inhaled deeply, drawing it all into her lungs. "Why do I want to be with you when I don't even like you?" She didn't look at him when she asked the question. "You know why, don't you?" She knew things; she had always known things. She knew he wouldn't lie to her about whatever was between them.

Rafael moved beside her in silence, his body fluid and powerful. She could *feel* his power. They walked past the large garden she had worked so hard to maintain. She noted absently that Paul had forgotten to water it. As soon as the knowledge shimmered in her mind, Rafael waved his hand and the water began to flow into the irrigation hoses. He did it casually, almost as if he didn't notice he did it.

"Why do I need to touch your mind with mine, to see you, when I've never needed a man in my life at all?"

His hand brushed hers again and this time their fingers tangled together. "Do you really want the answers to your questions, Colby? You must be very sure it is what you want. The answers you will get are not what you are expecting."

She stopped walking, her body very close to his. She had to tilt her head to look up at him. Colby took a moment to think it over. She sensed he was going to reveal something monumental, something terrifying. Was she strong enough to take it? Colby *needed* to know. She took a deep breath and nodded. "I think I have enough mysteries in my life right now without this one. Tell me the truth."

His hand framed her face, his fingertips unbelievably gentle as they brushed her face. "I look at you, Colby, and I see the most beautiful woman on the face of the earth. Inside and out you are beautiful. I know you better than anyone else could ever know you, because I can see into your thoughts and read your memories. The very light in you, your tremendous capacity for loving, humbles me."

She looked at him steadily, trying not to drown in the depths of his black, black eyes. Looking at the intensity, the hunger there, it was impossible not to believe what he was saying and his words robbed her of her breath, of her ability to stay focused. She shook her head to ward off his spell. "Tell me about your life." She found she was holding her breath; she didn't want to hear about Rafael and other women. She wanted to know about *him*. Who he was, what he thought, what mattered to him.

"You matter to me. Ginny and Paul matter to me. Honor matters." His black eyes, dark and brooding, moved over her face. His fingers drifted down her silken curtain of hair before reluctantly releasing her. "Honor is the only thing I had left to me, Colby, before you came into my life." He looked away from her, avoiding her eyes to look up at the high shadowy peaks surrounding them. "I belong in the rain forests, up in the mountains, far from people, where it is much safer for them ... and for me."

Colby kept her eyes on his face, determined to know the truth. There was something truly solitary about him, something so alone it touched her heart. She had an overwhelming desire to gather him into her arms and comfort him. "I don't see what is so wrong with needing your own space. Sometimes, there is such a bombardment of information overwhelming me that I can barely hang on. You are much more sensitive than I am, I can tell. If you read minds, the emotions must be overwhelming."

He rubbed the bridge of his nose thoughtfully, shaking his head at her. "Naturally you would give a plausible reason for my behavior. But it is not so, *pequena*, I do not have the excuse of being bombarded with emotions. In truth, although I can read minds, I felt nothing at all until I met you."

Colby continued to walk. The soft breeze was soothing, a perfect backdrop for serenity when she was struggling to understand what Rafael was telling her. "I don't understand. How could you feel nothing? You mean you never fell in love? What? What does that mean?"

"I mean it in a literal sense, Colby," he continued gently. "Touch my mind, look at my memories." He didn't sound ashamed, he sounded matter-of-fact, as if he casually discussed his sins every day, not as if he was baring his soul to her, as if he was ripping his heart out and handing it to her.

He knew he could no longer continue without her. He knew he was too selfish to end his life, and in any case he had all but tied her to him. He had no idea of the consequences to her should they be separated. He had not officially bound them with the ritual words but he had exchanged blood with her on two occasions. She was partially in his world. And she needed him. She was lonely in the midst of her beloved family. And they were using her up, her generous, compassionate nature and unique gifts. Without those talents, it would not have been possible for Colby to run the ranch on the defective equipment as she had been doing these last few years.

There was a vampire in the area, probably drawn by her use of her psychic talent. And there was Nicolas, so close to turning it was terrifying. And Rafael truly did not know how much longer he, himself, could endure without claiming her. More than all those reasons, Rafael knew he had never wanted anything for himself in all his long years. He wanted Colby and he wouldn't give her up.

She reached out to him, for the first time really seeing beyond his expressionless mask. His handsome face was different when she really studied him. There were lines etched into his sensual features that hadn't been there before. There was a sorrow in the depths of his eyes as if he was suffering. Instantly her heart melted and Colby tightened her grip on his arm.

"What is it you don't want to tell me, Rafael? Don't you think it's just better to get it out in the open?"

Colby. Direct, to the point. He tucked thick silky strands of red-gold hair behind her small ear. "You have so much here, Colby. You are willing to give so much of yourself to those you love. I want you to love me. I am not deserving of your love. I have not only done nothing to deserve it, but I have made your life more difficult. I need you. I know I will not always be easy to be with. I am a very dominant man, sexually and otherwise. I want you to be mine. All mine." He said the words starkly, without embellishment, totally vulnerable, aware she could crush him easily with one word, one look. "But I want you to love me, I need you to love me."

Everything in Colby responded to the directness of his plea. He looked so alone, tall and straight, his black eyes alive with some terrible inner pain. "Why? Why do you need me to love you, Rafael? You have everything." He wasn't overwhelming her with romantic endearments, or even using the highly charged sexual chemistry between them to persuade her, and that, more than anything else, had her complete attention.

"I have nothing without you. Before I came here, Colby, my life was one endless bleak moment after another. I am alive when I am around you. I can feel emotion, I know I care for the Chevez family, I feel affection for them, I *care* what happens to them. I *feel* for my brothers, my people. I do not want to return to a barren world, I cannot." His black eyes moved moodily over her upturned face. "You are a miracle and you are not even aware of it."

"I haven't done anything to be a miracle," Colby reminded him quietly. She waited in the darkness for what would inevitably come. She knew there was something else, something he didn't want to tell her.

"That you exist is a miracle for me, Colby." He gestured with his hand, the long slow sweep taking in a wide circle. "This is my world, Colby, the night. I have lived long alone and I cannot do so anymore." He bowed his head as if infinitely weary. "I thought I might be strong enough to allow you to slip away from me. I have thought long on this, but I cannot." He looked at her directly then, his head coming up, standing tall and powerful, his black eyes burning a brand into her mind. "I cannot, Colby."

"Rafael, stop talking in riddles. What is it?" She could hear her own heart beating wildly. She could feel the desperation in her mind and body as every single cell needed to comfort and assure him. But he was changing her life. She knew it instinctively, she knew he was warning her, not reassuring her. Whatever he was *not* saying was something terrible. So she simply stood there looking up at him. Waiting.

Rafael stood one moment looking curiously vulnerable and the next his expression was grim, determined. Sheer arrogance. He dragged her into his arms and took possession of her mouth with his. She tasted a desperate need, a terrible hunger, and something far more frightening. She gave herself up to him, clinging to him, returning the hunger in his kiss, reassuring him even as she feared where he was leading her. Her hands crept up to his neck, bunching his hair in her fingers.

"Tell me, Rafael, can't you feel how much I want you?" She wanted to give him the courage to tell her, wanted to give herself the courage to listen. She whispered the words into his mouth, against his lips, holding her body very close to his.

He lifted his head then, his black eyes glittering at her. He looked every inch a tall, dark predator. "You cannot just want me, Colby, you have to love me." There was a finality about his words, something in his voice that warned her she was in danger.

She stood in the silence, listening to the wind whisper to her, feeling it on her face, her body. His face was still and etched with a deep sorrow she couldn't quite comprehend. He looked as lonely as her beloved mountains. Colby lifted a hand to his lips, her fingers gently smoothing the lines. "What is it, Rafael? Say it aloud, say it here in the night where it's just the two of us while we belong together. Right now."

Tiny red flames flickered in the dark depths of his eyes. His fingers shackled her fragile wrist, lightly, loosely, as if chaining her to him when he expected her to run from him. "I am of the night, Colby, of the wind and the earth. I can soar as the eagle or take the shape of a jungle cat. My people are as old as time itself. I am not human."

For a moment her mind was perfectly still, not comprehending, not wanting to take in what he said. She blinked up at him as the words settled into her mind. Her gaze fixed on the flames in his eyes. "If you are not human, Rafael, what are you?" She shouldn't have believed him, but she sensed the danger in him, the predator, she sensed his differences. The way the Chevez brothers acted suddenly made perfect sense. They knew he was different. And they feared him.

She wasn't running from him, she didn't even attempt to pull away, but he heard the slamming of her heart and he saw the gathering apprehension in her eyes.

"I am Carpathian. My original homeland is in the Carpathian Mountains. In the thirteenth century, our prince asked for volunteers to go to distant lands to protect the world from the evil branching out. My brothers and I were already warriors with much experience and we answered the call."

She stood very, very still. The words "thirteenth century" echoed through her mind.

"We are rather like normal human children in the first years of our lives. As we become teenagers our gifts and talents begin to emerge.

The elders teach us to shape-shift, to use our gifts. At that time the sun begins to become a problem for us."

She drew in her breath sharply, her eyes never leaving his face. "Like it is becoming for me. It isn't because of the fire, is it?" Shape-shifting. He had used the term casually, in the same way he had mentioned the thirteenth century. He wasn't insane and Colby wished he were. She took an involuntary step backward, her hand going up to cover the mark throbbing on her neck.

He shook his head slowly. "No, Colby, your sensitivity to the sun is not because of the fire. I brought you partially into my world, and I have no choice but to bring you fully into it." He said it very quietly, implacably, irrevocably. His black eyes watched her carefully. She felt him in her mind, that same watchful stillness, judging her reaction.

She held her ground, looking up at him steadily. "You think I'm just going to let you take me over?" Her words were soft, like the night wind, but it was a threat, the first real threat Colby had ever made in her life. "I love my brother and sister; I will never let you take me from them. I hope we understand one another."

He nodded, his eyes very black, very empty. "You have strong gifts, Colby, but you have no concept of my power. I mean it when I say I have no choice. You have no concept of how strong the pull of the darkness is, the insidious whispering of power. The call to feel. Just feel. Such a small thing humans take for granted. I thought there was nothing worse, but it is not so. Emotions bombard me; I cannot seek the solace of the earth because you are aboveground and my soul cries for yours. I have no anchor. I cannot hold out much longer. There is too much at risk."

She lifted her chin. "I don't know exactly what you're talking about, Rafael, I'll admit it, but it doesn't matter, don't you see that? I don't matter, you don't matter, only Paul and Ginny matter."

His white teeth gleamed in the darkness, a predator's warning. "You think I will allow you to trade our lives for theirs?" His voice was very, very low.

Her heart thudded painfully and for a moment she could scarcely breathe. Was he actually threatening her brother and sister? He seemed invincible there in the darkness and she didn't even know what he was, what he was capable of doing. She sensed his power, she *felt* his power clinging to him, vibrating in the air around him. "What are you saying, Rafael? I don't like riddles."

His hand moved up to shape her face. Colby stepped away from him before his fingers could skim her skin, before his touch could seduce her into acceptance. His hand fell to his side. "I am incapable of harming those children," he said softly, his voice a whiplash. "They are a part of you. I have offered my protection to them. You persist in seeing me as your enemy when you are surrounded by the real enemy."

She stood quietly with the wind ruffling her hair and her heart as heavy as a stone. His pain or hers? Colby wasn't certain if it was one and the same. "I'm sorry, Rafael." She shoved a trembling hand through her silky hair. "The ground seems to be shifting out from under me and I honestly don't know what to think." She waved a hand to encompass the mountains surrounding them. "This is my world. This ranch, the children. My entire world. What's happened between us is frightening. I behave differently around you. It isn't me. You have to understand that. I'm not who you want."

He smiled at her. Gently. Tenderly. "Colby." Her name was a soft ache in the darkness of the night. "I have waited close to two thousand years for you. Only you. Without hope, without color or emotion. I cannot go back to a barren world. You are here in front of me and our time is now. I will not allow it to slip through our fingers. You cannot conceive of the monster I can become without you. You sense it lurking, watching, waiting even, but you do not realize its potential."

"You have the ability to mesmerize with your voice."

"I see no reason to deny it. I did not seduce you with my voice.

You are my other half, you feel it, you know it. I live in you and your need is as strong as my need." He moved then, glided, a silent predator, his arms gathering her against his body and his dark head descending until his mouth claimed hers. Hot. Dominant. Hungry. An urgent demand.

The moment his mouth fastened on hers, Colby felt the flames licking at her skin, inside her skin, deep within her body. The heat built, a fiery inferno that turned her blood into a molten liquid that pooled low in her body and consumed her mind with a dark desire she would never escape. It moved through her body, wicked, sinful, a treacherous craving that deepened and spread, until she was consumed with the need to touch him, taste him. To give him everything. Her denials were gone, lost in the fire of his hot mouth and hard body.

It wasn't enough with his mouth welded to hers, she had to feel the heat of his skin beneath the pads of her fingers exploring every muscle, every indentation. She wanted nothing between them, not even a thin layer of material to cushion the thick hard evidence of his need for her. The surge of power vibrated in the air, so that electricity crackled and snapped. His shirt floated to the ground while her hands found the fastening of his trousers. She pushed impatiently at the off ending jeans, wanting them out of the way, needing them gone. Once again the air crackled and he was naked in the moonlight, the silvery beams illuminating the hard planes of his body. He looked magnificently male, a masculine sculpture dedicated to pure carnal pleasure. Made for it. Needing it.

Colby gasped in awe, running her hands over him, while deep inside the aching need blossomed into a ferocious hunger that bit at her and clawed until her body raged at her. She was sharing his mind, knew they were both beyond control, but it didn't matter to her. She looked up at him, at his black, merciless eyes, eyes alive with hunger and desire, an insatiable lust bordering on obsession. She understood; she felt the same.

Rafael parted the threads of her cotton top so that the buttons went flying in all directions. His hands moved up to loosen the clip in her hair, tossing it aside so that it lay unwanted beside the small round buttons. His hands skimmed up her rib cage, settling on her breasts as he dipped his head to feast on soft, creamy flesh. Colby's soft cry was muffled as his mouth closed over her nipple, wet and hot and suckling strongly. Answering liquefied heat throbbed and burned deep inside her, a molten pool of beckoning anticipation.

Rafael's hands glided over the curve of her hips, sliding her jeans from her body, leaving her open to his hungry gaze. The surge of power came again as she kicked off her shoes and pushed aside her clothes so her body was skin to skin with his. "Touch me, Colby," he commanded softly, as his teeth teased and scraped along sensitive skin. "I need your hands on me. Touch me."

Her hands were on his hips, tracing his hips bones, the sharp edges, the defined muscles. He groaned as his body grew fuller, heavier, at the brushing of her skin against him. "I want to touch you, Rafael," she answered truthfully. She loved the way he thrust his mind into her mind, the erotic pictures very vivid, very graphic.

His mouth at her breast was numbing her mind, turning her body into liquid heat, a fire so exquisite she wanted to burn out of control, could only burn out of control. Deliberately she danced her fingers along the hard thick length of him, cupping the weight of him in her hand, squeezing gently until the air rushed out of his lungs and he lifted his head with a soft growl of animal pleasure.

It wasn't enough, she wanted to bring him to his knees, this creature of dark power, a master of seduction who had left his brand deep inside her so that no other could ever possibly take his place. She wanted him to feel the way he had made her feel. So close to the fire she burned init. Colby caught at his hips, dragged him closer to her so that the warmth of her breath had his teeth snapping together. Her tongue tasted him, a slow, seductive swirl, deliberately intimate, following the smooth velvet-soft contours, exploring the thick knob while her teeth nibbled as if she might take a bite. She had no real idea of what to do, but she could follow the instructions in his mind, and the guidance of his hands. Each ragged breath he drew encouraged her.

His hands fisted in her hair, the growl deepening in his throat. She wanted him this way, on the edge of violence, with no restraint, therein the night with the stars scattered overhead and his powerful body trembling because of her. Because of the silken heat of her mouth, tight and moist, taking him the way her body would take his. Deep inside, suckling him the way he did her. His body belonging to her, for her pleasure, to bring him to a fever pitch, to be able to drag the throaty growls from him and feel his body thrust helplessly into her. His fists tightened in her hair, dragging her head closer to him while she deliberately drove him careening toward the edge of control.

He said something, something hot and erotic, dragging her head up to find her mouth with his. He waved his hand and a blanket of thick grass lay beneath her as he shoved her back onto the ground, following her down with his hard body. Grasping her legs, he jerked her to him, so that her legs were spread wide, leaving her open and vulnerable to him. He was kneeling and he simply tugged her legs over his broad shoulders and bent to find her hot, wet core with his probing tongue.

Colby's body imploded, fragmented, rocking and bucking in his hands. She cried out, her fingers clutching at the grass stalks for something, anything to hold on to.

"Not good enough," he said softly, impatiently. "Again, Colby, again and again and next time say my name. Know who I am. Say it." It was an order, a threat. His mouth found her again, buried deep, stroking, caressing, teasing. Very deliberately he slipped his finger over her, inside her. At once her body responded again, sending her spiraling out of control so that she gasped for mercy, clawing at the grass for an anchor.

He left his finger deep inside her, pushed farther so that his palm was pressed against the heat of her entrance. He bent to kiss her flat belly, his teeth nipping, his tongue swirling over her peculiar birthmark. Her muscles clenched tightly in answer around his finger. "That is what I need to feel, *meu amor,* I want you to need me more. Even more." Watching her face he inserted a second finger, stretching her tight sheath, pressing deeper into her as he bent his head to her breast thrusting so temptingly at him. Her body shuddered in answer, bathed his fingers in a hot cream, clenching and tightening, rippling with life.

"Rafael," she gasped his name. Aching. Needing. On fire.

He bit lightly at her breast, sucked at her flesh, thrust his fingers deep, withdrew, thrust again. There was satisfaction in her cry as his movements triggered an even wilder release. She nearly sobbed as her body ground against his hand.

Rafael leaned over her, pressed his throbbing body against her, thick and hard, wanting her to feel him. "Not yet, Colby. Who am I? Say my name, tell me. Tell me what you want from me. Only me. No one else, just me." His voice was a dark sorcerer's tool, velvet soft, a seduction of senses, husky with his own dark hunger. His tongue flicked over her nipple, his teeth scraped over her pulse, swirled a caress even as his fingers stretched her further, sunk deeper into her core.

Tears swam in her eyes. "I can't do this, I can't take any more. It's too much." Her body was alive with a thousand nerve endings, tiny pinpoints of pleasure swamping her to the point of pain.

"Yes, you can." His teeth teased the pulse in her neck, his breath warm in her ear. "Let go, give yourself to me, all the way, Colby. I want all of it, everything that is you. I will not take anything less from you. All of you. You want me. You need me the same way I need you. Your body needs mine."

Her breath caught in her throat and the feel of his mouth against her skin was almost more than she could bear. "Yes, Rafael, now." She choked the words out as her body rippled and quivered and spiraled out of control again.

He brought her legs to his waist, pushed his hips against her, keeping her thighs wide to accommodate his larger body as he pressed into her hot, wet, welcoming sheath. A soft sound escaped her throat as he pushed into her. Even with his fingers preparing her, stretching her, her body was tight and resisting against his thick hard length. "All of me, *querida*, take all of me," he urged softly, insistently. His beautiful voice was husky with his need, his face an etching of desire and hunger, his eyes burning with intensity.

She cried out, her voice scattering across the sky as he deepened his stroke, joining their bodies together. It was his name, her mind filled with him and her soul claimed by him as he took possession of her body. The release was fast and ferocious, overtaking her like a freight train before she could get her breath.

Rafael had no mercy, surging forward, burying himself deep while the fiery friction built again and again, intense and hot, a firestorm consuming them both. He needed all of her, the essence of her flooding his bloodstream, and deliberately he bent forward, knowing her eyes were on his face, wanting her to see who he was, to know what he was.

10

Colby read the hunger in Rafael's eyes, the predatory flame leaping to life. There was a helpless fascination in watching the fangs lengthen in his beautiful mouth, his white teeth gleaming as his head slowly descended to her body. His hips moved, a hard, long stroke that had her gasping even as his teeth teased at her pulse. Her heart jumped, her body tightened around his, her muscles clenching. Her breath seemed to stop. Her body seemed to go up in flames.

His teeth sank into her, a white-hot lance of pain, of pleasure, a whip of lightning dancing through her body, heightening her senses, so erotic's he thought her body would fragment into tiny little pieces. His hair brushed her skin like silken tongues, his body was wildly taking hers, the friction so exquisite tears leaked out of her eyes and she could only lay beneath him, her hips rising to meet each frenzied thrust.

He was everything to her in that moment, belonging to her, his body, his mind, his heart and soul. She accepted him as no other ever could. The wild untamed part of him that was pure predator, the man wearing the thin veneer of civilization, the creature of the night who must have blood to survive. And he was accepting of her, of her nature that demanded she care for her brother and sister, shoulder the responsibility of the ranch, of her strange differences, telekinesis, the accidents of her youth, starting fires, the rigid control she placed on herself. Total, unconditional acceptance.

His tongue swept across the tiny pinpricks and he closed his mouth over hers, sharing the exotic taste of her, sharing his need, as the flames began burning out of control, over them, through them. He felt her tightening, clenching, and he roared with his own release, his hands gripping her possessively as her body took his over the edge of all control, all reason. All sanity.

Colby lay beneath him, aware of the combined pounding of their hearts beating out the same exact rhythm. Aware of the thick carpet of green grass under her that had not been there before. Aware of the stars glittering overhead like a canopy of jewels. Aware of his hard body, still joined with hers. She couldn't move, her body so sated, so completely drained of energy she was at peace, serene in the midst of the violence of their coming together. Colby was relaxed despite the earth-shattering sex and the revelations he had so casually made.

It was Rafael who shifted first, easing his body out of hers, moving his weight off of her. His hands framed her face, holding her still as he bent his dark head to hers. He kissed her gently, tenderly. She tasted the edge of hunger in him. A faint smile curved her soft mouth. "Go away before you kill me."

"Again," Rafael said softly, a demand. A command. The need to bring her into his world was a living breathing monster in his mind and body. He knew he wanted her to accept him, but if she didn't, if persuasion didn't work, he would take what was his and damn the consequences. "I want you again."

Colby twisted away from him, pushing up on her hands and knees in the soft carpet of grass in an effort to get up. "You're killing me, I can't, I can't move." Her body was rocking with aftershocks, her breasts aching, her mouth swollen with his kisses.

He moved with blinding speed, a large jungle cat bringing down its prey, his body blanketing hers, his arm circling her narrow waist, dragging her hips back against him. The firm muscles of her bottom were pressed tightly against his heavy erection so that he grew even harder. "I will never get enough of you, not in all the long centuries to come." He bent his head to the smooth line of her back, trailing kisses along her spine. "This is for all time, *querida,* can you feel it? How right it is? How perfectly we fit together." Rafael closed his eyes and slowly eased into her, inch by slow inch. It amazed him how tight she was, how hot, how her muscles were so delicate yet gripped him, milking his body with the expertise born of a true life-mate.

Colby gave herself completely, without inhibition, moving with him, meeting each powerful surge and thrust with one of her own. It was impossible to think, to hold anything in her mind when there was only room for pure feeling. Her body had a mind of its own with him, moving in perfect rhythm while the lightning danced and sizzled and electricity arced all through her. It was the first time in her life she had ever been completely out of control, giving herself up to him, pouring everything she was into him, for him, for herself. She felt her body tightening around his, the earth-shattering release a long endless series of shocks, fragmenting body and soul. The only safe anchor was Rafael's arms as he held her tightly to him, his body and soul soaring with hers.

Colby collapsed forward, on her stomach, exhausted, unable to move, her fingers fisting in the carpet of grass. "Since you are very, very old, this can't possibly be good for your health." She turned her head slightly to look at him, her eyes dancing with laughter. "Has there ever been a recorded death from too much sexual activity?"

He lay over her, his head beside hers. His black eyes shimmered with amusement. "I do not think I recall such an event, but if you like, we can try."

Her lashes fluttered. "I can't move. I think I'll stay right here in this nonexistent grass, which by the way, is very cool. Can you make my front lawn, that ugly brownish patch, into this?" She patted the grass with her clenched hands.

He kissed her shoulder, savoring the feeling of her small, soft body beneath his, the imprint of her firm bottom, her narrow waist. He could live forever buried deep within her, her body beneath his. "I can command the earth to move for you, or bring the rain if you need it."

"Let me get my hay in first," she said pragmatically. She turned her head to look at him. "What are you, Rafael, are you a vampire?"

He shifted his weight to lie quietly beside her, his arms locking her to him. There was no fear in her mind. He had deliberately allowed her to see him with his true predatory nature and yet she wasn't afraid of what he might be. He nuzzled her neck. "I am not the undead, Colby; I am Carpathian, and once bound to you there is no chance that I might turn to such an evil creature."

"You think you can become an honest-to-God vampire?" She opened her eyes wider to study his face, although she didn't move a muscle, too tired to make an effort.

"There is such a monster. Our males can turn vampire and prey on the human race, and on our own species. They are wholly evil and must be destroyed. We have hunters in every land." His hand found her bottom, needing to touch her while he told her of his world. His fingers began a slow, soothing massage. "There is a vampire somewhere close by in this region. I've hunted them all of my life, and I feel him. They are capable of murder and the most vile of acts."

"Pete?" She held her breath, waiting. If she hadn't seen Rafael's fangs lengthening, if she hadn't read his mind, she would think they were both insane.

He bent his head and nipped at the soft expanse of flesh so that she jumped beneath his sharp teeth. "Not Pete. A vampire would have killed him ... differently. But the vampire is up to something. Nicolas, my brother, is far too close to turning to allow him this hunt. He needs to be back in the rain forest, near my other brothers where we can all aid one another."

"Why would he be close to turning? You mean turning vampire?" Colby couldn't help the sudden memory of Nicolas invading her mind, of his cold eyes and merciless expression. In that moment of touching minds, she knew Nicolas De La Cruz was as close to a killing machine as she ever wanted to get. Her heart slammed painfully in her chest. She had touched Rafael's mind and there was a large part of him thatwas much the same as Nicolas.

"Colby," he said gently, "I tell you these things to relieve your fears, not add to them. Our males lose emotions and colors after two hundred years. We exist, but we do not live. I was sent out to kill the vampire, yet each time we make a kill, the whisper of darkness calls to us with more urgency. When the kill is made during the taking of blood, we feel. To someone with emotions, that is nothing, but when you feel nothing, century after century, it is everything. I do not want Nicolas to make a kill."

"What about you, Rafael?"

"You are my anchor. You will prevent me from turning. It is much safer for me than it is for Nicolas." He leaned over her. "Why are you believing me so easily? How can you accept the things I am telling you so readily without fear?"

"Because I've touched you, Rafael. I've looked into your mind and touched your memories. You can't hide something that intense from me when you're sharing my mind. I admit I don't understand everything I've touched on, but you aren't a killer of humans. And you are powerful—the things you can do are much more extreme than what I can do." She rested her head on her arms. "In a way, it's very comforting." The feel of his hands moving over her bottom, his fingers massaging her muscles, soothed her deliciously sore body even as deep within her, pooling heat felt sinfully wicked. She was too relaxed, too sated to care.

Lying beneath the stars without a stitch of clothing, with his finger marks on her body and signs of his possession on every inch of her, held a sultry, primitive satisfaction. She could feel the weight of his eyes, the burning intensity that filled that terrible emptiness inside of her. For a moment she thought of what her life would be like after he went away, returned to his own land, and her heart nearly stopped beating. The breath left her lungs in a terrible rush. She went very still. This night would have to last her forever.

His hand tangled in her hair. "Tonight I want to show you my world so you will understand why I have no choice but to do the things I must."

His tone warned her. A soft velvet, but there was steel in it. Something implacable, something immovable.

"Why do I get the feeling I'm not going to like this?" She made a supreme effort and turned over so she could stare up at the glittering stars scattered over her head. When his hand reached for hers, she entwined their fingers together. "You can't be out in the sun, can you, Rafael? That's what the Chevez brothers were worried about this morning when you came to help fight the fire—the sun had come up." She leaned close to brush his shoulder with her mouth. "You suffered to stay and comfort me, didn't you?"

"I had to be with you, Colby." His voice was husky, touching her deep inside as his body had. "I cannot bear your unhappiness. And if you are in danger, I can do no other than see to your safety. Pain is a part of life; you learn much in centuries of living. Pain is momentary, but enduring every moment of a barren existence is intolerable. I cannot go back to such a thing. I was closer to turning than I had believed. I know this because I feel it in my brother Nicolas now. You felt it in him.

His darkness when he was so close to you. He frightened you—I read your memory of your meeting with him."

Colby knew he was telling her much more than she was hearing, than she was understanding. She didn't touch his mind, preferring to allow her brain to process the information at its own pace. She didn't want to fear him, not now when her body was vibrating with a thousand sensations, when she was more relaxed and happy than she had ever been in her life. "If I never say it again, Rafael, thank you for this night. Thank you for caring enough to lend us the money to save the ranch. And thank you for accepting me the way I am, for making me feel accepted."

"You sound as if you are saying good-bye to me, Colby." His voice was gentle. "Did you think to wonder why your skin burns in the sun? Why your eyes are so sensitive? Why you need to sleep in the middle of the day?"

She sat up, her palm over the dark brand of his possession. She could hear the sudden beating of her heart, loud in the silence of the night. He sounded as if she were becoming what he was. "Taking my blood would do what? What are you saying?" She pushed down panic, fought to stay calm. There was something terrifying in the way his black eyes moved over her body. She looked around for her clothes, suddenly feeling more vulnerable than ever.

"Taking your blood would not affect you so. We exist on the blood of others. The women you think I sleep with hold no interest for me, other than as prey." He said the words starkly, watching her reaction closely. "If you were in my mind, you know I take sustenance from humans."

She reached for her shirt, feeling more threatened than ever. His hand caught her wrist, held her still. His gaze was very direct, very black as it moved broodingly over her face. "You belong with me, Colby. This night has proved that to both of us."

There was enormous strength in his grip. More than the viselike shackle of his fingers, there was the feeling of restraint, as if she were a prisoner, not a lover. She swallowed the tight knot of fear welling up. "Let go of me."

"A few moments ago you thanked me for the night, now you fear me."

"I have reason to fear you," she pointed out and waited for him to deny it.

His gaze didn't leave her face. "You knew that the first time you saw me, but it didn't stop you from wanting me. Did you ever ask yourself why?"

She made the mistake of struggling. Colby didn't know why she did it. Rafael was the type of man to respond aggressively to a struggle and he was far stronger. She found herself lying in the thick mat of grass, staring up at the stone carving that was his face. She swore she heard a growl rumbling in his throat, and his eyes blazed with fire.

"Do not do that," he hissed. He brought his hand up to span her throat and bent his head slowly to press a kiss to the corner of her mouth. "I would never hurt you, Colby. *Never.* I am incapable of harming you."

She took a breath. Let it out. Forced her mind away from panic. "I gave you acceptance, Rafael. I acknowledged what you are. Why are deliberately scaring me this way? What more do you want from me? Do you think I lie in the field with any man who comes along? I've done things with you I never even thought about. I let you do things to me I never considered doing with another man. I even let you take my blood. I watched fangs lengthen in your mouth and let you sink them into me."

His mouth moved to the spot on her neck. His tongue swirled

there. "And it was erotic, was it not?" He bent his head to the mark over her breast. "I want all of you. You are giving me only a part of you and I refuse to accept that."

"It's all I have to give you. I'm sorry it's not enough for you, but you knew that I had responsibilities going into this. I told you I wouldn't trade Ginny and Paul's future for anything."

His tongue flicked over his mark on her. He lifted his head, his black eyes glittering. "And what do you think a vampire would do to Ginny and Paul?"

For some reason, unbidden, came the memory of being trapped in the mine with a living, breathing monster. It had been as trapped as she was, pinned beneath the rubble, but clawing at the dirt to get to her. She remembered the sound of it hissing and gurgling, the glowing eyes, demonic in the blackness of the mine. The stench had been horrific, evil permeating the mine shaft so that she was sickened by it. She had inadvertently burned the thing, her fear causing flames to lick over its trapped body so that it screamed horribly. She still woke with nightmares, drenched in sweat, hearing the echoes of those cries. Had it been a vampire? Could she have encountered one in her youth? Ginny and Paul would never survive such a creature.

"I'll protect them," she whispered fiercely. "From you, your brother, the Chevez brothers, and a vampire if necessary. Let me up, Rafael. I mean it."

He didn't move, his wide shoulders blocking the sky, his heavy muscles rubbing along her skin causing every nerve ending in her body to come alive. If it was possible, his eyes darkened more, robbing her of breath. "You do not get to close your eyes to what is between us. I told you I would have all of you and I meant it. If I kissed you and took your body right now, when you are afraid and when you are angry with me, you would let me because you want me. You need me in the same way I need you." He leaned close so that his breath was against her mouth. "You are not complete without me. That is why you let me have your body, Colby. It is the only reason. You need me. You wanted sex to be enough, but it is not enough and will never be enough."

"What then?" She asked him the question quietly, no surrender in her defiant gaze. She would *not* trade the children for her own life. Whatever he was asking, the price was too high.

"I am going to bring you wholly into my world."

Colby might have been expecting it. She had considered briefly he might ask her, but the way he said it with his hard, implacable resolve was terrifying. Hearing the words said aloud was far different from turning the idea over, however briefly, in one's own mind. For a moment she was paralyzed, lying beneath him like a sacrifice. Her body had betrayed her long ago, soft and pliant, belonging to him, alive beneath his hands, beneath his body, ready for him even when he was holding her captive.

"What have you done to me?" She didn't even recognize herself. He could take her right there, in the midst of her fear with her heart breaking and she would enjoy it. "This isn't love, Rafael. No matter what you think, it isn't love."

"It is love to me." His hands smoothed over her bare skin, shaping her curves, feeling her response to him. "You have my body and my soul. You have all of me. I want all of you. I will not take less."

"What have you done?" she repeated, refusing to give in to hysteria.

"To bring a human life mate wholly into our world it requires three blood exchanges. The woman must be psychic, which you are."

She stared up at him in horror. "You exchanged blood with me?"

"Of course. You are my lifemate. It is natural. You become the very blood in my veins as I am in yours."

She closed her eyes briefly to block him out. "You gave me your blood?" It was a whisper, maybe even a plea. She didn't want it to be true, yet her eyes had burned in the sunlight and her skin had blistered. Her mind needed the touch of his mind and still did. "Damn you, Rafael, you had no right to give me your blood. You know I have a ranch to run. You don't have the right to arbitrarily make decisions for me. I don't care what you are, I have rights and you just stepped way over them. How many times? How many times did you do that?"

"Do not judge me by your human standards, Colby."

She shoved at the wall of his chest. "Get the hell off of me. Get off me or I'll scream until someone hears and comes running." She was furious, more furious than afraid of him.

"Do you think I will allow anyone to take you from me? I am more animal than man. More monster than guardian. I am capable of things you cannot conceive of."

"And you think telling me this furthers your cause how?" She shoved again. "Get off of me!"

His hand pinned her wrists together and he pulled her arms above her head. "Kiss me, Colby."

"Go to hell, Rafael. I don't care what you do to me. It won't make a difference. I decide my fate, not you."

He bent his head toward her mouth. Colby turned her head away and bit at his shoulder hard. At once heat flared between them. Fire raced through her body. It was maddening and perverse and she didn't want to give in to it. He kissed his way down her throat to her breast. His mouth was tight and hot and he scraped his teeth along her tender skin, lending an edge of pain to the pleasure. Her body reacted with more heat. More fire. With urgent demands. The pressure built fast and sharp deep within her, needing release.

Rafael refused to give it to her, tending her breasts with his hot mouth, massaging with his hands, taking small nips with his teeth and laving with his tongue. He held her down easily while she clawed at his back, her hips frantically trying to align with his body for relief. Deliberately he fed the sexual frenzy in her mind, heightening her pleasure, sharing his own. The way it felt to have her skin against his skin, moving beneath him like satin and silk. The way it felt to take her breast in his mouth, to stroke her body until she cried out for him. He shared the feeling of holding her beneath him, doing as he willed with her body, a body that belonged to him. He shared what it did to him to feel her fingernails in his skin, her hands bunching in his hair, wanting him, wanting more.

He kissed his way down her belly, his hands massaging her breasts, his thigh holding her in place. She sobbed as he plunged his fingers deep into her wet core. She moved against his hand, but he refused to allow her release. She swore at him, tugged at him, but he shook his head, wanting her to know what it was like, the terrible hunger inside of him every time he looked at her. The needs, dark and intense, that bordered on insanity when he grew hard and thick and needed her body under his. He didn't want her to come to him unaware of his demanding nature. He would try to learn tenderness for her, but he knew exactly what he was like and what he would insist on from her.

"Give yourself to me," he whispered, dragging her legs around his shoulders. His eyes glittered like black obsidian as they met hers. Then he lowered his head to her hot, waiting core.

She screamed, clawed at his back, tugged at his hair. "I did. I have," she pleaded when he stopped time after time, keeping her teetering on the edge of release.

"I am taking what is mine," he replied. "There is a difference."

"You're being a bastard," she pointed out and screamed again when he deliberately renewed his attack.

When she was sobbing, certain she couldn't take it anymore, he lifted her legs even higher, holding firmly to her ankles as he thrust hard into her. A deep long stroke of possession. He buried himself deep inside of her, deeper than he'd ever been, forcing her to take all of him. He filled her, pushing through soft, swollen folds, slick with welcome, hot with need. She couldn't move in the position he held her, could only lift her hips to try to meet the hard, deep thrusts of his. Fire raged in his blood, burned in his belly. Thunder roared in his head. She was so hot and tight he thought he would explode. His body was no longer his own, but a part of hers and he shook with the pleasure and pain of their forceful joining.

"I claim you as my lifemate." He bit the words out, gasped them aloud, as he surged into her tight channel, again and again, over and over, never wanting to stop. The fierce conflagration was burning out of control, spreading like a firestorm through him. "I belong to you. I offer my life for you. I give to you my protection, my allegiance, my heart, my soul and my body. I take into my keeping the same that is yours."

He was killing her with pleasure. Waves of it crashed over her, through her. She climaxed so many times, so hard; she shook as the sensations ripped through her. As he spoke she felt a curious wrenching in her heart. Her soul. As if something was weaving them together inside of her. As if his ferocious lovemaking and his words combined together to weld them into one complete person. "Stop!" Panic welled up. He held her ankles tightly, keeping her open to him, shattering her, taking her apart and remaking her so completely there would never be any way to go back to what she had been.

Mercilessly he thrust into her, over and over, ruthless hot hard strokes, each designed to take him deeper, to tie her to him in every way possible. "Your life, happiness, and welfare will be cherished and placed above my own for all time. You are my lifemate, bound to me for all eternity and always in my care."

She saw his face, the sensual lines etched deeply, the conviction and implacable resolve, and knew he had done something terrible. She felt it. She knew it. She saw it in the glittering black of his eyes, in the harshness of his expression even as he drove her out of her mind with sheer pleasure. She felt his body hardening and thickening deep inside of her. He threw back his head and she caught the glint of his white fangs as he cried out hoarsely, pumping into her, filling her, sending her body into a wild orgasm that blasted her entire body into a million fragments.

After a while she became aware of lying in the grass with her legs spread, up in the air, his fingers circling her ankles like vises. She tugged to get free. His breathing was ragged, matching hers. He slowly loosened his hold on her and lowered her legs to the ground before slumping over the top of her.

Colby lay beneath Rafael. Her heart slammed so hard she feared it would break through her chest. Her body continued to ripple with aftershocks, pleasure shattering her so that she couldn't move, but lay sprawled out in the grass afraid of the terrible craving his sexual needs had set up in her. She could never find anyone who would do this to her body and soul. How could she lie awake at night and not feel his hands on her body? Not feel him driving into her over and over again until they were both screaming for mercy? Tears burned, but she didn't know if it was from sheer ecstasy or from a bone deep hunger that only Rafael could assuage.

"Did I hurt you?" He didn't think he could ever find the strength to stand up again. His fingers brushed gently at her tears.

"I don't know. I won't know for a few hours." She was dazzled by the colors in the sky, the stars and the moon and the variations she'd never noticed. Her body sang, still gripped in the aftermath of their frenzied joining.

He lifted his head from her breast and looked into her eyes. "You are a very stubborn woman."

"You are a very pigheaded man." She pushed the silky black

strands of hair from around his face. "You don't like anyone saying no to you, do you?"

A small smile curved his mouth. "There is no reason to say no to me. And I especially do not want you saying no to me. You are my woman. My lifemate."

"But that doesn't mean ownership," she told him. Her fingertips were gentle on his face. "You can't *force* me to love you, Rafael. I need to know more about you. I see into your mind and there are things that don't make sense to me."

"What you see in my mind should not make any difference, *querida.*"

Colby stirred, pushed at his body, annoyed with his arrogance. "You're heavy, Rafael. Move." His fangs had not retracted and she was becoming nervous again.

He kissed her throat and pushed away from her to sit up. "It is only because you are so small. You need to eat more."

She looked at him from under her lashes. "I can't eat anything lately. Do you have anything to do with that?"

"Yes." One did not lie to one's lifemate.

Take her. Make her yours so we can leave this place and go home. Nicolas was hunting prey. His voice whispered in Rafael's mind. It was obvious he didn't understand why his brother was not simply forcing the woman to do his bidding.

It is complicated.

Nicolas sighed. *You forget who and what you are. Do you want the vampire to kill her? To destroy the people on this ranch? If you allow this rebellion to continue, she will be the death of us all. We will be without honor.*

Colby managed to find her blouse, although she had no idea where her bra was. "Is he talking to you?"

"My brother? Yes."

She slipped her arms into the shirt, wincing a little. She was sore from the strength of his fingers. Her body still held the stamp of his possession. "What did you say to me? What were those words you said? They sounded suspiciously like a ritual of some kind." She cast him a wary glance as she crawled toward her carelessly discarded jeans. "What *exactly* did you do?" The buttons were gone from her blouse, so she knotted the tails together under her breasts.

"I bound us together in the way of my people."

He sounded smug. Arrogant even. Colby bunched her panties in her hand and threw them at him. "You ripped these."

"You do not need them." His arms wrapped around her and he pulled her back against his chest as she tried to wiggle into her jeans. Teeth nipped and scraped at her neck. "You should never wear clothes."

"That will go over big with the rest of the world. What ritual?" She leaned against him for leverage as she pulled the jeans over her bottom. She was sensually sore everywhere, inside and out. And of course, his hands had gone straight to her breasts, cupping the weight in his palms through the gap in the edges of her blouse. "Is it ever enough with you?"

"Apparently not. Maybe you should not get dressed just yet."

She turned her face up to his throat and lay against him, savoring being in his arms. In another few hours she would have to work nonstop, but she had the night with him. All she had to do was convince him not to bite her anymore. "As it is, I'm not certain I can walk." She stood up, using his shoulder as an anchor while she tested her legs. It was strange to look at him, to know the things he'd done to her, with her, to know she'd screamed his name, begged him for more, pleaded with him to consume her, and yet not feel in the least embarrassed.

Rafael stood up in one smooth motion, clothing himself in the way of his people. She gave a small gasp and stepped back. "How did you do that? Even your hair looks clean and combed." She lifted a hand to her own hair with a small frown. "I'm afraid I look a bit on the used side. I need a shower and a hairdresser."

"You look beautiful, Colby. You are always beautiful, especially when you are screaming beneath me." There was a wealth of satisfaction in his voice. He held out his arm in front of her, his gaze on her face. His skin rippled, and feathers erupted as a wing developed, a huge expanse of wing much like that of a harpy eagle.

Colby sucked in her breath. "It was you. I let you into my house."

"Into your bedroom." The feathers disappeared, leaving behind muscle and sinew. He leaned close to her, his fangs very much in evidence. "Into your body. I am stealing your heart."

Because he already had her soul. She knew it now with a strange certainty, in the way she knew things, He owned her body and her soul. He wasn't finished or satisfied. He wanted her heart and he wanted her mind. Colby shook her head. "You aren't thinking straight, Rafael. Think with your brain, not overactive portions of your anatomy. Realistically, how do you think this is going to end?" She swept her arm to encompass the ranch and the high mountain peaks. "You love Brazil and the rain forest. You and your brother want to go back. You *need* to go back. This is my home. It's all I've ever known. I have to hold it in trust for Paul and Ginny. I've fought a good part of my life to keep this ranch running. Do you really think I'm going to walk away from it and run off with a man I barely know because we have great sex together? I may be a ranch girl, but I have brains in my head."

He stepped closer to her, his body posture suddenly aggressive. "You think realistically, Colby. Do you really think I am going to walk away from the *only* thing in this world standing between me and the loss of my soul? Standing between me and utter darkness? The monster roars at me every rising. Whispers to me in the middle of the night, calls tome when I hunt, and when I take blood from my prey. I will *never* give you up. I am taking you with me when I return to my homeland. You will come with me as my lifemate whether you agree or not."

She glared at him. "You are such an arrogant savage. Is that the way men in Brazil get their women?"

"No, it is the way Carpathian males get their women. The ritual words to bind them are imprinted on them before birth. Once found, he can bind his woman when she refuses to see reason. It is what safeguards our men and keeps our species alive."

She tasted fear in her mouth. He was serious. And he was closer. She hadn't seen him move, but he was there, a breath away, and there was something terrible in his eyes. She couldn't look away from him, mesmerized by the sheer force of his personality. She swallowed hard and shook her head. "Don't, Rafael. Don't try it. I'd fight you and I can be destructive. One of us might get hurt and I wouldn't want that, not after what we've shared. I don't have the control that you have."

His fingers curled around the nape of her neck with exquisite gentleness. With tremendous strength. She knew he could snap her neck if he desired. "Then do not fight me, *meu amor.*"

A prickle of unease went down her spine. Her mouth felt dry and her heart pounded out of control. She took a step back. He glided with her, almost a dance, matching her every movement.

"Rafael." She heard her protest through the sudden roaring in her ears.

His body jerked. His eyes went wide with surprise. He shoved her away from him with such force that she was literally lifted into the air and flew backward. She saw the blood spraying from his chest. Colby's scream was cut off as she landed so hard it knocked the wind out of her. She lay several feet from him, staring in horror as he turned to face away from her. She saw the gaping hole in his back, the river of blood. She hadn't heard the sound of a gun and she was certain she hadn't done such a thing.

11

"Good evening, Rafael."

The silken evil in the crooning voice made Colby's breath catch in her throat. She jerked her head around to stare in horror at the monster standing at the edge of the clearing. "Paul!" A low cry escaped when she saw Paul held as a shield in front of the creature.

Her brother's eyes were wild with fear, his breath coming in gasps of dread. There were bruises on his face and lacerations on his knuckles. His shirt was torn and she could see marks on his chest. A powerful hand, corded with steely tendons, clutched his throat in an unbreakable grip. One long sharp fingernail pressed against Paul's jugular and, even from the distance, Colby could see the blood trickling down Paul's neck.

Rafael! Oh, God, what is it? She had never seen anything so unmistakably evil in all her life. It resembled a man, or something that had once been a man, but the tight, mottled purple flesh that clung to its skull appeared more dead than alive. Red eyes gleamed like burning coals out of the hideous face and long terrible fangs flashed in the lipless slash of the creature's terrible mouth. Dozens of serpents coiled around the monster's limbs, seemingly growing out of his flesh. Rows of sharp, piranhalike teeth filled the snakes' gaping jaws and they hissed and undulated with open menace.

One of the serpents, fully extended from the monster's arm, was slowly retracting back toward its master. Bright red blood covered the snake's awful head and Colby's dazed mind made the connection. The mutated serpent had attacked Rafael, its razored teeth slashing through the flesh of his back, driving straight toward his heart.

That is a vampire. Rafael's voice was edged with pain. *How badly are you hurt?* He ignored her question. *Do not draw its attention.* Even as he spoke the warning, the vampire's grip on Paul tightened.

Her brother cried out and Colby held up her hand, wanting time to stop, wanting her world back the way it had been just moments before. "Don't." She made the plea softly as she got to her feet. Her gaze shifted to Rafael. She had no idea how he was still standing with a gaping hole in his back and blood running down his body.

I was so centered on you I did not feel his presence, querida. I have not made such a mistake since I was a youth. His voice was weary, but calm. *Stay behind me where he cannot get a clear field of vision to you.*

"Colby?" Paul sounded young and frightened.

The vampire shook him, digging his fingernail deeper so that the boy cried out in terror and pain. More blood trickled. With a small sob, Colby rushed forward. Rafael caught her as she tried to get past him and pushed her behind him.

Oh, God, Rafael, what about Ginny? They were at the house alone together while I was with you. There was guilt and fear in her mind.

Ginny is safe, fast asleep in her bed with her dog guarding her, Rafael reassured her.

"You are Kirja Malinov." Rafael gave a small bow. "It is long since we met."

The creature laughed harshly, the sound grating on Colby's ears. "I knew you would remember. You have grown careless, Rafael."

You know each other? Colby was incredulous, unable to look away from her brother and the hideous vampire who held him.

We were friends once.

"So you have come for justice, Kirja. Had I known, I would not have been otherwise occupied and would have prepared a fitting welcome." There was complete confidence in Rafael's voice. Colby glanced at the blood running down his back and shuddered with terror.

His words, or perhaps his demeanor, seemed to anger the creature. "Look at your sister, boy." The vampire shook Paul. "She's his whore now. She will do anything for him, even sacrifice your life for him." He pointed to a scrap of cloth on the ground and Colby's ripped panties floated toward Paul's face. Her bra leapt from a bush and wound obscenely around the boy's arm.

Paul stared at the silky underwear with a frozen expression on his face.

"He can make her do anything for him. Look at her, see his marks on her, know what he's done to her. I told you he would make her his slave."

There was pain and shock in Paul's eyes, condemnation on his face. Colby gasped at the disgust in his expression. Before the hurt and embarrassment could take her over, she allowed her natural power to flood her body, her brain. She needed to save Paul more than she needed to defend her choice of lovers.

The evil one is using his voice to persuade Paul, she heard Rafael tell her. *This is an ancient master vampire, nearly impossible to defeat. Wait until I can align my power with yours.*

Rafael sighed aloud. "I tire of your game, foul one."

Tell me what to do to help you. Colby was shocked at how she could speak to him mind to mind. It seemed to come naturally as if they were so connected now they were one person. If Rafael was a killer of vampires, she would let him take the lead, but it had better not take too long. She couldn't always contain the build up of power when she was angry. Right now she was close to rage. The sight of the evil creature stroking the side of Paul's neck with his sharp talons brought out every protective instinct—and more rage than she'd ever known she was capable of feeling.

The vampire hissed between his jagged, brown teeth. "The great Carpathian hunter defeated by his own carnal pleasures. There is some justice in that, I think." His bloodshot eyes glared at Colby. "You can choose which one you want to save. Your lover or your loved one." He cackled as if he'd made a great joke and the sound was so grating she felt her skin crawl.

Gather up handfuls of soil, as rich as you can find, and use your saliva to mix it. My blood flows in your veins so you will carry the same healing agent. Pack the soil into the wound in my back but do not allow the vampire to see what you do. Remember, your power is greater than it was, enhanced by stepping partway into my world. There is no question we must save the boy. Think only of that and not of me.

Nothing Rafael said made sense. Pack dirt she spit on into an open wound? She shuddered to think of the bacteria she would introduce. Rafael should be falling down, not standing there looking cool and calm and completely in control. His mind was firmly lodged in hers, she felt him there, commanding her to do as he bid. Colby tried not to see Paul, forcing her mind away from the sight of that wicked sharp nail poised to kill.

She backed away, shaking her head, stumbling and falling in the deepest of the night's shadows, her hands clawing for fresh soil behind a fallen log. Colby let one sob escape as she bent her head, pretending to be sick while she spit into the dirt she had gathered. Terrified for Rafael, she packed it hastily while the vampire snarled and snapped at her with his ghastly stained teeth.

"Get up!" he yowled. "Get up and make your choice before I do it for you."

Colby staggered to her feet, but kept Rafael between her and the sight of her brother as she advanced. Closing her eyes, she pushed the soil pack deep into the gaping hole in Rafael's back. He didn't wince. He didn't indicate in any way the pain that must have shot through his body. Instead, he sent her warmth and reassurance.

"There is no question of a choice," Rafael said quietly. His voice was beautiful, clear and strong and brushed with magic. "I would never allow anyone to trade the life of a child for my life." He didn't look at Colby, but she felt him stirring in her mind. *I will force Paul from his arms. He will expect the attack to come from me, but I will use you. Keep looking at him. The Chevez brothers and Nicolas are on the way so do not despair.*

It was the complete confidence he exuded that allowed Colby to keep panic at bay. She had always thought his voice beautiful, but when he spoke to the vampire, she couldn't help but want to hear him speak again and again. There was enthrallment in his voice, conviction. For all of Rafael's faults, she knew she was looking at the difference between good and evil.

"It is not your choice to make. Let us see if your woman prefers to keep you alive," the vampire snarled. His talon traced a line around Paul's throat and left behind a thin trail of blood.

Colby cried out and stepped toward him again, the power sweeping through her, but Paul was in the way and he would get hurt. She didn't dare retaliate.

Paul began to sob, calling out for Colby, begging her to help him.

Reading Colby's agitation, Rafael waved his hand toward Paul. Immediately the boy became quiet, his face slack, his eyes glazed. *He does not know what is happening, so there can be no fear,* Rafael sought to reassure Colby.

What are our chances of saving him? It took every ounce of self-control she had not to hurl herself at the vampire. Strangely, she trusted Rafael to save Paul. She was in his mind and saw his resolve, his absolute determination. He would sacrifice his life for her brother. She swung her head to look at him, her hand going to her throat. It was in his mind. Whatever he was planning more than likely would get him killed, but he intended that Paul would live. A protest welled up.

Look at him. Do not take your eyes off of him. The command was sharp and imperious, a being dictating and used to absolute obedience.

Rafael was far more than human and she felt his power. Colby kept her gaze fixed on the vampire. What was he waiting for? Why was he prolonging the agony?

They feed on terror and the pain of others. He is enjoying his moment of watching the fear in you as you wait to see which one of us he kills. It is the absolute power of life and death, the controlling of others, that feeds him now.

Thunder rumbled and lightning dazzled her, forking across the night sky. Clouds spun dark webs overhead. Her skin prickled and she knew somewhere in the rocks above them were the Chevez brothers. She forced herself to keep from shifting her gaze in inquiry toward Rafael. It was his mind that had provided the information, the knowledge that they had high-powered rifles trained on the vampire.

"Choose!" the vampire snarled, his claw poised over Paul's throat. The mutated serpents immediately became agitated, lusting to kill, lusting for blood, raising ugly heads and undulating in excitement.

Something moved beneath the ground. Colby felt the ripple beneath her feet and knew immediately more of the ghastly creatures guarding the vampire were preparing to attack. She clenched her fists. *What are you waiting for? He has more of those hideous things, I feel them moving beneath us.*

Rafael ignored her. "Foul one, do you think to take this woman and repair your soul with her? That makes no sense. She would never submit and would cut out your heart someday."

The vampire laughed, the sound ugly and harsh after the purity of Rafael's voice. "She is of no use to me. She does not have the talent I seek. Why would I wish to be like you? Serving others when you should be ruling them?" Contempt sharpened his features and heightened his evil appearance.

"You? Seeking a talent?" There was taunting amusement in Rafael's voice. "Why would an ancient need a human's talent? You are acquiring a certain reputation and if it becomes known you need a human to succeed in your plans, your reputation would be that of a laughingstock."

Colby winced. Rafael was deliberately stirring the vampire to greater heights of agitation. But he was also stalling for time.

"I care nothing for what hunters think of me. I have no respect for those of power who subjugate themselves for lesser beings." The vampire waved his hand to encompass the ranch. "I take humans as fodder, cattle such as they use for prey. I use them and reign over them. They do my bidding as I will it. They live or die as I will it. You are so weak you do not even take your lifemate, willing to put your life, hers, and your brother's life in danger. You do not deserve to live," he sneered. "What became of you, Rafael? You were always a leader, yet you allowed Vlad to send you scurrying to do his bidding."

The sharp-toothed serpents erupted through the ground right at their feet, striking at Rafael and Colby with tremendous force. Simultaneously, thick thorn-covered vines burst through the dirt to wraparound the striking serpents. She could feel Rafael generating the defense through the vines. Colby stumbled back, but Rafael held his ground, still facing the vampire.

Now! He sent her the command, but it wasn't only to Colby. She found she was connected through Rafael to both Chevez brothers and to Nicolas. Vines broke through the surface, hungrily reaching for Paul, dragging him from the vampire and wrapping him up in a thick cocoon. The angry serpents smashed at the plants, eager to get to the boy, but as fast as they broke the fibrous stalks, more replaced them, these covered in thorns that slashed the serpents and embedded deep into the coils.

As Paul went down, Colby felt Rafael and Nicolas take hold of her power, tear it ruthlessly from her, hurl it with terrible force at the vampire. Fire burst through the sky, a blowtorch of white heat and raging red-orange flames, generated by Colby, fed by the De La Cruz brothers. Colby heard her own scream and knew the moment Rafael and Nicolas directed the Chevez brothers to shoot with their high-powered rifles.

The fire incinerated several of the serpents, but the vampire was already gone, leaving nothing at all, not even a vapor trail or a blank spot to mark where he had gone. Rafael waved his hand toward the sky, turning in a circle as he did so. Colby found she was holding her breath, waiting for something terrible she knew was coming.

Lightning forked in a violent display as the clouds spread out, thinning as if a giant veil was stretched across the sky at Rafael's command. Colby blinked several times to try to see what he was so interested in. She thought he should be worried about the snakes slithering across the ground toward him at a rapid speed. Instead, he watched the sky patiently. His hands continued to flow in a graceful rhythm and she heard his voice whispering words she didn't understand.

Something moved at the edge of a cloud, something dark and shapeless. She swore Rafael commanded the lightning, slamming a bolt from ground to sky, streaking like a spear toward the dark spot. A hissing curse signaled a hit, but retaliation was swift. The ground shook. Colby went rigid.

"Rafael, he's stampeding the cattle." The snakes and vines seemed to be everywhere, an obstacle course between her and Paul. She had thought her brother safe, caged inside the thick, fibrous stalks, but he was helpless in the face of the mindless animals thundering toward them.

Rafael turned his attention to the ground, waving his hand so that the vines withered and the creatures blackened, smoking, but still alive, mouths gaping wide, snapping teeth together in frustration as they continued to fight to get to the hunter.

Go, querida, get him clear. Juan, Julio! Help Colby.

Colby hesitated for only a moment. Rafael was weak, but determined to save them. She hated to leave him, but Paul stood no chance against the stampeding cattle, locked in the vines the way he was. She ran to him, skirting around the slithering snakes as they tried to obey their master even as the heat seared them from the inside out. She knew the terrain, knew the cattle were heading down the steep gully that led right to where they were all gathered. She could hear them now, bellowing in fright, and she could see, off in the distance, just below the ridge, an ominous red-orange glow. "Paul." Heedless of the thorns, she began yanking vines away from her brother.

The attack came from behind Rafael, a rush of wind and flapping of wings. Great unnatural bats darkened the sky, racing toward Rafael, ferociously beating the air around him with outstretched wings, claws extended as they reached for him.

Colby couldn't watch, terrified he was going to go down under the weight of so many creatures. She held on to Rafael's calm reassurance and concentrated on freeing Paul. Rafael had allowed her brother to wake from his enthrallment and he was already trying to dig his way out from the prison made of plants. She focused on the vines, blocking out her fears and thinking only of moving the thick stalks. The vines opened, stretching apart to allow enough space for

Paul to crawl out. He staggered to his feet and caught Colby's hand as she tried to drag him quickly out of the path of the oncoming cattle.

As they ran, she screamed for Rafael to get out of the way. The ground trembled under the heavy hooves and she could see the terrified cattle as they thundered over the slope and raced down the gully toward them. Gasping at the sight of the herd maddened with fear as great orange-red flames leapt in between each animal as they ran, she pushed Paul up onto a rocky ledge and turned back for Rafael.

Rafael! Her cry was in her mind, not aloud. He was holding his ground, the hordes of sharp-clawed bats inches from his body, unable to get through some invisible barrier to tear apart his skin and bones. She could feel the terrible strain on him as he held off the creatures, called down rain to put out the fires springing up around the cattle, and battled with the vampire hidden somewhere close by. She took a step toward him, frantically trying to figure out how to help.

Do not distract him. Nicolas was just as calm, just as confident, and just as imperious as Rafael. His voice was in her mind, a reminder of the closeness of the brothers. There was something very chilling about Nicolas and, rather than intimacy, he only added to the threat she felt was all around her.

"Colby!" Paul caught at her, dragging her up onto the ledge as the cattle swept down the valley.

She couldn't take her eyes from Rafael. He exuded power and confidence even in the face of a stampede. His expression never changed as he controlled the elements, his body ravaged by the loss of blood. He never yielded for a moment to pain or fear. She was in his mind, sharing the battle. And she knew Nicolas shared both of their minds. She could feel him there, coiled, waiting to strike. She knew, through Rafael, that Nicolas was moving toward them at a fast speed and that he was *flying through the air*.

Flashes of light streamed from the cloud cover toward Rafael. He deflected the white-hot spears and launched an attack of his own, sending a hail of silver slivers of lightning rocketing back toward the vampire. A tree uprooted behind Rafael, falling toward him with huge, outstretched branches.

Colby tried to scream a warning, but Paul clapped his hand over her mouth roughly and nearly slammed her into a boulder. She had no time to reprimand him as she caught sight of a flaming spear spinning through the air aimed directly at her heart. She kicked back, struggling against Paul's unusual strength as he held her immobile.

She felt the sudden shift in Rafael's attention as he realized she was in danger. He immediately sent the hidden barrier that protected him from the vampires' batlike creatures in between her and the oncoming spear. The spear bounced off the barrier, but he was instantly swarmed with bats, clawing and digging at his skin and face.

Colby drove her elbow into her brother's ribs with the intention of leaping off the ledge to go to Rafael's aid. The first of the cattle rushed through the gully, others following so that the narrow strip was filled with the large, heavy bodies. She tried to shield her brother from the mass of huge bodies as they rushed past, pressing close to him as the ground shook. The rain poured down, extinguishing the fires and sending billows of smoke into the air. She felt Paul grip her shoulders hard, his fingers squeezing viciously. Before she could cry out in protest, he picked her up off her feet and flung her into the center of the stampeding herd.

Instinctively, Colby curled up in a tight ball, hands over her head to protect herself from the flying hooves. Shockingly, nothing touched her.

The ground shook, but not a single animal kicked her as they thundered past. She heard the sound of voices and knew the

Chevez brothers were turning the herd, trying to calm them before they reached the steep cliffs rising to the east.

Colby cautiously lifted her head. Nicolas stood beside her, his face a grim mask. He reached down and hauled her to her feet with casual strength. At first her legs were shaky, refusing to hold her, but he paid no attention, dragging her with him almost at a run to his brother.

Rafael stood upright, although she couldn't see his body for the hundreds of creatures clinging to him, clawing at his flesh, digging into the wounds on his body. With a cry she tore herself away from Nicolas, reaching for one of the furry animals ripping at his face. Before she could touch it, Nicolas clapped his hands and issued a command. The bats fell to the ground and were incinerated. The noxious odor made Colby gag, but she ran to Rafael.

Rafael staggered. Colby wrapped her arm around his waist. "I'll get you to a doctor." She didn't see how it was possible for a doctor to help him. Most of his skin was scraped from his body. She'd never seen such injuries. She looked around frantically for the vampire, expecting an attack immediately. "Where'd he go? Can you see him?"

"He is long gone," Nicolas said. "He will not fight all of us." His hands were gentle as he reached for Rafael.

Paul ran up to them, swinging a tree branch toward Rafael's head.

"Don Nicolas!" Julio Chevez called out in warning.

Nicolas caught the club and twisted it easily from the boy's hands, sending him sprawling to the ground.

"The boy is tainted, Rafael. He reeks of the vampire. He is no more than a human puppet. I will dispatch him quickly and convert the woman for you. You will go to ground and heal properly." There was absolute resolve in Nicolas.

Colby could see he had already dismissed Paul and would kill him without a single thought of remorse. She flung herself in front of Paul. "Don't you dare. Don't you come near him." Paul was taller than she was, but she spread out her arms and called up every ounce of power she had in her. She didn't want to protect Paul, she wanted to go to Rafael, to save him, do anything it took. She hated standing there, shielding her brother, when Rafael was so broken. She felt her heart was shattering into a million pieces as she looked at his ravaged face.

Meu amor, I would not allow Paul to be harmed by my kin. You should know better. The stirring in her mind was weak, as if Rafael was fading, leaving her.

She was frightened, not knowing who to run to, who to protect. "Rafael's dying, Nicolas," she said. "Is that what you want, to have him try to fight you with his last dying breath? What kind of a person are you?"

Rafael's tall, muscular frame crumpled. He went to the ground on his knees, held there swaying a moment, his eyes glazing before falling forward facedown.

Colby had no memory of leaping to catch him, but she was under him, cushioning his fall, his large frame taking her down with him. Surprisingly, she didn't slam into the dirt as she expected. Nicolas floated Rafael gently to the ground, turning him just before his body hit hers, his head pillowed in her lap. She couldn't prevent the shudder of fear when Nicolas loomed over her.

Juan and Julio stepped up on either side of Paul. "Don Nicolas, please do not force us to make such a choice. This boy is *família*. He is under Don Rafael's protection, as is Colby. This protection should be yours as well."

There was a small silence. Even the night seemed to hold its breath. Insects ceased their wild calls and the cattle stopped their restless motion.

"The poison can perhaps be driven from his system, but I will have to take his blood." Nicolas made it a threat, staring straight at Colby.

She didn't trust him and wished Rafael was fully awake to tell her what to do. "Rafael says he can't lie to me—can you?"

"Say yes or no," Nicolas replied harshly. "He will suffer with the acid of the vampire's blood and he will crave the taste of human flesh. He will rot from the inside out and the vampire will be able to use him to defeat us all."

Paul burst into tears, his hands pressed to his stomach. "I do burn inside, Colby. And there's a buzzing in my head that makes me feel crazy. Is he saying I'm going to be a cannibal?"

"Then do whatever you have to do, but don't you harm him or I'll hunt you down and drive a stake right through your ice-cold heart," Colby warned.

Nicolas ignored her threat and knelt beside Rafael. She watched in disbelief as he tore open his own wrist with his teeth and shoved the wound against Rafael's mouth. He looked at her with empty black eyes as he forced his brother to swallow the ancient blood. "He should have taken you immediately instead of catering to you the way he did." His voice was a harsh whip, lashing her when she was holding Rafael's head in her lap, her fingers tangled in the long silk of his hair and his blood soaking into her jeans.

"I don't like you very much either," she snapped. "How are you different from that monster? My brother is innocent. He didn't ask to have that horrible creature kidnap him and infect him with poison. I didn't ask to be your brother's lifemate. I have my own life here, my own responsibilities. Why should your rights be more important than mine?"

Nicolas leaned close to her, his eyes flat and diamond hard. "Because if you don't find your lifemate, you will not turn into a monster that will be absolutely evil and live for the death and pain of others. I will. I am not human. Rafael is not human. We have fought centuries against the darkness. You could relieve his pain so easily. You could ensure that he would never face that moment in time when he might succumb to darkness, yet you are too stubborn, too selfish to give him what he needs. And because of that, you foolishly risk the lives of your brother and sister and your neighbors and others you don't even know. Worse, you risk my brother's very soul and the souls of my *família* and myself. In the end, he will have you, so taking this risk is senseless. I would take you, if you were mine, and get it done." There was a distinct snap to his teeth as if he might lean over and bite her neck right there.

Colby's heart pounded harder in her chest, but she faced him squarely, trying to be honest with him. Struggling to understand. She wanted to understand when she saw him giving his own blood to his fallen brother. More, the thought of Rafael turning into such a hideous monster as the creature who had attacked them was inconceivable. "I can see from your point of view. Can you see from mine? I'm not Carpathian. I didn't even know you existed until a short time ago. I don't know Rafael. I don't know much at all about him other than he's different, with tremendous powers, and that he can control me in ways that scare me to death. I have a brother and a sister I love and a ranch that I swore to my father on his deathbed I would keep for them. I didn't have any concept of the consequences you're describing. I haven't lived centuries and I haven't known of vampires other than in movies."

"Now you have seen one. Now you know the consequences to Rafael and you know the things I say are true. What are you going to do about it?"

"I don't even know what you want me to do, Nicolas," she answered honestly. "How do I protect Rafael? He talked of bringing me wholly into his world. What does that mean?"

"Could you not tell the evil one was striking at you? If he

succeeds in killing you, he has destroyed Rafael. He used the boy to try to kill you," Nicolas pointed out.

"I didn't try to kill her," Paul denied, his face very pale.

"Yes, you did," Nicolas said calmly. "And if the poison is not removed from your system, you will try again and again until you succeed. Colby, as long as you are human, the vampire knows you are vulnerable and he has a chance to kill Rafael through you."

"How would my death be killing Rafael?" She asked it, but she already knew the answer through her own fears and grief. She struggled to contain it, but she couldn't entertain the idea of losing Rafael. Her mind refused the possibility because her heart knew she wouldn't survive.

"You know," Nicolas said softly.

"Don't even think about it, Colby," Paul snapped. He doubled over in pain, holding his stomach. "Don't let them do anything to you. Can't you see what they are?"

Julio slipped his arm around the boy's shoulders. "They are great men and have protected us from the vampire, Paul. Nicolas is the only one who can save you from the acid inside of you. No doctor could cure the effects."

Nicolas stopped Rafael from feeding, closing the wound in his wrist with a swipe of his tongue. Colby couldn't help the shudder that ran through her body at the matter-of-fact gesture.

"I must take Rafael to a place where he will be safe and I can heal him," Nicolas said. "He has bound you to him and you will suffer greatly for the separation. I can stop that by converting you, but then you would have to rest in the earth with him. Choose now. He needs care immediately."

"If I have to make an immediate choice then I have to stay with my brother and sister and see to their safety," Colby said. There was challenge in her voice.

"You will grieve for him. You will believe he is dead and you will feel a strong call to join him. You cannot harm yourself, no matter how desperate you feel. Reach for me and I will aid you should it become necessary." Nicolas reached down and easily gathered his brother into his arms.

"Wait!" Colby said frantically. "What about Paul?" Her brother could no longer stand, but had to be supported between his two uncles. Doubled over, he sagged helplessly, groaning in pain.

"I will return to take the poison from him. Know this, sister kin: in doing so, he will be tied to me for all time."

It sounded like a warning to Colby, maybe even a threat. Her hand went to her throat in self-defense. "Should I wait for Rafael?" She kept her gaze fixed on his, refusing to be intimidated, wanting the truth.

"That is up to you." He cradled Rafael in his arms, almost as if his brother were a small child instead of a very large and dangerous man.

Colby reached out to touch Rafael's face. He felt cold. Lifeless. A scream welled up in her mind, but she forced it back down. "He's alive?"

"I will not allow him to die. Do I return this night?"

Colby looked at her brother's face, saw the twisted hatred in his eyes, and shuddered. "Please," she whispered, looking away from Paul. "Hurry."

"Traitor! Whore!" Paul threw himself at her, his fist raised, his expression demonic.

Julio caught him and dragged him away from her. "Shall we take him to the house, *senhorita?*"

Paul fought his uncles, growling and snapping his teeth at them. Then he suddenly subsided, looking around him, blinking his eyes to clear his vision. "Colby?" He sounded young and confused. "What's happening to me?"

"You're ill, honey." She tried to comfort him, but tears were clogging her throat and burning behind her eyes. She could no longer touch Rafael's mind. She felt the loss deeply, as if someone had ripped out her heart. She could barely breathe, let alone think. She wanted to scream and claw at the earth, dig her way down to where his body would rest.

Instead, she lifted her head to find the Chevez brothers watching her with compassion. "Let's get him home," she said wearily.

"Juan will see to the cattle," Julio said. "I'll watch over you and Paul and Ginny."

Colby stumbled after him. She could see better in the darkness than she'd ever been able to see, yet she was off center, feeling blind and deaf. "Does this kind of thing happen often?" *What were those terrible creatures and how badly was he hurt, Nicolas? He was so torn up, lost so much blood.* She hadn't kissed him. Hadn't tried to hold him to her. What if Nicolas was more monster than man?

I am more monster than man, Nicolas confirmed. His voice was soft in her mind, distracted. She could hear a chant repeated, old, ancient words with a soothing rhythm of power. *I am healing him, giving him more blood, and then I will put him in the arms of the earth to heal.*

Julio glanced back at her as he propelled Paul forward. "Do you need my help, Colby?" When she shook her head, he continued, "Yes, I've witnessed many battles between the vampire and the hunters. This vampire is not like the others. He is much more powerful and cunning."

Colby wrapped her arms around her waist as she walked along the trail back toward the ranch house. Rafael had walked this path with her, holding her hand, making her feel the most beautiful and desired woman in the world. When he focused on her, nothing else seemed to matter. She tried to replay what Nicolas had said about conversion, but her mind was too scattered.

"Do they often get hurt?" Colby asked.

Julio shook his head. "Vampires are all different. The hunters are very powerful, very experienced. Rafael is a great fighter—together with Nicolas, or any of his brothers, they rarely sustain injuries. This one"—he shook his head—"this is one they call a master vampire, an ancient who has escaped justice many years. Zacarias, the eldest of the De La Cruz brothers, thinks a master vampire is an ancient of their kind. One long in the world and experienced in battle who finally succumbs to the dark call. The master will not stand and battle, but he'll use human puppets to do his bidding. He'll call lesser vampires to him and use them as pawns. And he mutates other species into evil incarnate. You saw a sample of his work."

"You're very nervous. What aren't you telling me?"

Julio looked at her with dark, worried eyes. "Nicolas can take the blood and help with the pain, but until the vampire is dead, Paul will be connected to him. He can still try to use Paul. Nicolas will be the only one standing between Paul and what the vampire wants from him. Nicolas is powerful and ancient, but he is very close to the end of his time. He also must rest during the daylight hours. It is dangerous forhim to do this thing you ask. If he does not, Paul will eventually die and you will be thankful."

Colby pressed her fingers to her pounding head. She needed Rafael's reassuring touch. *He is safe beneath the soil. I have fed and will meet you in the barn. I do not want the child to see what we must do to aid her brother. You must be certain. He can and will harm you if the vampire reaches him and programs him. I can run interference, and I can remove the pain, but I cannot break the tie between them.*

He was offering to kill her brother. It was his voice, so flat and empty, that made her ill. Made her feel Rafael's barren existence starkly. She could almost see the darkness creeping inside of him, staining his soul, taking him over. She closed her eyes but she couldn't block out what was in her mind.

I will watch him until you have a chance to kill the vampire. She made her decision.

Rafael has much to answer for. There was a bite to Nicolas's voice.

Rafael has tried to give me time. Is that truly such a terrible thing? Tears burned in her heart. Had she caused all of this? Was it her fault Rafael lay as the dead beneath the earth?

I feel his love for you. It has sustained me, yet it cannot soften me. He has given me hope by sharing his feelings for you. His emotions are intense and difficult to manage. He is uncomfortable with the presence of other males near you, myself included, yet he tries to ignore those dangerous emotions and allow you the space you need to come to him.

Is it my fault? she persisted.

Silence answered her question as she pulled open the door to the barn and faced Nicolas and his black, merciless gaze.

12

Paul sat silently in the corner, his uncle very close to him. Colby couldn't help but note the protective posture. In that moment, Julio looked heartbreakingly like her stepfather. She glanced anxiously toward the house. "I want to check on Ginny."

"The girl is fine, sleeping peacefully," Nicolas said. "If you want this done, we do it now."

She tried not to bristle at his abrasive attitude. "I wasn't stalling. I happen to be genuinely worried. This hasn't been the best night of my life so far. You might deal with vampires on an everyday basis, but their existence is news to us." She sent a reassuring smile toward her brother.

He tried a grin, looked down and caught sight of her peach-colored bra still wrapped around his arm. At once his expression changed, became dark and ugly. Paul unwound the lacy garment, holding it away from him with two fingers, up, so everyone could see. It made Colby acutely aware of the fact that she wore nothing at all beneath her thin shirt and that the buttons were missing. Even so, even in the midst of her utter humiliation, her mind tried to reach for Rafael. The moment she realized she couldn't touch him, there was only emptiness and grief. Fear shook her heart.

She followed the movement of her bra as Paul tossed it away from him as if it were something so disgusting he couldn't stand to look at. He suddenly lurched away from Julio and caught up a pitchfork, lunging at Colby in one motion.

Colby never saw Nicolas move, but he was there in front of her, taking the weapon from Paul and dragging him into his terrible embrace.

The air rushed out of Colby's lungs as she saw his fangs lengthen, and without preamble he sank the teeth into Paul's neck, her brother going still, under the influence of his mind. She shuddered, feeling as if those sharp fangs were going into her neck. At that moment she hated Nicolas. Hated herself. Hated Rafael. How could she just stand there while some creature she barely knew took her brother's blood so coldly?

What is he doing? Rafael was weak, too weak. She could feel the low pulse of his lifeblood as he stirred in her mind.

His alarm wasn't for Paul. It was for his own brother, for Nicolas. She felt it as if it were her own alarm. She felt the surge of love and warmth that spanned centuries. It flooded her body, took over her heart and soul so that she wanted to reach out to Nicolas, to stop him. What he was doing *was* dangerous to Nicolas, not to Paul. Nicolas was deliberately ingesting vampire blood when he fought every minute of every day against the beast that already stained his soul and fought for supremacy.

"Wait!" Colby couldn't choose between the two brothers. Her own, or Rafael's. They were intertwined, both bound together now in her mind. Paul's life versus Nicolas's soul. It was a terrible choice.

Do not waste your worry on me, either of you. Nicolas's voice brushed at the walls of her mind. *I will hold on and return to our brothers for your sake, Rafael. You share with me the emotions you feel for this woman and this boy. It is enough for me to continue until I reach our home. Go to sleep, Rafael, and allow the earth to heal you.*

She actually felt Nicolas's love for his brother through her tie with Rafael. It was a strange shared path. For the first time she could see him as something other than the cold-hearted monster trying to rip her brother and sister from her arms. Nicolas was real to her. She could see him through the heart of Rafael. Memories of Nicolas welled up and she knew it was deliberate on Rafael's part.

How many times had he stepped between humans and death, at risk to his life and soul? How many times had he tried to protect Rafael and their younger brother from the terrible battles? He had been wounded countless times. He had killed countless times, each time tearing pieces from his soul.

Colby closed her eyes. She didn't want to see it, didn't want to view him as anything other than the emotionless predator she'd first thought him. She was already confused enough. And there was Paul, standing in his embrace while Nicolas took more and more blood, until Paul's face went pale and he sagged in the hunter's arms, dizzy and weak, but still so unnaturally willing to do as Nicolas required him.

She felt the exact moment when Rafael succumbed to his need for rest and healing. He pulled from her mind and left her bereft. She sank down onto a bale of hay and pressed both hands to her churning stomach as she once again watched Nicolas with her brother. He swept his tongue across Paul's neck, closing the pinpricks as if they'd never been. There was no mark. None at all. Her hand crept up to the mark on her neck that never seemed to fade, never went away.

We can leave a mark if we desire, yet not leave evidence if we choose. Nicolas read her thoughts as easily as Rafael; but where, with Rafael, it was an intimacy, with Nicolas it seemed invasive. The cold black eyes swept over her, so different from Rafael. So utterly alone and separated from everything going on around him. *Rafael chooses to leave his mark both as his warning and and his commitment. He will protect you even when he should be resting beneath the earth.*

She recognized the mild censure, but for the first time was able to look past that to the terrible burden Nicolas carried. "What do you have to do now, Nicolas?" she asked.

"Push the poison through my pores and rid my body of the vampire's taint." Her brother was still under his enthrallment. Nicolas helped him to sit on the floor of the barn. "Vampire blood burns like acid. The boy would not have lasted very long. There is something here I have never come across before." Nicolas's eyes drifted closed and he sought inside his own body to break down the compound that had infected Paul and now lived within his own veins. "There is something else here, some small parasite that should not be. It is mutated, much like the serpent the vampire used to attack Rafael."

"Where did the vampire come from?" Colby asked, sickened as beads of blood began to push through the pores of Nicolas's skin. It was a sight she would never forget, never get out of her mind. She tried to distract her thoughts, anything to keep from screaming as the blood seeped onto the floor of the barn and stained the hay dark red. She wasn't squeamish—she'd grown up on a ranch—but her stomach lurched all the same.

"Do not look," Nicolas said harshly. "You are going to draw Rafael from his slumber again and his wound is deep. He must be given time to heal."

"I'm sorry. I've never seen such a thing." She *needed* to touch Rafael. It wasn't just something she wanted. Everything in her reached for him, yet there was only emptiness. She wasn't altogether certain she could stand being away from him and that was alarming, especially with Nicolas telling her his injury was grave and needed time to heal. She wasn't a selfish person, yet it seemed so imperative to disturb him, to call to him so she could feel the brush of his mind in hers.

Nicolas sighed. "He should have converted you and spared you the hell you will have to endure. You must not harm yourself."

"I'm not the type," Colby said, but she was beginning to wonder if that was true. "Is it hurting you?" She couldn't imagine Paul having to go through such a thing.

"Yes." His voice was without inflection. He gestured toward the blood-soaked hay and Julio immediately brushed back everything that hadn't been touched, leaving a circle of bare wood exposed with the bloody hay in the center. Nicolas shoved open the door to the barn and stared up at the sky. At once lightning forked.

To Colby's horror, an orange-red ball streaked toward them, drawn by Nicolas. It incinerated the vampire blood, burning hot for an instant and then simply disappearing as if it had never been. She blinked several times to make certain she wasn't hallucinating.

"This is too bizarre for me." She backed away from Nicolas. "Is Paul going to be okay now? Can I put him to bed?"

"I want to attempt to heal him. The vampire infected him with his blood and his insides are going to feel like someone took a blowtorch to him," Nicolas replied.

Colby could see how pale and weary he was. The lines were deeper than ever in his face and his eyes as cold as ice. She shivered. "You need to feed."

"Yes."

Colby glanced helplessly at Julio. After what Nicolas had done for Paul, she felt she had no choice but to make the offer, and it was the last thing she wanted to do.

Julio shook his head. "I will give Don Nicolas blood while you put young Paul to bed. Then I'll help Juan tend to any injuries the cattle sustained."

"Julio, you and Juan must stay here," Nicolas decreed. "Watch the boy, particularly during daylight hours. I have to rest and I will not be able to monitor him."

Colby paused as she reached for Paul. "What does that mean? Didn't you just remove the vampire's blood from him?"

"Until the vampire is dead, Paul will always be tied to him."

Colby wanted to ask more questions, but Nicolas freed Paul from the enthrallment. Her brother got unsteadily to his feet, forcing her to wrap her arm around him and help him out of the barn.

Paul leaned on her heavily. "I feel terrible, Colby."

"I know, honey, you need to sleep."

He clung to her as she led him to the house and into his room. "I'm really scared, Colby. I've never seen anything like that."

"Me either. But we have Rafael and Nicolas and Juan and Julio to help us. We'll be safe. I'll get your boots off, Paul. Just lie down on the bed and sleep."

He closed his eyes the moment his head hit the pillow, not stirring even when she removed his boots and socks. He looked pale, his dark hair standing out starkly against his skin. She brushed the stray strands from his forehead with gentle fingers and bent to press a brief kiss on the top of his head. Paul stirred, touched her wrist. "I love you, Colby."

She hadn't heard him say that in years. "I love you, too, Paulo," she murmured, aching inside for him.

Colby returned to the barn and found Nicolas gently propping Julio against the wall. "Is he all right?"

Nicolas turned to look at her, his gaze sweeping over her so that she had to struggle to keep from shuddering. "Yes, of course. Julio is my *família*, under my protection. Ordinarily we do not take the blood of our human companions. He was generous to offer when the need was great."

"Nicolas, Rafael knew the vampire. And the vampire called him by name. I felt sadness in Rafael, more than sadness when they were fighting."

For the first time Nicolas regarded her with more than his cold expression. There was a faint expression reminiscent of Rafael in his eyes as if by struggling to understand their world she had gained a greater degree of acceptance from him.

"We knew one another as boys back in the Carpathian Mountains." Nicolas sat down beside Julio, the first really human gesture she'd ever seen him make. It was odd—she couldn't stop thinking of Rafael as human, yet she *never* thought of Nicolas in human terms. She watched as he took Julio's wrist and checked his pulse.

"I am fine, Don Nicolas," Julio protested.

"You must drink plenty of water and sleep."

"I have work to do," Julio protested. "I must watch the boy."

"Juan can watch the boy," Nicolas said. "You go to bed."

"Don't worry, Julio," Colby agreed, "I can help watch Paul. I know he might become dangerous and I'll be careful."

"You must do as Juan tells you," Julio instructed.

Juan entered the barn as Julio spoke and he immediately helped his brother up. "I'll take him to the house."

"The guest room is the middle bedroom," Colby said. She wanted to learn more. She *needed* to learn more, and somehow Nicolas's presence helped to ease the grief that overwhelmed her at times. She watched the Chevez brothers make their way out of the barn. "They're good men."

"Yes, they are, and that is no small compliment," Nicolas said. "I can read their thoughts and know the honor and integrity that lives in these men."

"Tell me about the vampire. Who is he?"

"Who *was* he, is a better question. The first thing you learn as a hunter is to separate the man you knew and loved as a friend from the monster who battles you with every intention of killing you. Kirja is such a man. His brothers and mine were the best of friends. It is unusual in our society to have brothers so close, yet our two families did. Our parents were friends and we were raised very similar." He gave a soft sigh. "We were very competitive, a little rougher and more defiant of the rules of our society, so we stuck together. Kirja and Rafael were particularly good friends. They were always in and out of scrapes and always competing to see who could do something first. It was a goodtime, although my memories fade. Rafael and Riordan kept those memories alive for the rest of us." Nicolas dropped his head into his hands, rubbing at his temples.

Nicolas. Rafael's voice once again brushed in their shared minds. *You have grown weary. You must rest.*

"He sounds so faint, so gone from us." Colby's heart pounded in alarm.

Nicolas lifted his head, leaned back against the wall. *You are not resting properly. Shall I command you to sleep, Rafael? Why do you persist in sleeping so lightly when you know you are mortally wounded?* The bite was back in Nicolas's voice, making Colby wince.

Those I love are vulnerable aboveground and I want to hear should they have need of me. I begin to see why my life mate is reluctant to commit her life to mine. It is a form of hell to lie helpless beneath the earth when those you love are in danger. Rafael's voice was a thread of sound, but he was calm, almost peaceful.

Go to rest, Rafael, or I will do the one thing you asked me not to do and break my promise to you.

Colby looked at the lines etched so deeply into Nicolas's face. She had seen him through Rafael's eyes and now she saw those lines as badges, a man bound by honor, a man ravaged by his destiny but determined to continue to protect the people he loved through memories.

You ease his burden, querida. For that alone I will always love you.

Colby closed her eyes to savor his voice, the caress in her mind that slipped through her body and wound around her heart. She ached to touch him. To make certain he was all right. Even now, even with his terrible wounds, he was stroking her mind and body, reaching out to soothe her, reaching out to his brother.

She blinked back tears. She was beginning to fall in love with him. She didn't know how it was happening; he wasn't the kind of man she would have ever allowed herself to look at.

I am the only man for you.

You are too dominating. You like your women to say yes to everything you dictate.

Only when it comes to sex. And when I am right.

Nicolas's breath came out in a slow hiss. "Merge your mind fully with his." It was more than an order; it was a dare.

Without giving herself time to think it through and back out, Colby merged her mind fully with Rafael's. Instantly she was flooded with pain, a great tearing pain that clawed at her insides, her skin, even her mind. She saw more than that; she saw his child-hood memories of a small boy running with a friend in the hills, trying to shape-shift, and falling from the tree branches, laughing together. She felt the terrible burden of knowing she would have to kill that friend, rip his heart from his chest, with the memory of that boyhood smile and kinship of centuries weighing on her.

With a small cry, she pulled out of Rafael's mind, staggering back, reaching behind her for support. Nicolas was there, although she hadn't seen him move, easing her down to a bale of hay.

Colby! Rafael's cry echoed hers.

I had no idea you were in such pain. Go to sleep at once and I mean it, Rafael. How could anyone live through such a wound? She pressed her hand to her heart. The vampire had tried to jerk the organ backward through Rafael's body using the serpent's strong jaws and razor teeth.

"I should not have told you to do that," Nicolas said. "I regret few things, but that was not worthy of me. My brother will retaliate."

"What does that mean?"

A faint smile touched Nicolas's mouth and was gone. "He just severely reprimanded me and it was not fit for your ears." He sank down beside her. "In truth, I have not thought of the Carpathian Mountains in years. South America has become our home. I do not even remember what the current prince of our people looks like. He was young when we were sent out to hunt the vampire."

"Was Kirja sent out as well?"

Nicolas nodded. "Vlad Dubrinsky was prince at the time. He was a great ruler and we all looked up to him. He sent all five of us to South America and sent the Malinov family to Asia."

"Five of them?"

Nicolas nodded his confirmation.

"Have all five of them turned vampire?" Colby asked. Why would the De La Cruz brothers hold out so many centuries against the whisper of dark power yet the Malinov brothers succumb?

"I thought them long dead. I have heard nothing of them for centuries. Most of the hunters hear rumors of those who have turned vampire and the Malinov family has never been mentioned. My brothers and I have been so cut off from our people it did not seem unusual. Brazil, our ranch, the rain forest became our world."

"And none of you have wives?"

"Lifemates," he corrected. "We have lifemates and we must find them. You are lifemate to Rafael. My youngest brother, Riordan, has found his lifemate in the rain forest, which shocked us all, but gave us a small hope to continue."

"How do you know for certain? I'm not certain. I feel drawn to Rafael—in fact, obsessed with him. That's frightening for me. I just don't respond to men that way."

"It is not obsession, although I have heard it feels that way.

When I touch your mind, I feel your confusion and fear of him. We are all the things you think we are—powerful and dangerous and capable of great destruction—but we are not capable of harming our lifemates."

"Only ruling them?"

"You are not used to being submissive to a male."

"I'm not submissive, it isn't in my character. How can we possibly be compatible? Is it possible there's a mistake?"

"There cannot be a mistake. You restored colors to him, and, through him, to me. I have not seen colors in hundreds of years. You gave him his emotions and, through him, you gave them to me. I could feel what he felt for you, the tremendous love in his heart and his need to protect and watch over you. I want to feel those emotions for myself."

"How can I possibly be his"—she hesitated and then tested the word—"lifemate, when I was born human?"

"I only know that women who are psychic can be successfully converted to Carpathian and these women can also be lifemates to the males. I have not yet met Riordan's lifemate, but he tells me she is a descendant of the jaguar race."

Colby smiled. "My brother says I can be catty, but I doubt if I have any jaguar in me. I couldn't jump very high when I was playing sportsin high school."

"We had school of sorts." Nicolas folded his arms across his chest. "We had to learn to shape-shift first. It was not nearly as easy as we thought it would be."

"That might be kind of cool," Colby admitted. "I like the idea of flying. I used to wish I could fly. Believe me, when you've been on a horse for eight hours, it gets old."

"I remember the first time Rafael attempted to turn into a wolf. It was the very first thing he tried and he was not successful. Part of him was covered in fur and part of him had legs where there should not be legs. We were all there, of course. We all ran together, the De La Cruz brothers and the Malinov brothers. We were all howling and falling on he ground, rolling around like idiots, but then when Ruslan, the eldest of the Malinovs, began laughing and pointing, my oldest brother, Zacarias, went after Ruslan for making fun of Rafael. We ended up in a huge brawl. Mind you, the entire time, Rafael was still caught between man and beast."

Colby couldn't help but laugh as Nicolas related the story to her. He provided very vivid pictures of the incident for her. Rafael looked so young and uncertain, not at all like the dominant man she was tied to. "What about you? What was the first thing you tried to shape-shift into?"

There was a small silence. The mask slipped back over Nicolas's face. He shrugged his shoulders carelessly, but she didn't think it was a careless gesture. "I do not remember."

"You recalled Rafael's first time so vividly." Even to the colors of the trees, the individual leaves, the smells and sounds. She'd heard the hum of insects in his mind.

He stood up. "It was Rafael's memory, not mine. You gave him back those things and he shares with me."

Colby studied his mouth. There was a cruel edge to it, a remoteness in his eyes. "You're very close to turning into one of those monsters, aren't you?" she asked. Her heart ached for him. Ached for Rafael.

"Yes. Without the memories my brother shares with me, I would lose this battle."

"And yet you came to his aid even though you knew if you battled the vampire you would go a step closer. And you took the vampire blood from Paul, when it could have pushed you over the edge. Why did you do that, Nicolas? I wasn't even nice to you."

"You are *família*. You are a Carpathian lifemate and must be protected by all Carpathians. And I love my brother. I may not feel it anymore, but I know it is there, buried deep, and I will not allow anything to happen to you."

"I will never forget the risk you took on our behalf, Nicolas, and if it becomes too difficult and you need to see colors and feel emotions, I don't mind so much the sharing of our minds."

There was a small silence. "It is no small thing you offer, sister kin," he said softly. "Carpathian men do not share with others, not even kin. My brothers and I are unusual because we had no choice but to bind together to overcome the call of the beast. I know you fear Rafael's hold on you and you have yet to commit your life to his. Why do you offer this to me?"

It was complicated. She didn't know if it was watching him push the poisonous blood through his pores after taking it from Paul, or watching him give his brother blood, but she was very conflicted. She certainly wasn't going to make a commitment to a life of living underground and sucking blood from living human beings—the very idea made her shudder—but she couldn't leave him so starkly alone any more than she could stop herself from thinking of Rafael.

"You stayed here talking to me because you knew I would never make it through the night without him, didn't you?"

"Yes."

"That's your answer, Nicolas. Maybe I feel the need to protect you for him, just the way you feel it for me."

They were silent a moment. Then he spoke again. "I have a vampire to catch."

"How can you find him?"

"Now that I know who he is, he will be easier to track. I know his ways. It has been hundreds of years, but he had certain patterns, all of us do, and he will keep to some of his."

"Rafael wants you to wait." She had sensed Rafael's concern and it hadn't just been because he was afraid Nicolas would make another kill and be that much closer to succumbing to the insidious whisper for power.

"I cannot take a chance that he will strike against you. He will be locked in the ground during the daylight hours, longer than I will be, but he can use his human puppets to try to kill you."

"You mean Paul."

"I am guessing he has more than one. This vampire is ancient and cunning. He is a skilled fighter and knows all the tricks. A master vampire has no pride to guard, unlike a fledgling or even a slightly experienced vampire. He is willing to run away, to sacrifice pawns so that he might live, and he is called master because he reigns supreme in battle and the magic of our kind."

"Why would he want to live such a terrible existence?"

"The pain and terror he derives from the suffering of others, from killing, gives him a rush. A high. Like a human drug. It is addicting. He lives for that one moment."

"How do you kill a vampire?" She was trying to stall him. It was getting close to dawn. Surprisingly she wasn't tired. She had plenty of time, before the sun became too high, to do the morning chores.

"*You* don't." His voice was very stern.

"Your women never fight the vampire?"

"In any species there are always exceptions, but our women hold the light to our darkness. They will fight to defend their lives and the lives of our people, but they do not hunt. We have too few women and our hunters are solitary. If we divide our attention to keep a woman safe, it is an additional risk to ourselves."

"I could feel Rafael's resolve. He was willing to die to keep me alive, to keep Paul alive. He knew if he fought the vampire he might be defeated."

"Kirja is a very powerful fighter. He had a reputation for hunting. He has grown in strength since that time. His blood was different and I would very much like to know why. Something is not right here, Colby."

"I still want to know how to kill one. I'd feel better if I knew it could be done."

"Not with a rifle. Juan and Julio could have slowed it down by shooting it in the heart, but it would not kill it. The heart has to be completely removed and incinerated or it will find its way back to its evil host. The body is then incinerated so there is no hope of regeneration. The blood of a vampire burns like acid, Colby, and they can command with their voices just as Rafael and I can. Leave them alone."

"Did Rafael use his voice to seduce me?" She looked him straight in the eyes, needing an honest answer.

"I do not know what Rafael chose to do to bind you to him, but if I had a lifemate, Colby, I would use my voice, my gaze, and everything else at my disposal to make her mine. I would not take any chances. My woman will do as she is supposed to do."

"I hope your woman is an Amazon," she muttered under her breath. She could see she had kept him as long as she was able to. He walked out into the cool of the night and she followed him. "I already feel the need to touch him again," she confessed, rubbing her hands over her arms. "Is it going to be like this all the time?"

She hated weakness in herself, and grieving over Rafael as if he were dead just because he wasn't touching her mind was a terrible weakness.

"Yes. I will help during the nights, but stay close to Julio and Juan during the day. They will help you as much as possible. Remember everything I said to you. You *must* survive."

"I don't plan on anything else," she assured him.

Colby watched in wonder as Nicolas simply dissolved. At first his human form shimmered, became transparent so that she could see right through him. Tiny droplets of mist formed and he was nothing but vapor, streaking through the air away from her toward the hills. She blinked several times, trying to make her mind accept what she'd just seen.

The moment Nicolas was gone, she let out a sigh of relief. She hadn't realized how tense she was. She needed to be alone, to be with the familiar chores that might make her feel normal again, even if just for a few moments.

She went to the makeshift stable, surprised at all the work the Chevez brothers had accomplished while she slept that afternoon. Sean Everett must have sent both materials and additional men over to get a shelter up so quickly. She sighed again, this time for her pride. It seemed to be going right out the window. She didn't even know what was happening on her ranch anymore.

Colby spent the next couple of hours attending to the horses and treating burns. Most of the burns were nearly healed, and the horses already seemed stable again, a remarkable achievement when they'd been so traumatized. She became aware then that she heard a slight noise, the door to the kitchen open and close. She caught a glimpse of the dog running up the slope and took a deep breath. The day was already starting. Juan and Julio would be up soon, in spite of their need for sleep. And in a few hours she would be going to bed and leaving Paul and Ginny in their hands.

She rubbed her hand over her eyes. Rafael had no right to bring her partially into his world when she had such responsibilities. She was trapped between the two worlds now, with no clear way out of either one and no idea what to do about it.

She forked hay to the horses and filled the water basins with freshwater. The shelter constructed to keep the horses out of the heat was solid and, as the sun came up, it protected her skin as well. All the while she thought of Rafael. Her body ached for him and her mind refused to think of anything or anyone else. Colby had no chance to solve problems when all she could think of was wanting to touch Rafael, to see him, to know he was alive and well. She was disgusted with herself, but it didn't stop the tears tracking down her face or the terrible grief welling up unexpectedly and often shaking her to her very core. She worked steadily, trying to use normal chores to make her feel normal again. It was the only thing she could think to do. She was just finishing and about to go to the hay field when she heard the kitchen door again. This time Paul's steady footsteps could be heard walking across the yard toward her.

Colby shook off the sudden dread. She needed a few hours alone without worrying about whether or not her brother was suddenly going to turn into a monster in front of her eyes. She didn't want to watch him every minute. She turned to greet him with a determined smile, grateful for her acute hearing.

"You've been crying," he said immediately.

"Feeling sorry for myself, nothing bad," she explained. "What about you? You should still be in bed. Can't you sleep? You aren't hurting, are you?" Colby pushed back her hair. Paul *looked* fine, but it made her nervous to know that the vampire could still use him. It was difficult to forget the memory of his young face twisted with hatred as he threw her into the herd of stampeding cattle. What did you say to a boy who'd been bitten by a vampire and tried to kill his own sister? How did you comfort him? She was out of her depth.

"I'm fine, I just had too many nightmares. I don't want to sleep, even though I'm exhausted." He handed her a piece of paper. "Ginny already went out for a walk this morning. She took King with her. She said she'd water the garden and make breakfast when she gets back. It's hard to think about things as mundane as breakfast and chores."

"I saw King taking off and thought she'd just let him out and had gone back to bed. She likes to pick berries for breakfast, but I don't like her going off too far with all this going on."

"I could go after her," Paul offered. "I don't like it either."

Colby didn't want Paul out of her sight. "We'll just let her have a short walk and if she isn't back in a half hour, we'll casually walk after her so she doesn't think anything is wrong."

"What about the vampire?" he asked uneasily.

"He can't be up this time of day; the early morning light is too much for him. We should all be safe." And Paul was with her, so he couldn't be used unknowingly. The sun was barely out but her skin felt it. She rubbed her arms. There was an awkwardness between them that had never existed before.

Paul patted several of the horses as they moved restlessly. "I helped put this shelter up yesterday with Sean's men and Juan and Julio." There was pride in his voice.

"It's wonderful." She didn't mention money. Paul needed to feel good about something.

"How are the horses doing?"

"They seem to be recovering fast. I like to see Juan and Julio working with them, whispering in their ears the way Dad used to do." Colby exchanged a smile with her brother. "I love watching them do that."

"Me too," he admitted. "Did they go back to the Everett ranch to get some sleep?"

"No, they're both in the house. I put Juan in Dad's room and Julio in the guest room." She smiled at him.

"I can't believe the horses are so much better already. How do they do that?"

"I think it was Rafael," Colby said. "Every time he's visited with them, they're improved. I think he uses some kind of healing technique on them."

An awkward silence fell over them. Paul pressed his hand to his throat. "I can still feel him, Colby."

"I know, Paul. I'm trying to figure out what we're dealing with here. We can't exactly go to Ben and tell him there's a vampire on the loose—he'd lock us both in a mental ward."

Paul shrugged, attempting a smile. "He's been wanting to do that for years. It wouldn't be anything new."

Colby turned her head, movement catching her eye along the slope just above their ranch. Her eyes were already burning and it was early morning. The sun wasn't even high, yet she could feel the light poised to stab at her. She squinted, shading her eyes. "What is that, Paul? An animal dragging itself?"

Paul swung around, his eyes tracking the slope. Immediately he stiffened. "That's King, Colby. He's hurt." He took off running, streaking across the yard toward the injured dog.

13

The dog crawled toward them, dragging its body along the ground. When King saw them approaching, he flopped into the dirt and whined, his dark eyes looking at them with trust.

Paul knelt beside him and ran gentle hands through his fur. "He doesn't have any wounds that I can find."

A chill went down Colby's spine. She leaned closer to stare into the dog's eyes. "He's drugged, Paul."

There was a small silence. Paul shook his head adamantly. "It wasn't me. I swear. I woke up remembering everything this morning, Colby. I don't remember the things Nicolas showed me I did when he was removing the vampire blood, but I knew I lost little parts of time. I haven't this time. I didn't drug the dog. I didn't."

Colby put a hand on his shoulder. "That's not even important right now, Paul. What's important is that King was with Ginny. Take King into the house and leave him on her bed and wake up both of your uncles. Tell them to saddle a couple of horses and follow us, then get out here fast. I won't wait long."

Paul scooped up the dog and raced for the house. Colby pushed down fear. Ginny was probably picking berries near the pond. Ignoring her heightened senses and the alarm skittering down her spine, Colby tore at the tack, hastily bridling the mare. Without bothering with a saddle she flung herself on its back and rode up to the house. Paul was already waiting for her. Juan stood behind him, his shirt unbuttoned and concern stamped on his face.

"What is wrong? Where's the child?"

"I'm going to go looking for her now." Colby reached her arm down and Paul took it, swinging up behind her. "The dog's been drugged and I'm really worried. Get Julio and bring a couple of rifles. I can use all the help I can get." Not wanting to wait any longer, she dug her heels into the horse's sides, whirling it around and urging it into a dead run toward the spring.

As they topped the rise, Colby slowed the horse while she scanned the area. There was no sign of life. It was quiet, too quiet. Colby's heart slammed against her ribs. Fear choked her. Not Ginny. Colby would not allow any harm to come to Ginny. If anything happened to her, Colby didn't know what she would do. Fighting back a sob, she reined in, practically shoving Paul off the horse. "You look for a sign. If you see anything, anyone, you shout but stay to cover. Understand, Paul? Stay covered. If anything happens to me, go to the sheriff. Go to Ben. Don't trust anyone else."

"But—Colby?" White-faced, he stared up at her. "I couldn't have done this. I couldn't have hurt her, could I?"

"You didn't do this," she said. "You're in as much danger as Ginny. Be careful, Paul, and don't trust anyone. I wish to hell I knew what was going on."

"What if something awful has happened to her? I don't think . . ."He trailed off. He couldn't face a vampire again. Not for Colby. Not for Ginny. Not for anything.

"Do what I say." She kicked at the mare again, riding across the meadow to the far hillside, where she began casting about for a sign.

Meu amor, why are you so afraid? Your terror awakens me from even the deepest of sleeps. Rafael's voice was a soothing caress in her mind. She nearly went to pieces the moment he touched her mind with his. She actually felt his hand brush her face and realized she was crying.

It's Ginny. The dog was drugged and she went alone for a walk. It should have been safe. The vampire is locked in the ground, isn't he? She needed the reassurance.

He is in the ground but he can use puppets. Where is Paul? He asked it carefully, knowing how she would react.

It wasn't Paul. If it had been Paul I wouldn't be so worried—I know he'd fight against it. But I can feel that something is wrong, Rafael.

I will come to you.

No! Colby's gaze was riveted to the ground, looking for signs. *You're badly wounded and I can't take care of anyone else right now. Stay where you are and let me find her.*

I'm coming to you and the little one. His tone was implacable.

Paul checked the spring first. If Ginny had come this far she would have been thirsty. The first thing they always did when they were out walking was go to the spring for a drink. There was no print of Ginny's small boot in the wet ground, but his heart nearly stopped when he saw the clear outline of a man's boot. A good two sizes larger than his own foot, Paul knew neither Colby nor he had made that track. It might be from one of his uncles, but they wore a distinctive boot with a different tread and neither had such a big foot. Alarmed, he scanned the ground for anything that would give him a clue as to which way the man had gone.

A few minutes of scouting around and he found a faint trail. Not much, a partial track, a twisted leaf, a snapped twig; once he found a cigarette butt. Suddenly he dropped to his knees beside the imprints in the dirt, a low cry of alarm escaping. His hand reached of its own accord to touch the small boot print. It was definitely Ginny's track; he would recognize it anywhere. The larger boot had covered hers. For just a minute indecision warred in him—he wanted to yell for Colby, but feared whoever had taken Ginny would hear him and hurt her. The tracks were fresh. He began to follow the tracks, staying low, keeping to cover, careful not to disturb the dirt and send dust into the air. He hoped his uncles or Colby would come after him soon.

Rafael burst from the ground. He gave a guttural cry as shafts of sunlight raked across his skin like knives. He shapes-shifted immediately to protect his sensitive eyes and body from the burning sun. The wrenching of muscles and bones reopened his wounds so that droplets of blood sprayed across the sky and settled on the ground. He chose the form of vapor so he wouldn't have to continue to protect his eyes. Holding the form in his weakened state was precarious and left him with little energy to provide cloud cover. Nicolas had found rich soil deep in the mountains, but far from the ranch, and had put Rafael to ground there, in the hopes that the rich minerals would heal him faster. It had been a perfect healing ground, but it meant traveling a distance with his body already drained of strength. Using his tremendous iron will, Rafael pushed aside the clawing pain and streaked across the sky toward Colby, leaving behind a trail of red mist.

Colby dismounted, dropping the reins so the mare wouldn't move far while she studied the ground with a puzzled gaze. There was something wrong but she couldn't put her finger on it. Squatting down, she ran her hand over the dry earth as if that would give her a clue. She made herself take several deep, calming breaths. Hysteria would not help at this point. She had to believe Ginny was off playing somewhere completely oblivious to their concern. She quartered the ground carefully, frowning as she discovered a clean break in a tiny twig of a small bush. She touched it with her fingertip. Ginny's height. She would have brushed it running by. But where were the tracks? A bruised leaf a few feet away convinced her Ginny had come this way. She shook her head. This was crazy, there should have been more. Where was the trail? It was too elusive, as if Ginny had flown, and only touched down lightly in obscure spots, like a small wraith. She shuddered, clamping down on her imagination and the terror that threatened to consume her any moment.

I am on my way. I do not see why your fear is growing when you see that she has passed that way. Rafael was calm and rock steady. She latched onto his strength as an anchor.

Tracks aren't made like this, Rafael. I see her boot tracks in the dirt, and farther on, a rock kicked over. There would be more obvious signs of her passing. She tried to convey to him what she meant, showing him memories of tracking animals.

Where are Juan and Julio? All of you should be armed and you should stay together. His voice hadn't changed, but she sensed his uneasiness.

They're on the way. She hoped it was true.

"Colby!" It was a cry, a plea, a small child seeking adult reassurance. She hadn't heard Paul use that voice since he was about six years old.

She leapt to her feet and spun around to spot Paul. He staggered toward her, his face a pale, twisted mask of anguish. He dropped to one knee, burying his face in his hands.

Colby's mind went mercifully blank as she covered the distance between them in a flat run, flinging herself down beside him, drawing the lean, trembling body against her protectively. "Tell me, Paulo." Incredibly gentle, her voice still held a wealth of authority.

She felt Rafael go still, felt him wrap his arms around her to give her strength.

"The tracks, hers and his. I followed them. There's—there's a—a . . . " He broke off, sobbing wildly, tears coursing down his cheeks. He buried his face again in his hands, refusing to look at her.

Colby gripped his shoulders, shook him hard twice. "Tell me!" Fear was choking her, making it impossible to breathe. "Paul! For God's sake, did you find Ginny?"

Paul lifted his face, staring at her with haunted eyes. Colby held her breath. Rafael held his breath.

"Paul." Colby touched the tears on his face. "What is it?"

"A grave!" Paul shouted. "I found a grave."

There was a sudden silence. Shocked, Colby was completely still for a minute, the thudding of her heart slamming in her ears and a scream tearing up from her heart. "I won't believe it," she said, shoving him away, stumbling to her feet.

Wait for me. Rafael redoubled his efforts for speed in spite of his injuries. She was nearly hysterical. He should have taken the children's blood so he could know where they were at any given time. The thought of that small child hurt, perhaps dead, struck at his heart and soul until he wanted to echo Colby's silent scream.

Colby took off running in the direction Paul had come from. She saw the large boot prints where a heavy man had overtaken Ginny, the broken, bruised bushes where she'd struggled, the deeper imprint of the man's tracks as he'd carried her. The tracks twisted back into the shelter of a dead-end canyon. Off to the left, in between two large boulders, was a small mound, fresh earth piled up and more scattered around, small rocks placed carefully on top to prevent animals from digging it up.

Rafael. Rafael. Oh, God I think she's dead. Colby ran forward, screaming a denial, hurling the rocks away in a terrible fury, tearing at the earth with bare hands.

Do not do this yourself. I am so close, meu amor. Let me do it for you. She didn't stop, couldn't stop until her fingers touched something solid. She stopped breathing, stopped thinking, her mind nearly numb. She became aware of everything then, the tears on her face, the dirt on her clothes, the material in her hands. Burlap. Reluctantly she pushed the remainder of the dirt away to uncover the sack.

I can't breathe, Rafael, I can't breathe. She was going to be sick.

"No, you are not." She hadn't even heard Rafael arrive. He was simply there beside her, a hand on her shoulder, his breath warm and reassuring against the nape of her neck. "Look closely at the bag, Colby."

She could barely see through her tears. Then she was sobbing aloud, wildly, uncontrollably, gratefully, joyously. "It's a hundred-pound sack of oats. Not Ginny. Oats." She turned around into the haven of his arms, buried her face against his chest, and cried with sheer relief.

"She's alive," Rafael said. "I scanned the area and there is something evil here, but she is alive. I feel her presence."

"Not Paul," she whispered, clutching at his shirt.

"Not Paul, *querida,*" he confirmed, his hands gentle as he helped her to her feet.

Colby turned to look at Paul. He was several yards away, clutching a tree for support, his face buried on his arm. "It's not Ginny," she called. "It isn't her, Paul. It's a hoax. Thank God, it's a hoax."

Paul lifted his head, staring at her as if she was crazy, then he ran forward on trembling legs, stumbling over the uneven ground to see for himself. They clung together laughing hysterically, their relief so great they were a little crazy for a few moments.

Colby sobered first, reaching again for Rafael. It was only then that she really looked at him. His face was ravaged and raw from the deep claws of the vampire's mutated creatures. His shirt hung about him in dirty shreds, the skin of his chest angry and lacerated. Blood stained his shirt and seeped from his wounds. His eyes were red and swollen even in the early morning light, a testimony to his loss of strength.

He stood tall and straight and so torn up her tears began all over again. "Rafael, you shouldn't have come." He was so wounded, his great strength utterly diminished, yet still he had come to her aid. She bit her lip, wanting to touch him, wanting to hold him close and soothe the worst of his pain. "You don't even have dark glasses."

"And where are yours?" He took her hand, his thumb moving over her skin as if checking for burns or blisters.

"I don't know, I forgot them. I still have to find Ginny. I should have known. It was right there in front of me, but I was so frightened. That's what they were counting on. I'd be so scared I'd believe the obvious." She touched his face gently. "Rafael, you have to go back. There's Julio and Juan. I'm not alone now." She couldn't help herself, she wrapped her arms around him and leaned into him, careful of his wounds. "Thank you for wanting to be here for me."

"You *must* go to rest, Don Rafael," Juan said, dismounting. He took in the tracks, the opened grave and sack of oats. Rafael stood very close to Colby, a purely protective gesture. "Have you found young Ginny?"

Paul flung himself into Juan's arms. "I didn't do this. I know I didn't do this."

Rafael quieted him with a touch. "No, Paul, you didn't do this. There is a puppet at work here, a very evil being. I will not leave until the child is found. She is somewhere in that direction." He pointed back toward the area where Colby had been casting around for sign. "Juan, you and Julio get to higher ground and use the scopes. Make it look as if you're heading out of the area to check the cattle."

"You think someone is watching us," Paul said. "I don't understand this. Ginny's still missing; he must have her with him."

Rafael nodded. "I do not think they are together. Ginny would fight to give his position away. I think the two of you were lured out here deliberately."

Paul met the red-rimmed eyes. "You think they want to hurt Colby. Can the vampire use me to hurt either of my sisters?"

"Paul," Colby objected.

Rafael put a restraining hand on the small of her back. "During daylight hours the vampire cannot give you any orders. He can program you ahead of time, but cannot continue to do so during the day. Nicolas is watching over you. I will not allow anything to happen to any of you."

Paul squared his shoulders. "What do you want me to do? If this man has Ginny, we have to get her back."

Colby shook her head firmly. "No, she went off in the other direction. Somehow he lured her over there, I'm not sure how, but we'll find her over that way. He erased her tracks and did a darned good job of it too."

"How?" Paul asked.

Colby shrugged. "All he had to do was wait for her to start for the spring and somehow get her to switch directions. Once she was out of sight, he got rid of her tracks on that side and any evidence that she'd passed that way. He left her tracks leading in this direction, covered them with his own, and smashed bushes to make it look like she struggled."

"And he used the sack of oats to make his prints deeper in the dirt so we'd think he was carrying Ginny," Paul said.

She nodded. "I should have figured it out right then. It would have saved us a lot of grief."

"Why, Colby?" Paul asked plaintively. "Why is the vampire doing this to us? Where did he come from and what does he want?"

Colby looked up at Rafael. "That's a good question, Paul, and I don't have the answer. It makes no sense."

Rafael sighed. "The vampire has effectively destroyed the man's brain. He's rotting from the inside out. To him, what he is doing may make perfect sense, although to us it is elaborate and vile. He cannot think clearly anymore. He tries to obey his master's bidding. More than likely his master did not say to kill the child so he is concentrating on drawing out his target."

As much as she wanted Rafael there, he was swaying with weariness and she could see blisters rising on his skin. She touched his mind, as soft and delicate a probe as she could make it. Instantly she was driven to her knees, the pain so excruciating her heart stuttered.

Rafael's hands were gentle as he lifted her to him, but his eyes were stern. "Do not do that again."

She blinked back tears. Tears wouldn't find Ginny and they wouldn't stop the pain for Rafael. "Paul, I need my rifle. Take the mare and go back to the house and bring me my gun and extra ammo and a canteen."

"You'll find Ginny?"

"Absolutely I'll find Ginny."

Paul hesitated. "But what are you going to do with the rifle?"

"I don't know yet," Colby replied honestly, "but this is going to stop. Now go."

He turned away, took two steps, and turned back. "What if you're both wrong, Colby? What if he has her?"

"I'm not wrong, Paulo," she told him. Colby had been reading tracks most of her life; she was certain she could find her sister.

"You know what we are through your link to Nicolas," Rafael pointed out. "I am telling you, Ginny is not with the vampire's servant and for that we can all be grateful. I sense his presence in one direction and hers in another. Colby hopes to send me away because I am not at full strength, but I won't leave her until everyone is safe. You have my word of honor."

Paul hugged Colby, needing to, needing her strength, deriving comfort and reassurance from her the way he'd done most of his life.

Colby watched Paul scramble out of the canyon and begin to make his way back toward the ranch house before she turned back to Rafael. "You look like you're going to fall over. I'm a good shot, Rafael. If it isn't the vampire, I can take care of it."

"They eat human flesh, Colby," he said, gesturing toward the direction they thought Ginny had taken. "You find your sister and I will destroy the vampire's evil creation."

"What are you going to do?"

"Let him think you are alone. He will come after you. I do not like using you as bait, but it is the only way when I am so weak, *meu amor.*"

"I don't mind being bait to get Ginny back. Are you certain Ginny's alive?"

He took a deep breath, scenting the air. "She's alive." Rafael's large frame shimmered. "It will be easier for me to endure the light in the form of mist. I will be close, Colby."

She knew he would be. Rafael was in excruciating pain, yet he had still come to her when she needed him.

He is taking a terrible risk. Nicolas's voice was harsh in her mind. *Soon the lethargy will overtake him and he will be unable to move, and without cover, he will die.*

I won't let him. She couldn't change Rafael's mind once it was made up. She could only try to locate Ginny quickly and get them all out of the climbing sun.

Colby began a slow, methodical search of the ground. She kept her eyes glued to the dirt, moving in an ever-widening circle. In a shallow depression behind the boulders she discovered a partial print, the worn left heel, an old rusty shovel. It was one she recognized. She and Paul had discarded it months earlier after the handle had broken.

It took twenty precious minutes to find where the man had lain in wait, his elbows making twin impressions in the grass on the knoll. He had watched the trail long enough to smoke three cigarettes. Conscious of the sun's position, she carefully examined the ground, sure that the vampire's puppet had some method of transportation. Again she used up precious time she knew Rafael didn't have unraveling the trail as she backtracked him. A few hundred yards from his vantage point she found where he had left his horse.

Rafael. I've seen these tracks before. They belong to a man working for Clinton Daniels—his name is Ernie Carter. I ran into him near where I found Pete's body. His eyes were red and swollen and he felt evil. Could he have killed Pete? The idea that this man had been anywhere near Ginny terrified her.

It is likely.

Colby examined the trampled grass, found where the horse had grazed and its droppings, and knew that Ernie had been there for sometime. She could see a clear impression where the heavy grain sack had rested against rocks, the weight crushing the grass beneath it. She bit her lip reading the story easily, the short strides taken away from the horse, obviously burdened. Ernie had laid out the scene and had gone back to the knoll to observe his handiwork. She found the telltale tracks, his distinctive heel mark where he'd spotted her tracking him and he'd whirled around, the longer strides indicating he had run to his horse.

He's somewhere close by. He definitely spotted me and could be stalking me now. For a moment her shoulder blades itched, expecting an impact any moment.

He is to your north, on foot now, moving through the brush. Neither Juann or Julio has a clear shot at him.

Colby flung up her head, an unfamiliar coldness sweeping through her, an iron resolve. The vampire had not only done this to her, he had put Paul through something no one, let alone a child, should have to go through. *I can't think about him, Rafael, I have to find Ginny. Please don't let anything happen to Paul. Promise me.*

Querida, Paul will not be harmed by this evil creature. I have him now, and I will destroy him. Paul comes now with your rifle.

At once her heart stilled. Rafael was determined to go into battle. He was mortally injured. By all rights he should be dead, not running around hunting for a servant of the undead.

She held out her hand for the rifle and Paul tossed it to her. He dropped the mare's reins and swung down, handing her the box of ammunition. "Have you picked up her trail yet?" he asked.

Colby shook her head. "This man's a skilled tracker. He's brushed out her tracks for a good quarter mile through the brush. I want you to work out the trail, Paul, but it will be dangerous. You'll have to pretend you're me and you'll be the bait. I'll work my way through the brush to get a bead on him. Rafael's hunting him, but he's badly injured and the sun is already up. I can feel how tired he is and how difficult moving is becoming for him."

"What if she's . . . " Paul trailed off .

Colby shook her head as she thumbed shells into the rifle. "She isn't, Paul. Rafael says he's certain she's alive. What about you?" She paused, her gaze meeting his solidly. "Can you resist anything the vampire might have programmed into you?"

I am with him. It was all Nicolas said, but it was enough to reassure her.

Paul nodded. "I won't hurt Ginny. Nothing could make me hurt her." He put the canteen strap around his neck. "And Nicolas De La Cruz is in my mind. He's awake, so I guess it will be all right."

"Take my hat and my long-sleeved shirt. Stay in the brush so he thinks you're me. He has to believe that, Paul, can you do that?"

Paul took the hat and shirt, frowning as he did so. "You're already burned."

Colby ignored his comment. "I'm counting on you, then." She took off running, her body low to the ground, using as much available groundcover as she could, working her way north. She knew Ernie was working his way toward her in the hopes of killing or capturing her. He was good, but he made mistakes and one of them was his continual need for nicotine. She could smell the cigarette burning as he smoked it somewhere ahead of her.

Without long sleeves to protect her arms, branches scratched her skin and, even with the cloud cover overhead, she could feel blisters forming. Her eyes burned, tearing continuously, and she knew Rafael was suffering even worse. She flattened her body in the midst of brush, crawling along an animal trail through the branches.

What do you think you are doing? There was a distinct snap to Rafael's voice, as if he had bared his teeth.

I'm protecting you. Paul is playing me and he's nearly as good a tracker as I am. This man isn't going to get close to either one of you.

I forbid this.

"Forbid away," she muttered aloud. He was weak, nearly the walking dead, his body so ravaged and torn, but he was too stubborn to admit it. He needed help whether he knew it or not. She crawled closer to where her quarry had settled into the rocks, waiting for her. Waiting to kill her. A chill went down her spine as she realized that was the man's single goal—to get to her.

Colby... There was a warning note in Rafael's voice, a promise of retaliation.

Just do your thing and let me do mine. This is who I am, Rafael, so if you're thinking about hooking up with me for any length of time, get used to it.

This is who I am, Colby. You put yourself in danger at any time and I will wrap you up in an impenetrable barrier where nothing can touch you. It will take a great deal of my strength when I need it elsewhere.

She muttered an imprecation under her breath, calling him

several names, none of which were complimentary. The man was impossible, even when he was on the verge of death.

She had pushed through the bushes a little farther and saw the vampire's puppet. It was definitely the same man who had been with Tony Harris on her property near the mines. Her stomach lurched as the thought came unbidden that he had tried to feed on Pete's body, that he must have been the one to kill him. Ernie Carter looked enormously strong, but disheveled, his clothes torn and rumpled. He was drooling and one eyelid drooped over his eye. He watched Paul through a pair of binoculars, but continually wiped at his streaming eyes.

Colby felt sick that she had to do the same. She was somehow related to the man. Once, he'd been just like Paul, innocent, until the vampire had taken a hold of him.

Not so innocent, Rafael denied. *His mind and memories are rotten. Stay still, he is suspicious. Paul does not move as you do and he is noticing something is not right.*

Ernie suddenly cursed aloud, tossed the cigarette to one side, and lifted the rifle to his shoulder, aiming at Paul.

Colby tucked her rifle into position, finger on the trigger. She was an excellent shot, but she'd never killed anyone before. With a sinking feeling, her finger began to tighten. She knew she didn't have a choice. The sun blinded her, coming out from behind the cloud and striking her in the face. It was all she could do not to cry out in pain as thousands of needles seemed to penetrate her eyes. She blinked rapidly to clear her vision, desperate to get off a shot before the stalker could hurt Paul.

"Paul! Get down!" She screamed the warning, knowing she was giving away her position, but uncaring.

Ernie immediately turned toward the sound of her voice and fired off several shots. The bullets whined through the air, thudding into the dirt feet from her. Colby squeezed the trigger, half blinded by the sun but determined to lay down covering fire for her brother.

Simultaneously, she heard the rifle fire from two other guns and knew Julio and Juan were doing the same. The vampire's servant slipped back into the trees, crawling on his belly through the brush toward his horse. Colby caught glimpses of him, but couldn't get a clear shot. Her heart nearly stopped when Rafael stepped into her line of fire, his back to her. Fresh blood was a giant pool on the back of his shirt.

No! No, Rafael. He was too weak. She could feel the terrible drain of energy. *Nicolas! Oh, please, tell me what to do!* She screamed for his brother in her mind. Colby got her feet under her and ran, clutching her weapon, determined to help Rafael. She could see Juan and Julio sprinting down the slope, converging from two directions, trying to get to him. She hit something solid and fell backward, finding herself seated on the ground, a barrier blocking her. She could touch it, but she couldn't see it.

Ernie lumbered to his feet, his red-rimmed eyes swollen nearly shut, but his head snapped around as he located his target. He brought the gun to his shoulder, although Rafael was only an arm's distance from him. Rafael caught the barrel and twisted the weapon from the man's grasp, tossing it away.

The vampire's puppet screamed, a ghastly sound of rage and hatred, and rushed Rafael like a linebacker. He managed to wrap his arms around Rafael, sinking his teeth into the hunter's chest and his fists into the wound in his back. He tore a chunk of flesh from over Rafael's heart and spit it out.

Colby tried the rifle, shooting at the barrier, hoping to shatter it, but it remained in place. She could only watch in horror as the mutated human tore at Rafael a second time.

Rafael didn't flinch away, but rather caught the man's head in his hands and wrenched hard. The sound of Ernie's neck snapping was loud in the early morning air. Colby drew air into her lungs in relief, but to her horror, Ernie didn't fall. Rafael shoved him backward. The zombie-like creature lurched forward, his head twisted at a peculiar angle. He roared, spewing spittle as he attacked.

Colby's heart pounded in her chest. Her fists gripped the rifle so hard her hands went numb. She'd never felt so helpless in her life.

Surprisingly, the vampire's servant was fast, but Rafael side-stepped, slamming his fist deep into the man's chest. He stood there, eye to eye with the puppet, his hand buried deep, then he withdrew it. The sound was loud in the still morning air, a sucking sound that made Colby sick. Rafael stood there with Ernie's heart in his hand, blood running down his arm. The body swayed and folded in on itself in slow motion.

Colby turned her head away from the sight, her heart slamming in her chest. She didn't belong in a world where men tore the hearts out of chests and bit each other in the neck and turned human beings into cannibals and puppets. She felt faint and dizzy, pressing her hand to her forehead, wiping the beads of sweat away.

I am sorry you had to witness such a destruction of life, meu amor.

Rafael's voice brushed along her nerve endings, a sensuous touch of velvet over her skin, in her mind. Seducing her senses. She shook her head, wanting to think clearly. Needing to think clearly. Part of her felt she might be going insane.

A flash of lightning drew her attention. Rafael drew from the sky the same orange-red ball of energy that Nicolas had manipulated, incinerating the man who had once been a human being. He tossed the heart to the ground and did the same to it, also bathing his hands and arms in the energy.

He took a step toward Colby and staggered. Gasping, she slammed at the barrier with the rifle butt. "Get it down now!" Her third swing met with no resistance and she ran to him. "Damn you!

Don't you ever do that again. Don't you ever take away my choices like that. I could shoot you myself."

Juan and Julio were nearly to them. "Find Ginny," she yelled and caught at Rafael. "You take my blood right now. This second."

He shook his head. "It is too dangerous, *meu amor*. I need too much. Hunger claws at me. I could hurt you. I will not take the chance."

Colby was so angry adrenaline surged through her bloodstream. She yanked the knife from her belt and slashed her wrist. "Damn you, don't say no to me." It hurt like hell, and turned her stomach over so she had to fight against the waves of nausea. She thrust her arm to his mouth. "Take the blood before I pass out or get so mad I stab you and finish the job."

The smell of blood hit him hard, and before he could stop himself, Rafael grasped her wrist and latched on. The adrenaline-laced blood hit him like a fireball, rushing through his system, giving him a false high instantly. He gulped at the liquid, his cells crying out for sustenance. The red haze spread through his mind and the beast rose up, roaring for more. His ravaged body demanded the means of regeneration and the blood poured into him, hot and sweet and addicting.

She felt the drain, actually felt the blood rushing from her body into his. Her wrist burned and throbbed and she could feel the puncture of his teeth. She couldn't prevent the involuntary tug as she tried to get her hand back. His grip tightened painfully, fingers digging into her skin with bruising force. Colby closed her eyes and tried not to look or feel anything at all.

Stop him. Nicolas's voice was so distant and faint Colby could barely catch it. *Force him to stop before it is too late.*

"Rafael." She yanked at her wrist hard, trying to break loose from his grip. "Let go of me. You're hurting me." Her legs went out from under her and she sank down.

"Don Rafael." Juan Chevez shoved the barrel of his rifle beneath Rafael's jaw. "Let her go or I will shoot."

There was a moment of silence. Colby's heart pounded. Inside, she could hear herself screaming a denial. She'd rather be dead herself than lose him, but fear lived in her as Rafael stroked his tongue across her wrist and lifted his head to look at Juan. There was death in the black eyes and little else.

Colby's arm fell free of his grip. Before she could think she leapt to her feet and shoved the rifle away from Rafael. "No, Juan. He doesn't know what he's doing." She tried to touch Rafael's mind, but she could only hear a strange roaring and, very distantly, a wrenching cry of sorrow. Rafael's fingers wrapped around her throat. Time stopped. Her heart beat too fast and the air rushed from her lungs.

Without warning Rafael collapsed, going down hard and taking her with him. He was gone from her mind. Colby frantically took his pulse. "Is he dead? Juan, there's no pulse. He can't be dead." She tried to roll him over to give him CPR.

Juan stayed her with a hand on her shoulder. "It is the sun. He is too weak and he must be protected, put in the ground. We have to attend his wounds as best we can and cover him with earth. When Don Nicolas rises this evening, he will take him somewhere safe."

She lifted Rafael's head and to her shock, his black eyes stared at her, filled with intelligence and remorse. He seemed paralyzed, unable to move. His heart and lungs appeared not to be working, but he was alert. "Should I pack his wounds like I did last night?" She didn't want to look into Rafael's eyes and she didn't want to touch his mind.

While Juan dug a place in the cool earth near the pond, she packed the wounds with soil and her own saliva. He never spoke and she felt numb. His wounds were terrible. It didn't seem possible for anyone to recover from such a thing. She hated helping Juan roll him into the shallow grave and had to look away when his body was covered.

Colby staggered to her feet and began to run through the brush, uncaring that the jagged branches and prickly thorns tore at her skin and clothes. She needed to find Paul and Ginny. She needed to be with someone sane, someone normal. Her mind couldn't accept what Rafael could do. He should be dead, yet he had ripped out a heart with his bare hands. He had nearly killed her and might have killed Juan. Instead of taking him to a doctor, she had packed the gaping holes with dirt and saliva and buried him on her ranch.

Paul and Ginny sat in the small grove of pine trees, Julio standing guard. Both looked tired and dirty and so familiar she burst into tears.

Rafael couldn't comfort her, locked beneath the earth, his body already leaden and his heart ceasing to beat. He could hear her crying, knew he had nearly killed her and that she knew it as well. Juan had obeyed him, putting her protection above all else, and for that he would always be grateful. He was so close, the monster growing in him when the ritual words should have made him safe. Had he waited too long? He wanted to reach out to her, hold her, kiss the tears from her face and reassure her he would never harm her, but he no longer knew if that was true. Lying beneath the earth, he found his anguish over Colby hurt far worse than any of his physical wounds.

Aboveground, Colby clung to Paul and Ginny, desperate to get them away from a world she didn't understand. Ginny began to tell her all about her frightening experience, following the sound of a hurt animal and being trapped in a deadfall. The sound of her voice did nothing to help the terrible dread that invaded Colby's heart.

14

"We've got work to do," Paul shouted, hitting the flat of his hand on Colby's bedroom door. "Are you going to lie in bed forever? Half the day is gone! Julio drove Ginny to visit the Everetts and Juan's already bringing in the hay. Let's go!"

Colby threw back the covers, her hands shading her eyes. With each passing day her sensitivity to the sunlight seemed to get worse. She showered quickly in cool water, trying to make the terrible heaviness that invaded her body disappear. Three nights had gone by since Rafael had been left to heal in the ground, three days and nights of sheer hell. She tried to sleep during the day, from ten in the morning until about four in the afternoon. It should have been a relief, but she was plagued with endless nightmares. She had even visited the area where she and Juan had buried him, but he was gone, taken somewhere else by his brother to heal.

Colby had dream after dream of Nicolas drawing the vampire's blood from Paul's body. It was a ghoulish nightmare that left her shaky and frightened. The moment she closed her eyes, she could see blood pressing through Paul's pores, and some sort of parasite in his bloodstream, wiggling like worms over his body. When she wasn't dreaming of Paul, she dreamed of Ginny lying in a shallow grave, her eyes wide open and accusing. Sometimes she had dreams of Rafael smiling at her as he ripped her throat open with his teeth. Most of the daylight hours she lay in her bed, waiting for the lethargy to pass, trying not to think of Rafael and how terribly hurt he was. She prayed for undisturbed sleep, her mind always racing to find a way to keep her sister and brother safe.

She often woke up crying, her heart a painful ache in her chest, her mind numb with grief. She was sick to death of grieving and being afraid. And she hated the way everyone watched her, as if she might do herself harm at any moment.

"Come on, Colby, you've got to wake up! You told me to get you up no matter what, so haul it out here." The kitchen door banged hard and Colby winced. With Ginny visiting at the Everett ranch with her new friend, Paul's dishes from breakfast and lunch were in the sink. Just the sight of the partially eaten food as she made her way slowly through the kitchen made her nauseous. Her body hated to work this time of day, no matter how much she willed it to be normal.

Colby could barely cope with the separation from Rafael. Half the time she felt as if she were going crazy. Nicolas reassured her through the long nights, and the Chevez brothers reassured her during the day. She was certain Nicolas was sharing her mind, helping her through the waking hours, and it felt like an invasion whenever she thought about it too much. She silently screamed for Rafael, thought of him, needed him; and having another person know just how obsessed she was with him was humiliating. She could barely function she was so grief-stricken.

Rafael had a lot to answer for. How the hell did he expect her to run a ranch and take care of two children when she was such a mess? She might need to see him, but she dreaded the moment she would have to face up to him and tell him it was over. It had to be over. She couldn't live in his world. It was far too dangerous and violent.

She stumbled across the yard to the corral where Paul held the bridle of a mean-looking bay. She was so sensitive to light now, she wore sunglasses to protect her eyes even in the evening. It took courage to face the light and she found herself wondering how Rafael had managed to stay with her when the stable had burned, and worse, when Ginny had gone missing. He must have been in agony. She was only partway into his world and it felt as if a thousand needles were poised to stab her eyes.

She watched the horse dance nervously, its eyes red-rimmed and suspicious. Paul already had the saddle on him. Colby had always believed in going for the meanest horse first and Paul was obviously following her philosophy to the letter.

"You have him?" Colby looked at the animal, at the way it was throwing its head, the way the eyes were regarding her with wicked intent. She tried a soft whisper, her mind seeking to soothe the animal, but it shook off her usual calming effect.

"I've got him," Paul reassured her.

Taking a deep breath, she swung into the saddle. The moment her weight eased into the leather, the animal exploded wildly, violently, head plunging, rear rising, shrieking angrily. It went stiff -legged, rising high and slamming to the ground with bone-jarring strength, whirling like a demon possessed. Without being fully set, Colby had no chance to keep her seat. She was launched like a missile, her slender body slamming into the hitching post. She crumpled and landed in the dirt facedown.

"Colby, look out!" Paul's hoarse cry sent her instinctively rolling toward the safety of the fence, hands up to protect her head. The ground shook under the pounding hooves as the animal reared and struck at her repeatedly. One slashing hoof struck her right thigh as she made her escape.

Instantly there was the echo of two cries in her mind. *Rafael.* His voice was a soothing balm and worth any price. He was alive. And Nicolas, reprimanding her yet again.

Her entire leg was numb. She lay still, staring up at the dusky sky, trying to get control of her racing heart and rapid breathing. Although it was late afternoon, she could feel the last of the sun's rays burning on her skin and her body still felt sluggish and drained. She should have waited another half hour or so before attempting her work.

"God, Colby." Actual tears were in Paul's eyes as he flung himself down beside her. "You're bleeding bad—tell me what to do. I don't know what to do."

Colby pushed herself very gingerly up on one elbow to stare at the ugly gash soaking her leg with blood. She swore softly, fighting off nausea. "I'm going to live, Paulo, but it's going to need stitches." She clamped the edges of the wound together, forced herself to press hard. "Go get a couple of towels and a tray of ice. You'll have to drive the truck into town. Call ahead and tell Doc Kennedy to wait in his office—I don't want to go to the hospital and run up another bill." She bit the words out between her teeth. Her leg had gone from numb to a burning torture.

Paul ran for the house. Colby's face was so pale she looked like a ghost. He would never forget, as long as he lived, the sight of her small slender body so fragile in the dust under the huge, maddened animal, the sickening sound of a hoof meeting flesh. He tore open the refrigerator, caught up the towels and the truck keys, made the hurried, breathless call, and was back at Colby's side in minutes.

"Does it hurt much?" he asked anxiously as he watched her apply the ice to the wound. In all her injuries, Paul had never seen so much blood on his sister. It was bright red and Colby was pressing very hard, her teeth biting deep into her lower lip.

She managed a lopsided grin, pushing at the hair tumbling

around her dirt-streaked face. The action left a smear of blood on her temple. "You'll need to help me, Paulo, my leg's kind of numb from the shock of the blow." She was gritting her teeth, wishing it had stayed numb, but it was better than telling him she was going to pass out from the pain and blood loss. "Bring the truck close and I'll be able to get in."

Colby. Her name came out of nowhere, soft and beautiful, wrapping her up in safe arms. Tears burned in her eyes at the caress of Rafael's voice in her mind. She ached for him. Missed him so much. Just hearing his voice made her feel complete.

I'm okay. You still sound tired. Are you supposed to be waking yet? Rafael sounded far away and it was an obvious effort to reach her. It made Colby feel treasured that he would try. She knew his wounds weren't fully healed and that his hunger raged in him, but he reached for her anyway. She *hated* the melting sensation, when she was so angry with him for causing her problems. She didn't want to need to hear his voice or feel his touch. And she didn't want to think of the violence he was capable of.

I cannot come to you for another hour. Show me what you have done. I feel the pain in you. It is severe enough that you woke me from my slumber.

She took a deep breath and made herself look at the horrendous gash in her thigh, lifting her hand and the towel of ice away from her skin. She heard his gasp of alarm and immediately covered the wound. *Paul is taking me to the doctor in town. No big deal. A couple of stitches.*

I will come to you as soon as I am able.

She lay back because it took too much energy to do anything else, turning her head to observe the horse. He was trembling, pawing the powdery earth, still fighting the saddle, his body dark with sweat. As soon as the truck pulled up next to her and Paul jumped out, Colby indicated the animal. "Look at him, Paul, something's wrong with him. He just isn't acting normal."

"He's a killer," Paul snapped, glaring at the horse, totally out of character for Paul with animals. "Someone ought to put him down."

"He's drugged, Paul. Look at him again, he doesn't know what's going on."

"Who cares, Colby? Forget the damn horse, let's get you to the doctor."

"Not yet. Go call Dr. Wesley, tell him we're leaving and to bring some help with him, he'll need it. I want the horse taken care of."

"You've got to be kidding me. I'm supposed to call the vet while you lie there bleeding all over the place?" Paul protested, concern in his eyes.

"Paul." There was infinite weariness in Colby's voice.

Reluctantly Paul obeyed, relating the details hurriedly to the astonished veterinarian. It seemed an eternity before Paul was able to half-lift Colby into the truck. Shaking and rattling, the old pickup truck sped toward town.

Colby yelped more than once while the doctor cleaned, stitched, and bandaged the gash in her thigh. She endured lectures from her doctor and a nurse wielding a syringe and felt she could recite the dangers of tetanus by the time they were finished. The cut was deep and the wound had swollen considerably; she would be uncomfortable, but she'd had worse injuries.

With Paul's support she limped back to the truck, ruefully looking down at her dirty, bloodstained, and torn jeans. She knew her face was streaked with dirt, her hair falling in a jumbled mess down her back. She glanced at her brother. "Have you ever noticed how wonderful I always manage to look?" she asked him with a poor attempt at a smile. She nodded toward the sleek Porsche parked down the street.

Paul followed her gaze, recognized the woman disappearing into a small, pricey boutique. He looked from the perfection of Louise to his sister, staring for a moment. Beneath the dirt and blood, there was something extraordinary, something he had never really seen before.

"You're so much prettier than her, Colby, there's no comparison. Really, there's not."

Colby found herself smiling in spite of the ragged way she was feeling. "You're some brother, you know that? I'm going to lie here and rest while you go get my prescriptions for me and I'll contemplate how perfectly wonderful you are."

"I'll move us a little closer," he said, reaching for the keys.

"You're not moving me anywhere near that shop—the pharmacy is next door to her perfect little Porsche. You could use the exercise."

"The ultimate sacrifice," Paul groaned. "Cowboys aren't supposed to walk anywhere." He pocketed the little slips of paper and helped ease her into a more comfortable position. "You're looking a little green around the gills under all that dirt, Colby. Are you sure you're all right and I can leave you?"

"I'm fine, Paulo," she reassured him. "Just leave the door open so I don't panic and try to climb out the window."

"I'll be right back." Hastily he started down the street.

She watched him go, weariness washing over her. The worst part was that endless work was still waiting for her. With Juan and Julio helping, they were finally beginning to catch up with the work. An injury like this one would interfere with the ability to do the necessary riding and training of horses as well as the day-to-day upkeep on the ranch.

What had been wrong with the bay? Could he have been drugged the way King had been? Ernie was dead. He couldn't have done it. She didn't want to think that Paul might have done it. She tried to remember exactly how the horse had looked before she had climbed into the saddle. It was inexcusable. She hadn't noticed the animal's distress; she'd been too upset over Rafael. It always came back to that. Rafael and his hold on her.

"Hello again." A soft voice pulled her out of her reverie.

Colby looked up to see the woman with startling green eyes who had offered to help her when Rafael had been so possessive. She flashed a quick smile. "I always seem to be in trouble, don't I? I'm Colby Jansen."

"Natalya Shonski." The woman smiled, her face lighting up. She indicated Colby's leg. "Looks painful."

"Trust me, it is. I wanted to thank you for what you did the other night. Most people would have just walked on by."

"You were afraid of him," Natalya said. "I could feel it."

Colby pushed her hair from her eyes and gave the woman a wan smile. "I'm still afraid of him."

Natalya leaned in the door to examine Colby's neck. "He's one of the hunters, isn't he? Do you have any idea how dangerous they are?"

Colby's palm instantly pressed against the bite mark, holding Rafael to her. "How do you know about them?"

Natalya hesitated, choosing her words carefully. "I had the bad luck to run across their counterparts on more than one occasion." Natalya watched her closely to see if Colby understood.

"I just had my first encounter a few nights ago." Colby shuddered. "It's nice to know I'm not losing my mind. I thought maybe I was making the whole thing up." Relief flooded her, an eagerness to talk to this woman who knew what she was going through, who didn't think she needed to be locked up. "How did you find out about them? Half the time I still don't believe the whole thing."

"What does the hunter want with you?"

Colby's fingers pressed deeper against Rafael's mark on her. It was always there, as fresh as the day he made it, never fading and always throbbing as if calling to her. What did he want from her? Sex? If only it was just great sex. She could handle that.

She remembered the sound of his laughter moving through her

mind. Low. Sensual. A temptation. Her lashes swept down. He ruled her sexually; it was true. She couldn't overcome her need for him. "I'm not completely sure." She tried to be truthful. To her utter surprise Colby found herself blinking back tears. "I'm a mess, Natalya. He's bound me to him somehow and I can't stand being apart from him. I hate feeling this way."

Natalya glanced around and kept her voice low. "I wish I could help you, Colby. Here's my cell phone number. I'm leaving soon. If you want to come with me, give me a call. I can't stay in one place too long."

"I have a brother and a sister to protect."

"If there's a hunter in the area, there's a vampire close by. You can't protect them from a vampire."

"How did you know Rafael was a hunter?"

Natalya lowered her voice even further. "I have a birthmark on me, low, right over my ovary on my left side. It looks like a dragon breathing fire, and when a vampire is close, or a hunter, or even one of the human puppets, it burns."

Colby inhaled sharply and touched her left side. "Where did it come from?"

Natalya shrugged. "I was born with it. It's saved my life on many occasions."

Colby rubbed her thigh, just below the laceration, in hopes of easing the pain. "There's a vampire in the area and Rafael says he's different than others, more powerful."

Natalya frowned. "Can they kill him?"

"I don't know. Rafael was injured and the vampire got away. I think Rafael hurt it, though."

Natalya sighed. "I kind of liked it here. I didn't really want to leave yet. I haven't learned to kill a vampire yet. They keep coming back. Watching Dracula movies all the time isn't all that helpful."

"Rafael and his brother, Nicolas, are originally from the

Carpathian Mountains. You might find help there," Colby suggested. "Nicolas told me they have to be incinerated. It was pretty gross. He said they rip the heart from the chest and incinerate that as well."

Natalya straightened up slowly. "I wish I hadn't asked." She looked at Colby. "Are you sure you're all right? Can you handle this? It's been hard for me and I don't want you to feel as alone as I've been."

"I honestly don't know. He talks about conversion."

Natalya scowled. "Bringing you over? Can they do that? I know the vampires usually kill. They often keep women around for a while, enjoying their fear, but they always kill them. I've tried a couple of times to rescue them, but they're insane. They want to bite me and they try to drink blood and I've even seen them try to eat human flesh. I don't know, Colby, it sounds dangerous."

"It feels dangerous. I'm having trouble with the sunlight, and without the Chevez brothers—they came from Brazil with Rafael—I wouldn't be able to keep up with the ranch work. I have to sleep during the day now."

"Do you want to get away from him?" Natalya asked.

Colby sighed, feeling close to tears. "I don't think I can. I don't honestly know what I want. I'm very afraid, but I'm so obsessed with him. If I'm away from him, he's in my mind until I think I'm going insane." She looked at Natalya. "I don't have a craving for any kind of food, let alone human flesh."

"He isn't a vampire," Natalya assured her, "but these hunters are dangerous. He isn't human, Colby, and no matter how much he relates to you as a human, he is still different, with an entirely different set of rules."

"I'm afraid," Colby admitted in a low voice, astonished at just how afraid she really was. Rafael had deliberately seduced her. He had brought her partway into a world she knew nothing about, and he'd taken her partway out of the world she was familiar with. It was terrifying and yet she couldn't imagine her life without him. And that in itself was what was so frightening.

"You can come with me, all of you," Natalya offered. "It isn't much fun running alone. And we might all be safer together."

And I would find you. There is nowhere to go that I cannot find you. There was a bite to Rafael's voice, a warning.

Colby felt a shiver run down her spine. "He can hear me."

Natalya pulled away instantly, looking warily around. "I have to go. I don't dare stay here. Good luck." She backed away from the truck.

Colby fought down the urge to grab her hand and keep her there. "Be careful, Natalya," she called, shoving the small piece of paper with Natalya's cell phone number on it into her pocket. She wanted to run away too. There was fear in Natalya's eyes and an absolute resolve to get away. Whatever the vampires wanted from her, she wasn't going to give them. Colby just wished everything would magically return to normal. She closed her eyes again and counted to ten, knowing Paul had run into one of his friends and was talking instead of rushing the pain medication back to her. So much for his concern.

"Don't tell me Annie Oakley fell off of her horse!" Tony Harris leaned into the truck, his handsome features mocking.

"You're just what I needed to make my day complete, Tony," Colby told him tiredly.

"What happened?" He moved closer to stand in the open doorway, his weight across her body as he bent to examine the thick, rather bloody bandage. He was pinning her against the seat, his arm pressed tightly and very deliberately into her waist. He whistled, glancing up at her, his dark gloating eyes revealing his enjoyment of her predicament. "Maybe I should take a look at this; it seems to be bleeding." His hand was on her thigh, fingers pressing into swollen flesh.

"If I scream, Tony, half this town will come running."

"No one can see with me blocking the view," he said. "Scream away, I'll just say your leg hurt and I was trying to help."

"As if they'd believe your word against mine. Go to hell, Tony. And get your hands off me." Colby swung at him, but her movements were hampered by the lack of space.

He dodged the blow and laughed at her. "You leave your rifle at home, Colby? What's wrong, where's all that cold haughty disdain you love to dish out?" His hand was back at the bandage, hovering there while he watched her closely, enjoying her helplessness.

"Shut up, Tony, and get out of here."

His fingers inched closer to the wound on her leg, pressing that little bit harder.

"This isn't funny, Tony." Colby tried to not to look at his hand.

"Oh, yeah, I think it's really funny. You always thought you were better than me, haven't you, Colby? So now you've got your rich man and you think that proves you're too good for someone like me, but you know what I think? I think you're nothing but his paid whore. I'm going to show you what a real man makes you feel like."

Before she could elude him, Tony bent down, clamping his mouth to hers, deliberately grinding her teeth against her soft inner lip. One hand remained on her leg, right beside the swollen laceration in warning.

Colby forgot everything, her weariness, the pain in her leg, the fact that she was parked on the main street of town. It was one thing to put up with Tony's sick innuendos and bullying; it was an altogether different proposition for him to physically touch her. Their feud had started in the schoolyard when Tony, two grades ahead of her, had been unmercifully teasing a boy in her class. She had hit him right in front of everyone. When he had retaliated, Joe Vargas, Ben, and Larry Jeffries had all instantly jumped to her defense. Over the years Harris had threatened and harassed her, but he had never laid a finger on her.

Her right elbow slammed into his solar plexus and her left hand caught the back of his curly black hair in a wicked grip, in an attempt to jerk his head away from her. To her horror he was suddenly catapulted from the truck as if unseen hands had lifted him bodily and thrown him down. Then she was staring into Rafael's black, black eyes. She caught her breath at the stark menace concentrated there. Tiny red flames were glowing, fierce and unnatural. He looked a demon, a predator, vicious, cunning, more animal than man. Nothing in her life had ever frightened her like the grim emptiness revealed in his eyes. She was looking at death. And she knew he could very easily kill Tony Harris.

No! No, Rafael, you can't. Deliberately she used the more intimate means of communication to call the man back into his body, his brain. She was looking at a natural predator. He was already turning away from her, back to Harris, who lay sprawled in the street.

"Rafael, let it go," she called aloud, struggling to slide off the seat, her heart pounding in a kind of terror. She swore softly under her breath as her leg took her weight, jarring her entire body.

Tony leapt up, doubling his fists as he spat in the street.

Rafael coolly and quite brutally slapped Tony Harris open-handed, a hard, powerful blow that staggered the man as he rushed forward. Rafael continued to slap him, delivering blow after powerful blow, walking the cowboy backward down the street. Each blow had Tony stumbling off balance, a jarring, humiliating punishment. Colby had witnessed a thousand brawls, but this was completely different. It was a savage, yet cold-blooded attack, a brutal display of power that held everyone motionless, standing on the sidewalks simply gaping at the drama.

Colby went hobbling after them, anger beginning to smolder as her heart accelerated at the realization that Rafael could have dropped Tony Harris with one blow. This was a public punishment. Rafael would have killed Tony, coolly and without remorse. He preferred to kill him, but refrained because Colby would never have condoned murder.

It didn't help that she was drinking him in, her body flaring to life. She could feel every cell, every fiber of her being reaching for him, needing him, *craving* him like a drug. She *detested* the control he had over her body and mind. Did it show? Natalya had looked at her with pity and she felt scorn for herself every time she thought of the way she had been so grief-stricken, almost to the point of harming herself. She had been forced to reach out to Nicolas, someone she didn't altogether trust, in order to get through each night.

"Let them go," Paul yelled, grabbing at her arm, out of breath from his headlong dash through the street. She was limping and didn't seem to notice her teeth were clamped together in pain.

Colby shook off her brother. "Shut up!" she snapped.

Paul halted immediately. Colby's hair was red for a reason. She could go up in flames if someone pushed her too far. He regarded De La Cruz with intense satisfaction. He was about to be publicly put in his place. The crowd was certainly big enough.

Colby caught at Rafael's arm, momentarily taken aback by the sheer hardness of it. It was like clutching a piece of iron. "Stop it, Rafael, right now!" She attempted to place herself between the two men, but Rafael glided around her easily, keeping his body squarely in between her and Harris. It only made Colby angrier. "I don't want you handling my problems. You understand me, not ever again. This is my business." She understood power, understood, better than most people, the need to stay continually in control, but she was so angry with both men she attempted to drag Rafael away from Tony by his arm without much success.

Harris took the opportunity to stumble away, clutching at his smashed face with both hands. Over the top of Colby's head, Rafael watched him go, red flames still flickering in the depths of his eyes.

"Damn it, Rafael." He was making Colby feel like a fly buzzing around him. She slugged him in the chest, all her pent-up anger behind her well-thrown punch.

He stood towering over her, blinking down at her as if seeing her for the first time. Slowly amusement crept across his sensual features, warmed the bitter ice in his eyes. *Did you hit me, querida?* His voice was soft, sexy, intimate there in the middle of the street, making her blood heat and body clench, and that made her angry enough to want to strike him again.

"Don't be funny." She would not be charmed by him. She would *not* feel her body melting and pooling with hot heat. "You stay out of my business. If I don't want Tony Harris mauling me, I'll handle it myself. You've made the situation ten times worse; the entire town knows something happened, thanks to you. In case you've forgotten, you're in the United States, *not* Brazil, and here we call the sheriff ."

He picked her up easily, casually, right there in front of everyone, cradling her against his chest, moving back up the street toward her truck with effortless long strides. "You know I would not stay away when you are injured, Colby." His voice whispered over her, velvet soft, irresistible. Magic. There was possession in his burning gaze, and something else, something wild and primitive, as if he wasn't yet finished with Tony Harris. "And I am not about to allow another man to put his hands on you."

Colby reached up to touch his mouth. Her fingers trailed over the lines etched so deeply, lines of strain and weariness that had not been there before, reminding her he had awakened before Nicolas said he should. There were faint marks on his face, slowly receding but evidence of the claws that tore at him. He had suffered terribly to provide a barrier for her. She smoothed her hand over his heart, wondering if the bitemarks were still there. Something softened inside of her when she didn't want it to. "I can handle Tony Harris," she said more gently than she intended. "Our laws don't allow people to just go out and kill someone because you don't like what they do."

"Our laws are very clear." There was no emotion in his voice, just a dead calm and a merciless slash to his mouth.

"Tony's a bully."

"Tony is going to learn a lesson he should have learned a long time ago or he will not be around to bother women anymore."

"Don't, Rafael. I know you could really hurt him, even from a distance, but it isn't right. Just don't." Her temper was rising in direct proportion to the pain in her leg and the implacable set of his jaw.

"If you want me to say I will not touch this man, I cannot lie to you and I refuse to make such a promise. If this man ever attempts to lay his hands on you, he will not get another chance. Ever." He said it with complete finality.

"How very macho. I'm really impressed. So is Louise. For God's sake, put me down, I feel like a fool. I'm quite capable of walking." To her horror tears welled up out of nowhere. Damn the man. The entire town was looking on, smirking at her, right under Louise's gloating gaze.

"Stop struggling, Colby, or I will command you to do so," he bit out. "What did you expect me to do, *querida?* I could not allow that poor excuse of a man to touch you. You are bleeding and in pain. I am your lifemate and it is my duty and my right to see to your care. I intend to do just that."

She felt it then, deep inside him, the volcanic rage that had not been allowed near the surface when he faced Harris. Barely leashed, barely controlled. Her large eyes were swimming with tears and it added to the fury burning in his gaze as it roamed over her face. "I just want to go home, Rafael." *Away from here, away from you.* It slipped into her thoughts before she could prevent it.

A muscle jerked in his jaw. *I will never, ever, give you up. Not now, not ever. We should be past this.* There was a lash to the quiet whip of his voice.

Past this? Are you crazy? I have a few issues, you know. Like you pulling a man's heart right out of his chest. That isn't done, Rafael.

He deposited her very gently on the seat of the pickup truck, ignoring Paul's black scowl. "Move, kid, I'm driving." He said it softly, but there was something in his voice, a warning note that had Paul shrugging helplessly at his sister before jumping into the back of the truck.

Nothing dared defy Rafael's power and the truck started up immediately.

"Do you know how to drive?" Colby asked.

His black eyes flicked over her and then he stared at the road, driving straight through town, narrowly missing Tony Harris as the man stood by his car. "You were thinking of leaving me. And you defend that poor excuse of a man."

"Of course I was thinking of leaving you." She glared at him. "Do you think I'm nuts? And damn Tony Harris. Do you think this is about him? It isn't about Tony, Rafael, it's about you nearly killing me. Do you think I'm going to fall into your arms and trust you not only with my life, but with Paul and Ginny's lives?"

There was a small silence. "I can explain about that, Colby."

For the first time Rafael seemed hesitant. Her eyebrow shot up. "I don't want to take a chance that Paul might hear. Let's wait until we're at the house. But you *are* going to explain. All I'm thinking about right now is the way my leg is hurting," she added and knocked on the window. Paul slid it aside. "Hand over the pain pills. I'm taking all of them."

Paul put the bottle in her hand and Rafael took it out. "You do not need those."

"How do you know? It hurts like hell." She glared at him. "You're making me crazy. You really are. You did something to tie us together and then you got yourself nearly killed and left me to go sleep in the ground. Give me the pills."

"No. And you do not need to chastise me, I have done so enough for both of us."

"Maybe enough for you, but it will *never* be enough for me." She let her breath out slowly and lay back against the seat. "My leg really hurts, Rafael."

"I am aware of it. I feel what you feel, remember? It is not good to use such medications; you are partially in my world and your body will reject such things."

"Like the way it's rejecting food?" she asked, glaring at him.

He glanced down at the bandage. "The doctor sewed your leg. Very barbaric."

"Should he have packed it with dirt and spit in it? Maybe shoved me in a grave and left me there for a few days?"

"Just be quiet." He knew she had a mad desire to leap out of the truck. She was confused and agitated and the pain was making her feel sick. "I'm pulling over so I can relieve the pain in your leg."

Colby didn't argue. If he could take it away, she'd be more than grateful. He found a small sheltered area on the winding road and pulled off so he could focus his attention completely on Colby. Rafael sent himself seeking outside his body, allowing it to fall away and leave behind a light, pure energy, traveling into her body to heal her from the inside out. He took his time to repair her leg carefully, ensuring the swelling was gone, the ragged edges would become seamless, and the injuries to the muscle and tissue inside were healed.

When he pulled back into his own body he leaned over her, touching her leg with gentle fingers. "Does that feel better?"

Colby could only stare up into his dark eyes, drowning there like an idiot when she wanted to be strong. Her leg felt perfectly fine, but the lines in his face were etched deeper than ever. "You shouldn't have done that."

"I had no choice." He bent to kiss the corner of her mouth, her eyelids, the tip of her nose. "You scared me. Do not ever do that again." He reached for her wrist, the one she had slashed open to save his life. He brought it to his mouth, his tongue moving over the faint scar.

The intimacy of it sent heat curling through her body. "Rafael, you need to heal more yourself." She could feel hunger beating at him, a living, breathing monster that roared for attention. "You should take care of your own needs."

"I am taking care of my needs." His voice was low and husky, a seduction on all of her senses.

The shadow was the only warning, dark and ominous and filled with a black kind of evil as it loomed over the two of them. The door jerked open behind her, nearly spilling Colby out of the truck. She screamed in shock and horror as her brother, his face twisted into a mask of hatred, lunged at her with a knife.

15

Rafael moved too fast to be seen, placing himself between Colby and Paul. Savage growls emerged from Paul's throat and he slashed wildly with the weapon. Rafael clamped down hard on his wrist, easily removing the knife, and at once, Paul's expression changed. He blinked rapidly, his eyes clearing, becoming aware, and he gave a startled cry of recrimination that tore at Colby's heart.

"Colby!" He sounded like a lost child, the little boy she had loved so much, had cared for all of her life. "What am I doing? What have I done?" He didn't struggle in Rafael's grasp. Tears filled his eyes and tracked down his face. His entire body shuddered.

"Honey." Colby reached out to him, wanting to comfort him.

Paul jerked backward out of her reach. "It is me! The vampire did something to me when he bit me, didn't he? That's why Nicolas wanted me dead. He knew I was going to hurt you." He turned to look Rafael straight in the eye. "Could I hurt Ginny? Was I the one who did something to the horse to hurt Colby?"

Rafael probed the boy's memories and saw him finding his sister's bra in the barn where it had been forgotten. The undergarment had triggered the hidden compulsion buried deep in Paul to kill Colby. He saw the boy prepare a syringe and shoot the horse full of drugs before saddling it and waking Colby. He pulled out of the boy's mind and let out his breath slowly. "Paul," he spoke gently, "this is the kind of thing vampires thrive on. It is not you. They take someone good and try to get them to perform acts that the person would never conceive of doing. You cannot remember because it is so against your nature to harm either of your sisters. He couldn't twist you into something evil. He can only use you when you are vulnerable."

Paul backed away from the truck. He didn't remember jumping out of the back or tearing open the door behind his sister. He didn't even know where the knife came from. "I love my sisters. I'd rather be dead than hurt either of them."

Colby made a single sound of distress that tore at Rafael's heart. She tried to slide out of the truck and go after Paul, but Rafael caught her hand and held it to him, never taking his eyes from the boy. *Querida, allow me to try. He is ashamed of what he's done and terrified he might succeed.* "Paul, we know you love your family and that you would never do anything to harm them."

"I did, though. I did." Paul turned as if to run, but Rafael was faster, holding him there, his arms locking around the boy.

"Listen to me." Colby recognized the compulsion in Rafael's voice. "Now that we know what he has done and who he is, we can better stop him. He cannot have you. You belong with us. You are *família*, family to us. You will be the one to bring about his downfall if he continues to try to use you."

Paul burst into tears, sobbing wildly, burying his face against the Carpathian. Rafael found himself comforting a teenager, a human boy, his heart reacting right along with Colby's to Paul's unrestrained crying.

"I saw what the vampire did to you. He was hideous. And his

teeth going into my skin." Paul shook with revulsion. "I have night-mares."

"I have hunted the vampire a long time. I know you think he is invincible, but I have destroyed more than you can imagine over the years. I was careless, feeling too many emotions, and was not as wary as a hunter should be. The vampire took you with the intention of using you against us, but found you much stronger than he expected. You could have killed Colby in her sleep, anytime during the after-noons." That was not strictly the truth; Paul could have *attempted*, but Nicolas had provided safeguards to her room while she slept and the Chevez brothers had watched Paul closely. Paul had never made the attempt in spite of the vampire's compulsion. "Your character proved too strong for him. All these days and nights have gone by, yet only now, when I was close to rising, did you succumb to the demands."

"But I hurt her."

"You had to obey him. Paul, look at me." Gently Rafael held him at arm's length until the boy's shattered gaze met his. "You know I am far stronger than you, and far faster, yet you attacked when I was here to stop you. He did not defeat you and yet you are a boy, a human thwarting his plans."

Paul bristled a little at being called a boy, his pride surging forth. "I'm sixteen," he said and stepped back, wiping at his eyes.

"Yes, you are, and I am counting on the fact that you have been shouldering a man's responsibilities. You are definitely mature enough to understand the stakes and what we have to do."

Paul glanced at Colby, a quick, nervous shift of his eyes. He straightened his shoulders. "Tell me how to stop this."

"We have to kill the vampire in order for his hold on you to be completely gone, Paul," Rafael explained. "In the meantime, I can aid you in the same way Nicolas can."

Nicolas hasn't been much help so far, Colby was compelled to point out.

Nicolas prevented him from outright killing. Rafael was gentle, but firm. *Without his interference, Paul would be in bad shape.*

*He is in bad shape. I'm in bad shape. My ranch is in bad shape. My life is a mess ever since all of you came here. Did that vampire follow you here . . . ?*Colby trailed off, her mind racing. The accidents on her ranch had started long before the Chevez brothers had come to make their claim on Ginny and Paul. She couldn't blame them for that.

"Whatever it takes," Paul said. "Whatever you want me to do."

"It may mean leaving here, Paul," Rafael said.

Colby stiffened. "We're not leaving, Rafael."

"We have no choice, Colby," he said. "Until the vampire is destroyed, all of you are in danger. Paul, most of all. We need to put distance between them."

Colby suddenly felt trapped. She turned her face away from Rafael and looked up at the craggy peaks of her beloved mountains. "You're talking about sending Paul to Brazil, to the Chevez family, aren't you?"

There was absolutely no expression in her voice, but Rafael felt the surge of adrenaline, of resolve. "There are five of us in South America to protect Paul and his sanity. Across such a distance, the vampire could not so easily direct him when he is vulnerable. He will have his uncles and cousins to look after him during the sunlight hours and all of us when the sun is down."

"Paul, get in the truck," Colby said.

The boy hesitated, but she was giving him her fiery gaze, so he climbed into the back, still unsure and confused and very upset.

Rafael started the truck. "Colby, you cannot run away from your feelings for me. Vampires are utterly evil. This is a dangerous situation."

"I'm well aware we're all in danger," she replied stiffly. His black eyes flicked over her, just once, but sent a shiver down her spine. She was afraid of him, afraid of his control over her. She slid the window back in place to give them a semblance of privacy. "I don't know what my feelings for you are. We have sex. Great sex, but still, I don't really know you. You deliberately seduced me, Rafael. Don't deny it. You did. I'm lonely and I was easy prey."

"I have no intention of denying I seduced you. Why should I? But you would not have responded to me the way you did if I were not your lifemate."

"Rafael, any woman would be seduced by you. You're very sexy and an incredible lover. It has nothing to do with being lifemates."

"*I* could not be seduced by any other woman," he said quietly. "You belong with me. The rest will have to come later."

"What rest? The part where I do everything you say?"

"No, that needs to come now."

She glanced at him to see if he was attempting a joke. She didn't feel any amusement on his part and she had the sinking feeling he was very serious. "Here's the thing, Rafael: vampires and Carpathians aside, I believe in compatibility. I speak my mind, make my own decisions, and go my own way. I also think things all the way through. You want to make up my mind for me. Why would you think we're even remotely compatible?"

His black eyes slid over her a second time. Hot. Possessive. He robbed her of breath with that single seductive look. Colby had to look away, out the window, her fingers twisting together hard. He could look right through her and *own* her. Once he kissed her she seemed to lose her own will. Colby pushed at her throbbing temples.

She tentatively touched his mind with hers. Emotions swirled, violent and turbulent and unlike anything she was prepared for. Rafael intended to have her at any cost. He was every bit as ruthless as she first thought, maybe more so. He would have his way and do what he thought best to protect her in spite of her fears and misgivings. Colby pulled out of his head, more afraid than ever. Rafael didn't like anyone telling him no and he believed he had a right to her.

How could she survive with him? He lived so differently, thought so differently. He was a mixture of animal, instinct, Latin male and dangerous Carpathian hunter. She was the epitome of an independent woman, yet she could no longer trust her own judgment around him. She wanted to be with him more than she wanted anything, but she was losing herself. She *needed* to be with him and yet she knew he would rule her. She wasn't the type of woman to be ruled. She closed her eyes, trying to keep her mind blank, not wanting him to read her confusion.

Rafael thought of a hundred arguments, a hundred explanations, but none of them would matter. Colby feared what he was and she feared his hold over her. After she had witnessed his nearly losing control, she had every right to fear him. She didn't even trust his purpose with her brother and sister and he couldn't really blame her. He and his brother had come with the sole intention of removing Armando Chevez's family to the ranch in Brazil and that purpose remained the same. Colby had clearly read that resolve in his mind. She was trying to keep from thinking, not wanting him to read her thoughts, but she planned on calling the sheriff as soon as she was home and talking things out with him. She trusted Ben like no other.

He felt the rising of something dark and deadly. The beast roared and his fangs exploded in his mouth. He kept his gaze fixed on the road, opening the gate with a wave of his hand and closing it behind them with a clang of steel and a rattle of chain as it slipped back into place.

They rode in absolute silence up to the ranch house. Colby slid out of the truck and made her way up to the house, annoyed that her leg felt completely better. She couldn't ignore that Rafael could heal her, that he had nearly died to save her and Paul from the vampire. That he had come to her when he was in terrible pain, near death, to help find Ginny. But could he be manipulating her mind in some way to believe all those things had happened when they hadn't really? Was it possible everything was an illusion? Standing alone in the living room, she touched the throbbing mark on her neck with her fingertips, stroking a caress over the pinpricks. Both Rafael and Nicolas were capable of powerful mind exploitation; she'd seen them use compulsion and enthrallment on others. Their eyes, their voices, everything about them shouted power.

The nape of her neck tingled. Her breasts began to ache and heat pooled in secret places. She closed her eyes briefly before turning around, knowing he was there in her living room. Rafael leaned one hip lazily against the wall, his black eyes watching her.

"Where's Paul?" Was that her voice? She could barely speak, her mouth was so dry. She couldn't look at him and not want him. It had to be compulsion. She had never been a woman to be obsessed with a man. She kept her hand over the bite mark that never seemed to fade on her neck.

"The Chevez brothers are taking him over to the Everetts'. He can visit with Ginny and calm down. Sean's good for him, a very steady man, and his uncles will watch over him. It will give him a few hours of relief. The vet left a note for you. He's taken the horse back to his clinic. I made certain the chores were done for the evening." He held out the veterinarian's note.

Wary, Colby stayed where she was. It was the way he looked at her. He was so handsome, so tough and hard yet completely sensual, and his gaze was hot and possessive when it rested on her. And so hungry for her. It made her feel as if he saw only her. That only she existed for him. Her body responded to the dark intensity of his look no matter what her brain said.

"I still have some things to get done. I need to make a few calls and go over the bills," she said. Her voice didn't even sound like her own. She felt behind her for the wall and gripped it as tight as she could.

"I am not going to go away."

"If you were just asking for my body, Rafael, I'd give it to you. But you're trying to take all of me, and I don't want that." She spread her hands out in front of her and stared down at the small white scars from repairing too many fences and handling too much barbwire.

"I am not going to go away."

"I have to have room. You aren't letting me think or breathe. I have to try to figure out what we've gotten into. I'm sorry it isn't what you want to hear, but I'm asking you to leave."

He raised an eyebrow. "Why do you persist in thinking I would ever leave you?"

She tried a careless shrug and just managed to pull it off. She didn't want him to go, but he couldn't stay. He devoured her, ate up her personality until she didn't recognize the woman who would do anything for him, be anything for him. "Maybe because you look human and you seem to be a fairly reasonable person. If a woman asks you to leave, I would imagine you would comply."

"I cannot leave you and you do not really want me to go. I can smell your scent calling to me. I am like the great cats in the forest, or the wolf running free. I claim what is mine and I hold it to me. Your fear is of little consequence."

"Does that type of line endear you to women you go out with?"

"I only go out with you so you will have to answer that." He suddenly straightened, a show of muscle and fluid strength.

"No, it doesn't endear you to me at all. I want you to leave." Because if he didn't, if he stood there looking the way he was looking, she was going to go up in flames. She was all too aware of her body's reaction to him. She had to figure out whether she believed in him, or even trusted him, before they went any further.

He shook his head. "You think to be rid of me. You have no idea of the power I possess, or the lengths I would go to keep you."

"And you have no idea what a stalking law is," she said. "But you're right, I don't have any idea of your power. How can I trust that any of this is real?"

"You believe this is all an illusion?"

"I don't know what to believe. You came here to get Paul and Ginny. Suddenly they're in danger and my entire world is upside down. Surprise—the big solution is to take them to Brazil with you. How very convenient is that? I'm not going to just accept it all without really thinking it through. That's who I am. Live with that." Her eyes challenged him, dared him even. She needed Ben, needed to talk to him desperately. She was out of her mind, baiting Rafael the way she was.

"I suggest you stop thinking of this other man." His voice was very low, almost a purr, but fear blossomed deep in her stomach and spread.

"Ben is my friend. If you stayed out of my head, you wouldn't know I was thinking about him," she pointed out.

His eyes hadn't blinked once; they were totally focused on her. He was mesmerizing her, as efficiently as a cobra mesmerized prey. She stood her ground because she had no other choice. She would not allow him to take her over.

"What do you think would happen to you if I disappeared? You have gone through hell without me these last few risings, yet now you are so willing to do so again. Could you have managed without my brother's aid?"

She winced visibly. "There you go, Rafael. No, I wouldn't have managed and that tells me something important. It isn't normal not to be able to go a few days without seeing someone. Or feeling them inside your head. That's where you are, inside my head, and I can't get you out. It isn't right."

"How do you know what is right? You purposely keep our relationship physical. You do not touch my mind to find out who and what I am. You do not want to know."

His tone was mild but her stomach tightened at the way he kept watching her. She suddenly realized she was completely alone in the ranch house and he had arranged it that way. "You keep it physical, Rafael. The way you look at me and touch me. You're a very physical man and you don't take no for an answer, not when you want me."

"Well, at least we understand one another," he said.

"No, we don't," she burst out. She paced the length of the room and then swung back to confront him. "You act so calm, like everything is normal, Rafael. You tried to kill me. Okay, let's just say for the moment we put aside you ripping the heart out of a man's chest and the fireball you pulled from the sky. We'll just shelve that for the moment and go right to the fact that you nearly killed me. I saw it in your eyes. You might have killed Juan as well."

Rafael's dark gaze met hers. "That is true."

"You told me you could never harm your lifemate. If I'm that person, how is it possible? Your own words make you a liar, or very much mistaken about this entire thing." He had scared her to death. Even now, just thinking about it made her go cold with fear.

"In order for you to understand how such a thing is possible, I have to tell you about myself and my brothers. Even when we were young, not yet two hundred years, we knew we were different from most other Carpathian males. We challenged every rule, pushed every limit. We reveled in our power and strength and when the prince gave us orders, we obeyed, but we questioned. Zacarias was our acknowledged leader, first and always before our prince."

"So you were the bad boys of the community."

"More than bad boys. We chafed at the restraints placed on our kind. Our closest friends were the Malinov brothers. They played rough the way we did, reveled in battle, in challenge, and we had long discussions on why our species should be dominant over mankind. We knew we had power and it seemed wrong to us to allow our prince to keep our strengths secret. As we grew in strength, fighting the vampires and learning our craft as warriors, we grew closer together and questioned the authority of our leadership. We even discussed overthrowing the Dubrinsky family and taking over leadership."

Colby sank back into a chair, her legs rubbery. Nothing he had said so far was giving her confidence in him and their relationship. "You actually plotted to overthrow your ruler?"

"In an interesting discussion kind of way. It happened over a long period of time before any of us thought about it seriously. Eventually, the night our prince sent us away from our homeland with no chance of ever finding a life mate—at least that was what we thought then—we did discuss turning vampire and whether we would be strong enough as a unit to keep from turning on one another as vampires do. We could separate and scatter to recruit others of our kind, using one code name. That way, it would appear as if the same person was in several places at once."

Colby thought of the horrific monster holding Paul in front of him, sinking his teeth deep into her brother, the mutated creatures undulating all around him. She pressed her hands to her stomach. "Where does the part where I understand come in?"

"I am trying to tell you our natures were darker, more animalistic, even more predatory than many Carpathians. It has only been the fact that my brothers and I have remained close, that we had a pact with one another and have kept to it. We did discuss these things, but in the end, it came down to one thing. Honor. We refused to live without honor. The Malinov brothers felt the same way. Our decision did not make it easier for us to conform to the rules. I have a predatory nature. You have not committed your life to mine. I need you as an anchor; I need that commitment from you so that our souls can fully merge."

She jumped up. "Now you're blaming me for what happened. Your predatory nature might just rear its ugly head again and next time you'll kill me, or Paul, or my sister."

A slow hiss of impatience accompanied his exhale. "I have told you things I have never told any other person and yet you do not see that in sharing this shameful part of myself, I was giving you a gift. You would never have found it buried deep inside of me. I chose to be honest. Nicolas is right, there is no other way than force with you."

She moistened her dry lips with the tip of her tongue. He was seething beneath his deceptively lazy demeanor, a swirling cauldron of heat and fire. He made her burn just looking at him. His eyes smoldered one moment, were icy cold the next. Colby let her breath out slowly. "What are you going to do?" She hated that her voice came out a whisper.

"Fortunately for you, your good friend the sheriff has arrived without you calling him. You have gained another reprieve."

Relief swept through her instantly. She sank back down into the chair. She had no idea the tension in her had coiled so tightly. She blinked and he was no longer at the wall near the doorway, but crouched at her feet, looking up at her. "Be very careful with this man, Colby. I am angry beyond your imagining and I need you in more ways than you think. I would not want an innocent man to suffer because you push me too far."

She twisted her fingers together. Perversely, a part of her was disappointed and she was honest enough to recognize the fact. She was drowning in her body's need for him. Her mind wanted to touch his. She ached for him and wanted his arms around her.

Holding herself apart from him was difficult and wearing. "Don't hurt Ben," she whispered.

His fingers caught her chin in a firm grip. "Then do not do anything to set me off. Admit I am not human. Let yourself admit that much and it will become easier to accept that I do not have entirely human characteristics. I was born and bred a hunter, a seeker of prey. It is what I do and what I live to do. Every instinct I have is that of a predator."

"Okay." Her gaze shifted away from him. "You aren't helping your cause. Why do you deliberately try to scare me? I'm already afraid."

"Because you should be afraid. You are not facing a civilized man who understands the laws and abides by them. Our own laws, based on our predatory makeup, rule us. If I do not do what my instincts tell meI must, I endanger too many people. Weighing that against your reluctance, when I know in the end the outcome will be the same . . . "

"You don't know that," she interrupted, attempting to jerk away from his tight grip. She was always astonished at his strength, yet he never seemed to hurt her, even when he was rough. His touch sent butterflies winging in her stomach.

"I do know it. The only way it will change will be if I am dead."

His words took her breath. Sent a dark dread creeping through her body. She blinked away tears, hating that just the thought of his death tore at her emotions.

The knock on the kitchen door was loud but brief. Ben's voice called out to her. "Colby? You home? Doc said you had a bad cut on your leg and the vet said the horse was drugged." He was walking through the house.

Rafael scowled his distaste at the easy familiarity of the other man. He reluctantly allowed Colby to pull her chin away from his hand and stood up, looking more a jungle cat than ever.

"I'm in the living room, Ben," Colby answered, her gaze on Rafael. She couldn't look away if she tried. He was too overpowering, filling the room with his presence, breathing all the air and taking up all the space.

"How bad is it this time, honey?" Ben asked as he entered the room. He paused for a moment when he saw Rafael lounging against the desk with his arms crossed and his legs stretched out in front of him lazily. Immediately the tension in the room went up several degrees.

Colby rubbed her hand over her face. "I'm fine, Ben. Thanks for worrying about me. Paul and Ginny are at Sean Everett's ranch at the moment and I'm just resting." *Why not just say something? Have Rafael arrested for stalking her?* She pressed her fingers to her throbbing temple and shook her head at her own foolishness. She didn't have the kind of strength it took to get Rafael out of her life. Maybe she could do it for her brother and sister, but not for herself. She was beginning to despise herself.

Querida. His voice was soft, compelling. Terribly intimate whispering in her mind. *You are beginning to understand, to accept. You face so much for others without fear and yet you cannot accept anything for yourself.*

When he did that, when he spoke in that voice in her mind, she turned inside out and wanted to burrow inside of him and be everything he wanted and needed.

"We've got trouble around here, Colby. I should have listened to you when you were talking about all the accidents happening on your ranch and old Pete's disappearance." Ben removed his hat and sank into her one good rocker. "I've had three people disappear from town and another two from a couple of ranches."

Colby glanced at Rafael. The news obviously didn't surprise him. *Vampires have to feed and when they feed, they kill their prey.*

A chill went down her spine. He was so calm about it, so

accepting and matter-of-fact. So *removed*. As if his feelings weren't involved.

I have not had emotions for centuries. I do not feel when I hunt the vampire. I would not be able to kill that which was my friend over and over.

"Was there evidence of foul play?" Colby asked, watching Rafael. Did he even feel for the victims? For their families? She couldn't see evidence of it. *What did you feel when you tore out that poor unfortunate man's heart?* Because it could have been Paul's heart. He could have been hunting her brother. The vampire had bitten him, tried to use him in the same way as a puppet.

I felt nothing at all. He would not lie to her. She insisted on scaring herself and making her life so much more difficult than it needed to be.

Would you have been so dispassionate had it been Paul? It was not Paul.

"Colby, are you listening to a word I'm saying?" Ben demanded.

"I'm sorry, yes, it's just so awful. We've never had murders and disappearances here before."

"I talked to Tony Harris." Ben's hard-edged gaze fell on Rafael.

Colby had to admit Rafael didn't look impressed or in the least bit remorseful. "I have no idea what got into Tony. He was far worse than usual."

"Luckily for Mr. De La Cruz, he admitted he had assaulted you," Ben said. "I felt like giving him a good beating myself."

"Tony *admitted* it?" Colby was shocked. She glanced suspiciously at Rafael. Had he planted a compulsion in the man to tell the truth? Rafael's dark features remained expressionless.

Ben nodded. "I had a long talk with him about all the things going on here. I've been suspicious that his boss wanted your ranch and that he was the cause of some of your accidents here."

"I thought of that, Ben," Colby said, "but as much of a bully as

Tony is, he's ranch. He's one of us. I couldn't see him doing that to the kids and me. I've known him my entire life."

"And you've always looked down on him."

Colby spread her fingers out in front of her. "Maybe that's true. He's always been such a bully. I hate the way he talks to me."

"He's had a crush on you for years, Colby," Ben said.

She glanced at Rafael. She couldn't help herself, although she didn't want to look at him. She could feel his gaze, hot and possessive, on her body. *Stop looking at me like that.* The plea burst out of her before she could stop it. He made her want him without touching her. Standing across the room, looking cool and nearly bored, he could look at her and reduce her to raging hormones. *I hate it. I hate what you do to me.*

"I don't believe that, Ben. He was always nasty to me. Nasty and sarcastic. He always calls me the ice princess."

"Everyone knows he's had a thing for you, Colby. And he is nasty and sarcastic. I'm not saying Tony Harris is a great guy—he's meaner than a snake—but he seems to think you should be with him and he's damned angry that you're not. It was fine when he didn't feel he had a rival, but everyone knows you're carrying on with De La Cruz"—Ben jerked his thumb toward Rafael—"and Tony's nose is out of joint."

"That doesn't give him the right to put his hands on me."

"No, it doesn't, and I would have arrested him if you'd made a complaint. And if I'd seen what he did to you I would have done what De La Cruz did." He looked at Rafael. "You've made an enemy for life. Tony doesn't hold too much with the law."

Rafael shrugged, uncaring. "Did he have anything to do with the accidents happening on Colby's ranch?"

"I think so," Ben said. "He skirted the issue, but he didn't altogether deny it either. I think his worm of a boss tried to get her place cheap and Tony went along with it. Twice, in the course of the conversation, he said maybe Colby wouldn't be so high and mighty when she realized she needed a man to help her. I think in his twisted way, Tony thought he could force Colby to ask him for help."

"As if!" Colby all but snorted. "I'd never ask that rat for help. You should have seen him when he thought I was alone out by the mines. He and that ..." She trailed off, biting down hard on her lip. She didn't want to talk about Ernie Carter, or think about Rafael standing, covered in wounds, his fist buried in the man's chest. She closed her eyes, feeling sick.

Ben shrugged. "Tony has delusions, Colby, but I think he had opportunity and in his own twisted way, motive."

She sat up straight. "You don't suspect him of killing Pete, do you?" Tony was many things, but he wasn't a murderer. She didn't want to try to tell Ben there were vampires and puppets in his county. He would lock her up in a padded cell, but she couldn't have Tony arrested for murder.

"Tony isn't smart enough to commit murder and get away with it. He drinks too much and he talks when he's drinking. No one would help him cover up a murder."

Colby let her breath out slowly. "If it's that worm Clinton Daniels causing all the accidents to my ranch, how are we going to catch him? He'd send Tony or one of his other men—he'd never dirty his own hands."

"Whatever you're thinking about doing, Colby," Ben warned, "don't."

"Well, someone has to stop him. I'm not going to be happy putting Tony in jail if Daniels put him up to it."

Rafael, always a shadow in her mind, touched on her plans, irritated that Ben could read her so easily. He caught her thoughts, meeting Daniels casually for a drink, flirting with him, trying to get information on tape from him. Could she kiss him? She wasn't certain she could go that far.

I do not think so. I would have to kill him. Rafael was matter-of-fact about it. *And then you would have to deal with my wrath.*

Spare me the male drama. This is serious. Clinton Daniels is a snake. I've struggled for months trying to hold things together.

"You stay away from Daniels, Colby," Ben said. "I'm not putting up with your shenanigans in the middle of dead bodies and disappearances."

Colby grinned at him. Ben had used his sternest voice on her. "Ben, darling, no one says 'shenanigans' anymore."

She felt the darkness then, heard the roar of a beast. Rafael turned his face away from her, staring out the window, his back to them, but she knew fangs exploded in his mouth. He was fighting a dark instinct that seemed to be riding him hard.

What? She pushed a hand through her hair, irritated all over again.

You call this man by an endearment when you will not even contemplate the possibility of caring for me. How do you expect your lifemate to react?

It was almost a snarl. Her heart thudded hard against her chest. *Ben? You're jealous of Ben? Are you nuts? Ben thinks I'm loony. He loves me like a sister or something. And I love him back the same way.*

Do not speak to me about loving another man when you refuse to love me.

Rafael, Ben does not try to take over my mind and rule me like I'm some brainless sex toy. Maybe you should try to learn a little something from him.

Ben does not try because you do not belong to him.

"Oh, for God's sake!" Exasperated, Colby jumped up. "Men are idiots. I can't take this. I really can't. Ben, go away and take Rafael with you."

Ben looked completely confused. "You never make any sense, Colby."

"I make perfect sense, Ben. Men don't make sense. I need rest. I'm upset and I'm cranky and frankly if you don't get out of my house, I'm setting the dog on the both of you." She glared at Rafael, her hands on her hips.

He straightened slowly. It was a lazy movement, but catlike and sensual. Or predatory and sensual. Colby couldn't decide which. Whatever it was, she could hardly breathe with him staring at her. Devouring her. Stripping off her clothes and claiming her with his black hungry eyes. He took one step toward her and stopped abruptly, the smoldering intensity fading from his gaze, replaced by ice-cold calculation. She instantly felt the darkness creeping through the sky, invading her lands.

What is it? But she already knew. It was out there, maybe watching, maybe after Paul again. The vampire had risen.

He knows I am not yet at full strength and he wishes to test me in battle. The vampire will always take the advantage.

"Then don't go. Stay here with me." Colby crossed the small distance between them, catching his arm. "Wait until you're stronger." It was perverse, and totally an about-face, her emotions swinging wildly out of control at the thought of Rafael in danger. She couldn't stop herself from clinging to him even though she'd wanted him gone only moments before.

Ben threw his hands into the air in exasperation. "Two minutes ago you were throwing us out and setting the dog on us, now you want us to stay. Colby, get a handle on your emotions."

Rafael bent his head toward Colby. He framed her face with his hands. "You know I have to go, *meu amor*. Paul is in too much danger to let this pass."

"Then call Nicolas."

He pressed his forehead against hers, blocking out Ben, the vampire, everyone, until there was only them. Colby and Rafael. "You know I cannot. He is too weary, too far gone. He fights the darkness every moment."

"He'll fight it more if anything happens to you," she whispered. "Rafael, don't go alone. That's what he wants."

"Do you know something about these disappearances, De La Cruz?" Ben demanded. "If you're meeting someone dangerous, I'll go with you."

Rafael didn't turn his head, but kept his gaze fixed on Colby's. "I thank you for your concern but I must handle this problem alone. Perhaps you could drive to the Everett ranch and take Colby with you. Tell Juan and Julio to watch the boy."

He kissed her. Took possession of her mouth the way he did with no coaxing, no light foreplay, instead claiming her, branding her, his mouth hot and hungry and demanding a response. Colby wrapped her arms around his neck, her body melting into his, completely oblivious to Ben's presence.

Rafael put her from him and turned and walked out. Colby went to the window to watch him go. He simply dissolved, was no longer there, but she caught sight of a harpy eagle winging across the sky.

"I hope to hell you know what you're doing, Colby," Ben snapped.

"I hope so too," she said absently.

"Come on, I'll take you to the Everett ranch."

"I can't go, Ben, but will you make certain Paul and Ginny are safe?"

"Are you sure?" He shoved his hat on his head.

"Very." She didn't turn her head, just watched out the window until the giant bird had disappeared behind the foliage of the trees. Her heart sank. "I have too much to do."

"Be careful, Colby, and take care of that leg."

She'd all but forgotten about her leg. Rafael had healed the cut.

Long after Ben had driven away Colby continued to stare out the window intothe night, blinking back tears. She finally put her hand into her pocket and pulled out the crumpled piece of paper with Natalya's cell phone number.

16

*R*afael. *Come out and play with me.* Harsh laughter echoed across the valley and rang in the mountains. Clouds spun dark webs in the sky overhead as the harpy eagle winged away from the ranch toward the higher reaches.

Always a pleasure, Kirja, Rafael answered. He pitched his voice low, a soft melody of purity he knew would grate on the ears of a vampire.

I miss the old days when I had a challenge occasionally. Most vampires are so easy to defeat for one with my skills. Deliberately he taunted Kirja, playing on their old friendship, the days of boyhood dares and one-upmanship.

You will not find me so easy. There was arrogance in the tone.

Rafael caught a faint scent and switched directions, using a slow, steady circle. *I would hope not. You were a great fighter, Kirja, always one of the best. There would be no joy in an effortless victory.* Rafael flattered him, knowing vampires were very vain. Kirja had always been especially competitive.

Join us. Your brother Zacarias was wrong to say we should live with so-called honor. He was brainwashed by a ridiculous code. The prince sent us away because he feared our power. Why do you think he kept Lucian and Gabriel? He knew he would never defeat our combined strength. He cowered behind their protection, knowing already, even then, we were stronger. Join us, Rafael. You can have any woman you choose. You do not have to hide from our prey, but you can use them the way they should be used, as servants to do our bidding.

And you would welcome me after all this time? After I have hunted and destroyed so many of your pawns? Kirja was much closer now, somewhere just ahead, in the thick grove of trees. His presence was a foul stench in the crisp air. Rafael could see where the grass had shriveled, retreating from the presence of evil. Kirja had always favored surprise simultaneous attacks from both above and below. He couldn't stage his preferred ambush in the thicker groves—the trees would hinder his efforts—yet perversely, the groves were exactly the place Kirja's presence seemed the strongest. Rafael didn't trust the evidence Kirja left for him to find.

From his position in the sky, Rafael studied the ground below him with a keen eye. The groves of pine trees formed a large, loose ring around a small cleared area. Kirja's scent was strong in the trees. Rafael knew he would expect the hunter to approach through the clearing in the form of an animal or reptile. It was unlike Kirja to give away his presence as he was apparently doing in the trees and Rafael mentally shook his head at his old friend. He must have fought unwary hunters, those without much skills in such things, to believe Rafael would fall for such a trick. Rafael would not go out in the open in any form where he would be vulnerable to the style of attack Kirja favored.

Still in the form of the harpy eagle, Rafael made a wide circle around the area and in midflight shifted into a much smaller bird, one native to the mountains. He landed in the tree with the thickest foliage and the most interwoven branches. Hidden among the branches and other resting birds, he listened to the whisper of the leaves and the quake of fear running through the tree trunks. Insects, frogs, and other small creatures rustled in the twigs on the ground as they tried to creep away from the clearing. He watched several lizards transverse the wide open space, skittering in stops and starts through the grass, freezing often and testing the air and feel of the earth before they rushed forward, only to stop again.

Rafael took in the signs of distress. The lizards felt the threat, but couldn't identify it. Safe within the flock of birds, he waited.

I await you, Rafael. Have you decided you cannot dispose of me without your big brother to protect you? There was a sneer, a challenge in Kirja's tone.

Rafael sent his voice to the south, careful not to give away his presence in the grove. *There is no honor in defeating the vampire. It is merely a job, Kirja. Well you know the truth of that. Whether it takes one hunter or ten makes no difference. We mete out justice according to the law.*

Above the clearing, where the clouds spun dark threads, the sharp eyes of the bird picked up a glinting flame at the edge of the turbulent mass. Kirja was up to his old tricks and the battlefield was already prepared.

I tire of waiting for you, Rafael.

Rafael duplicated the grove of trees, a difficult and extreme feat that only the oldest and most powerful Carpathians could execute. Trees sprang up in the clearing, long spearlike roots stabbing deep into the ground, winding to form a barricade beneath the earth, while the branches spread out, lifting arms to the sky, forming a nearly impenetrable barrier.

Shrieks of pain and anger rose from the ground as Kirja's serpents burst through the surface, an ugly mass of scales and teeth, writhing and coiling as they tried to escape the relentless roots. They thumped against the ground, striking repeatedly at empty air, sinking their razor-sharp teeth into each other in a mindless need to kill anything close.

Insects swarmed up from the ground, millions of them, large scorpions and a river of ants, a poisonous army determined to kill everything in its path. Rafael countered the move with nature, setting the sap running from the trees and spreading into a lake of liquid amber, trapping the lethal little bugs and containing them within the battle zone beforethey could spread out and cause harm.

That was not nice, Rafael. How unkind to all those living creatures.

Have your memories of me faded so much that you make them up? I was never nice, Kirja, nor have I ever learned how to be.

Join us. The voice whispered the temptation. *Fulfill your destiny. You were always greater than Prince Vlad, and now his sniveling son, Mikhail, has taken his place. He has no one who can adequately protect him. Gregori is too young and not experienced with ancients. He hones his skills on the young, never realizing we exist. He is complacent in his battle skills, thinking he knows all, yet he has only managed to defeat lesser vampires. Those he thought were true masters are our puppets to be used for fodder to gain our goal. You and I both know Gregori is nowhere near our skill and could never defeat us. Join us, Rafael. Accept your true destiny.*

The vampire attacked from the sky, raining fire on the clone trees, slamming bolt after bolt of lightning into the large tree trunks so that they burst into flames and blackened under the heavy assault. The trunks split apart, some falling under the blasts from the sky. Rafael nodded the bird's head toward the spinning clouds, releasing the rain to put out the fire.

The droplets fell, dark and ugly with acid, hissing as they burned through the trees and foliage on the ground, withering every plant in their path and burrowing deep into the earth, infecting the very soil with poison.

Very nice. Rafael kept his admiring tone coming from the south, wanting Kirja to believe he was orchestrating the battle from a distance.

I thought you would like that. Kirja gave the impression of taking of bow.

Rafael stared up at the sky from the refuge of the bird's body within the grove of real trees. The rain ceased abruptly as a wind came from the south, ferocious as it hurtled with hurricane force through the acid clouds, scattering them across the sky, bringing with it a churning storm. Lightning forked in the clouds and crystal-clear rain fell once again, pouring down onto the fires and leaving a crisp, fresh scent behind.

Lucian and Gabriel have risen. They will battle for their prince. Falcon is alive, as is Traian. They will fight.

They have gone soft. They have women to protect. Hunters lose their edge when they worry over the loss of a lifemate. We hunt and worry about no one so we have the advantage. Join us, Rafael. Our ranks grow strong while the hunters allow their numbers to dwindle and their skills to weaken. Most are artisans, forced into service by the prince, not true hunters. I have destroyed thousands of them. Call to your brother and join us. We will not be defeated.

The rain turned from water to ice, a storm of spearing icicles dropping from the sky, piercing the trees from every direction, driving through bark to the very heart of the trees with the intention of killing them. Slivers drove through the bushes and foliage, seeking targets, hoping to find Rafael should he be hidden there.

Inside the body of the bird, a safe distance away from the ice storm, Rafael smiled. Kirja was in rare form, on the run, but fighting back, turning each weapon to his advantage as he tried to score against Rafael.

Seems like old times.

I live to hear the shriek of the trees when the ice pierces their hearts.

You always enjoyed feeling the power of holding life or death over living things, Kirja.

As did you, Rafael. Do not fool yourself. Your nature demands domination over others. You know you are a powerful being and forcing yourself to submit to lesser beings chafes at you every moment of your existence. Join us. They cannot hold against our growing ranks.

Rafael knew there was an underground labyrinth here. He had spent time in the caverns and beneath the surface in the rich soil. He had listened to the whispered songs of the earth and knew there was an abundance of water flowing from various sources. He called them together, a whisper of command, certain Kirja directed the battle from beneath the surface where most of his traps might protect him.

First the trickle began. As tuned as he was to the earth, Rafael could feel the slightest vibration as the underground river began to form, water pouring in from all directions until it was a powerful, moving force. He directed the current so water pounded through the ground to the area he was certain Kirja occupied. In the churning waves he sent jagged roots pistoning, deadly spears hidden in the depths of the frothy waves. The water would saturate the soil, diluting the poisons Kirja had injected, allowing plant life to grow once again after the vampire was gone.

The underground river swelled to a monstrous rapid, roaring through the ground, sweeping aside everything in its path. A scream of rage and pain shook the ground and several trees exploded, raining sharpened stakes throughout the cloned grove of trees. Blood bubbled up through the dirt, pooling into a smoking, noxious puddle, a sure sign the vampire was injured.

From his vantage point in the tree just to the east of the cloned trees, Rafael waited for Kirja to surface. There was no way he could withstand the power of the water rushing underground or the sharp roots shooting through the river with deadly intent. He would have to emerge.

Water burst through the earth, geysers spewing high into the air, boiling hot as if fed by a simmering volcano. Great globs of mud spat from the holes, still bubbling with heat as they flew through the air in all directions. In the midst of the steam, a darker column rose, shooting toward the clouds. The edges of the shadowed vapor trail gleamed a deep red.

At once Rafael attacked, slamming a barrier across the sky so that the vapor hit it hard and clung to the transparent surface much like droplets of condensation. He sent heat pulsing through the barrier, drying the condensation, forcing the vampire into another form.

Immediately the sky blackened, with a huge swarm of killer bees that began attacking every living creature, whether insect or mammal, massing over the bodies in clumps and flying at the trees and shrubbery in a frenzy of hate and rage.

Rafael sent a voracious backlash, sucking all the oxygen from the air over the grove of cloned trees. The bees fell to the ground, inches deep, covering the soil, a carpet of bodies, dead and dying. From the ground rose a transparent dark shadow. It streaked to the nearest tree, sliding inside the blackened trunk. At once the remaining leaves withered and shriveled into brownish black curls. The branches gnarled and knotted, great tumors bursting through bark, the wood splitting in places as the evil swelled.

Rafael slammed a lightning bolt from sky to tree, going for a direct hit and quick incineration, but even as the tree split in two, the shadow within leapt to a neighboring tree.

Kirja. This is so unlike you. I am on your heels. Do you feel my breath on your neck? Does it itch between your shoulder blades? As he spoke, Rafael slammed another bolt, a jagged whip that blew the tree into pieces. Once again the shadow slipped into the next tree. *Why do you run? I thought you wanted to play, old friend.*

Hot lava poured through the vents the geysers had opened, spewing up from beneath the earth, ejecting ash and fire high into the air. Molten rock exploded and slammed to earth as fiery meteors. Trees burst into flames and beneath the earth the river turned to a stream of lava.

I can play. Gnashing teeth accompanied the words. *You will not like how I play this game, Rafael. You should have taken the chance I gave you to join our ranks. You will die a horrible death, but before you do, I will destroy everything and everyone you care about. That is my promise to you.*

Rafael kept his sharp gaze fixed on the trees as the vampire's shadow raced from one trunk to another in an attempt to make it out of the cloned forest to safe ground. Wounded, he fled, staying to cover so Rafael had no chance of getting a clear space to deliver a mortal blow. Kirja couldn't hide in the trees; the twisted, gnarled branches gave him away each time, bursting open to reveal the venom so that it oozed like sap through the splits.

To combat the fires and hot destructive lava streams, Rafael called on the clouds to darken and at once snow poured from the sky, great volumes, a swirling blizzard that only added to the steam obscuring his vision. He cooled the lava rapidly, taking to the air, wary of traps, but knowing Kirja had no choice but to run. He shape-shifted, using the sharper eyes of the harpy eagle as he circled above the cloned forest, now burned and damaged. The snow and rising steam made a nearly impenetrable veil, but he caught sight of a dark shadow at the very edge of the grove emerging from a twisted tree. Droplets of blood stained the snow as the vampire disappeared into what could only be a lava tube, a tunnel formed by the stream, leading deep into the caverns. Gases normally flowed through such tubes once the lava began to cool, but obviously Kirja still had enough power and energy left to blow a forceful wind in front of him and clear his path.

Cursing softly, Rafael followed. It was dangerous to follow a wounded vampire, especially such a master at battle as Kirja. Rafael pressed him hard, unwilling to give him the time to throw up a defense. He was not going to risk losing Colby and he knew Kirja, knew he would never forget that bitter promise of retaliation. Kirja would one day, even if it took a thousand years, find a way to revenge this battle. Even as a boy he had always evened the score against perceived slights. Rafael had wounded him and that would never be forgiven.

You betrayed our friendship. Kirja spat the words, a venomous poison in his voice. He was moving fast. Rafael caught the impression of the sloping tube, the blackened ropy surface as the vampire rushed toward the safety of the mountain interior. *Just as you betrayed it so many years ago by allowing that fool Vlad to send you to your doom. He isolated us on purpose. You know he did. He literally sent us into exile while his chosen ones took the women and lived the life meant for us.*

Rafael remained silent as he flew into the tunnel, shifting into the smaller form of a bat. Whatever trap Kirja managed on the run would be flimsy and in the smaller body Rafael would have a greater chance to avoid an ambush. The lava flow had twisted and turned as it formed the tube, making it difficult to see ahead. Rafael relied on all of his acute senses to warn him of impending danger.

Rounding a turn, the surface of the tube abruptly went from the nonthreatening roped *pahoehoe* surface to the *'a' a* shell, a loose rubble with knifelike protrusions and sharpened spikes. Kirja had ensured that the surface was honed to a razor edge to cut anything moving through it. The tube narrowed as it descended beneath the earth and forged deeper into the caverns beneath the mountain. Rafael, even in the form of the small bat, was forced to slow down.

He tried something he had not done in centuries. As small boys, Kirja and he had tried to "see" through each other's eyes. They had essentially done so without using a blood exchange. Instead, they had followed the mental path and tried touching other senses. It had been successful with practice. Although rusty, Rafael was far more powerful than he had been as a child. He reached out to touch the vampire's brain. The connection was almost instantaneous and Rafael wasn't prepared for the mass of churning hatred and cunning. Kirja was stumbling over the uneven surface, attempting to close the tube behind him. He was far weaker from his wounds than Rafael would have guessed, or he would have been using more power. The undead was conserving for a fight if needed.

Taking a breath, careful to keep his touch light, Rafael pushed through the icy rage and rotten core to try to find sight. He needed to be able to see ahead of Kirja, to set up an ambush of his own. It took only seconds to see the long expanse of blackened lava he needed. At once he weakened the surface several yards ahead, keeping the outer layer looking smooth and even, but paper thin. Beneath the surface, he pooled the lava, a makeshift dam that wouldn't hold long, but might give him an edge.

Rafael pulled out of Kirja's mind as gently as possible, not wanting to give away the fact that he'd made the contact. He knew the exact moment the vampire stepped on the thin surface, cracking it and falling through. A hideous scream shook the walls of the precarious tunnel and the noxious smell of burning flesh permeated the air. Rafael rounded two corners and found himself staring at the vampire only a scant few yards away.

Kirja was pulling himself from the hole. Most of his legs were burned to bloody stumps, the skin falling off in ashes. He raised his hate-filled gaze to Rafael. *Your woman will suffer as no other woman has ever suffered.* He made the promise in a harsh, hissing voice, all pretense at friendship long gone.

Rafael rushed him, going for a kill, determined to separate heart from body. Halfway to the vampire, the entire tube collapsed and above it, the underground cavern itself. Tons of dirt and rock rained down between them, driving Rafael back. He was forced to use his power to keep from being buried under the debris, forming a protective cave around him and waiting for the earth to settle.

Kirja was in no shape to attack Colby or the children. They were safe while the vampire healed, but he had to get to her. He had run out of time. Colby had to be brought fully into his world, where Rafael could protect her from revenge. Even digging through the debris would not net him a vampire. He knew Kirja, knew he would find a hole and crawl into it, maybe waiting years to rise before attempting to exact his vengeance, but he would eventually make his move. Now or later, it would happen.

Rafael reached to touch Colby, to assure himself she was waiting at the Everett ranch where he had sent her. To his shock, she was in the bar. For a moment he simply stood there in outrage, buried under the mountain, the earth above him ravaged by the battle between two ancients. Colby hadn't listened to him, hadn't paid any attention when he tried to warn her. She hadn't wanted to hear him.

He made his way through the dirt and rock until he found where he had last seen Kirja. There was no blind spot. No trail of blood. Not even a scent. In the closed-in cave he should have smelled the taint of vampire, but Kirja was an ancient master and he could conceal what he was when he desired. There would be no following him and taking advantage of his wounds.

Back above ground, Rafael cleared the evidence of the storms. He incinerated the damaged trees and sent the underground streams back where they belonged. The lava was gone as quickly as it had been wrought, back in the small pool beneath the sleeping mountain. When it was done and he had cleaned himself up, he turned his attention to his most important task. Seducing Colby and taking what was rightfully his.

Natalya sat in the darkest corner of the bar, with her back to the wall, her gaze moving constantly over the crowd. She nodded when

Colby sat down. "You know everyone, don't you?" There was a wistful note in her voice.

"Pretty much, yes."

"Must be nice. I can never stay anywhere for very long." Natalya leaned close. "I can't take a chance on one of the hunters finding me."

"Why? What do they want with you?" Colby asked, rubbing at her suddenly throbbing temples. "I have to have some answers or I'm going to go out of my mind. I'm honestly at the point where I can't tell reality from illusion. Are there really vampires? I encountered a horrible creature, but I swear I might just be going insane and I'm being fed illusions. Mass hysteria." Briefly she covered her face with her hands before looking again at the other woman. "I wanted to talk to Ben about this—he's the sheriff, a friend I've relied on all my life—but do you know how insane this all sounds? He'd lock me up and throw the key away."

Natalya regarded her with compassion. "I'm sorry, I know how difficult this must be for you. I wish I could help you."

"You said if I wanted to come with you . . . " Colby trailed off as Natalya shook her head.

"He can follow you. You said he talks to you." She indicated Colby's neck. "He took your blood. You're having problems because he must have given you his. He won't let you go. I know little about the hunters, other than that they have tremendous powers and can become the very thing they hunt." She tapped her fingernail on the tabletop. "I don't honestly know how to help you. I thought about it a lot after we spoke, but I can't come up with any answers."

Colby pressed her hand to her neck, holding the bite to her and hating the gesture. "I don't honestly know if I could leave him. I'm so worried about Paul and Ginny. Paul was bitten by the vampire and the vampire tries to use him to hurt me." She couldn't touch Rafael with her mind. She tried over and over, but he was closed off to her. She didn't know if he was injured, or dead, or simply protecting her. Her skin crawled. "It's like some terrible addiction. I think about him all the time. I'm a strong person, but I can't get over him." She looked up at Natalya pleadingly. "I've got to either trust him or find a way so I know the children are safe. I think it's too late for me."

"Where is he?" Natalya looked around again. "I can't imagine him giving you too much room when you aren't giving him what he wants."

"Right now he's gone off to battle the vampire. He says if he doesn't destroy it, the creature will always have a hold over Paul."

Natalya nodded. "I'm afraid he's right."

The music in the bar blared, reverberating through her head. Colby pressed her glass of ice water to her forehead. "I hate being so indecisive. I've lived my entire life knowing what I was supposed to do and doing it. All of a sudden I don't have any idea which direction to turn. Suddenly the ranch doesn't seem very important next to Paul's life. I just want Paul and Ginny to be happy and to live normal lives."

Natalya studied Colby's face. "What is it? Why did you come here?"

Colby sighed. "I wanted to run away with you. Take the kids and go. And I want answers. I need them and I think you can give them tome." She tapped the tabletop with her fingernail, beating out a rhythm of nervous energy. "You know that mark on you? The dragon? You said it was a birthmark? I have a mark like that. It's very faint and unless you're looking for it, you'd never know it was there. It doesn't get hot like you said yours does, but I have one."

There was a long pregnant silence. Natalya shifted closer, staring at her incredulously. "Are you certain? You should have told me when we last spoke."

"It means something, doesn't it?" Colby asked.

"Has the hunter seen it?" Natalya's voice was nearly inaudible, in spite of Colby's enhanced hearing.

"His name is Rafael."

"I don't want to say his name. I don't want him to turn his attention to me. Has he seen the mark on you?"

"It's very faint and it fades at times, so even I have a difficult time finding it. Why would saying his name turn his attention to you?" Colby asked.

"Where is the mark located?" Natalya asked, ignoring Colby's question.

"The same place you said yours was, over my left ovary. Is that how the vampires identify us? Does that mark call them to us? I know you know things. I need to know them. I'm not asking for myself, Natalya, but for my brother."

"Have you allowed the hunter to make love to you?"

"You know I have."

"Then you have a fading mark of protection or he would have spotted it. It hides itself from him."

Colby had the desire to stand up in the middle of the bar and scream. "You aren't making this any easier for me. Just tell me what's going on."

"If you have the birthmark on you, you're related to me in some way. We have an old, ancient lineage. There are very few of us." Natalya obviously was choosing her words carefully. "The hunter cannot see that mark, so it must be hiding from him."

"*Why* can't he see it?" Colby nearly hissed the words from between clenched teeth. "Why won't you tell me? Can't you see I'm desperate? I *can't* be away from him. I don't know how to reverse whatever he did to me, and to be honest, I've gone past the point of wanting him out of my life. I have a terrible feeling I'm halfway in love with him. He does things so wonderful, so heroic, it's heartbreaking. Please tell me what you know."

"Unfortunately I know only what my father told me and it isn't much. I've lived a long time, Colby, and I don't age much. You think I'm about your age, but I'm much older. I have rare talents. I can touch something after you, or anyone else, and I can 'see' where you've been. I can read the history of objects and I'm telepathic."

"Can you shape-shift?" Colby asked bluntly. "You're describing this same species. Why would you have to hide from them?"

"The birthmark. Anyone born with the birthmark must stay far from the hunters and vampires or they will kill us. It is some ancient rule."

Colby dropped her head into her hands, remembering the feel of Rafael's tongue tracing her birthmark, a seductive, erotic exploration that made her shiver with need. "I don't think so, Natalya. I think you're wrong." Rafael had to have felt the faint outlines of the mark. It was raised slightly. Even if the birthmark could try to hide itself, he had lapped at it several times, his lips moving over it until she wanted to scream for him to give her release. But later, he had tried to kill her. She rubbed her throbbing temples. "I don't know anything anymore. Has a hunter ever attacked you?"

"No, I avoid them, just as I avoid the vampires. There was some kind of feud between my family and the hunters in ancient times and it has carried over into this time." Natalya leaned back in her seat. "My understanding is, one of the hunters' women, Rhiannon, left her husband to be with a very powerful man. There was a rift between the two factions and war broke out. Rhiannon had triplets, two girls and a boy. She died when the children were young, but their father taught them to avoid the hunters and vampires. Her son is my grandfather."

"And the two girls?"

"They disappeared. No one knows where they are. My father thought it possible the hunters found them and killed them."

"Where do I fit in to all of this?" Colby asked.

"My guess is, you're my niece. My brother took up with a woman briefly but then left her. You have his look and maybe that's why I was drawn to this part of the country. The woman owned a ranch around here."

"Your *brother* is my father?" Colby felt more agitated than ever. She couldn't imagine Rafael killing her because a woman left her husband however many years earlier. "Where is he now?"

"He's dead." Natalya's tone made it clear she wouldn't give out any more information.

Colby couldn't feel anything for a man she'd never met. Armando was her father and she would always love him. "Just how old are you, Natalya?"

"Does it matter? You aren't going to leave him. You already know that. You just aren't willing to trust him with your brother and sister. I can't take them with me, not without you. They wouldn't be happy and we'd all be in danger. I can shield myself and get in and out of places without the hunters or vampires detecting me, but unless the vampire that bit Paul is killed, they will always be tied together." Natalya's head suddenly went up alertly. "He's close. Either him or the other one. I have to go, Colby. I'm leaving town immediately. Good luck to you."

"Thanks for giving me someone to talk to." Colby knew Rafael was near. Every cell in her body had gone on alert. The nape of her neck prickled as if, already, she felt the warmth of his breath. "Be safe."

"Good luck, Colby. I'll be thinking of you." Natalya reached out and touched her, just the lightest brush of her fingers, but warmth sprang from Natalya to Colby. There was recognition in the touch. Natalya drew back and nodded. "We're definitely related. Please be very, very careful."

Colby nodded. "You too." She watched Natalya make her way quickly through the tables toward an exit, her heart beating with anticipation. She knew the exact moment Rafael entered the bar. He was alive and that was all, in that moment, that mattered to her. He didn't look around—his gaze found her immediately. He stood across the room from her, exuding sheer sexy male confidence.

Her stomach muscles tightened. Her breath stopped. Tiny flames of arousal licked through her as she felt the weight of his eyes from across the bar. He was alive. He seemed unhurt. And when he looked at her, there was stark hunger, a potent desire that rocked her to her core. He began to walk toward her, never taking his gaze from her. He moved with a sensuous grace that started her heart pounding in time to the music. He walked right through the crowd as if no one existed but her, watching her the entire time. No one bumped him and no one got in his way. He simply held out his hand for hers. "Dance with me."

She watched fleeting emotions flicker across his face and dark shadows shift in his eyes. Before she could stop herself she reached slowly out to him, mesmerized as always by him. He pulled her up and drew her against his body hard, fitting her close so that she could feel the hard bulge of his arousal pressed tightly against her. His body was hard, his arms strong, and his heart beat out a rhythm beneath her ear. She felt safe and protected. She felt threatened and frightened. It was insanity at its worst to dance with him. She was giving herself to him.

Heat spread from his heavy erection outward, catching them both on fire. She felt weak with wanting him. His hands, at her waist, slipped lower to her hips, to press her body more tightly, increasing the friction between them as they swayed slowly around the dance floor.

I don't see any blood on you. Did you find the vampire? She wanted to just drift away with him on a rising tide of lust and need.

We met. He managed to get away, but I marked him. Why did you come here to meet this woman?

She started to lift her head from his chest, but his hand caught the back of her head and held her to him. It wasn't his words or even his tone that alarmed her; it was a glimpse of his thoughts, quickly hidden from her. For just a fraction of a second, she caught temper swirling in him and something dangerous.

Let me hold you, Colby. It has been a long evening and I just want to feel you in my arms. He bent his head to her, his mouth nudging aside her shirt to burrow against the warmth of her neck. She shivered in his arms in reaction. His tongue swirled over her pulse and his teeth scraped roughly, seductively back and forth.

Colby was afraid she was melting in his arms. She had pressed a kiss against his chest, turned her face up to his throat so she could feel his skin beneath her lips. She was shaking with need for him. Her womb clenched and she was slick and damp with invitation. She wanted his clothes gone so she could examine every inch of him, see for herself that he wasn't hurt.

Come away with me. I want to take you to the hot springs up in the mountains. Just the two of us. I need you tonight, meu amor. This once, do not argue or protest. Do not say no, just come with me and let me have you.

The music faded away. Some of the bar patrons left the dance floor while others stayed as the next song picked up the tempo. Rafael's body urged her from the floor toward the exit. She could feel the heat of his palm burning like a brand through her thin blouse. "Paul and Ginny . . ."

"Are safe," he finished, his voice rough with raw passion. "Come with me, Colby. Of your own free will. Give yourself to me." He bent his head and deliberately teased the nape of her neck with his teeth, scraping gently, a small nip and swirl of his tongue heating her blood.

Beneath the thin layer of her shirt, her breasts ached, felt uncomfortable in her bra, the nipples tight hard peaks painfully rubbing against the lace. She felt her body go weak and damp with invitation. She wanted him right there. That moment. Hunger raw and sharp and terrible. "Yes." She said it softly, but he heard. She knew he heard because his hand bit possessively into her hip. He urged her toward the door. Her heart pounded in anticipation.

17

Outside, in the cool night air, Rafael abruptly turned to Colby, his hand fisting in her hair, holding her head still as he bent to her, his larger body aggressively caging hers against the side of the building. He was hot and hard and hungrier for her than he'd ever been. "I do not know if I can wait. We have to get out of here before I take you here and now." His voice was a rough whisper, as he slanted his mouth over hers, his tongue sliding over the seam of her lips, tasting her, demanding entrance. He caught her soft moan in his mouth and his temperature soared several degrees.

In the parking lot? Colby didn't care if they were in the parking lot. There were too many clothes between them. She heard her own whimper as he licked at her, his teeth teasing her full lower lip, and then his tongue sank back into her mouth again. His erection was pressed tight against her stomach, her breasts mashed against the muscles of his chest. She was beginning to lose touch with reality the way she always did with Rafael. The hand gripping her hair in a tight fist, holding her still while his mouth dominated hers, was just on the edge of rough. He kissed her like a starving man, drowning in need for her. As if he couldn't wait. Could never get enough. Her body reacted, hot and slick, drenched in need.

The parking lot, the field, who the hell cares? I want to tear your clothes off. Why are you wearing a bra? His hand skimmed lightly up her stomach to cup her breast, his thumb caressing her nipple, teasing and tugging beneath her blouse. *Do not ever wear a bra again.*

Her breath caught in her throat. She pushed into his hand, fighting back a moan of need. "We can't. Someone will come out here and see us."

He could shield them, but he couldn't do the things to her he wanted to do if they remained at the bar out in the open. With more impatience than finesse, he wrapped his arms around her and took to the air, his mouth still commanding hers. She whimpered, tried to struggle, but he held her still, kissing her until it didn't matter that they were no longer on the ground.

Colby circled his neck with both arms, clung tightly to his body, closing her eyes and giving herself up to the shocking sensation of his mouth. Her body melted against his. The heat, created by the thick bulge pressed tightly against her stomach, was generating a wild response in her. The lower half of her body was hot and heavy, pressure building fast. She rocked against him, rubbed along his body, all the while her mouth welded to his. His tongue mated with hers, exploring the velvet interior of her mouth, stroking and caressing until she felt him in every cell of her body.

Rafael had to touch her skin or he was going to go out of his mind. He wanted to make it to the hot springs, where the soil was rich in minerals and he could ensure she was safeguarded while the earth healed her body and completed the change. It had all been so important until he saw her. His body had hardened until every movement seemed painful and he knew he had to have her again and again. She was addicting, with her soft skin and her silky hair.

She was such an independent woman, steely strong under all

those soft curves, with a will like iron, until he touched her. Then she was his. Completely his. She fought him for so long. She was still fighting him, but not when he kissed her, not when he had his hands on her. He enjoyed the feeling of power, of being the one man she couldn't resist. He fed on that, needed it from her.

Somewhere over the mountains, he tore her shirt from her body, wanting the feel of her skin beneath his palm. Colby didn't protest, rather threw back her head, a strangled sound of need escaping, as his mouth trailed down her neck, licking and taking tiny bites that sent tongues of fire racing over her skin and sizzling through her body. She always seemed to do this to him, the moment his body came into contact with hers. Lust rose sharp and dangerous, out of control. His body burned him alive from the inside out, raging with needs and wants he could never get enough of. There would never be enough ways to take her, to have her, and eternity wouldn't be long enough to satisfy him.

Rafael. She whispered his name plaintively, pleading with him to set them down, uncaring that they flew through the air to an unknown destination. She writhed against him, wrapped one leg around his thigh to rub her pelvis over him seeking relief.

With one hand wrapped firmly around her waist, he bent his head to her bare breasts, forcing her upper body backward. Her hair blew in all directions, whipping in the wind, stinging her face, reminding her where she was. "We're going to hit a tree or something. Put us down." Her voice came out husky with desire. Lust poured through her veins, thick and burning with an intensity that left her shaken. "You have to, I need you right now."

The breathless plea in her voice shook him. His mouth brushed her breast, tugged at her nipple. She screamed and arched her body further to give him better access. Fire radiated from her breasts through her entire body and created a throbbing, urgent hunger between her legs.

Rafael heard the pounding of her blood rushing through her veins beneath her satin skin, calling to him, beckoning with erotic promise. His blood pounded with the same intensity, the same beat, throbbing and pulsing through his heavy erection in anticipation. He hungered for her. For all of her. He hungered for his body to be buried deep in her tight, hot channel, his mind firmly in hers and her blood flowing into him like nectar. If he wasn't careful they were going to fall out of the sky and tumble to earth, locked together in a passionate embrace.

He took them to ground, grateful they'd made it to the hot springs. The moment his feet were on the ground, he ripped the off ending jeans from her body, tore them into strips, and hurled them away from her. His eyes darkened as his gaze slid over her possessively. "You are so beautiful." Her body was flushed with arousal, with need for him, desperate hunger in her eyes. He could see the wet, slick evidence of her desire glistening between her thighs and it was all he could do not to drop to his knees and feast.

Colby watched as he deliberately removed his clothes the human way. He kicked aside his shoes, his hands going to the waistband of his jeans. She could see the enormous bulge pushing for freedom against the tight material. Her breath nearly stopped when he unbuttoned the jeans and shoved them off of his hips. He never took his eyes off of her, watching her with hungry intent. His face was etched with desire, his eyes black and his mouth a sensual slash.

"Come here to me, Colby." His hand circled his heavy erection, absently stroked, a casual, easy movement bringing him more pleasure.

She went to him, half mesmerized by the size and shape of him, half hypnotized by the stamp of dark sensuality stamped on his features. Her tongue darted out, swept over her lower lip as she watched his hand slide over the thick hard length. His gaze never left her, compelling her forward, drinking in the sight of her breasts swaying as she halted in front of him.

He lifted his hand to cup her face, his touch gentle. He bent his head slowly toward her, his lips drifting down her cheek to the corner of her mouth. His tongue traced her lips. "I love your mouth. I could kiss you forever." His other hand brushed her breasts, sent tiny flames dancing over her skin.

Colby was so conscious of that second hand, traveling lightly over her breasts, the pads of his fingers barely skimming, yet so arousing, moving over her belly, circling her navel until her breath caught in her throat and his fingers tangled in small fiery curls.

"You are so wet and ready for me, *querida.*"

She couldn't stop the small sound escaping, a plea for more. He was barely touching her, yet he was sending her temperature soaring.

The hand cupping her face slid to her nape, reached up and tangled in her hair, pulling her head back to expose her throat. His mouth slid over her pulse. His teeth nipped, a small stinging bite, his tongue instantly swirling a soothing caress. Her body nearly convulsed, every muscle tightening, her womb contracting. "Tell me what I need to hear, Colby." His mouth moved up her chin, teeth nibbling at her lower lip. "Tell me."

"You know I want you." How could she not? His fingers slipped inside of her, pushing deep so that she cried out with pleasure, writhing against his hand, desperate for relief. The fingers withdrew, making her frantic.

"It is not enough for me." His voice was very quiet, whispering over her like a stroke of heat. His tongue teased her throat again, moved lower to the side of her breast. She felt the sharp bite of his teeth, edging pleasure with pain just before he drew the creamy mound of flesh into the hot cavern of his mouth.

Colby caught at his shoulders for support, her knees threatening to give out. "What do you want from me, Rafael?" His fingers thrust deep, so that she rode the edge of a climax but couldn't quite make it over the edge.

"You know."

It wasn't fair to ask for a declaration of love, of commitment, when she was trying so hard to make sense of it all. Rafael didn't believe in fairness. He believed in getting his way, using any means possible. And when it came to sex, she knew she would do anything for him. He knew it too. It was there in the heavy-lidded glittering eyes. His hands were magic and his kiss could shred her self-control. Colby's chin rose a fraction and she flipped her hair over her shoulder, her gaze dropping to his erection. He was huge and hard with need. The moment she looked at him, the moment she moistened her lips, she felt the hitch of his breath.

Her hand dropped to circle the thick bulge, fingers skimming lightly. She licked her lips again, watching his reaction as her thumb glided around the base of the velvet head. He barely took a breath as she went to her knees in front of him.

She allowed her tongue a brief exploration, licking a sensual circle and teasing the base of his swollen head. He shuddered, a rough groan escaping. His fingers sank into her hair, bunched there, and dragged her closer to him even as he thrust into the hot cavern of her mouth. Her tongue curled around him, danced and teased. His fists tightened in warning. "You are pushing me over the edge of my control, *pequena*."

Her mouth was hot and tight, her tongue flattening to vibrate along the sensitive base of his thick, velvet-over-steel tip. His hips jerked, his muscles clenched with pleasure. His incisors ached to lengthen but he controlled the need. He thrust forward, holding her head, wanting control back but unable to make himself ruin her obvious pleasure. She started a fire in his groin that spread through his belly to every part of his body. Her tongue curled and lapped until he was out of his mind.

For a moment demands pushed their way into his mind, but she was inexperienced and not quite ready for all the eroticisms he was hungering for.

Rafael pulled her head back and stared down into her eyes. They were brilliantly green, darkened with passion, with need. He ached with his love for her, with his need for her commitment to him. He drew her with him to the large boulders surrounding the hot springs and simply caught her around the waist and lifted her onto one of the flattest rocks. His hands jerked her thighs apart and pressed into the entrance to her slick folds. She was so hot he was afraid they'd both burn. She tried to push herself forward, to impale her body on the hard length of him, but he held her still.

"You forgot to tell me something. Something very important."

"This isn't funny, Rafael." How could she want him when he wanted everything his way? "Give me time."

He leaned over her, his hands flat on the boulder, bracing himself above her, his body refusing to enter hers. He just held them both there, on the edge of madness. "I am in your mind. I see what you feel for me."

"Then I don't have to say it, do I?" Colby managed to slide down on the rock, but he clamped his arm across her restless hips and held her. Now she was trapped between the hard edge of the boulder and his hips. He gave her an inch, enough to make her scream in utter frustration.

"Because you belong to me. I want to hear you admit it."

She was near tears and that would be worse. "Fine. I belong to you but I don't have to like it."

"And you love me." He pushed deeper into her tight folds. "Tell me you love me, Colby."

"You can't command me to love you, Rafael. Isn't it enough that

I'm here with you? That I can't keep my hands off of you?" It was humiliating to have him hold her against the rock while she ground her hips against him, nearly begging him to take her.

"Whatever you think, this is me making love to you. Not having sex, making love," he reiterated. He pushed deeper into her body, watching her pupils dilate with pleasure. "I love everything about you, *querida*. I am not ashamed to admit it to you. I love the way you burn for me and the way my body grows hard and hot and ready for you every time I lay eyes on you. I love the way you take care of your family and even the way you think you can defy me. Stop being a coward and admit you love me."

"Stay out of my thoughts. It's bad enough that you try to force me to do whatever you want. If you need to hear me say it before I even know my own mind, compel me to say it," she said, staring up at the raw intensity of his face. Her heart pounded in fear as they stared at one another, as his eyes glittered with danger.

He sank into her all the way, burying himself so deep he could feel her womb. Pinned against the hard rock, she could only accept the rough thrust of his hips, her body a tight fiery inferno surrounding his. She looked beautiful, her face and body flushed, her lips swollen with his kisses, her eyes glazed with passion. For him. His fingers tightened on her. "You are such a gift, Colby." He could barely take in that she was real, that she was his. That after this night he would always have her. There would be no going back.

He drove hard, surging into her over and over. She was such a tight fit. He could actually feel the way he stretched her folds as he impaled her. She writhed beneath him, trying to lift her hips to meet him, to be slammed back at each furious thrust. The smooth boulder cradled her buttocks but refused to give so that they came together in wild heat. Every thrust sent agonizing pleasure careening through his body, through hers. He could feel her become hotter, wetter, feel the passion spiraling through her mind until she was dazed with the need for release. Joy surged through him, shaking him with the need to satisfy her. She cried his name, pleading with him, a half sob that had him driving his flesh into hers, branding her his for all time.

The orgasm tore through her body, encompassing every fiber of her being, taking her heart and soul and mind. Colby felt shattered, fragmented, by the mindless, endless pleasure that rippled on and on until she knew she would never be happy without him. She felt his eruption, the hot jetting release that sent more tremors through blood and bone, through every cell until even her vision blurred. She buried her nails deep into his arms, trying desperately to anchor herself while the world rocked around her.

Rafael leaned his body over hers, his breathing every bit as harsh and desperate as hers. Their hearts beat together, a crazy syncopation as they tried to draw in the night air. Colby lay back against the rocks, his head pillowed on her breasts. She was beginning to feel the effects of making violent love against hard stone. "Ow."

"Ow?" he repeated and lifted his head to look at her.

She peeked at him from beneath her lashes. It was a mistake. He looked darkly sensual, his face sinfully sexy. His eyes were dark with passion, with possession, and still far too hungry. She shook her head. "We can't. I mean it. This rock is hard. I didn't notice before, but I'm not going to be able to walk."

"And I thought cowgirls were tough." His tongue lapped at her nipple and her small muscles clenched around him. He was still hard, still buried deep inside her, and wanted to stay that way.

"Not this tough." She looked around her. Several small waterfalls poured into the hot springs coming up from the ground, cooling them enough to use as a spa. "I haven't been here in years. It's miles from my ranch and I'm always too busy to get out this way. I'd almost forgotten it was here."

Ferns covered the ground and surrounded the large flat boulders forming the ring around the basin. "It is beautiful here. I thought you might like it." His teeth teased and tugged just to feel her reaction.

She pushed at his shoulders. "You have to stop. I can't take any more right now. I think you killed me."

His tongue stroked over her breast, curled around her nipple. He lifted his head and smiled at her. A slow, sexy smile. "Not yet."

"No." She said it firmly, though her blood was already thickening at the wicked glint in his eyes. "I can't move. I think I'll just lie here all night, draped over this rock. You go do whatever needs doing and let me sleep." Perversely, when he slipped out of her, she felt bereft. There was no stopping the small sound of protest.

"You need to get in the spring or you really will be sore." He lifted her as if she weighed no more than a feather, cradled her against his chest, and carried her to the steaming spring. He paused, the same sensual smile teasing her senses. "Unless you want me to lick you better. My saliva acts like a healing agent."

Colby circled his neck with her arms. "I could like you when you act like this, Rafael." She kissed his throat, nibbled her way to his jaw. "Why don't you act like this all the time? Sweet and gentle."

He waited until her lips teased the corner of his before turning his head to capture her mouth. His move was aggressive and commanding, taking possession, his tongue spearing deep and tangling with hers in a wild mating. Her heart jumped and her blood sang. He lifted his head, black eyes glittering at her. "That is why. I know you. Inside and out, I know what you need, maybe better than you do. You like me rough."

Colby pulled back to stare up at his face, etched with stark possession. "Is that what you think, Rafael?" Her tone was very serious. "Is that what you think you read in my mind?"

"You would never respect a man you could dominate, Colby. You are a strong woman and you require a man who can make decisions, not be overwhelmed by the strength of your personality." He answered her just as seriously.

"Rafael, I can't be submissive to you. It isn't in my character—don't you see that as well? I have to have some control, some partnership, or it would never work between us. I could never love you. I know I'm sexually addicted, but I want to be in love with you as much as you want me to be. I just can't make that leap knowing you don't respect my judgment."

"*Querida*, why would you think I do not respect your judgment? You are in a situation you cannot possibly understand. It makes sense to rely on my judgment until you have gained the knowledge and power necessary to cope with our world."

There was such love in his voice, such a wealth of tenderness, her heart turned over. If he could only be like that all the time. She closed her eyes as his teeth teased her pulse and her body responded with a fresh wave of heat. "I would like to explore the sexual addiction to me. It sounds most interesting."

"Great. Now you're telling me I'm kinky." She leaned back and stared up at the stars. Maybe she was. The things he did to her body were inconceivable with anyone else, but with him, she melted every time he came near her. "Maybe I am, but only when it comes to you."

"I like you kinky," he whispered against her neck. Against the pulse beating in her throat. "I need to taste you tonight, *meu amor.* Give yourself to me."

"No way." She shook her head even as her body went weak at the sensual brush of his voice. Deep inside, her muscles clenched and her womb throbbed. She could feel heat building and it had nothing to do with the hot springs. "Last time you got all vampy on me and scared me to death. Sink your fangs into someone else."

His mouth moved down her throat, his tongue lapping at the small dip in her shoulder. His teeth scraped back and forth in a particularly erotic way. She closed her eyes. "Make sure it isn't a woman, though."

He waded into the water so that it lapped around his thighs. His laughter vibrated against her neck, teeth teasing. "I want you again."

"You always want me, you're wearing me out," Colby said.

"Again," he insisted, easing them both down into the steaming water. "Wrap your legs around my waist." His eyes were dark with passion as he took possession of her mouth, licking at her lips, taking teasing bites until she was kissing him back, her arms sliding around his neck, her breasts pressed tight against his chest.

He sat with his back against the side of the natural basin, pulling her down onto his lap, dragging her legs around him so that he could spear into her tight channel as she settled over him. He swore softly, against her neck. "*Deus*, Colby. You are so hot and tight. It feels like heaven." His hands guided her hips into a slow, rocking rhythm. "That is perfect. You drive me out of my mind."

She started to sit straight, to ride him with a leisurely pace, but his hands slid up her back, pressing her close, keeping her against him. His mouth moved over her shoulder, licked at her, blazing kisses across her skin. "I have to taste you, *meu amor*. There will be no mistakes this time. Give yourself to me. It will be such pleasure." His sinful voice whispered temptation. "You have no idea how much I need you. No one else will ever need you or love you the way I do. They will never understand your needs or your hunger." His tongue swirled over her pulse, just along the swell of her breast. His teeth scraped seductively. "Give yourself to me."

Steel ran through his arms, yet he held her with a gentle possessiveness, even more persuasive than the way her body was rippling with fire. His breath was warm on her skin, and each tiny bite made her muscles clench and tighten around him. The desire to give him whatever he wanted, whatever he needed, pulsed through her.

"I am not going to shield you, *pequena*." His voice was rough with passion and she felt him grow thicker and harder, his hips thrusting upward to meet her lazy ride.

His obvious heightened arousal only fed her own. She cradled his head, his hair a silky slide over her skin. His tongue swirled and her muscles tightened and gripped. She felt the fresh flood of liquid heat, of excitement, burning between her legs. Her heart beat once, twice. His fangs sank deep, white-hot pain lashing through her body to give way to sheer erotic pleasure. She gasped, threw her head back, a soft cry escaping as every nerve ending in her body sizzled to life. She thought she could feel sparks igniting as he thrust deeper. The force began to build and build until she thought she might die of the pleasure. She began to pick up the pace, needing release, but his hands slid to her hips, rocking her gently, preventing a climax, keeping her teetering on the edge of madness.

It was an incredible luxury to hold her naked in his arms, her body riding his while he drank the nectar from her body. She was scorching hot, surrounding him with velvet heat, her muscles gripping him tightly, squeezing and massaging until his head roared with lust and love. Her blood sang in his veins, burned through his body until he felt complete. He swept his tongue across her breast, closing the twin pinpricks, his body thickening even more.

He found her mouth with his, poured everything he felt for her into his kiss. She tightened her arms around his neck, kissing him back as she slowly slid up and down the hard length of him, sending shudders of ecstasy through both of them. "I love you, Colby. You are everything to me." He whispered the words against her lips. His heart was pounding out of his chest in anticipation. She was all soft skin, all heat and fire, a haven for him. Her body was made for his and he took the greatest joy in knowing he could make her scream in pleasure.

His fingernail lengthened. His hand shook with the enormity of the moment. Colby would be his for all time, joined in his world, her life twined with his, the miracle of his species. The ritual words had bound them, but he had been too close to the beast. He was always too close to the beast for anything less than a full commitment between them. For one moment time stopped. His heart thundered in his ears. She would hate that he was taking this decision from her. He read her mind, knew she was searching for a way to bridge their two worlds. This would anger her, but if he took her to his home, brought her fully into his world, he knew he could make her happy, devoting himself completely to that end. He would have ample time to persuade her to get over being angry with him. He needed her more than any other, and she did love him; she just couldn't admit it to herself or to him, but he read it in her mind.

He bent to press his mouth against her ear, whispering a command to her, rocking her body with small thrusts of his hips. The water lapped at them with sizzling heat, but it only added to the erotic world he was floating in.

Her mouth traveled down his throat, her teeth nipping his skin, his body swelling, stretching her tight sheath impossibly at the little stinging bites. Fire ripped through him as he slashed his chest with the sharp nail and caught the back of her head to force her to drink. Her body moved subtly, naturally sensual, even under his thrall. Her tongue swept over his chest and he shuddered in reaction. Her mouth moved, drawing the essence of who and what he was into her body. His blood spread through her like molten lava, moving slowly to every cell, invading muscle and bone and tissue, spreading to every organ until she was truly his. He felt the completion of their union and the terrible tension finally faded from his soul.

When she had taken enough for a true exchange, he slowly separated her mouth from his chest, commanding her to sweep her tongue across the slash to close it. He kissed her hard as he removed the hypnotic spell, thrusting his tongue deep into her mouth while he speared upward with his hips, keeping her riding the edge of a climax. He swallowed her soft moan, urging her into a harder, faster rhythm.

Colby wound her fingers in his silky black hair. He made her feel so beautiful, so incredibly sexy, as if he could never get enough of her. He made her feel as if she were the only woman in the world. "Maybe I do love you," she whispered, making the confession against his neck, her tongue tasting his skin. She rocked back, holding her body away from his so she could look into his dark eyes. Insatiable hunger blazed back at her. Possession. Love. It was stark and raw and rough like Rafael, but it was all hers.

Her soft words nearly drove him over the edge. It was a hard-fought battle to get her to admit she might feel something other than pure lust for him. Satisfaction spread.

"Lock your ankles around me, Colby."

She felt his hands on her bottom, lifting her more fully into him. She didn't think it was possible, but he stretched her more, leaving her gasping and calling his name. He took over, setting the pace, pinning her hips while he thrust again and again, driving her right through a violent release. The tight grip of her climax, fiery hot, took the last of his control. His entire body seemed to explode, his own release tearing up from his toes, pulsing through his groin as he emptied himself into her.

Colby collapsed onto his chest, her head resting on his shoulder. His arms slid up her back, held her close. His heart was strong and steady, beating wildly in tune with hers. She was beginning to like the concept of hearts beating together. She drifted in a haze of pleasure, her eyes closing while the hot water lapped at her sore body and Rafael made her feel safe and loved.

After a time he carried her out of the spring and laid her on her back on a thick carpet of grass. She opened her eyes to look up at the stars while he stretched out, naked, on his stomach, blanketing her. His body was wedged between her legs and he pillowed his head on her stomach. She tangled her fingers in his hair. "I'm so tired, Rafael."

"I know, *meu amor*. Go to sleep if you like. I want to look at you. I love just looking at you." He bent to press his lips against her navel. His fingers moved possessively over her skin. He loved touching her as much as he loved looking at her. Almost without thought, he sought the outline of her birth mark. For some reason, this time, the outline was more pronounced. He could trace the pattern. Shock rippled through him and he raised his head to stare down at the small fire-breathing dragon. His breath rushed out of his lungs, fingers dug into flesh, along her hipbones. "You are Dragon seeker. *Deus!* You have the mark of the Dragon seeker clan."

Beneath him, Colby stiffened. He was talking about her birthmark. She reached down in an attempt to cover it, fear spearing through her. He pushed her hand away, locking his arm around her hip to keep her pinned down. "You had to have been born with this mark. I have not seen such a thing in centuries."

"I was told you would kill anyone with such a mark." He didn't sound as if he was going to kill her. There was a silky caress in his voice that made her weak all over. He nuzzled the birthmark, his tongue stroking over the shape and texture of it. She could feel his excitement pulsing through him.

"Who would tell you such a thing? Dragonseeker is one of our most powerful bloodlines. They are Carpathians with skill and cunning and gifted with battle sense as no others and their lifemates often produce female children. We thought the family had died out a long time ago. No Carpathian would ever harm a woman of the Dragonseeker lineage, nor would they wish to harm a warrior of that house."

She lifted her head to look at his black, gleaming eyes. He meant every word. She relaxed beneath the silken heat of his mouth, "Do you remember the woman in the parking lot of the bar? She heard you when you threatened to hurt anyone interfering with your business."

He nuzzled the triangle of curls with his chin, sending a wave of desire rushing through her bloodstream. "Yes, she heard me when I spoke telepathically."

"She has the same birthmark only hers reacts differently. She was taught to avoid hunters and her mark grows hot when one is near, just as it does when a vampire is close by. She told me that an ancestor, Rhiannon, left her lifemate, although she used the term husband, and went off with a powerful man. A war broke out."

"It is true that there was a war, but Rhiannon was kidnapped and her lifemate murdered. She was held captive by a powerful wizard . . ."

Colby groaned. "I don't know if I want to know this. Vampires are bad enough, Rafael. Please don't tell me there are wizards."

"Call them what you like. Powerful beings trained in the ways of magick. They were well versed in the old ways when safeguards and spells were plentiful and all things of the earth were worshipped and cherished. They were called wizards only to identify their teachings and skills. Rhiannon had begun to study with one of their most powerful teachers. He conspired to murder her lifemate and take her for his own. Most lifemates do not survive the passing of their mate. Her captor must have found a way to keep her alive for a time."

"Natalya claims Rhiannon had triplets, two daughters and a son, before she died. Natalya said that Rhiannon's son was her grandfather. Natalya also suspected that her own brother must be my father."

"What of Rhiannon's two female children?"

"She didn't know what happened to them. It was her father that taught her a hunter would immediately kill anyone bearing our birthmark. She also said the birthmark hid itself from you, that it would hide from hunters and vampires."

"Of course he would say that." Rafael pressed small kisses against the birthmark. "They would poison their children against us. What better revenge than to keep the line from the Carpathian people, when we need them so much?"

"Why would the birthmark hide from you?"

"I suspect it knew how strong the beast in me really was and reacted to that. Most of the times I have spent with you, I have barely managed to control the darkness in me. It would seek to protect you from me as long as I was near embracing the temptation of our darker side, but there is no longer need."

Colby's stomach gave an uncomfortable lurch. Her skin felt oversensitized and something fiery hot swept through her insides, searing every organ in her body. Rafael lifted his head alertly. She could see knowledge in his eyes. Colby pushed at him to get him off of her, the strange wave of heat scaring her. "It hurts to have you touching me." Her insides were suddenly on fire and she felt sick. She pushed at him harder, as the air left her lungs in a rush of flames.

Colby's eyes went wide with shock. Rafael felt the first wash of guilt. It wasn't a comfortable feeling and one he'd only experienced since meeting her. He rolled over, settling next to her, his arm caging her without touching her, his eyes watchful.

"What's happening to me?" Knowledge mixed with her pain. "You know, don't you? What have you done this time?" The breath left her body and she nearly convulsed, her body going rigid as pain gripped her. Nails bit deep into his arm.

"Just breathe, Colby." He hadn't expected the conversion to be so violent. His heart twisted. What if something went wrong?

"Answer me! God, at least you can tell me what you've done to me."

"You are beginning to go through the conversion." Her pain swirled inside of him, mixing with guilt and terror for her.

"I trusted you." Her eyes were accusing, ravaged with pain and betrayal. She gasped the words, half sitting, attempting to twist away from him as she made the accusation. "How could you ever tell me you loved me? Do you think this is love? You wouldn't know love if it slapped you in the face. Love isn't betrayal and it isn't domination, robbing me of free will. I was trying to get to you in my own way and you took even that from me." The pain twisted like a knife inside of her and her eyes clouded. "I trusted you," she whispered again, her voice breaking.

Rafael stiffened. It hadn't been like that. He knew he had to convert her for all their sakes. He wouldn't carry dominance that far. Was he such a monster after all? The next wave was already building, rushing through her like a fireball, scorching skin and organs. She broke into a sweat and blood beaded on her pores. He whispered her name, brought cooling water from the waterfall to bathe her face. She turned her face away from him, clearly not wanting his help as her body went rigid with the next terrible blossoming pain. It swept through her, searing everything in its path.

Fear lived and breathed inside of her. She pushed herself up, tried to crawl away from him, a hurt, wounded animal. He caught her in firm hands, his insides churning with bile. He had done this to her, in his own arrogance believing he had the right to her. He had no idea of the suffering the conversion would cause and it sickened him.

The pain was excruciating. Colby's eyes were glazed and her body writhed. "Did you do this to me so you could take Paul and Ginny?" She made the accusation hysterically. "You really aren't any different from the vampire controlling Paul."

The hurt in her eyes, the suggestion of betrayal shattered his soul. Did she see him like that? Did she honestly believe he could do this to her to get the children from her? His soul shrieked in reprimand, in horror at him for what he'd done. He felt moisture on his face, knew he shed tears, knew he had committed an unpardonable act. She had been making her way to him but his lack of patience could very well have destroyed his fragile hold on her emotions.

He bent over her so she could see he told the stark truth. "I love you more than my own life, more than anything on this earth. I had no idea it would be like this. I swear I am telling you the truth. I am more sorry than you will ever know for bringing you into my world without your consent."

She looked up at his ravaged face, the bloodred tears seeping from his eyes, and her heart fluttered with forgiveness for one brief moment. The next wave hit and she turned away from him, writhing and convulsing, the fire burning her from the inside out.

Rafael could only remain helplessly by her side as the conversion took control of her body, forcing her to rid it of toxins, of everything human. His power meant little in the face of such pain. He attempted to take the pain for her, but it was impossible. They had no choice but to ride it out together. He tried to hold her, to comfort her, washing her, rocking her, murmuring as much encouragement as he could to her. All the while he felt he was dying inside. He couldn't take the pain from his lifemate. He couldn't take back what he'd done. He had to go forward now no matter the cost and he was afraid the price was going to be much higher than anything he'd ever considered.

When it was safe, he opened the mineral-rich soil and floated down into the depths of the earth, holding her in his arms. For the first time in centuries he found himself weeping hard, feeling lost and ashamed of his own actions.

18

Paul writhed on the bed, drenched in sweat, the sheets twisted around his body. "I won't do it. Colby! Colby!" He screamed for his sister and pushed both hands flat over his ears. "I won't. You can't make me."

Ginny sat up, looking around the strange bedroom. She was sharing a room with her friend Tanya. She could hear her brother muttering and sometimes shouting for Colby. Immediately she got up and, with a quick glance at the sleeping Tanya, hurried out of the room and down the hall to where her brother was staying. Juan and Julio were already up and coming out of their rooms. Julio extended his hand to her with a warm smile. Ginny hesitated a moment before she placed her hand in his. "I think Paul's having nightmares," she whispered.

"Does he have them often?" Julio asked with a quick glance at his brother.

She shook her head. "Not Paul." She knocked once and pushed open the door. Paul knelt up on the bed, his eyes wild, his chest bare. Only his pajama bottoms covered him. The sheet was a tangle on the floor, ripped in several places. Ginny could see Paul's skin was coated in sweat. He had a knife poised over his wrist. There were several small cuts on his arm and each trickled blood.

He shook his head hard, tears welling up. "Get out. Get out, Ginny. Hurry."

Julio caught Ginny to him and pushed her behind him even as he held out his hand to Paul. "You cannot do this thing, Paul. Give me the knife. Fight it. Fight what the vampire orders you to do."

Paul looked helpless, a small child seeking an adult's understanding. "I have been fighting, for hours now. I can't hold out any longer. I can't. Where's Colby? You have to tell her I tried to fight it."

"Listen to me, Paul." Julio pitched his voice low, keeping the boy's attention centered on him so Juan could begin to maneuver his way along the edge of the wall toward their nephew. "It's the vampire. He's trying to use you to hurt Colby. You don't want him to hurt your sister, do you? If he can succeed in taking your life, she'll never be the same. He knows Colby loves you."

Tears poured down the boy's face. "He whispers to me all the time. I've tried, but I can't seem to stop myself."

Ginny made a single sound of distress, drawing Paul's attention. He shook his head. "Please, Ginny. Please get out of here. I don't want you to see me like this. You can't watch."

Paul felt the vampire stirring again. Just before dawn the creature had begun to work on him. He seemed distant and weak, at times losing the contact. Paul had the impression he was injured in some way, but then he would renew his attack, whispering commands, demanding compliance. Demanding Paul cut himself over and over, insisting he take his own life. Paul fought hard against the commands, but the vampire wore him down. Where was Nicolas? Where was Rafael? Both had promised to help him.

The vampire gripped him hard in his thrall. He'd gathered his strength and made one concentrated attempt to force the boy into compliance. Paul's eyes opened wide, staring into space as he felt the undead move within him. For one ghastly moment he was aware of the creature in his head, looking through his eyes in triumphant glee. He felt the terrible bite of the blade into his flesh. It hurt, a searing pain that lanced through his body. Time stopped. In that heartbeat, five separate people were joined together. Nicolas and Rafael had taken Paul's blood and they were suddenly aware, brought out of their sleep, sharing his head with the vampire. They could all see one another; feel one another. It was sobering and terrible, the vampire elated, his evil laughter a harsh echo in Paul's mind.

Through Rafael, Colby joined them. Paul felt her awareness, the scream of anguish welling up. The terrible moment when he was conscious of Colby, buried beneath the ground, trying to claw her way up through the soil to try to reach the surface and get to him. In that heartbeat they were all together and the vampire threw back his head and laughed in triumphant glee.

Juan dove for Paul, knocking him back on the bed, wrestling the knife from him. Paul blinked rapidly to clear his blurring sight and to try to focus on what was really happening. The thought of Colby buried alive made him ill. His wrist burned and his uncles were tying him down so he couldn't hurt himself while they worked on stopping the flow of blood. Paul could hear Ginny crying, but he couldn't move, couldn't find his voice, could only lie still with his heart pounding and a terrible dread beginning to flood his brain. The vampire wasn't finished.

Colby. Rafael caught her to him as she struggled wildly, tearing through soil with her bare hands to get to her brother. He had placed her in a deep sleep. Nothing should have disturbed her. Nothing should have penetrated the safeguards to awaken her, yet she was frantic to get to Paul.

It is her Dragonseeker blood, Nicolas explained calmly. *She is far stronger than either of us realized.*

It was true. Rafael knew her bloodline provided the iron in her will and also enhanced the tremendous sexual hunger she couldn't overcome when she was around her lifemate. The bloodline was both her strength and her downfall. Her pain and anguish tore at him. *Querida.* He smoothed her hair, pulled her hands away from the soil. *Paul will not die. You cannot leave this place of healing.* He could still feel the fire in her body, her organs still undergoing the reshaping.

Get away from me! What have you done? Oh, God, Paul's hurt. I have to get to him. Help me get out of here.

Nicolas and I will go to him. Juan and Julio have him and Sean is there. You cannot leave the earth yet. You are not healed and the light would harm you. Rafael tried to provide a calm, cleansing breeze of sanity in the nightmare Colby found herself in. His hands were gentle as he tried to restrain her.

She didn't stop clawing at the soil. Rafael was forced to pin her wrists together. She was going to do damage to herself. *Colby, pequena, be calm. Nicolas is rising. We will stop him. You cannot do this without causing harm to yourself.* He tried to be reasonable, but she was breaking his heart. He wasn't a man familiar with his gentle, tender side and his fierce, protective nature demanded he force obedience.

Damn you, I don't care about myself. I have to get to him. He's hurt. For God's sake, Rafael, he tried to kill himself. He's only a boy.

Her distress raked at him, tore his heart to shreds. *I will make certain he is safe. Sleep, Colby.* He pushed hard with the command.

She didn't succumb, her Dragonseeker blood rising to protect her. *Go to hell, Rafael. He's my brother. If you don't get me out of here, I'll get out myself.*

He was enormously strong and there was no way to fight him

physically and win. *You cannot, meu amor. Sleep now.* This time he took command, not allowing her to use her blood or will against him.

I will not ever forgive you for this. She succumbed to his compulsion, reluctantly fading into the sleep of their people, but not before he felt the rift between them. It yawned wide, a great chasm that might not ever be bridged. And he couldn't blame her. For a moment, he lay beside her, holding her in his arms, his heart pounding with fear for her, for their future. There was steel in Colby. She might never be able to resist him physically, but if she made up her mind to keep from feeling anything else for him . . .

Rafael groaned. He couldn't blame her. He had converted her without her permission, forced her into his way of life, and while she was beneath the ground, the vampire had attacked her brother. He stroked her silky hair, his lips pressed against her temple. *I could not survive without you, meu amor. I know you are my heart and soul. Find a way to love me through all of this.* When he was alone thinking of her, when there was a knot of love in his throat so large he couldn't swallow at the thought of her courage and her strength, when he was longing to be with her, so aroused at the mere thought of her loving him, needing him, he thought of all kinds of poetic things to say to her. But when she stood in front of him, her green eyes blazing defiance and her mouth and body a sinful temptation, he lost all good sense and went for domination. How were they going to get through this one?

Rafael burst through the soil, the early morning light hurting his skin and eyes, but definitely tolerable. He shifted in the air, assuming his favorite shape of the harpy eagle, and began winging his way toward Sean Everett's ranch. Simultaneously he felt Nicolas rise, and knew he was heading for the ranch as well.

I should have considered that Kirja might retaliate against the boy. There was deep regret in Rafael. *I knew he was wounded and thought he would go to ground to recover, not use his last remaining strength for revenge.*

He will be in bad shape now. If we can find his resting place, we may be able to kill him before he can regain his strength, Nicolas ventured.

Rafael blistered Nicolas's mind with a string of curses. *Do you have any idea what I have done? She will not forgive me.*

She is your lifemate. Eternity is a long time even for a Dragonseeker to hold on to anger. Do you have an idea where the vampire has constructed his lair?

Maybe, Rafael said thoughtfully.

The ranch house was blazing with lights. He dropped low, into the front yard, shifting to vapor so he could easily enter the house and appear as if he'd come from his assigned bedroom. Nicolas met him in the hall and they hurried to Paul's room.

Sean Everett stood, grim-faced, his arm around Joclyn, while Julio comforted Ginny, who clearly refused to leave.

"Forgive me, Paul," Nicolas greeted. "I slept soundly when I should have been on watch."

"We thought you were safe," Rafael said. He closed his eyes for a moment, knowing he had no choice. Colby loved this boy. For her sake, for the child's sake, he had to be sent away where the vampire couldn't touch him should they fail in their efforts to destroy the undead. Colby would never forgive him. A dread began to settle in the pit of his stomach.

Paul lifted his head. His face was very pale, dark circles prominent under his eyes as he regarded the two Carpathians. "I held out against him a long time."

"I know you did. I am proud of you." Rafael reached out and deliberately circled the ragged tear in the wrist, his palm covering the gaping wound. "I have some ability to heal. Allow me."

Juan kept his hand on Paul's shoulder in a gesture of solidarity. "He fought hard, Don Rafael, Don Nicolas, and this time we were able to stop him. But what of next time?" He looked at them. "There will be a next time."

Nicolas nodded. "We must put distance between Paul and our enemy." He looked straight at Rafael, reading the fear of what it would do to Colby. Rafael's nod was nearly imperceptible.

"Would someone like to tell me what is going on?" Sean said. "Juan and Julio refused to allow me to call the doctor. By rights, Paul should be in the hospital where he can receive psychiatric counseling as well as medical care."

Nicolas shook his head. "Our old enemy has found us and he is attempting to use Paul for revenge. Paul has been hypnotized to do his bidding." He smiled at the teenager. "Paul is much stronger than any of us realized. I am proud of you."

"We should call Ben," Sean insisted.

Nicolas turned his head to look directly into Sean's eyes. "It is better we handle this alone. It was only an accident. The boy was careless playing with his knife and we do not want him to be food for gossip in a small town."

Sean nodded. "I agree it's best not to say anything."

"If we were to take Colby, Paul, and Ginny to Brazil, Sean, would you and your men be able to run her ranch? We would be willing to pay you to care for Paul and Ginny's property until they came of age. If neither wanted it and wished to remain in Brazil with us, we would sell the ranch to you if you desired the property," Rafael offered.

"Colby's going to be pissed," Paul whispered.

"Colby told you not to use that word," Ginny said, sticking her head out from behind Julio. Her eyes were very large as she looked at her brother. "What's Rafael doing to you?"

Rafael's hand remained wrapped around Paul's wrist. The angry-looking cuts seemed to be fading into the area Rafael's palm covered.

"Does it hurt?" Ginny persisted.

"Not anymore. Rafael's making it feel better."

"What do you say, Sean? Can you and your crew handle the extra acreage and work load?" Rafael asked. He knew what Colby would think and he knew what he risked by sending the children away, but there was no other choice. He wanted to rip something apart, wanted to destroy everything around him. He wanted to forbid his brother to send Paul and Ginny away, but he knew she loved these two children. Through her, he had learned to love them and, more than his own happiness, he had to put Colby first. And that meant sending Paul away to keep him safe. Now, this night. As soon as possible.

"We are talking a large amount of money, Sean. You will need to pay your men," Nicolas added as a further enticement, glancing warily at his brother, reading his tormented thoughts and feeling the tension rising in the room.

"What about Colby?" Sean inquired. "The last I heard, she was hell-bent on running the ranch herself."

"Rafael and Colby are getting ..." Nicolas glanced at Juan.

"*Casam-se,*" Juan supplied. "They are getting married."

"Naturally Colby and the children will return immediately to Brazil. Juan and Julio will make the arrangements to ship their belongings and horses home."

"And King," Ginny said. "I'm not going without King." She tugged at her uncle. "And I won't go without Colby." She sounded stubborn, a small replica of her sister.

Rafael raised an eyebrow. "I would never leave Colby behind, little sister. Have no fear of that."

"Are you certain about Colby agreeing?" Sean asked again, shocked that she might actually walk away from the ranch she'd spent her entire life on.

Nicolas turned his head and once again captured the man's gaze. "Colby wants to come with us more than anything else. She is with

Rafael and wishes to make her home with him. Naturally she will take the children with her."

"Naturally," Sean agreed. "If you really are making the offer, Nicolas, you know I'm always willing to do business with your family. I could use the extra acreage and I certainly have enough men to run both spreads."

"Colby is never going to agree," Paul whispered to Rafael. "You know she won't. She'll be furious."

"You let me take care of that, Paul. The most important thing right now is to get you out of the vampire's range so he can't harm you while we are hunting him. I'm going to have Juan help you pack and you and Ginny will leave this morning. We have a private jet and it will take you to our home far from this place. I will bring Colby as soon as possible." He glanced at Ginny. "And, of course, the dog must go too."

"But don't we need passports? I don't have a passport. I've never traveled anywhere." In spite of himself, Paul was excited at the prospect of being on a private jet, of seeing another country, of waking up in the morning and not having to work from sunup until sundown. He felt a little guilty, but he was eager to try it just once in his life.

"I'm not going without Colby and neither are you, Paul," Ginny declared, glaring at the men in the room.

Rafael reached a hand out to the little girl. "You are much like your sister, Ginny. She will come. She is with me and must accompany me to our home. There is an indoor horse arena and a swimming pool."

"I like my garden."

"We have a wonderful garden and you will be able to spend time with your uncles and your entire *família*. They are all very anxious to meet the three of you. Your dog will be welcomed and you can have as many horses as you like."

Paul suddenly tugged at his hand, trying to free himself from

Rafael's grip. He didn't seem to notice when Rafael tightened his hold and turned his attention completely on the boy. Paul went very still, his eyes glazing over. His body began to tremble and his expression went slack as if he were far away from them.

Nicolas moved closer to the bed. Rafael kept the physical connection to Paul. The self-inflicted wounds were all healed, but both Carpathians were in the boy's mind, feeling his emotions and reading his thoughts.

"What is it, Don Rafael?" Julio asked.

"Take the child out of here. Sean, put her to bed." Nicolas gave the order, his voice a powerful weapon.

Sean Everett obeyed, taking his wife and Ginny with him.

The Chevez brothers crowded closer to their nephew. "Has the vampire taken him over again?"

Rafael held up his hand for silence, his features grim. "The vampire is on the move. By rights he should be in the ground. He is badly wounded and the dawn is upon us. He has cloaked the sun with heavy clouds, but he should not be able to travel once the sun has risen. He has truly become far more powerful than most of his kind. Paul is tracking him."

"Good boy," Juan murmured.

"He is moving underground, not above," Nicolas said.

"Why would he be on the move?" Rafael mused aloud. A tightness was beginning to form in his chest. He glanced at Nicolas to see if he shared the sudden dread. Nicolas met his gaze with a dark sober one. "Colby." Rafael stood abruptly, his expression savage. "He is after Colby." Rafael's heart began to pound. Fear clogged his throat. Terror warred with rage.

"He knows where she lies," Paul said. He stared straight ahead, his eyes unfocused, but he said the words clearly. "He is making his way to her and he wants me to know he will kill me after he kills her. Then he will kill Ginny."

"He will not have the chance," Nicolas assured him. "Will the safeguards hold?"

"He is ancient. We invented the safeguards." Rafael's hands trembled. He itched to tear out the vampire's heart. The ground rolled ominously. Outside the building, lightning lit up the sky and the crash of thunder shook the house.

"He cannot possibly move fast and the light will slow him."

"Nothing stops Kirja." Rafael was already dissolving into a vapor, streaming from the room toward the early morning sky. *When he is determined.*

Outside the sky had turned black, matching his turbulent rage. *Colby! Wake!* He issued the command with tremendous force, the force of a powerful ancient.

He felt her instant response. Fear slammed into her, into him through her. The fear of being buried alive. He took hold of her with ruthless force, calming her mind. *Kirja hunts you. How he does this thing in the early light, I do not know, but it is past the hour he should feel leaden. You are no longer human. You must get past all human fear and know you can do this. You are Carpathian.*

Her reaction was to keep her eyes tightly closed, but a swirl of anger drifted through her. *Where's my brother and get me the hell out of the ground.*

Rafael felt the familiar clenching in his gut, the brush of fire through his veins. Colby had a temper and it always fascinated him, always aroused him. And he knew she would need it—that iron will and determination, the anger that pushed her when others would give up. *Paul is safe and Nicolas guards the children.*

I feel the vampire now. He's burrowing through the soil, like a mole. The ground is screaming. Get me out of here.

So the early morning light *was* too much for Kirja, but why wasn't he leaden as he should be? Rafael tore across the sky, speed uppermost in his mind. *Your body is not yet ready to come out of the ground. You need the healing soil, querida. Can you still feel the fire raging in your organs? It is too dangerous.*

He's close. He felt malignant, violent, a weapon of hate and vengeance so evil Colby shuddered with fear. *Rafael, hurry.* There was the feeling of urgency in her. She felt something moving over her. An exodus of bugs, running from the malevolence in the vampire, trying to escape him. *Insects, they're everywhere.*

Rafael could hear the hysteria in her voice. *It is so like you to face down a bucking bronco yet be frightened of a couple of bugs.* He tried to be soothing and calm, when he wanted to rip out the heart of his enemy for putting her through such terror. He forced his mind away from the fear in her and sought to feel how close to her Kirja actually was. The migration of insects meant he was approaching her resting place. The safeguards would slow him down, but Rafael doubted if he could reach her before Kirja had unwoven the spells guarding her.

Damn you for this. There was a sob in her voice that tore at his heart. *I feel like I'm in a coffin. If you don't get me out of here, I'm going to lose my freaking mind.*

Rafael began to throw barriers in Kirja's path. A solid wall of granite rock, impossible to break through. He would be forced to go around it and he had to be getting weaker. Whatever he had found to allow him to continue moving after the coming of the dawn could not possibly last long. The Carpathian people would have heard of such a feat and moved to counter it.

Please, Rafael. Please get me out of here. I swear whatever I did, I'm sorry.

She was weeping now, clawing at the soil. He could feel her heart pounding, accelerating until he feared it would burst. Her pleas only served to madden him. He wanted to weep with her.

Colby! Stop it. Stop crying. You can do this. You have to do this. I cannot bring you out of the ground. I want you aware so I can use you to fight him off if needed. You have power. You will do this. Stop crying and pull yourself together. His voice was a merciless command. He issued a warning, a deliberately harsh decree, rather than soothing her. She reacted exactly in the way he would expect from her. He felt the surge of anger at him.

The bugs are crawling in my hair, you bastard. In truth she could feel thousands of tiny legs moving over her fast, rushing away from the area and that was nearly as frightening as the insects touching her body.

She was fighting to stay in control. Rafael began to draw on the minerals from the volcano. He built a chamber of diamonds, first forming a roof over her head, a glittering transparent cavern, just large enough to keep her from feeling as if she were buried alive, and small enough that he could manage it quickly. The diamond fortress would keep Kirja out. Colby would be able to see the vampire, and it might be possible to further harm or even destroy the vampire using her sight.

What's happening? Colby touched the hard rock forming rapidly around her. *Rafael please. Really, I'm not going to be able to do this. You have to get me out of here. I don't understand why you won't take me out of the ground. Is it the birthmark?*

He read the desperation in her mind. Was he burying her alive? Leaving her to die a terrible death? Terror was returning fast. Her pleas were far worse than her anger. He had never felt so tormented in his life. His heart ached, a physical pain, and his belly churned with fury while fear was a knot in his throat.

You can open your eyes, meu amor. You are safe now. He cannot get pasta chamber of diamonds. They are too hard. He is far too weak. When he pushes his way through the soil, I need you to look at him, keep your eyes on him at all times, no matter what he does. Can you do that, pequena? He couldn't prevent the gentle coaxing note from creeping into his tone. He ached to hold her close to him, to comfort her.

Colby opened her eyes with slow reluctance, terrified of seeing the dirt and bugs. She was lying in a rich, black soil, but encased in glass. She lifted her arm to touch the wall, shocked at how heavy her limbs felt. Not glass. Crystal? Her breath caught in her throat. Diamonds. He had constructed a fortress of diamond to keep her safe. She wasn't ready to forgive him, she doubted if she ever would, but at least she wasn't going to have a heart attack now, if she didn't look up to see the dirt over the top of her prison. *Are you certain Paul is alive? That he's all right?* She would *never* forgive him for holding her captive beneath the earth when her brother needed her.

Rafael allowed his memories to replay for her. *His love for you and Ginny is very strong. Kirja did not take that into account.*

Colby was caught by a sound. By a feeling of being watched. She turned her head and there he was. Her heart stopped beating, and then began to thump frantically inside her chest. She had never seen such male volence and twisted hatred on anything or anyone's face before. The creature no longer appeared human. He had dragged himself through the mountain to reach her with the sole intent of killing her. Spittle ran down his chin, and his eyes glowed a fiery red. He was bloody and horribly burned. His chest had several puncture wounds.

Kirja reached for her with long, twisted stiletto like fingernails. He attacked the wall with a hard, driving stab, his red-rimmed eyes staring directly into hers. The talon shattered. The vampire screamed. He threw himself against the barrier.

Colby winced and tried to scoot back from the hideous creature. Only then did she realize she was naked and the undead could see her, vulnerable to his inspection. It made his grotesque leer all the worse.

He held up a hand, fingers spread wide as he stared at her throat. Slowly, oh, so slowly, he began to close his fingers. She felt the crushing squeeze, closing like a vise around her neck. For one moment she panicked, fighting for air.

You are underground, buried alive, remember, pequena? You do not need air. I am almost to him and do not want to give away my presence.

Her lips pressed together. Rafael was right, she was buried alive, something he was damned well going to answer for. She didn't need air. Let the undead try to strangle her. Deliberately, with defiance, Colby came up on her knees, tossing her long hair as a taunt. She didn't even care that she was naked. If the damned vampire could resist the terrible lethargy, so could she. Ignoring the way her insides burned like hell, she brought up her chin and her eyes blazed right back at him.

This was the terrible creature that had tormented her brother. He had tried to kill Rafael, but he was in for the shock of his life. The vampire had never met an honest-to-God cowgirl. "We breed them tough here," she said as she allowed her fury at everything that had happened in the last few weeks to come together into a raging inferno. "And we don't lie down for anyone, not even vampires."

Flames licked along the dirt floor of the tunnel Kirja had burrowed through to get to her. As if fed by a ferocious wind, the tongues of orange-red sprang to life, leaping high, enveloping the vampire in a whirling firestorm.

Colby! The command was sharp. Angry.

The vampire screamed, howled with rage and pain, too weak to continue the battle. He dared not remain longer; his strength was ebbing fast. He scurried through the tunnel, heading away from the hot springs, away from the rich soil that would heal his wounds. He needed a resting place where the hunters would never think to look. They knew he was severely injured and that he would have to have time to rejuvenate. He would need prey close as well as shelter and rich soil. He moved in the opposite direction fast, using every ounce of remaining strength to flee before Rafael could find him.

Rafael's reprimand was a slap in the face. Her own rage boiled over. *It's just like you to leave me buried underground, you swine, a sitting duck for your foul-smelling friend, and then dare to yell at me for protecting myself!* Colby's fist clenched. She ached to smash Rafael right in his too handsome face. *I hurt so bad I want to throw up. Get me out of here.* She stared in horror as the vampire's broken fingernail began to vibrate, to scrape at the diamond chamber encasing her. *I am so not kidding, Rafael. Hurry up. Now his fingernail is alive. It's scratching at the wall.* She didn't want to be afraid, but the thing seemed alive, determined to get at her. *Get me out of here!*

Rafael flinched at the undiluted anger in her voice, at the way it swirled in her body, but at the same time, his blood thickened and heated.

You're impossible. I'm in the middle of a crisis here. One you put me in, Rafael, and you're thinking about sex. You're perverted. Get me out of here. Colby began to run her hands over the surface of her diamond cage, opposite to the scratching nail, hoping to find a weak spot and crawl out. When she couldn't, she concentrated once more on focusing her fear and anger on the ghastly thing. It blackened slowly, smoked, and finally burst into flame. Pressing a hand to her wildly beating heart, she sagged against the wall. She just wanted to go home.

Your world scares me to death. Rafael, I need to see Paul and Ginny. Come get me out of here. She was weary of arguing, tired of being afraid. And her insides were beginning to feel as if someone had taken a blowtorch to them. She wanted comfort. She needed it. She deserved it.

Rafael wanted to gather her into his arms and hold her forever, but he had to find Kirja and destroy him. He would only have a scant hour or two to find the vampire's hiding place before his own lethargy would take over. He hardened his heart against the weariness in her. *You will remain beneath the ground as I have commanded and go back to sleep and heal properly.* It was a decree, a command delivered with hard authority. He issued the order and followed it with a hard push, one that sent her sinking into sleep, but not before he heard her curse him soundly.

In spite of the gravity of the situation he felt the warmth of joy spreading through him. So this was what it was to have a lifemate. The calm, bleak emptiness of his previous life had been replaced by a roller coaster of emotions. Love yes, but also aggravation, worry, the fiery clash of tempers, and an incredible wanton desire. At least, now, he always knew he was alive.

He circled slowly above the ground where Colby lay, looking for signs of Kirja burrowing through the earth, but as always with the ancient vampire, there was no sign of his passing. Rafael shifted into his human form as he dropped to the ground, running his hands over the ground, feeling for a vibration, feeling for the telltale signs of the undead.

His fingers curled into a fist. He might just introduce Colby to how pleasurable a punishment could become after this mistake. He had to kill Kirja. The vampire would take his revenge and she had eliminated Rafael's chance of easily trailing the creature back to his lair.

An owl hooted, a soft cry in the night. The sound beckoned to him, an unusual call from this bird of prey. Not a near miss, not satisfaction, but a calling. Wary, he raised his head and looked cautiously around. Even with his acute vision, it took a few minutes to spot the large owl tucked high in the branches of a fir tree several yards away.

Rafael straightened slowly. It was no indigenous owl in the tree. The bird regarded him from his position high in the branches. It wasn't Nicolas—he was with Paul and Ginny, helping to get them ready for the move to Brazil. He would put them on the private jet and get them out of the country, using his hypnotic voice to get them through the red tape quickly.

"You may as well come out of the tree and tell me what you are doing here."

The raptor immediately spread its wings wide and spiraled down, shifting before it touched the ground. A tall man with wide shoulders stood regarding him. "I have not seen you for far too many years, Rafael." He stepped forward and gripped Rafael's forearms in the familiar gesture of one warrior greeting another.

"Vikirnoff Von Shrieder. I thought you had long ago met the dawn."

"I have often thought of doing so, but I had my brother to watch over. Nicolae has found his lifemate and now my time grows short. I have one last task to complete before I rest. What of you? What of your brothers?"

"Riordan has also found his lifemate. There is hope with the knowledge that some human women can be converted. My lifemate, Colby, is human."

"I was drawn to this place by the sound of the earth screaming, yet now there is no evidence of a vampire."

"He has vowed to kill Colby. I must destroy him. He has managed to take the blood of her younger brother and reaches out to use him against us." As he spoke, Rafael continued to search along the blackened terrain for hints of the vampire's passing.

"Then I will hunt with you. It will be like old times." Vikirnoff reached up to pull his nearly waist-length hair to the nape of his neck, securing it with a leather tie.

"Colby carries the mark of the Dragonseeker. She is a descendant of that lineage." Rafael sent his senses deep into the earth, stretching first north, then west where the fertile soil might draw Kirja to heal.

"We thought the Dragonseeker line long gone from us. A good alliance between two powerful houses. The prince will be pleased." Vikirnoff scanned the skies.

"How is it you came to this place, Vikirnoff?"

"I am following a woman. Nicolae and I, through accident, became aware that a master vampire had put out the word to his pawns that this particular woman was necessary to him. I have been trailing her with the intention of warning her and protecting her." He pulled a photograph from his pocket. "Have you seen her?"

Rafael reached for the picture but Vikirnoff retained possession of it, holding it up so Rafael could see it. His thumb moved in a small, involuntary caress over the beautiful face. "I am certain I am close."

"She was here, tonight, talking in the bar with Colby. Colby said this woman, Natalya Shonski, told her a hunter would kill anyone bearing the mark of the Dragonseeker. She is not only running from the vampire, but from you."

"She, too, bears the mark of the Dragonseeker clan? Why would she believe such a thing?"

Both men cast for signs along the ground. They laid their hands over the earth, willing the soil to give them news. They listened to the wind, to the rustle of the leaves in the trees. Even the insects and night creatures usually told tales, but there was no lead to the vampire's trail. It was as if he had vanished into thin air.

"If what she said is true, Rhiannon had triplets, two girls and a boy. They are not children of her lifemate, but of the wizard Xavier. He held her captive for some time, no one knows how, but she somehow managed to join her lifemate in another world, leaving the children behind. Or it is possible—even more, probable—that Xavier murdered her after the children were born. Xavier hated all Carpathians. He would have raised his children to fear us." Rafael shifted his focus to the south and then to the east. "This young woman you seek is a direct descendant. She has been long in this world, avoiding our people." He pushed his hand through his hair in utter frustration at finding nothing, no sign of the vampire. "*Deus!* This is getting us nowhere. Where would Kirja hide?"

19

"Kirja?" Vikirnoff swung around, slipping the photo into his shirt next to his heart. "He is the vampire?" There was a thoughtful note in his voice. "No wonder this one is difficult to find. Kirja was a great warrior."

"I fear he is involved in a conspiracy to kill the prince."

"I have spoken recently with Gregori and all of us suspect that a large army is massing against us. What of Kirja's four brothers? Do you have news on them?"

"I believe they are all involved, but I do not know for certain. When he talked, he implied it was so."

Vikirnoff examined a pile of boulders that had shifted slightly out of position. "What is off in that direction?"

Rafael studied the landscape. "The mines." His dark eyes blazed with grim realization. "Vikirnoff, he has gone to the mines. Colby told me they boarded the entrances up years ago because they were dangerous. No one goes there."

"So he wouldn't have access to ready prey?"

Rafael shook his head. "No, but he would be able to call the unwary to him. He is incredibly powerful."

Vikirnoff nodded. "I remember all of the Malinov brothers. They were very powerful even while young." His cool black eyes studied Rafael. "As was your family."

"We were good friends, and yes, we tested the limits of the law, but we agreed, all ten of us, my brothers and Kirja's brothers, that we would follow our prince and live with honor. I do not know why the Malinov brothers chose the dark path." There was a lingering sadness in his voice.

Vikirnoff glanced at him sharply. "He is no longer your child-hood friend. Let us hunt the undead, and remove the threat to you and your lifemate before the sun rises too high and forces us to ground."

They shifted at the same time, Vikirnoff choosing the owl and Rafael, the harpy eagle. Both flew low to the ground, scanning as they quartered the most direct route to the mines. Kirja would have stayed beneath the ground. However he had managed to be awake after the first light of dawn, Rafael was certain the effect couldn't last too long. Kirja would have prepared his escape route before he had launched his attempt on Colby's life.

Vikirnoff? Do you think it strange that the male child of Rhiannon died and yet there is no word on the fate of the females? Colby said she was told her father died, but not how or when. There was open spec-ulation in Rafael's mind.

Wizards were not immortal. They had longevity, but ultimately, death claimed them. It is one of the reasons they came to resent us. For all their abilities and power, they could not sustain their lives. The prince believed that was the motivation for kidnapping Rhiannon. Xavier wished her to breed with him, to give his children immortal life. Xavier wanted her blood for himself and for his heirs.

Through the harpy eagle's keen eyes, Rafael noticed a slight shifting of dirt, still fresh, as if a mole had pushed upward and dis-lodged the soil. He circled it. *What if Xavier succeeded? Rhiannon*

*would not have willingly converted him, but he may have found a way
to use her blood to convert himself. Colby is proof that the Dragonseeker
blood was passed to what appear to be humans. We do not know for a fact
that Xavier died or that his son and his grandson have died. The women
have been told this, but there are no details.*

Vikirnoff considered the possibilities. *You are saying it is possible
that our greatest enemy is alive and has adult children to help him continue his work.*

Rafael spotted the mines just ahead and flew higher, taking in a
wider range. Kirja would not go into the mines without safeguards
and numerous traps. He studied the ground and the entrances to
the two shafts, both blocked with massive boulders. *I think it is possible, yes. I do not believe that any child of Xavier would easily be killed.
And if they carry Dragonseeker blood, it would be more difficult than
ever.*

Rafael landed in the branches of a large fir, a short distance from
the mine entrance. Vikirnoff settled beside him. They studied the
area around them with sharp eyes before settling to earth and shifting into their Carpathian forms. From their position, they sent their
acute senses in every direction, paying particular attention to the
position of the boulders blocking the entrance as well as the structure of the sloping mine.

"This woman I am following," Vikirnoff ventured, "has vampires
hunting her. Is it possible they know she carries the blood of the
Dragonseekers?"

"I do not know. Colby carries the blood of the Dragonseekers,
but Kirja did not seem to have knowledge of it." Rafael studied
Vikirnoff's weathered features. "We are surrounded by treachery
these days, making it impossible to tell enemy from friend quite
often. This woman may be leading you straight into a trap."

Vikirnoff shrugged. "It is of little consequence. I am no fledgling
and have been long in this world. I have acquired a few skills along

the way." There was a hard edge to his face, a darker shadow moving in the black eyes. "I am not so easily killed." He shook his head. "Something about this is not quite right."

"I agree. It seems off-kilter, but I cannot say how."

"There is a substantial wind, yet the leaves of the bushes near the entrance of the mines do not even waver. They remain still when the leaves all around us are moving. The breeze should move all the leaves, not just those near us," Vikirnoff pointed out,

Rafael studied the phenomenon. "Are we perhaps looking at an illusion? A scene Kirja set up as a safeguard?"

"If so, it is one I have not seen in all my centuries of hunting. It is an extremely large illusion to hold while he lies sleeping beneath the ground."

"Kirja is no ordinary vampire," Rafael said. "He was never ordinary as a hunter, but showed exceptional skills as did all of his family. If any of the undead could do such a thing, it would be Kirja. And I doubt if he is resting."

Vikirnoff shifted, and in the familiar image of the owl, spread wings and took flight, spiraling over the area, dropping lower and lower as he circled the mines. *If it is an illusion, it is a good one.*

"It is," Rafael said aloud. He shifted once again into the eagle form, leaving the safety of the trees to fly over the massive boulders at the entrance. They looked real enough, but Rafael no longer trusted his sight.

The owl flew toward the largest boulder, feet extended as if to land. At the last moment, he veered off. *There is nothing there. I would have hit the ground.*

Rafael landed on the ground off to the side of the mine entrances. "We are going to have to forget sight and use our other senses to tell us where the actual entrance is."

Vikirnoff shifted beside him. "We could try going underground. Kirja has already made a tunnel beneath the earth."

Rafael shook his head. "Not his tunnel. He is a master at fighting beneath the ground. The opening is here. I will find it." He shifted once more, becoming a small unassuming bat.

Vikirnoff watched the dipping and wheeling of the bat. The night creature would be able to feel any objects in its path and know the exact distance to them. *Very simple, but very clever.*

It is an illusion. The entrance to the mines is ten feet to the left. We can go in through the cracks using mist. At least we know we are in the right place. He must be in there to have set up such an enormous safeguard. He could not hope to keep it throughout the daylight hours.

Vikirnoff joined Rafael in the same form, using the bat's radar to judge the distance to the boulders at the real entrance to the mines. They moved with care, streaming as a vapor trail through a large crack between rocks, making their way into the dark tunnel. It was safer to proceed as vapor, not touching the walls or ground where they might trigger a trap. That worked until they turned a corner and encountered a giant spider web. The strands of the web were closely woven. It was impossible for even vapor to slip through without disturbing the silky threads. A very small spider sat in the corner of the web.

The hunters shifted into Carpathian form to study the design of the thick web. It looked silky and fragile, a delicate work of art, yet Rafael felt the hairs on the back of his neck rise in warning.

"Have you seen this before?" Vikirnoff asked, keeping a wary eye on the harmless-looking spider.

Rafael inched closer, bending to look at the fibers. They appeared that of a normal web, yet there were no holes, no lacy effect. The design was solid and tight. He looked at the small spider to identify the species. It stared back at him. The bubble eyes blinked and Rafael found himself staring into the eyes of evil, of intelligence. Kirja stared back at him, venomous hatred and malevolence roiling in the depths of his glare.

Rafael leapt away from the web, dragging Vikirnoff with him as the tiny spider burst into a thousand spiders, all springing at them with poisonous fangs. Rafael incinerated the arachnids quickly, but not before quite a few of them managed to sink their poisonous fangs into his and Vikirnoff's arms and legs. The tiny bites left bloody swollen sores, seeping with venom, burning through flesh and tissue.

"He definitely knows we are hunting him," Rafael said as he pushed the poison out through the pores of his body. Beside him, Vikirnoff did the same. "Every step we take is going to be dangerous. Not only is he good at illusion, but he is a master of mutating a species." He scorched the last remaining spiders.

Vikirnoff nodded grimly. "In all my centuries of battling the undead, I have never faced a vampire this powerful. I think he is strong enough to kill us both if we come at him one at a time."

"Unfortunately, I think you are right," Rafael agreed.

They began to follow the tunnel as it slanted downward, taking them deeper beneath the ground. They tested each step with caution, all senses alert to impending danger. The beams were rotted and split above their heads. The large timbers supporting the ceiling beams also showed dangerous signs of age. An old track lay half buried along the ground. A collection of dusty, forgotten tools lay scattered across the ground.

"Why do I feel as if we are entering the devil's lair?" Rafael asked. He pitched his voice low.

"Because we are," Vikirnoff answered. "What is that noise?"

Rafael glanced at the ancient hunter. "It sounds like miners."

They rounded the corner and saw a dozen men working with pickaxes on the walls of the shaft. Several lanterns hung from the overhead beam, casting a dim yellow light over the workers below. As Vikirnoff and Rafael watched, two men manipulated a heavy, ore-filled car into place on the rickety rails. No one seemed to notice the presence of the two Carpathians.

The two hunters looked at one another. "It has to be an illusion," Vikirnoff said.

None of the miners turned at the sound of his voice. The men continued to work industriously, the sound of the picks hitting rock ringing through the shaft.

"They are wearing modern clothes," Rafael pointed out. He studied the scene in front of them, looking for the hidden trap he knew had to be there.

"It could be he is slowing us down, making the point we cannot trust our own senses."

"How did he set them in motion?" Rafael wanted to know. "If his illusion can tear into the rock, it can just as easily tear into us."

The pickaxes continued to ring out against the rock in a steady rhythm. Vikirnoff tapped his hand against his leg, following the pattern. "Do you hear that? Maybe something in the beat?"

Rafael crouched down, studying the scene from every angle. "Could be. He is tricking more than one sense. Sight, smell, hearing. He has done a superb job." There was admiration in his voice. "Look at the ground. There are no footprints in the dirt. They do not leave any evidence of their existence. See where the picks hit the rock?"

"The scene repeats itself as if it's looped," Vikirnoff said. "If we disturb it, by entering into it, would that trigger a trap, or dispel the scene?"

"He would not have gone to this trouble without some kind of a trap." Rafael rubbed his chin. "Unless it is a delaying tactic."

"If it is, it is a darned good one. You stay clear just in case I trigger an attack." Vikirnoff approached the miners with caution. None of them looked up. No one spoke. They continued with their work as if he wasn't walking in their midst. He glanced at Rafael. "Any ideas?"

"Take the pickax out of one of their hands and see if that disrupts the scene," Rafael suggested.

Vikirnoff stepped up beside a miner and easily pulled the tool from the man's hands. There was a brief moment of eerie silence as the ringing of the picks abruptly stopped. Immediately the tools fell to the ground and the men dissolved into skeletons, the bones sprawling all over the floor of the mineshaft. Scraps of clothing lay rotting and the smell of decomposing bodies immediately filled the already foul air.

"Well, now we know for certain what happened to the missing people from the town and outlying ranches," Rafael said grimly. "This is definitely Kirja's lair." He stepped past the grotesque scene, careful not to disturb the bones.

They moved down the tunnel in total darkness. Almost at once there was a rustle behind them followed by the rattle of bone clicking against bone. The hunters whirled around to face the army of skeletons rising from the floor, bones reassembling to form warriors wielding the pickaxes with menacing intent, the eyeless skulls staring straight ahead.

"The sound of the picks on the rocks had to be the trigger," Rafael said in disgust at himself. "If we had not disturbed the scene, the trap would not have been sprung." He moved away from Vikirnoff to give them both fighting room.

It was a disturbing thing to see the dead rise up to defend the very creature that had brutally murdered them. It seemed so wrong, so obscene, that Rafael actually winced when he gathered his power into a ball of energy and sent it careening into the midst of the skeleton army. The explosion rocked the mines, cracked rotten timbers, splintered beams overhead, and sent dirt and rocks falling on the dead.

Vikirnoff and Rafael hurried away from the avalanche of debris. The three remaining skeletons that had not been caught in the force of the explosion rushed the hunters, brandishing their pickaxes. Their bones clacked and scraped in a gruesome manner and their mouths widened into a horrible gape. All the while the eyes stared straight ahead, pitiless holes in the empty skulls. Lights sprang up along the walls, lanterns swinging as if set in motion by an unseen hand. A wind rushed through the tunnels, awakening the guardians of the undead.

"Not good," Rafael murmured.

A terrible wailing came from somewhere just ahead of them, the sound swelling in volume until it was a symphony of screams. Dark shadows slipped through the cracks in the rock and dirt forming the walls of the tunnels. Vikirnoff turned to face the skeletons and Rafael took up a position at his back, facing the shadows. The Carpathians waited, back to back, for the attack.

It came in a rush of wind and bones. Dark shadows crept over the beams and rock, wailing loudly as they came with outstretched arms and clawed fingers, grasping for the hunters. Rafael answered with a burst of shattering white-hot light. The shadows screamed in fear and horror, retreating from the brilliance into the deeper recesses of the mine.

Vikirnoff smashed several lanterns over the heads of the skeletons, dousing them with flames. The pickaxes lay harmlessly in the dirt, but the burning bones continued forward, determined to kill the hunters. "Mist," he ordered.

Rafael shifted simultaneously with Vikirnoff so that the skeletons rushed past into the brilliant light. The bones disintegrated, exploding into splintered fragments. The flames flickered and died. There was another eerie silence.

The hunters moved farther through the tunnel, proceeding with caution, shifting back to Carpathian form in order to utilize all of their senses. Rafael reached out with every sense he had, gathering information, allowing his brain to assimilate every smell and sound that came back to him. "We are running out of time. If we do not find him soon, we will have no choice but to seek rest and we cannot do so in these mines. It is his lair and it is well guarded."

"He is counting on that fact. All he has to do is keep us from finding his resting place until the sun is high," Vikirnoff agreed. "I have never fought a vampire with such safeguards."

"He has had centuries to perfect his skills." Rafael turned his head, listening to the rustles coming from behind them. "Do you hear that?"

"The skeletons are trying to re-form for another attack."

They were in a maze of tunnels and for a moment remained motionless, trying to get a feel for Kirja's resting place. "He is also very good at leaving no trace of his existence," Rafael added. He indicated the fungus growing on the walls of one of the tunnels. "That would be my best guess. That fungus is not growing anywhere else and I would venture it is another safeguard."

Vikirnoff peered closely at the strange warted growth. "I do not like the look of this, and there are millions of centipedes covering the floor. The timbers are rotted almost completely through. I say we do not touch anything as we go down this tunnel."

Rafael took one look at the carpet of centipedes. He swore in the ancient language. "Kirja is well aware we are close. I can feel him now. He cannot hide his hatred of me. He takes my hunting him far too personally."

Vikirnoff raised his eyebrow. "I cannot imagine why."

Rafael flashed a brief grin. "He knows my aversion to centipedes. A childish thing, but of course he would use it."

The eyebrow rose higher. "We are of the earth. How could a creature such as a centipede bother one such as you? You have dominion over such things."

"I had four brothers, Vikirnoff," Rafael pointed out. His form shimmered, became transparent, and shifted to that of a very small bat.

Vikirnoff followed suit, but not before he glanced back toward the tunnel where the bones were making frantic scratching noises as they tried to re-form to carry out their master's orders. *We will have to watch our backs.*

Only if we do not get to him. Once he is gone, all of his servants will cease to exist. I say we move fast. Watch that fungus near the entrance to this shaft on your right. There is something strange about it. Rafael used the bat's radar to calculate the distance to the plant, but it kept changing, as if the plant moved.

Something struck at the bat hard, clipping a wing and knocking it to the ground. The centipedes immediately began to feast. Vikirnoff shifted one wing, reaching down to drag the small bat from the grasp of the greedy insects. Bite marks covered the body and small patches of blood seeped from various wounds.

Rafael shook off the clinging centipedes, flapping his wings to gain height. *Thanks. Now we know what that fungus is. It has teeth.*

Probably poison.

I felt it go in. Burns like hell. He is close. Go to the right, Vikirnoff. Watch yourself. The fungus is everywhere.

There is a pocket of gas here.

He is behind that mass of boulders. I feel him. The centipedes are frantic to get at us and the fungus is snapping teeth like mad dogs. He has to be inside the chamber.

Rafael. I am trying to tell you gas is seeping out into this tunnel and filling it.

A trick. He is up to his old tricks. He loved to play with fire.

I do not want to get cooked. Vikirnoff was adamant about it.

It is time to let him work for us. I have an idea. Go back to the tunnel entrance. Rafael followed Vikirnoff and shifted back to Carpathian form just out of reach of the fungus and centipedes.

"What is the plan?" Vikirnoff asked.

Rafael gestured toward the heavy boulders guarding the entrance to the chamber at the end of the tunnel. "That is."

Soon, clones of the two hunters stood near the chamber entrance, centipedes swarming up their bodies and fungus striking viciously while Rafael directed the clones to unweave the complicated safeguards the vampire had erected around his lair.

As the clones worked, Rafael removed the remaining poisons from his body. The process went more slowly than normal; Rafael fed most of his power into the illusions he'd created. He had to make them real enough to generate body heat. "If we are lucky, Kirja will believe those clones really are us and if he does, he'll try to kill us by igniting the gas. We will not risk triggering another one of his traps and it will leave us free to unravel the safeguards."

"I hope he hurries because I can hear the skeletons heading this way," Vikirnoff said grimly. "I would recommend we levitate to keep away from his warriors, but he would have thought of that." He didn't say what they both knew. Time was running out on them. The sun was climbing higher outside the mine and both of them would soon be hit with the terrible lethargy of their species. They could not go to rest in the mine with Kirja so close. It would be far too dangerous.

"I cannot sustain the illusion and make it realistic and work the safeguards. You will have to unravel the guards. Stay well back from the entrance," Rafael cautioned.

Vikirnoff began the complicated procedure of unlocking the spell guarding the vampire's lair. Behind them the clack and rattle of bones grew louder. The floor rustled with dark, malevolent insects, and the shadows wailed at them, held off only by the white-hot light Rafael continued to maintain.

The explosion came without warning, rocking the entire mine. The trapped vampire had ignited the pocket of gas. A red-orange fireball roared down the length of the tunnel, incinerating everything in its path. It blew out everything inside the long tunnel, killing the carnivorous plants and searing the carpet of centipedes, leaving the shaft burned and foul smelling, but clear for the two hunters.

As the hunters moved cautiously down the now-empty mine shaft, Vikirnoff's hands flowed gracefully in the air as he hurried to unravel the vampire's safeguards. Rafael continued to feed energy into the white-hot light surrounding them, keeping the shadows at bay. More than once, the dark, amorphous shapes lunged at the Carpathians only to shriek and fallback when Rafael struck at them with the lasered beam of light.

"The last safeguard is down," Vikirnoff said.

"Stand clear. He will have something waiting in the chamber." Rafael pressed his body against the blackened side of the tunnel and waited for Vikirnoff to do the same before waving his hand to send the boulders rolling away from the entrance.

Gas and steam poured from the interior, carrying with it a noxious, foul odor. Bats with sharpened fangs followed, a dark cloud of them, swarming the hunters instantly. Vikirnoff flung up a barrier as he and Rafael peered into the heated cavern. The bats crashed into the invisible barrier over and over, smashing their bodies in frenzied need to carry out the commands of the undead. The hunters stepped onto the steaming floor of Kirja's lair.

The chamber was hot and the vaporous gas held traces of sulfur and poison. The Carpathians floated upward as the acids in the soil melted their boots, seeking to penetrate to their skin. "Good one, Kirja," Rafael muttered, shaking his head to rid himself of the lethargy seeping into his body and mind, making him careless.

They began to quarter the ground, seeking the exact position where the vampire lay beneath the poisonous brew of acid and foul soil. "Here, Vikirnoff," Rafael said, indicating a spot directly below him. "He is here."

The two began to unravel the final safeguards, going fast, but being careful to remain alert. Movement on the ground caught Rafael's eyes just to the left of where the vampire lay, a small spewing of dirt, a disturbance beneath the soil. As he watched, the same thing happened in a half dozen other places, until he and Vikirnoff were surrounded by a loose circle. The soil burst open in a dozen spots and ghouls poured out of the earth.

"Keep going, Rafael," Vikirnoff said. "I will hold them off." He was already dropping low, flying at a ghoul with tremendous speed. He wrenched at the ghoul's head, knocking the creature off its feet so that it landed hard in the poisonous soil.

Rafael concentrated on unraveling the last lock to get to Kirja while Vikirnoff's battle with the ghouls raged ferociously around him. Several times he heard Vikirnoff grunting as he took a particularly nasty hit, but Rafael remained focused on disassembling the vampire's final safeguard. The moment the last element clicked in place, the ghouls howled and shrieked in fury, redoubling their efforts to destroy the hunters. Vikirnoff kept the dozen zombies away from Rafael, giving him the time needed to peel back the layers of soil from the vampire's resting place.

And then the last of the soil fell away and Rafael found himself looking down into Kirja's hate-filled eyes.

For a moment there was an eerie silence. The vampire was utterly motionless, trapped in the earth by the terrible lethargy of his kind. *You will never win, Rafael. You are doomed.* The voice rasped with hate even as Rafael plunged his fist through the vampire's chest cavity and ripped out the blackened, rotted heart of his childhood friend.

Kirja screamed, and Rafael hissed as the acid from the vampire's blood burned through his skin and muscles right to the bone. He threw Kirja's heart to the ground, but before he could call fire to incinerate the decayed thing, it burrowed deep into the soil, making its way back to its host. Black hatred vibrated in the air between them, then triumph as the heart reunited with its host. Cursing, Rafael drove his fist a second time toward the vampire's chest, staring down into the red-rimmed eyes.

But it was no longer Kirja lying helpless in the earth. Rafael stared down at Colby, her beautiful face, her wealth of red hair, her incredible soft skin. For a moment he hesitated as he leaned over the undead.

"Rafael," she cried softly, "help me."

"Colby?" Rafael blinked in confusion and shook his head and for one uncertain moment, he hesitated.

Kirja struck. Rafael screamed and the illusion of Colby dissolved as the vampire's razor-sharp talons pierced Rafael's chest. Breathless with agony, he could feel the hand of the undead clawing for his heart, shredding through muscle and sinew with murderous intent. Kirja shrieked in triumph and Rafael screamed again as the tips of the vampire's nail gouged at Rafael's heart.

Pain swamped Rafael, excruciating pain the likes of which he'd never known in all the centuries of his existence. For one agonizing moment his muscles locked in spasms of torment, then he screamed again from another driving pain as Kirja's talons pierced the outer walls of his heart.

Blood spurted from Rafael's heart. There wasn't much time. He had to finish this now. Quickly.

He dragged himself over Kirja's body. The vampire once again assumed Colby's shape, but this time Rafael didn't hesitate. Once more he drove his fist deep into the vampire's rotten chest, crying out as the acid blood ate through the flesh of his already wounded hand. His chest was on fire, the vampire's razored claws shredding the muscles of Rafael's heart. Blood jetted out of his chest in great deadly spurts, but Rafael could not afford to stop his heart and shut down his body's functions to save himself. Kirja must be defeated.

Rafael would protect Colby and those she loved with his last dying breath. As long as Kirja remained alive, he would retain his hold on Paul and put Colby's family at risk. It had to end here. Now. Rafael would remove this threat to Paul, give the boy back to Colby in sanity and health. He would not fail her this time with yet another in a long line of selfish choices. He could give her this one gift even if it meant the loss of his own life. She was Dragonseeker, she was strong, she could go on without him as Rhiannon had. For a moment he wavered. Had it been a spell of Xavier's that had prevented Rhiannon from joining her lifemate? Would Colby survive his death? He had to believe it.

He felt Kirja's fingers close around his heart, the nails digging deep, lacerating, shredding. He heard his own screams echo through the chamber, but he hung on tenaciously. He would *not* fail her. His death was the only thing he had left to give her.

No! Nicolas shouted the command.

Faintly, from far away, Rafael heard his other brothers, but maybe that was an illusion, too. The voices of Carpathians near and far seemed to melt into a single voice crying protest.

Rafael held on grimly, dragging the black vampire heart from Kirja's chest. Blood loss had made Rafael extremely weak and the heart struggled wildly to get out of his possession and back to its master. He fought to keep the rotted organ caged in his hand. The acid burned through his skin to his bones, but that pain was nothing compared to the agony of Kirja's fingers literally ripping Rafael's heart to pieces.

Deep beneath the earth, Colby felt the rending and tearing of Rafael's heart. Her eyes flew open, her heart shuddering in shared pain and slamming with relentless terror against her chest. The pain nearly shattered her. *Rafael!*

The undead will not get your brother.

Rafael's voice was ragged, frayed with pain. In that instant she saw him in the dark of the mine with the ghouls fighting to get to him, with his arm and hand burned raw from the vampire's blood. And she saw the vampire's fist buried deep in his chest. She *felt* the fingernails ripping and gouging at Rafael's heart in an effort to kill him. For a moment time stopped. The world went utterly still. Realization struck her in that blinding moment.

She loved him.

All this time when she thought she was fighting him, she'd been fighting herself as well. Pitting her enormous will against her heart, the heart that had begun to love Rafael when he had rushed into a burning building on her behalf.

Rafael had freed her to be who and what she was born to be. She would finally be able to use her extraordinary gifts she had spent a lifetime hiding. She would be accepted for who she really was, not who she pretended to be. And in that moment of realization, Colby knew she could bear anything, sacrifice anyone or anything else, but not Rafael.

Tell me what to do! She issued the order to Nicolas. And it was an order. She began to claw her way through the earth to the surface. Every ounce of iron will she possessed, the will that was her birthright, that had been honed in her sweat and tears, the unbending will that had refused to let her believe she could come to love Rafael, that will she now focused on reaching him. She would save him. There was no other choice.

Stay with him. Do not allow him to separate himself from you. He will hold on with everything he is, not wanting to chance that you will die with him.

Colby concentrated on holding Rafael to her. She could see through his eyes and hear the wailing of the ghouls and the horrible cries of the vampire.

Deep in the vampire's lair, Vikirnoff continued his battle with the relentless ghouls, but he could sense how close Rafael was to death.

"Rafael," he commanded, "throw the heart to me now." He kept his voice calm in the midst of the chaos reigning. He knocked back another ghoul, but it rose to confront him again as the others closed in.

Kirja's razor-sharp fingernails worked to drag Rafael's heart from his body, a slow but extremely painful process. The strength was ebbing from the vampire, but it was draining almost as quickly from Rafael. He could barely move, barely think, his body failing to obey the dictates of his brain as blood loss and lethargy from the rising sun sapped his remaining, rapidly dwindling strength.

He felt Colby moving in him, searching for a way to aid him. He couldn't protect her from the pain in his body. He felt the blow of it, nearly driving her to unconsciousness, felt her regroup, accept the pain. Then her strong will rose up, the unwavering determination of the Dragonseeker blood.

You will not die! She made it a decree. An order. *Throw the heart to the hunter. Take my strength and rid the world of that disgusting creature. Now, Rafael. I won't let you go.*

Using the burst of strength, he did as she commanded, tossing the vile organ through the air to Vikirnoff. At once Rafael's strength ran out and he began to topple. It was too late for him. His heart was shredded, his blood loss too great. But Colby and Paul would be safe and Vikirnoff would get out of the mines alive. Rafael closed his eyes and let go.

Colby merged her mind with Rafael's. She was strong. She'd always been strong, so much so that her powers couldn't be managed in her human state. She felt them now, running through her body, and she took a quick inventory of her abilities. Everything was different now, with the special gifts of the Carpathian blood running through her veins. She reached for the power, embraced it instead of shrinking in fear from it. She would save Rafael, hold him to her with her last breath even though his life force was no more than a small, dim light flickering weakly, all but extinguished.

She held him to her with all of her strength, preventing him from falling to the acid inferno of soil in the chamber, at the same time, keeping his spirit from fading away.

Bring him to me. Hurry. She sent the order to Vikirnoff, on the mental path she found in Rafael's mind. *The soil is rich in minerals and it is our only chance.*

Vikirnoff incinerated the vampire's heart, stoically ignoring the acid burning his hand and arm as the blood ran down his skin. Kirja screamed horribly, his body going limp, his fist falling from Rafael's body with a horrible sucking sound. The Carpathian's lifeblood splattered over him. He grimaced and licked at it in a last, vain attempt to heal himself.

Vikirnoff directed a second white-hot ball of energy at the vampire.

Blackened noxious smoke rose and Kirja gave a final hideous, wailing shriek and his foul life at last found its end. Vikirnoff caught Rafael in strong arms before Colby could let him fall to the poisonous ground and sustain further burns. The moment the vampire was fully destroyed, the ghouls dropped to the ground, lifeless without their master to give them orders. The soulless shadows ceased their continuous wails and the bones dropped back to the ground.

There was an eerie silence followed by an ominous rumble that grew louder as the maze of mine tunnels began to shake. Cradling Rafael in his burned arm, Vikirnoff streaked through the tunnels, away from the lair of the vampire. Dirt and rock poured down and smoke spewed through the shafts. Walls closed in behind them as he winged his way to the surface with the wounded hunter. *I am on the way with him. The sun is climbing rapidly. He is mortally injured. In truth, I do not see how you can save him.*

Colby burst from the ground, the sun nearly blinding her. It didn't even slow her down. She cast around for the richest soil. *What do I need, Nicolas? Tell me what to do to save him.*

He told her, naming several plants, sending her images of what they looked like, and directing her where to find them. Ignoring the terrible burning inside her body, her streaming eyes and sensitive skin, Colby raced to locate the plants hidden in the dense forest. The trees helped to shade her from the sun's burning rays and Vikirnoff supplied cloud cover as he traveled toward her. As Nicolas guided her hands, instructing her in what she must do to save Rafael, another voice joined his, and then another and another. She couldn't get all of their names, but healers gathered from around the world to talk her through the process of saving Rafael.

If something should go wrong, Nicolas, you watch over Paul and Ginny. Colby was fully aware she was risking her life. She would be giving everything she was to Rafael, and should she fail, it would mean both of their lives.

There cannot be failure. Nicolas decreed it.

And then Vikirnoff was there, Rafael's torn, mangled body in his arms. Colby closed her eyes for one brief moment as tears welled up and horror clutched at her throat. She had been prepared for his terrible injuries, but not for the sight of her proud, invincible Rafael ravaged so utterly. Her heart and soul screamed a protest.

She reached for her powerful will, grasped her strength with every fiber of her being, and shook off the despair and pain and terror. There was no time for emotion, no time for hesitation or fear. She listened to the soft voices giving her instructions and she felt her power moving through her. Kneeling beside Rafael's torn body in the mineral-rich soil where Vikirnoff had opened the earth for her, she set to work. It was easy enough to work on several levels, using her telekinesis to mix the plants and soil while she shed her body, her sense of self, and became the healing ball of energy needed to enter Rafael's body.

All the while she held him to her, bound by her determination, refusing to allow him to escape into another world. His heart was all but destroyed, savaged by the vampire's talons, lacerated and shredded. She hesitated in dismay.

It can be done. The assurance came from one of the healers, a male named Gregori. *I will be with you every step of the way.*

I am here as well. A feminine voice, Shea, a healer.

A third voice, very distant and ultra feminine, added her support. *I am Francesca. You are of the Dragonseeker clan. Few have the gifts you have. It can be done.*

She heard Nicolas and his brothers urging her onward. Voices swelled in volume in her mind, chanting an ancient healing ritual. With determination, Colby bent to the task. It was no longer impossible—it was simply a matter of will, and she had that in abundance. Slowly, meticulously, she repaired Rafael's shredded heart. Her physical strength waned several times, but Rafael's brothers fed her every bit of energy they possessed. She even felt Paul's touch through Nicolas.

She was as ruthless in her demands on Rafael, forcing him to endure the pain as she repaired his heart then set to work on his other numerous grave injuries. She shared her mind with the healers, following the instructions they whispered in her mind as she closed every wound, removed every drop of poison. She would not relinquish Rafael to Kirja's power. The sun continued to climb in the sky and the effects were devastating on the Carpathians, but she was relentless, driving herself and the others beyond their endurance.

Vikirnoff, following the dictates of the healers, lay down beside his fellow hunter in the rich soil. He gave Rafael as much blood as he could spare, and helped Colby to pack the terrible wounds with the mixture of plants, mineral-rich dirt, and saliva. Colby was swaying with weariness, covered in blisters from the sun, and sagging to the ground when she was finally finished.

I have never remained this long awake. Vikirnoff looked at her with surprise. *You held us all together, refusing to allow even our strongest to give in to the lethargy of our kind. Rest now. If you can hold us, you will not allow him to die.*

"Damn right I won't," Colby murmured and slumped over Rafael.

Vikirnoff had just enough energy left to close the soothing soil overall three of them before they succumbed to sleep.

20

Colby awoke the moment the sun went down, turning to Rafael even as she opened the earth above her. She had repaired the worst of the injuries to his heart with her careful, meticulous work, but there was a long way to go to keep him from dying. She started working at once, sitting beside him in the depths of the pit with the walls of soil high around them, letting go of her body to enter his. His heart was attempting to heal itself, but Nicolas and the others had warned her that Rafael's wounds were so severe that not even a Carpathian as ancient and powerful as he was could recover without continual aid.

As she worked, she became aware of the voices joining with hers, both male and female, chanting the healing ritual. She gratefully recognized the touch of Gregori, and the much more feminine touch of Shea, both Carpathian healers. Colby followed their precise instructions for continuing the repairs to Rafael's lacerated heart. He had to be awakened and given blood, but his heart would continue to hemorrhage until the muscle had sufficient time to heal, which meant he could not stay awake for longer than it took to feed.

"I will give him my blood," Vikirnoff volunteered. He sat watching her, noting the absolute determination on her face.

"You already gave him too much this morning. Go find whatever you need; you're whiter than a sheet." Colby swayed with weariness. "I'll give him my blood and put him back beneath the ground where he'll be safe."

"I will return as quickly as possible to provide for you," Vikirnoff promised.

Colby nodded and sat with Rafael's head pillowed in her lap. She called softly to him, hating that he would be in pain when he woke, but knowing that he must feed in order to heal and regain his strength. She felt his brothers then, called by the need to respond even across half the world. She felt them attempt to shoulder Rafael's pain as he woke.

Colby bent to press a kiss on his forehead. "Don't move, just lie still. You need blood." She tore at her own wrist, uncaring of the pain, pushing the wound against his lips. He was so weak, she didn't even feel him taking the nourishment and it frightened her.

Do not give up hope. It was Nicolas who reassured her and each of his brothers murmured their names in her mind and added their reassurances to his. Somehow it gave her a sense of family to have all the Carpathians whispering encouragement in her mind.

What about Paul and Ginny, Nicolas? Are they all right without me? She worked to keep the wistful note out of her voice so it wouldn't upset Rafael. That world seemed so far away from her now. She hadn't been happy when told the news that the children had been spirited away to Brazil for protection—but she understood.

They are being spoiled by aunts, uncles, and a hundred cousins. They miss you.

She was grateful Nicolas thought to add the last.

Stop him now and put him back in the soil. That was Gregori, the healer. Colby could feel Rafael's spirit edging away from her as the pain grew intolerable. She halted his feeding, hesitating only for a moment before swiping her tongue across the ugly wound on her wrist. With Nicolas's help she sent Rafael to sleep and closed her eyes wearily, slumping against the soil, uncaring that she lay in what looked like a grave. All that mattered was that she keep Rafael alive.

"You need to feed." Vikirnoff's voice jerked her out of her reverie.

She felt her mouth go dry. Rafael put her under enthrallment, but she wasn't ready to relinquish that kind of control to someone else. "I don't know if I can," she answered honestly.

"If you do not feed, you will grow weak and you will not be able to hold him to you," Vikirnoff pointed out. "I will keep you from knowing."

Her heart slammed in her chest at the idea of giving Vikirnoff, a virtual stranger, that sort of control over her. With Rafael unconscious, she turned instinctively to his brother. *Nicolas! What should I do?* Nicolas was close to Rafael, her link to him. She had no one else to turn to in the unfamiliar situation. *I can't think about his giving me blood.*

Vikirnoff is an honorable Carpathian. Allow him to compel you. You must maintain your strength in order to sustain Rafael's life.

She felt another of Rafael's brothers move through Nicolas to reach her. Zacarias, the oldest, the strongest, the one the brothers all deferred to. She picked that out of Rafael's memories. *I will make certain no harm comes to you.* Colby was amazed at the incredible sense of family, of the love they shared for her through Rafael.

Over the next several risings she repeated the same ritual each evening. She sometimes woke in the night to lie with the soil open, Rafael's head pillowed in her lap, to stare at the sky and twinkling stars, her hands stroking caresses in his hair, willing him to survive, to come back to her. She devoted herself and her will completely to healing him. Vikirnoff supplied nourishment and she became comfortable with his presence, but never enough to submit her will on her own. Nicolas or one of Rafael's other brothers always had to be with her before she would allow Vikirnoff to place her under his enthrallment.

On the seventh evening Vikirnoff rose well before Colby and was already out of the earth when she awakened. She was competent at opening the earth now and she floated to the surface, clothing herself the way Nicolas had taught her. She would awaken Rafael as soon as she had gathered fresh herbs and healing plants. "Vikirnoff?" She looked around. He was always waiting to supply Rafael with blood. She found a single rose lying across the boulder near the hot springs. He was gone. That could only mean one thing. Colby spun around, holding the long-stemmed rose, her heart pounding in anticipation.

Rafael stood there looking fit, much more fit than he had a right to, but he bore the signs of his brush with death. His beautiful dark hair, falling halfway down his back, was streaked gray on his left side. His face was etched with new lines and there was a weariness in his eyes that had never been there before. He touched the scar on his chest from Kirja's attack. "Carpathians are not supposed to scar."

She drank him in. Tears burned behind her eyelids and she had to swallow several times to get rid of the lump in her throat. "Maybe I didn't heal you in the right way." She couldn't stop looking at him. He was so solid. So *alive*. "You look perfect to me." She didn't mean to blurt it out. He already wore confidence like a second skin.

"You saved my life."

Colby nodded. "Someone had to do it. You were a mess."

His black eyes regarded her without blinking. She'd forgotten how completely he could focus on her. Her legs turned rubbery, but she stood her ground, trying to look nonchalant. "Are you sure you should be up?" Her gaze drifted down his body and the air seemed to leave her lungs in a long rush. He was definitely up and seemingly fit.

A slow, sensual grin curved his mouth. His eyes darkened with a blatant sexuality. "Oh, I am very sure."

A blush stole up her neck to her face. "You know what I mean. You nearly died." There was a hint of accusation in her voice.

"I promise to be far more careful in the future, *querida.*" He couldn't get enough of looking at her. He took a step toward her and watched with narrowed gaze as she took a small step back.

"I don't think you can ever do something like that again. You scared me."

"I am sorry." His gaze met hers steadily. "For a lot of things. It was wrong of me to convert you without your permission. You were working your way to me and I grew impatient. I should have had more faith."

"Yes, you should have. I will never be happy without a full partnership, Rafael. I'm not the sort of woman to tolerate you arbitrarily making decisions for me." She wanted to be stern. It was necessary to get her point across, but he looked so alive, when he'd been so close to death for so many days. She had seen the battle in his mind and it had been horrendous.

"I am very aware of what kind of woman you are, Colby," he agreed quietly. "I will do my best to try to work on learning to be a partner."

"Well, work on it fast." She had so much more to say on the subject, but she couldn't think of what it was at that precise moment. All she could think about was touching the new lines in his face. His scar. She wanted to smooth the frown from his mouth and erase the worry from his eyes.

"I have to explain about Paul," he said, determined to make certain she understood why he'd taken the boy from her. "I had no choice but to send him away. Kirja was unlike any vampire we have ever encountered. He was a childhood friend. A close friend who knew the way I hunt. He was a powerful Carpathian and as a vampire he had become tremendously powerful. If we did not succeed in destroying him, sooner or later he would have succeeded in killing Paul, or using him to harm you or Ginny. I knew I was risking you not understanding, but I honestly felt it was the right thing to do, the only thing to do."

"I know." She had seen the struggle in his mind. In all the time she had spent healing him, she had merged often with him to keep him alive and she'd seen his strengths and weaknesses. She had seen his memories and regrets, the way he wanted to do what was right and best for her even if it meant risking their relationship. His actions were motivated by love, not by a sense of power. He seemed to have trouble expressing his love in ways other than sexual. Colby was certain she could spend the next few centuries helping him learn to communicate better.

"Colby, about the ranch. I want you to come to Brazil. We can hold the ranch in trust for Paul and Ginny, until they are old enough to decide where they wish to live. I would like them to know Armando's family. My family. And I would like for my family to know all of you. But if you cannot be happy there, we will come back and live together here."

It was a tremendous concession. A gift he was handing her. He wanted to go home. He *needed* to go home. His heart and soul yearned for the rain forest, for his ranch, for the things familiar to him. For his family, both human and Carpathian. But she was in his mind and she felt his sincerity. He would make every effort to do what made her happy. And Colby found it wasn't the ranch that mattered. It belonged to Paul and Ginny. She was more than happy to relinquish her share. If her brother and sister loved Brazil, she would love it. And if they needed to return to the ranch, she would return with them until they were of an age when they could cope on their own. But always, her choice was Rafael. She smiled at him. "I hope you have horses. I need to be around horses."

"We have many horses, *meu amor.*"

She tilted her head. "Are you absolutely certain you're feeling healthy and your heart is strong?" Her voice dropped to a sultry invitation.

"I am healed."

Colby looked up at the cascading waterfall pouring over the cliff above them. It provided a shimmering backdrop to the secluded grotto where the hot springs bubbled up, separated from the stream by well-worn rocks. Fern and moss covered the ground like an emerald carpet. She took a breath, allowing herself the luxury of taking in the beauty of the place, appreciating the richness of the soil that had helped to heal Rafael.

He came up behind her, his hands sliding down her back to her hip, pressing her against his larger frame. Colby reached up to encircle his neck, pulling his dark head down to hers. She had to lean back, to seek the excitement of his mouth. "Make love to me, Rafael," she whispered against his lips. "I nearly lost you and I need to feel you loving me." She turned in his arms, needing the comfort of his embrace. Needing to feel the corded steel running through his body.

"I always make love to you, *meu amor.*" He stepped back, the intensity and hunger in his gaze mesmerizing her. "With every breath I take, I make love to you." With gentle, sure fingers, he unbuttoned her blouse, his knuckles brushing her full breasts. "You always have far too many clothes on. I thought we agreed you would just run around naked for me." He pushed the blouse from her shoulders, hands lingering on soft swelling flesh, enjoying the pleasure of simply looking at her breasts before reaching up to remove the clips from her hair. He released the silky mass, his fingers running through it until the last braid was free to tumble unrestrained about her body.

He crushed the strands of hair in his fist, brought them to his mouth, his eyes never leaving hers. Watching her. Hungry for her. She had never once given herself fully to him, but he could see love in her gaze, in the flush of heat spreading under her skin. As always, wildness rose in him, but he fought desperately to tamp it down, sensing her mood, her need for not only a physical demonstration of love, but comfort as well. She had been so courageous. And she had chosen him. He kissed her again, peace settling into his bones, contentment in his soul. For the first time he lost the driven feeling, the need to conquer and take.

Rafael eased her jeans from her hips, his hands moving over her thighs until Colby felt weak with longing. She watched him, the raw desire in his eyes as he traced the contours of her body with evident enjoyment. His body crowded hers until she stepped back into the hot spring.

Colby slid into the water. Warm bubbles like champagne surrounded her, enveloped her body like a living blanket. The water supported her, moving up her flesh as she sank deeper into the mineral pool. The sense of weightlessness in the water, her hair floating like seaweed, and the backdrop of the waterfall made her feel sensual, a water siren luring her mate.

She watched Rafael as he waded to her, slowly reaching out to pull her wet body against his. His fingers curled around the nape of her neck, dragging her head to his so he could take possession of her mouth. Colby brought up one leg and curved it around his waist, sliding her body up and down his thigh to relieve the building pressure. The bubbles felt like tongues licking at her sensitized flesh. No matter how much she wanted to go slow, to feel his hands moving over her with tenderness, something in her responded to him with a wild, frantic desire that built fast and hot.

"*Meu amor,* you have no idea what you do for me. I am a strong man, *pequena,* a powerful man, but one look at you and I melt inside. My body not only craves the haven of yours, but my heart is full and there is light pouring into me. I had no idea what that meant even when it was discussed in my youth. All male Carpathians dream of having a lifemate—it is our motivation and drive to continue in the endless, barren years—but until I actually met you, I could not conceive of how I would feel. I cannot find the words to tell you what you mean to me."

Colby wrapped her arms around his neck, her fingers caressing the white streak in his silken hair. "You do just fine, Rafael."

"You deserve better. A poet. A man of beautiful words that could express what is in my heart."

"I no longer need the words, Rafael. I opened my mind to yours and I *feel* the love you have for me. I know the words in your heart because I can see them there." She kissed him, a long, slow kiss of seduction. "I want you. I want to touch you, to hold you, to feel you inside of me. I need to feel you alive and wrapped around me."

His mouth left hers to find her neck. "You are so hot, Colby. You always are wet and hot and needing me. I get so damned hard just feeling you want me."

She closed her eyes when his teeth scraped over her skin. She ground her body harder against his, riding his thigh. "We happen to be in a hot spring. I'm hot and wet for a good reason."

His teeth bit harder in a small, mock punishment. "I am the reason you are hot and wet and you know it."

Her hands moved possessively over his chest, fingertips lingering along the scar. "You're healed all right—you're back to your arrogance."

His lips teased her shoulder, sent a shiver down her spine as he lifted her and carried her from the water to a flat boulder. "I am most certain I am not unduly arrogant. I love the way you want me, Colby. Do you have any idea what that does to a man, knowing a woman looks at him and burns for him the way you do for me?" His teeth teased her pulse, tongue flicking over the sensitive spot.

"We've never had the problem of me not wanting you," she confessed, leaning in to kiss his throat, to trail kisses to the scar over his heart. Her hands moved over him, her fingertips tracing patterns over his chest and down his belly.

He lifted his head, closing his eyes, savoring her in his arms, her body entwined around his and her mouth soothing over the wound on his chest. His heart beat there because of Colby. The rhythm was strong and steady and if there was still pain with each beat it was mild, easily masked, and worth every moment with her.

"No, just with you loving me." Just saying the words woke a fierce violence in him. It roared through his veins until his arms tightened, forming a steel cage around her. With an effort, he fought back the need for domination. His mouth whispered over her skin, feather light; he teased at her bottom lip, dipped lower to find her breasts. He felt greedy lust rising sharp and terrible, but he refused to give in to it.

She moved with restless abandon, her skin rubbing against his, her hands claiming him, roving over his body possessively. It only added to the hot need building in him. Colby bit lightly at his shoulder, ran her tongue to his nipple, flicking it gently. She could read his fight to give her tenderness and it meant everything to her that he would try to hold on to his self-control.

His black eyes drifted over her face. Moody. Brooding. Starkly sensual. Her heart pounded in anticipation. Watching her closely, he leaned into her, his tongue flicking her breast, sliding to her navel as he dropped down in front of her, his hands tightening on her thighs. Already she was drowning in heat, in pleasure. His tongue lapped slowly over her pulsing sheath. She jerked, a gasp escaping as her womb contracted and every nerve ending went into hyper-sensitivity.

Colby had been so focused on his injuries, on saving his life and holding him to her, she still hadn't quite relinquished her link to his mind. She felt the fire pouring through his veins and the roar of need in his head. Lust mixed with love until the two emotions were intertwined. It fed her own desires, a well of pleasure bursting through her as his tongue stabbed deep and teased, flicking and sucking until she was writhing with her need, nearly delirious and pleading with him. He brought her to the brink of release over and over and pulled back until her hands fisted in his hair and she cried out his name.

"Rafael. I can't stand it. It's too much." She couldn't catch her breath, couldn't find the release she so desperately needed. "I can't take any more."

"You can take it. I am going out of my mind with wanting you. You have to feel the same way."

"I do. I am. Hurry!" she pleaded urgently.

Rafael kissed his way up her stomach, nipped at the underside of her breast while she frantically tried to wrap her legs around his waist and draw him close to her. He buried his face against her throat. "I love you, Colby. I will love you forever with everything that I am."

His voice was pure honesty, the sound curling around her heart until she felt herself melt. Deeply embedded in his mind, she also sensed his uncertainty. He didn't know for certain that she loved him completely, with every fiber of her being. She had held herself apart from him for so long, he didn't trust his reading of her thoughts. He believed he was seeing and feeling what he wanted so desperately to see.

"Rafael." She whispered his name softly, forced him to look up into her eyes. She held his gaze, wanting him to see her expression, the terrible emotion that she had held back for so long. "I've been afraid all this time of what I felt for you. It terrified me because I thought if I gave you my heart, there would be nothing left of me, that I would lose myself entirely. I thought that you wanted to own me, to control me, and I could never live like that. But when you nearly died, I realized it was too late. I love you, Rafael. I love you so much I think I might die without you."

Tears glittered in Rafael's eyes, but he didn't look away from her, didn't care that she saw how she had humbled him with her admission. He framed her face. "I want you to hear the words that bind us together. They are what make us truly one. You are my life, Colby, for all eternity." He brushed a gentle kiss over her lips. "I claim you as my lifemate. I belong to you. I offer my life for you. I give to you my protection, my allegiance, my heart, my soul, and my body." He trailed kisses to her throat, whispering the words against her pulse. "I take into my keeping the same that is yours. Your life, happiness, and welfare will be cherished and placed above my own for all time. You are my lifemate, bound tome for all eternity and always in my care." He lifted his head, looking into her eyes, seeing the same tears swimming in her eyes.

Colby smiled at him. "Those are the most beautiful words you could ever have said to me."

"I mean every one of them."

"I know you do."

Rafael's eyes darkened even more, his desire intensifying. He took her hard, plunging into her hot, welcoming channel deep and strong, a fierce thrust that had her screaming, her orgasm ripping through her body even as he began to surge into her with long, sure strokes. She gripped him with her slick hot muscles, so tight a single sound of sheer pleasure escaped his throat. The orgasm burst through her, over her, endless, until she could only sink her fingernails into his shoulders and hang on as he rode her with his fiery passion.

Rafael stared down into her face. Her head was thrown back, her long hair whipping around them from the breeze. Her legs were wrapped around his waist, her breasts swaying with every hard thrust.

She was a beautiful sight, giving herself up to him, making her own demands with her strong muscles. He could only stare down into her face, watching as his body took possession of hers, conquering even as she conquered him. Surrendering, even as he surrendered to her. He knew he would never forget that moment, her offering herself wholly to him and his heart twisted in his chest. She trusted him with her body, her sexuality, and now, at last, with her heart.

He wanted to give her everything, to pour into her body all the emotions he felt and could never express adequately with words. With every hot stroke, with each burning thrust, his body declared his love. He was utterly hers and always would be. The fire raged in him like an inferno, building and building until it was impossible, until he swelled inside of her, stretching her delicate muscles, and she was crying his name.

He erupted, pouring his essence into her, deep hard thrusts he couldn't control, every muscle contracting. Even his heart hurt, pounding with need and love for her.

Rafael turned, still buried deep inside her, to rest against the boulder. Colby immediately burrowed close, her mouth seeking the scar over his heart, lapping at it with her tongue.

"Stay still," she said. "I need to make certain you are all right."

Rafael threw his head back, staring up at the moon, Colby's legs wrapped tightly around his waist, his body buried deep in the haven of hers while she gave him imperious commands. He found himself smiling. Happy. At peace. He could feel her moving inside of him, working on his heart. He could feel the thrust of her breasts against his chest, the silk of her hair in a tangle over his skin. It didn't matter where they lived. Here, on this ranch, or in Brazil, his home, his sanctuary was this woman in his arms.

The moment she lifted her head he took possession of her mouth, a long kiss of tenderness, a whisper of love as he waded with her back into the hot spring.

Epilogue

"Rafael! Colby!" Ginny called, waving wildly. "Come see this."

Rafael swept his arm around Colby, pulling her beneath his shoulder, close to the warmth of his body, as they walked through the indoor arena to Ginny. She sat astride a dark mare, her face glowing with happiness over her latest accomplishment. "I can finally jump the way Julio wants me to. Look at me." It had taken Ginny several weeks to adjust to riding an English saddle, but she had practiced until she was very competent and her uncles had pronounced her ready to jump.

"She's beaming," Colby whispered to Rafael. "Look at her, she's blossomed here with all this family around her."

"She actually gets to spend more time with you," Paul said, coming up behind them. "Before, you worked so much we rarely had a chance to really talk to you, but now, we have you every morning and almost as soon as we come back from school."

"You seem to really enjoy Julio and Juan," Colby said. "You spend a lot of time with them." They reminded her so much of Armando she ached sometimes looking at them. She studied her brother, who looked so much like his father and uncles. He seemed older and more sober since his ordeal with the vampire.

"I'm learning a lot from them," Paul admitted. He waved at Ginny as horse and rider cantered around the arena. "They know so much about horses and they tell us stories about Dad when he was younger."

"Have we heard from Sean? Are things going well on the ranch?" Colby asked.

Paul nodded. "He called last night. He's got two couples working the ranch. Ben's doing fine. Apparently he had a long talk with Tony Harris and Tony admitted to causing most of accidents on the ranch, but he denies starting the fire."

"Clinton Daniels's man, Ernie Carter, was the vampire's puppet," Rafael said. "He started the fire."

Paul glanced up at Rafael and then his gaze shifted hastily away. "I suppose he did."

Through her link with Rafael, Colby felt the wince of shame in her brother. She frowned and put a comforting hand on his arm, but Rafael spoke before she could.

"I never had a chance to thank you for saving your sister's life." Rafael said it in his usual low voice, a whisper of power in every word he spoke. "The vampire would have killed her had you not been so strong."

Paul sucked in his breath, turning his head away, but not before Colby caught the struggle of emotions on his face. "I did terrible things. Nicolas offered to remove my memories, but I don't want that. He said I would sometimes feel the way I was feeling now, but not know why." He hung his head. "I'd rather know there was a good reason for it."

"You have nothing to be ashamed of, Paul," Rafael said. "You are entirely human with no psychic ability, yet you fought a monster who was so strong that not even our most powerful hunters could have defeated him alone. Even with the help of another hunter, I nearly died fighting him. But you, Paul, stayed strong. You delayed him, hindered his plans more than once, and in the end, you managed to warn us that he was going after your sister. You should be proud of yourself."

Paul nodded, but swallowed hard, his eyes still reflecting misery. He turned to meet Colby's gaze squarely. "Ginny saw me cut my wrist. I tried to send her from the room. I couldn't stop myself. I'll never forget her expression." He glanced at his younger sister as she rode around the arena, practicing posting.

Colby swallowed the sudden lump in her throat. "Ginny isn't a baby anymore, Paulo. And Nicolas took the memory from her mind. You did your best and that's all anyone could ever ask of you."

"I had my heart ripped out by the vampire," Rafael admitted. "You knew that, you felt it, but what you didn't know was I had already bound Colby to me. If I had died, she would have eventually followed me. If there is shame, it is mine, not yours. We couldn't be prouder of you."

"Is that why Nicolas allowed me to know about the Carpathian people?"

Rafael nodded. "And we hope Ginny will someday understand what her sister is. We hope the two of you will stay close to us, here in this country among your family."

A small grin lit Paul's eyes. "Are you planning on providing me with a niece or nephew to make it worth my while?"

Colby smacked him. "Very funny. I'm just getting used to the idea of all of this."

"Ginny wants you to have a wedding with a long white gown and all the trimmings," Paul pointed out.

Nicolas came up behind them. "*All* women seem to want those ceremonies. Why is that? Juliette, Riordan's lifemate, has brought this up many times and it makes no sense to me at all."

Paul laughed. "It wouldn't make sense to *you*, Nicolas." His banter with Nicolas surprised her, and more to Colby's astonishment,

Nicolas punched her brother in the arm. Paul just grinned at him and attempted to look superior. "Women like to dress up."

"*Not me,*" Colby denied firmly. "No one is getting me up in front of the world vowing I'll obey Rafael."

Rafael raised his eyebrow. "There is the promise of obedience in this marriage ceremony? Paul, we have to talk."

"That's never going to happen," Colby said.

"Paul." Juan waved at the boy to come to him. Paul immediately responded, running over to his uncle to listen to his advice on jumping.

Colby could hardly take her eyes off her brother and sister. "Have either of you heard from Vikirnoff? Where is he? Where'd he go? He didn't even give me a chance to say good-bye after he helped so much with Rafael."

"He is searching for the woman," Nicolas answered. "I believe he is on his way to the Carpathian Mountains."

"Do you ever think of going there?" she asked curiously.

"Someday, we will go back to visit," Rafael said. "But this is our home now."

Colby listened to the sound of Paul's laughter as he answered his uncle's teasing. It had become all too rare in their life. She watched Juan throw an arm around her brother's shoulder in a casual display of affection. Julio was applauding and shouting encouragement to Ginny. Both children looked far more relaxed than she'd ever seen them. She turned to find Rafael watching her with his dark, mesmerizing eyes.

"Is it good?" he asked.

"It's very good," she answered.

A Much-Abridged Carpathian Dictionary

This very much abridged Carpathian dictionary contains most of the Carpathian words used in these Dark books. Of course, a full Carpathian dictionary would be as large as the usual dictionary for an entire language (typically more than a hundred thousand words).

Note: The Carpathian nouns and verbs below are word stems. They generally do not appear in their isolated, "stem" form, as below. Instead, they usually appear with suffixes (e.g., "*andam*"—"I give," rather than just the root, "*and*").

agba—to be seemly or proper.
ai—oh.
aina—body.
ainaak—forever.
ak—suffix added after a noun ending in a consonant to make it plural.
aka—to give heed; to hearken; to listen.
akarat—mind; will.
ál—to bless; to attach to.
alatt—through.
aldyn—under; underneath.

ala—to lift; to raise.

alte—to bless; to curse.

and—to give.

andasz éntölem irgalomet!—have mercy!

arvo—value (*noun*).

arwa—praise (*noun*).

arwa-arvo—honor (*noun*).

arwa-arvo olen gæidnod, ekäm—honor guide you, my brother (*greeting*).

arwa-arvo olen isäntä, ekäm—honor keep you, my brother (*greeting*).

arwa-arvo pile sívadet—may honor light your heart (*greeting*).

arwa-arvod mäne me ködak—may your honor hold back the dark (*greeting*).

asti—until.

avaa—to open.

avio—wedded.

avio päläfertiil—lifemate.

belső—within; inside.

bur—good; well.

bur tule ekämet kuntamak—well met brother-kin (*greeting*).

ćaδa—to flee; to run; to escape.

ćoro—to flow; to run like rain.

csecsemő—baby (*noun*).

csitri—little one (*female*).

diutal—triumph; victory.

epci—to fall.

ek—suffix added after a noun ending in a consonant to make itplural.

ekä—brother.

elä—to live.

eläsz arwa-arvoval—may you live with honor, live nobly (*greeting*).

eläsz jeläbam ainaak—long may you live in the light (*greeting*).

elävä—alive.

elävä ainak majaknak—land of the living.

elid—life.

emä—mother (noun).

Emä Maγe—Mother Nature.

én—I.

en—great; many; big.

én jutta félet és ekämet—I greet a friend and brother (*greeting*).

En Puwe—The Great Tree. Related to the legends of Ygddrasil, the *axis mundi*, Mount Meru, heaven and hell, etc.

engem—me.

és—and.

että—that.

fáz—to feel cold or chilly.

fél—fellow; friend.

fél ku kuuluaak sívam belső—beloved.

fél ku vigyázak—dear one.

feldolgaz—prepare.

fertiil—fertile one.

fesztelen—airy.

fü—herbs; grass.

gæidno—road; way.

gond—care; worry; love (*noun*).

hän—he; she; it.

hän agba—it is so.

hän ku—prefix: one who; that which.

hän ku agba—truth.

hän ku kaświa o numamet—sky-owner.

hän ku kuulua sívamet—keeper of my heart.

hän ku meke pirämet—defender.

hän ku pesä—protector.

hän ku saa kuć3aket—star-reacher.

hän ku tappa—deadly.

hän ku tuulmahl elidet—vampire (*literally: life-stealer*).

hän ku vie elidet—vampire (*literally: thief of life*).

hän ku vigyáz sielamet—keeper of my soul.

hän ku vigyáz sívamet és sielamet—keeper of my heart and soul.

hany—clod; lump of earth.

hisz—to believe; to trust.

ida—east.

igazág—justice.

irgalom—compassion; pity; mercy.

isä—father (*noun*).

isäntä—master of the house.

it—now.

jälleen—again.

jama—to be sick, wounded or dying; to be near death.

jelä—sunlight; day; sun; light.

jelä keje terád—light sear you (*Carpathian swear words*).

o jelä peje terád—sun scorch you (*Carpathian swear words*).

o jelä sielamak—light of my soul.

joma—to be under way; to go.

joŋe—to come; to return.

joŋesz arwa-arvoval—return with honor (*greeting*).

jŏrem— to forget; to lose one's way; to make a mistake.

juo—to drink.

juosz és eläsz—drink and live (*greeting*).

juosz és olen ainaak sielamet jutta—drink and become one with me (*greeting*).

juta—to go; to wander.

jüti—night; evening.

jutta—connected; fixed (*adj.*). To connect; to fix; to bind (*verb*).

k—suffix added after a noun ending in a vowel to make it plural.

kaca—male lover.

kaik—all.

kalma—corpse; death; grave.

kaŋa—to call; to invite; to request; to beg.

kaŋk—windpipe; Adam's apple; throat.

kaδa—to abandon; to leave; to remain.

kaδa wäkeva óv o köd—stand fast against the dark (*greeting*).

Karpatii—Carpathian.

Karpatii ku köd—liar.

käsi—hand (*noun*).

kaśwa—to own.

keje—to cook; to burn; to sear.

kepä—lesser; small; easy; few.

kidü—to wake up; to arise (*intransitive verb*).

kim—to cover an entire object with some sort of covering.

kinn—out; outdoors; outside; without.

kinta—fog; mist; smoke.

köd—fog; mist; darkness.

köd alte hän—darkness curse it (*Carpathian swear words*).

o köd belső—darkness take it (*Carpathian swear words*).

köd jutasz belső—shadow take you (*Carpathian swear words*).

koje—man; husband; drone.

kola—to die.

kolasz arwa-arvoval—may you die with honor (*greeting*).

koma—empty hand; bare hand; palm of the hand; hollow of the hand.

kond—all of a family's or clan's children.

kont—warrior.

kont o sívanak—strong heart (*literally: heart of the warrior*).

ku—who; which; that.

kuć3—star.

kuć3ak!—stars! (*exclamation*).

kule—to hear.

kulke—to go or to travel (on land or water).

kulkesz arwa-arvoval, ekäm—walk with honor, my brother (*greeting*).

kulkesz arwaval, jonesz arwa arvoval—go with glory, return with honor (*greeting*).

kuly—intestinal worm; tapeworm; demon who possesses and devours souls.

kumpa—wave (*noun*).

kuńa—to lie as if asleep; to close or cover the eyes in a game of hide-and-seek; to die.

kune—moon.

kunta—band; clan; tribe; family.

kuras—sword; large knife.

kure—bind; tie.

kutni—to be able to bear, carry, endure, stand or take.

kutnisz ainaak—long may you endure (*greeting*).

kuulua—to belong; to hold.

lääs—west.

lamti (or lamt3)—lowland; meadow; deep; depth.

lamti ból jüti, kinta, ja szelem—the netherworld (*literally: the meadow of night, mists and ghosts*).

lańa—daughter.

lejkka—crack; fissure; split (*noun*). To cut; to hit; to strike forcefully (*verb*).

lewl—spirit (*noun*).

lewl ma—the other world (*literally: spirit land*). *Lewl ma* includes *lamti ból jüti, kinta, ja szelem:* the netherworld, but also includes the worlds higher up *En Puwe*, the Great Tree.

liha—flesh.

lõuna—south.

löyly—breath; steam (*related to* lewl: *spirit*).

ma—land; forest.

magköszun—thank.

mana—to abuse; to curse; to ruin.

mäne—to rescue; to save.

maγe—land; earth; territory; place; nature.

me—we.

meke—deed; work (*noun*). To do; to make; to work (*verb*).

minan—mine.

minden—every; all (*adj.*).

möért?—what for? (*exclamation*).

molanâ—to crumble; to fall apart.

molo—to crush; to break into bits.

mozdul—to begin to move; to enter into movement.

muonì—appoint; order; prescribe; command.

musta—memory.

myös—also.

nä—for.

naman—this; this one here.

nélkül—without.

nenä—anger.

nó—like; in the same way as; as.

numa—god; sky; top; upper part; highest (*related to the English word: numinous*).

numatorkuld—thunder (*literally: sky struggle*).

nyál—saliva; spit (*related to* nyelv: *tongue*).

nyelv—tongue.

o—the (*used before a noun beginning with a consonant*).

odam—to dream; to sleep.

odam-sarna kondak—lullaby (*literally: sleep-song of children*).

olen—to be.

oma—old; ancient.

omas—stand.

omboće—other; second (*adj.*).

ot—the (*used before a noun beginning with a vowel*).

otti—to look; to see; to find.

óv—to protect against.

owe—door.

päämoro—aim; target.

pajna—to press.

pälä—half; side.

päläfertiil—mate or wife.

peje—to burn.

peje terád—get burned (*Carpathian swear words*).

pél—to be afraid; to be scared of.

pesä—nest (*literal*); protection (*figurative*).

pesäsz jeläbam ainaak—long may you stay in the light (*greeting*).

pide—above.

pile—to ignite; to light up.

pirä—circle; ring (*noun*). To surround; to enclose (*verb*).

piros—red.

pitä—to keep; to hold.

pitäam mustaakad sielpesäambam—I hold your memories safe in my soul.

pitäsz baszú, piwtäsz igazáget—no vengeance, only justice.

piwtä—to follow; to follow the track of game.

poår—bit; piece.

põhi—north.

pukta—to drive away; to persecute; to put to flight.

pus—healthy; healing.

pusm—to be restored to health.

puwe—tree; wood.

rauho—peace.

reka—ecstasy; trance.

rituaali—ritual.

sa—sinew; tendon; cord.

sa4—to call; to name.

saa—arrive, come; become; get, receive.

saasz hän ku andam szabadon—take what I freely offer.

salama—lightning; lightning bolt.

sarna—words; speech; magic incantation (*noun*). To chant; to sing; to celebrate (*verb*).

sarna kontakawk—warriors' chant.

śaro—frozen snow.

sas—shoosh (*to a child or baby*).

saγe—to arrive; to come; to reach.

siel—soul.

sisar—sister.

sív—heart.

sív pide köd—love transcends evil.

sívad olen wäkeva, hän ku piwtä—may your heart stay strong, hunter (*greeting*).

sivamés sielam—my heart and soul.

sívamet—my love of my heart to my heart.

sívdobbanás—heartbeat (*literal*); rhythm (*figurative*).

sokta—to mix; to stir around.

sone—to enter; to penetrate; to compensate; to replace.

susu—home; birthplace (*noun*). At home (*adv.*).

szabadon—freely.

szelem—ghost.

tappa—to dance; to stamp with the feet; to kill.

te—you.

ted—yours.

terád keje—get scorched (*Carpathian swear words*).

tõdhän—knowledge.

tõdhän lõ kuraset agbapäämoroam—knowledge flies the sword true to its aim.

toja—to bend; to bow; to break.

toro—to fight; to quarrel.

torosz wäkeval—fight fiercely (*greeting*).

totello—obey.

tuhanos—thousand.

tuhanos löylyak türelamak sa e diutalet—a thousand patient breaths bring victory.

tule—to meet; to come.

tumte—to feel; to touch; to touch upon.

türe—full; satiated; accomplished.

türelam—patience.

türelam agba kontsalamaval—patience is the warrior's true weapon.

tyvi—stem; base; trunk.

uskol—faithful.

uskolfertiil—allegiance; loyalty.

veri—blood.

veri ekäakank—blood of our brothers.

veri-elidet—blood-life.

veri isäakank—blood of our fathers.

veri olen piros, ekäm—blood be red, my brother (*literal*); find your lifemate (*figurative: greeting*).

veriak ot en Karpatiiak—by the blood of the prince (*literally: by the blood of the great Carpathian; Carpathian swear words*).

veridet peje—may your blood burn (*Carpathian swear words*).

vigyáz—to love; to care for; to take care of.

vii—last; at last; finally.

wäke—power; strength.

wäke kaδa—steadfastness.

wäke kutni—endurance.

wä ke-sarna—vow; curse; blessing (*literally: power words*).

wäkeva—powerful.

wara—bird; crow.

weńća—complete; whole.

wete—water (*noun*).

WATER BOUND

For Lev Prakenskii, the last thing he remembers is being lost in the swirling currents of the ocean and sucked deeper into the nothingness of a freezing black eddy off the coastal town of Sea Haven. Just as quickly, just as miraculously, he was saved – pulled ashore by a beautiful stranger – but Lev has no memory of who he was – or why he seems to possess the violent instincts of a trained killer. All he knows is that he fears for his life, and the life of his unexpected saviour.

Her name is Rikki, a sea-urchin diver in the small town of Sea Haven. She always felt an affinity for the ocean and the seductive pull of the tides – and now, for the enigmatic man she rescued. But soon they will be bound by something even stronger – each other's tantalising secrets that will engulf them both in a whirlpool of dizzying passion and inescapable danger.

978-0-3494-0008-2

SPIRIT BOUND

Lethal undercover agent Stefan Prakenskii knows a thousand ways to kills a man – and twice as many ways to pleasure a woman. That's why he's looking forward to his new mission. He must go to the coastal town of Sea Haven and insinuate himself into the life of an elusive beauty who has mysterious ties to his past and a link to a dangerously seductive and equally elusive master criminal who wants only one thing: to possess her.

Judith Henderson is an artist on the rise: an ethereal and haunted woman whose own picture-perfect beauty stirs the souls of two men who have made her their obsession. For years she has been waiting for someone to come and unlock the passion and fire within her – waiting for the right man to surrender it to. But only one man can survive her secrets – and the shadow she has cast over both their lives.

978-0-7499-5474-1

Do you love fiction with a supernatural twist?

Want the chance to hear news about your favourite authors (and the chance to win free books)?

Keri Arthur

S. G. Browne

P.C. Cast

Christine Feehan

Jacquelyn Frank

Larissa Ione

Darynda Jones

Sherrilyn Kenyon

Jackie Kessler

Jayne Ann Krentz and Jayne Castle

Martin Millar

Kat Richardson

J.R. Ward

David Wellington

Laura Wright

Then visit the Piatkus website and blog
www.piatkus.co.uk | www.piatkusbooks.net

And follow us on Facebook and Twitter
www.facebook.com/piatkusfiction | www.twitter.com/piatkusbooks